PENGUIN BOOKS
MILA IN LOVE

Dina Mehta is one of India's most versatile and accomplished writers in English. Her first novel, *And Some Take a Lover* (1992), focussed on the divided loyalties of a Parsi family during the Quit India movement. She has published two books of short stories, *The Other Woman and Other Stories* (1981) and *Miss Menon Did Not Believe in Magic and Other Stories* (1994), and selections from the latter were presented as a theatrical experiment by Alyque Padamsee and read on BBC Radio 4.

Dina has also written several prize-winning plays, including *The Myth Makers* (1968), *Tiger Tiger* (1978), *Brides Are Not For Burning* (1979), *Getting Away with Murder* (1989) and *A Sister Like You* (1996). *Brides* won first prize in the BBC International Playwriting Competition, and was subsequently broadcast on the BBC World Service and staged in Madras, Bangalore and Bombay.

Her stories and articles have appeared in the *Independent*, the *Deccan Herald*, *Kaiser-E-Hind* and the *London Magazine*, and her scripts, including *When One Plus One Makes Nine / The Joke about Rabbits*, have been heard on Doordarshan and All India Radio. She was fiction editor at the *Illustrated Weekly of India* from 1976 to 1982, and has worked as a senior editor at *Parsiana* and *Voyage*.

Dina has two daughters and three granddaughters. She lives in Mumbai, where she is presently working on her third collection of short stories.

MILA IN LOVE

DINA MEHTA

PENGUIN BOOKS

PENGUIN BOOKS

Penguin Books India (P) Ltd., 11 Community Centre, Panchsheel Park, New Delhi 110017, India
Penguin Books Ltd., 80 Strand, London WC2R 0RL, UK
Penguin Group Inc., 375 Hudson Street, New York, NY 10014, USA
Penguin Books Australia Ltd., 250 Camberwell Road, Camberwell, Victoria 3124, Australia
Penguin Books Canada Ltd., 10 Alcorn Avenue, Suite 300, Toronto, Ontario M4V 3B2, Canada
Penguin Books (NZ) Ltd., Cnr Rosedale & Airborne Roads, Albany, Auckland, New Zealand
Penguin Books (South Africa) (Pty) Ltd., 24 Sturdee Avenue, Rosebank 2196, South Africa

First published by Penguin Books India 2003

Copyright © Dina Mehta 2003

All rights reserved

10 9 8 7 6 5 4 3 2 1

This is a work of fiction. Names, characters, places and incidents are either the product of the author's imagination or are used fictitiously, and any resemblance to actual persons, living or dead, events, or locales is entirely coincidental.

Typeset in Giovanni Book by Eleven Arts, Delhi-35

Printed at Chaman Offset Printers, New Delhi

This book is sold subject to the condition that it shall not, by way of trade or otherwise, be lent, resold, hired out, or otherwise circulated without the publisher's prior written consent in any form of binding or cover other than that in which it is published and without a similar condition including this condition being imposed on the subsequent purchaser and without limiting the rights under copyright reserved above, no part of this publication may be reproduced, stored in or introduced into a retrieval system, or transmitted in any form or by any means (electronic, mechanical, photocopying, recording or otherwise), without the prior written permission of both the copyright owner and the above-mentioned publisher of this book.

To Keki
from whom I learnt that
'the faith and the love and the hope are all in the waiting'
and to our daughters
Huzan and Rashna

part I

1

At the Taj Art Gallery this afternoon I thought I saw Rayhaan about twelve feet away, contemplating a nude on the wall. Tall as only he can be. As I stared beseechingly at his back my heart said: impossible, impossible! And so it was when the stranger turned round, for certainly this was not Rayhaan disguised in a toucan's beak above a romantic moustache. As I tore my gaze away from that wicked Parsi nose I was surprised to find the walls still perpendicular, the colours still ablaze on them. And suddenly I was ridiculous to myself. I was a scream.

'What's so funny?' asked Ritu as I held the catalogue of paintings to my twitching mouth.

'Nothing,' I said, biting on my hysteria. 'Let's go home.'

'But we've just come!'

'It's hot in here.'

'Mila, this place is air-conditioned,' Ritu observed sensibly. 'It's hotter outside.' But I strode ahead of her into the high dazzle of the day. I had to, for I saw myself waiting endlessly for Rayhaan, my fear that he would come equal to my despair that he never would.

In her chauffeur-driven car Ritu continued her protests. 'You said we'd have tea at the Sea Lounge.' She sat there holding her pregnancy like a giant coconut in her lap.

'Soni will give us tea at home.'

'And the shopping?'

'It's too hot.' Stubbornly I stared out the window. It had not been Rayhaan, but the encounter had left me badly shaken, as after a head-on collision avoided with a screech of brakes. I couldn't tell Ritu that

Bombay streets were no longer safe for me, that I dared not risk the shops and pavements for fear of a confrontation I courted and dreaded in equal parts. I felt my lower lip stick out like a camel's as I thought of all the letters I had written Ray over the years, famished for crumbs from his table. Striving after the literary in tone, achieving banality in effect. Clinging pathetically to the safe, editorial 'we', the camouflage wearing thin with each unanswered missive, the dissemblance not clever enough. To be in the throes of love and composition at the same time— *aaow*! Ritu was looking at me in amazement. Could she hear my lovesickness as distinctly as the mewing of a cat?

The car had slowed down near the gate to my house. The wheels were now treading the very spot where a fragile body had fallen years ago, and no one had been able to put Humpty Dumpty together again. 'It's okay if you don't want me to come up, Mila,' Ritu was saying as her silver Maruti stopped before my entrance.

'You're not to call me "Mila", I've told you,' I said curtly. 'But please do come up.' For a moment I thought she would refuse, but she heaved her blooming middle out of the car. On her last visit I had not been very cordial. She had annoyed me by arriving early in the morning without any intimation or excuse, then by getting up to use the telephone or the toilet at every crucial point in the anecdotes I dredged up to amuse her—not bothered if she beheaded them in mid-sentence. She had made cruel inroads into my time, but given me only a fraction of her attention. And she persisted in calling me Mila after I had decreed that people should now use my full name: Sharmila.

In my living room we settled on the hard slab of a divan with fat sausage bolsters. I turned to her. 'Did I tell you, Ritu, that I saw your brother in Los Angeles?'

She did not respond. With lowered eyes she was apparently counting the bangles on her right hand, all sixteen of them. Did Ritu still greedily collect boys (in her fantasies) as avidly as she acquired her finery (quite factually)? For a bride of seven months she did not look very happy. And none of the clichés about impending motherhood seemed to fit her. Did she have imperious pregnancy desires, a sudden excruciating yen for, say, Alphonso mangoes? Mint chutney? 'Does it move, Ritu?' In answer to the blank look she gave me, I added, 'The baby. May I put my hand there when it moves?'

Ritu sat up quickly from her recumbent position against the bolster, as if to shield her burden from my eyes. Her manner was so constrained as she mutely turned her face away that I wondered what had happened to the old garrulity. Once upon a time I had wanted to gag my school chum. Not that we had connected even then, but at least she had gushed like a water pump. Had pregnancy done this to her? Or wifely submission? I looked at her curiously. Had she fainted when her bull-necked husband first dropped his pants, like maidens do in Victorian novels? Virgins were known to turn frigid or mad after the initial night of terror.

'My brother is back from America.' Ritu suddenly found her tongue. 'Kishore calls himself Sudama Dasa now. He has a guru.'

'Guru!' I couldn't hide my grin. 'Ah, the son follows in his father's footsteps.' The pater, a brilliant manipulator on the stock exchange and owner of a chain of provision stores, also had a guru to whom, presumably, he submitted his dossier of frauds from time to time. On two separate occasions Mansukhlal Motichand had been raided by the Income Tax Department, but nothing had been proved against him, so adroit was he in the business of 'legitimate' roguery. And MM was reverent to the deity in his own fashion—nudged, no doubt, by His Holiness the guru into donating generously to temples and performing other deeds of piety. 'Your father must be pleased with his son.'

'Papa is not. He dislikes Kishore having joined ISKCON.'

'What the hell is ISKCON?'

But Ritu excused herself to go to the toilet. Did this constant pressure to pee make room for the baby?

'On the streets you will see Kishore in a saffron dhoti,' Ritu said on her return, 'with shaven head and a top-knot, white clay marks on his forehead, beads and flowers round his neck and cymbals in his hands.' Gloomily, she listed his frivolities. He must have found this a great way to frighten his mother, scandalize his sister, direct hostilities towards his father. 'He didn't even let us know he was coming to India. Mother is grieving, but not saying a word.' Plainly Ritu thought this a new vice to which her brother had abandoned himself, but to me Kishore in holy garb was a joke. The Kishore I had left behind in Bombay had zoomed around on a noisy motorcycle, bulky and colourful in floral shirts, goggles and a large go-go watch. And the Kishore I had bumped into in LA had wasted cheeks and steel-rimmed spectacles, his thick mouth inserted in the parenthesis of a thin Tartar moustache. The frayed voluminousness of his jacket hung away from his sunken frame, making him look decrepit enough to frighten a crow. He had been stoned out of his mind.

'You mean he's serious about this guru business?' I was fascinated by the novel turn Kishore's delinquency had taken. How my late Uncle Amrish would have relished this story!

'Kishore says the only valid life is a life of service to Lord Krishna, and you must be on duty twenty-four hours in His service because we live in the troubled Kali age,' said Ritu. It was her longest single essay in eloquence that afternoon.

I was astonished. 'But I thought he wanted to be a painter!' Kishore's early initiation into the world of art had been undertaken by a young artist's widow who let out rooms to boarders. Mrs Dev had been much maligned by her colleague in the trade, a Mrs Choksy, also a widow, who had been Rayhaan's landlady for five years. It was surely a case of professional jealousy: Dev was young and delectable, Choksy looked like something out of a dried-fruit store. Anyway, Kishore had gone to live at Dev's while still at college, whereupon his father had suspended his allowance. But evidently his stay with the lovely Dev had not cost Kishore a paisa, for though he never sold a canvas—his concept of art being too lofty to allow him to slog when not absolutely flagellated by inspiration—he looked well fed and, in time, even rotund. Like any artist worth his paint, Kishore had not kowtowed to conventions. Should silly scruples be allowed to stand in the way of emulating the work of a Raza or a Souza?

Obviously something had happened to change all that, but Ritu wasn't about to fill in the blanks for me. Her mind was full of Kishore the devotee. 'When he went to foreign he did it,' she was saying. 'Joined up.'

'The armed forces?' I tucked my legs under my denim skirt to hear her out in comfort.

'Joined this International Society of Krishna Consciousness, ISKCON. He may go back there when this worldwide festival that's brought qualified brahmins here to speak on the Science of God is over.' At this point Soni brought in two cups of masala tea and a platter of round yellow sweets.

But Ritu was too immersed in gloom to find solace in tea. 'He dances on the streets with those foreign women, throwing up his arms, leaping into the air, chanting holy names. The women wear saris.' She absently smoothed her own purple printed silk over her stomach. 'They are allowed to join the order only as devotees' wives. But not all are advised to marry. Kishore is to remain celibate.'

'He's taken his vows?'

'Very soon, he says.'

'Your tea, Ritu.' Reluctantly she took the cup from my hand. 'And have a jalebi while it's hot. What made Kishore do it, do you think?'

She shrugged. 'He didn't get home food there, and he craved the sweetmeats the temple prepared.'

I gave a yelp of laughter, then sobered up quickly as I glanced at my friend's face: it was clear that no irony was intended. And indeed, what could be more natural than food for the spirit being routed through the stomach? Than sweets offered in worship of a god returning sanctified to man for his gastronomical delight?

'And one foreign maharaj,' Ritu continued, 'helped Kishore to kick his drug habit.' She nibbled her succulent sweet mournfully. Even her appetite was not the same.

I sat up. 'That's remarkable, Ritu. I must tell my brother his buddy is back. Vikram will be pleased.'

'Vikram knows.' Here she got up to use my telephone. I could see her standing in the passage, thick-set, speaking loudly and volubly in Gujarati to her aunt. Apparently Ritu had a cousin of marriageable age, and strenuous efforts were afoot to find her a suitable boy. Lucky Kusum—she need never wear herself out in unmaidenly manoeuvres to grab a man. No enterprise was required of her, no amorous dexterity. She would get married in accordance with the stars, the dowry and the sovereign will of her parents. I rather envied Kusum, then chided myself for being schizoid in my convictions: on the one hand I was unwilling to pretend a modesty I did not possess, the beguiling innocence of the daughter of a respected brahmin which would net her (with a little help from approving elders) a mate for life. I'd rather get myself a job, thank you. At the same time, the thought of never acquiring a husband filled me with trepidation.

I had a smile ready for Ritu when she came in. I, too, was husband-high, I wanted to tell her, so how about organizing some tuft-hunting operations for yours truly? But for me her face was buttoned up. She had to leave immediately, she said; something had turned up. And she picked up her handbag and left.

It's been an abortive afternoon and I'm not sorry to see Ritu go: she always disorients me by putting me back in time when I want to leap into my future. But alone I am assailed by a wretched sense of futility. What a depressing business it is to be a perpetual virgin—a ballerina endlessly dancing Giselle—when I long to be a cat of quite another colour: a young woman marvellously gluttonous, insatiable. I bite into my third jalebi. Oh well, I had my chances as a student in California, but Sharmila the mouse ducked them all. Even there only Rayhaan would do, only Rayhaan, but meeting him now is one of the great improbables of my life, so here I sit, stuffing my face. Maybe his books have already been acclaimed under a pseudonym and he is a millionaire. Or perhaps his worldly possessions are as meagre as those Mahatma Gandhi owned in his lifetime; you never can tell with Rayhaan Sharma. But the havoc the brute has caused! The stupid waste, as I try faithfully to live my young spinsterhood—doomed to chastity by obstinate choice, impenetrable by preference.

After the fifth jalebi I begin to feel sick. Where the hell is everyone? Dad's in Delhi—with his mistress?—attending a printers' conference. Aunt Roma is staying the week with a sick friend in Pune, the ministering angel that she is. My mother is in her 'heavenly abode', as they announce in death-anniversary ads in newspapers—which reminds me, I have yet to check on today's 'Situations Vacant' columns. That should occupy me till Vikram gets home; then big brother is going to squire me to a party.

I uncoil on the divan. As I pick up the *Times* from the shelf that forms the underbelly of our coffee table, I wonder what keeps Vikram so late at work these days. That lovely girl, Urmi Someone, at her computer in the market-research section only two partitions away from his air-conditioned cell? No, no, my brother is an office grub above reproach, schooled prematurely in virtue, secure against all vulgar perils. When I asked him yesterday if he indulged in certain audacities, he turned a faint pink, then coughed discreetly into a thin orphan's wrist. And some of the sad primness of a lonely child forced too early into adulthood returned to his face . . . But certainly he is not the boy I used to torment. Vikram no longer walks in the discomfort of weakness. Besides, he *knows* that at the time of the trouble I had not run out of choice, jumped continents in search of an easy nirvana abroad. My expatriation had been a tearing away from familiar possessions and patterns that had defined me. An upheaval, an epic flight, a tragedy . . .

I am crumpling the news pages in my hands. God knows I don't want to summon my past. Sharmila now wants no backsliding; she must get on with her life, forward wind. But to ignore Mila is to line her up in rebellion against me, allow her to gather enough power to fly in my face one day. I know that. So where, in my vanished years, do I locate her?

2

No, Mila is not to be ignored. Nervously I look over my shoulder. The years recede like a tide . . . and adrift in shallow water I come to rest on the day after her thirteenth birthday.

Late in the morning Mila lay prone on her bed. Roma-aunty fussed, worried, prodded, cajoled, even shook her at one point, but she did not stir. Or speak. When the aunt left the room, the niece shot up and fell back in bed in one fluid motion, gleefully waving her legs in the air. As soon as she heard footsteps Mila pulled her limbs under cover, made them drugged and heavy. Quiescent as a saint she lay there, with a profound myopic squint fixed on the green wig of the tamarind tree outside her bedroom window.

At 10 a.m. Soni, who had been with the family since Vikram's birth, dried her gnarled hands on her sari, did up her wisp of hair in its customary knot and hastened on swollen feet to Babulnath Temple. There she fervently tried to coerce Lord Shankar into delivering the child from evil. But when she returned home two hours later Mila was still in bed, with Roma-masi hovering over her like a wingless angel.

Muttering volubly, Soni passed an anxious and faithful hand over Mila's brow, causing the girl an excruciating private snigger, quickly suppressed. The Evil Eye was cast on mama's darlings with black beads threaded round dimpled wrists to ward off ravening spirits, and not on a schoolgirl safe in the land of sturdy forearms and a jolly-good game of netball. The reason Mila was sulking in bed this morning had nothing to do with the Evil Eye but with the devil in her. A report of her birthday crimes, filed with Father the night before, was pending his judgement. When he came to kiss her goodnight he must have been tired, for he had not alluded to her misdeeds and Mila, who had been framing extenuating sentences in her head, fell asleep in a dazzle of reprieve. But she knew her conduct would be reviewed with impeccable calm this morning, and by malingering in bed she hoped to escape the arraignment she dreaded.

'Mila?'

She started at her father's voice and, forgetting her self-imposed rigidity, sat up in bed. Aunt Roma gave a bitter, half-startled look, then scurried out of the room. Close behind her Soni made a wheezing exit, accompanied by the agitated jingle of her bangles.

'Mila,' said Father, 'why are you still in bed at this hour?' She dropped her head. She could remember nothing of her rehearsed excuses. 'May I sit?'

'Oh yes.' With alacrity she moved to make room for him, but kept her face averted. His next question was unexpected. 'Do you miss your mother very much?'

'Yes,' Mila looked up. Suddenly she was angry. 'Yes! Why don't you let her come home?' Then her heart began to race uncomfortably. Had she betrayed herself? Three days ago she had secreted herself in her parents' bedroom to read a letter that had arrived for him from Panchgani, where her mother had been exiled by a cruel decree, *his* decree. 'Why have you sent me away?' her mother had written somewhere in the middle of the page. 'Please, Naren, let me come back,' occurred again and again. In the longest paragraph on the reverse side she wanted to know if love always altered with time; and, most poignant of all, if it was unbecoming for a man to keep 'even a faded wraith of affection' for the wife of his youth? Mila had read a terrifying fear of abandonment in these words. With shaking fingers she had stuffed the letter back into its cover and fled the room.

'She'll be back,' her father was saying gravely, 'when she is well enough to come back.'

'But she's well now, isn't she?' Mila's question held a plea in it. One morning a month ago, her mother had left for Grandma's hilly retreat on the Western Ghats, and since Mila hadn't even known Mother was ill again, her precipitous departure had come as a shock. In the following week Nanima had dispatched her younger daughter Roma to help Father with the children. Clearly, in her own home daughter Roma was dispensable. 'Mother must be fine by now,' Mila said obstinately, 'just fine.'

'No. She needs time to recoup from the illness, and we must give it to her.'

I don't believe you, Mila wanted to scream at him. Mother isn't ill! *You* keep her from me! But even with her thoughts in a tumult of protest came the memory of a tight mouth, an unwavering stare. Of the inexplicable, dissociated remark, the sudden verbal spate that rose unbearably higher and higher . . . But this was disloyalty, treason, and on the bed Mila flinched away from it. Aloud she said in a trembling voice, 'And how much longer will she be away?'

'Another month or two, I expect.'

'A month or two!' Mila stared at him, appalled, trying to quell the mutiny within, when her mind gave a mighty lurch and filled her with the memory of a dream she did not wish to remember. She lay on her back on a sad grey beach, a smell of water in her nostrils. She could not breathe because of an intolerable weight on her chest and she was being pushed slowly, mercilessly, head first, into a black sack. She had sensations of moving underwater, then shooting rocket-like to the surface, blood pounding in her head, a clogging and roaring in her ears. And above her like a sagging cloud was a beautiful face wearing a distorted smile composed equally of love and hate . . . Then miraculously Mila was out of the sack, and she heard voices against the roar of the sea and the scream of the wind. Her eyes had opened on the rain at her window. Her throat was painful and her voice had remained hoarse for days. Her father was roughly shaking her awake in her own bed, a terrible anxiety in his eyes, sweat beading his forehead in fragile bulbs.

Mila now felt the sweat break out on her upper lip. '. . . the quiet of the hills, the cool crisp air and the complete rest,' her father was saying. 'Shivani needs these things to get well.' His gaze, sombre with assessments, held hers. 'And while she's away you mustn't be unhappy.' He paused, groping for words. 'For happiness is not something we can get from other people, Mila. Not something we can hack from a tree, like a jackfruit. We create it. We make it happen. Like a spider weaves a silken web from her own substance. You understand?'

As usual, his gentleness destroyed her defences, her stiff, blind rebellion. Mila looked at him wide-eyed, hoping he could *see* the depth of her passion to please him. If she couldn't convey that to him, she was infirm indeed! At the same time, a part of her was still confused, resentful. Why did he never berate her? Punish her? If only he would urge a penance on her, she would gladly obey. Walk barefoot to the temple like Nanima, bearing water, coconut and flowers. Even refuse second helpings of Soni's brinjal curry because *he* asked her to deny herself. But here was something he wanted her to *be*! What did that mean?

'Otherwise, what we feel we haven't got, we demand from other people.' He took her hand in his. 'And because *they* can't give us what we are looking for, we become aggressive. Unkind. Rude to a friend under our own roof.' Oh-oh, he was at last enumerating her latest sins. Mila snatched her hand away, conscience-stricken.

At her party the day before she had been nasty to Ritu, who had arrived in the middle of a boisterous round of 'dog-and-the-bone' in which Mila's side was winning despite the encumbrance of Baimai Buhariwalla, who always moved in slow motion. At the end of the game, flushed with victory, Mila had approached Ritu, standing so cool and aloof in her pink salwar-kameez, hair bunched on her head like a pagoda. Ritu's sharp eyes had travelled over the birthday girl with devastating effect. Feeling herself dismantled in bits and segments, Mila began to hate the crushed white organdy frock that circled her knees. Then her plump knees. Then the white bow askew in her straight, unbraided hair. Of course her hair was all wrong. Then the tortoise-rim glasses like two moons on her moonface. Mila was in despair over her face.

Primly, Ritu had declined to join them in 'Simon Says', which was now in full swing under Nellie D'Souza's exuberant commands. Instead, Ritu had pulled Mila to one side to whisper about Mr Topiwalla, who was their new maths teacher and also an aberration, being the only odorous male in the supremely feminine world of the Catholic nuns at the convent. 'Have you noticed his eyes?' Ritu began tremulously.

'No I haven't,' snapped Mila, fidgeting to get back to the girls, 'only his goatee.'

'Goatee?' Ritu looked startled. 'What's a goatee?'

'Beard, stupid.' Mila had looked round for an escape route and noted that Aunt Roma was bringing out the eats on the dining table.

'You think beards are sexy?' Ritu had undeniably been corrupted by the English-language 'romance' magazines and trashy novels they smuggled into class.

'No, I don't "think beards are sexy",' Mila mimicked her.

'But you are in love with Topi,' Ritu said in a dying voice.

'As if!'

'I bet you are,' persisted Ritu, who always bored Mila with her inaccurate and highly seasoned descriptions of love, of close encounters with amorous and randy boys from which she always emerged haughty, her virtue intact. 'In love with Topi. No?'

'I'm not, you duffer. But you are!'

Ritu looked stricken. 'Here, take your birthday gift,' she thrust a tiny package in Mila's hands. 'It's *Nights of Love*, perfume straight from Paris, frightfully expensive. I'm going home . . .' But her eyes had strayed to the dining table. Ritu looked slinky in pink satin, but had the appetite of a Bhima. Or perhaps she suffered from tapeworms? 'Immediately after the eats,' she amended.

'Oh, don't bother to wait!' cried Mila. This last bit was overheard by Roma-masi. She had clucked and disapproved, admonished Mila and coaxed Ritu into staying on, inundating her with pakoras and fat wedges of chocolate cake, and with fluttering despotism even placed an idiotic paper cap atop the artful tiers of hair. Ritu left immediately after third helpings of everything, and the tattling aunt reported the sorry incident to Father immediately after the party.

On the bed he lightly touched Mila's hair. 'When upset we don't think clearly. We are troublesome to someone who's left her own home to be with us and help us out.' Mila was silent but contemptuous. Did Roma-masi really think she could take Mother's place? Her aunt was gentle, without animal spirits, formed for devotion. A sense of mystery surrounded beautiful Shivani, but Roma's existence was neatly tucked away among household things. And she was silly. Always trying to please Father, guessing at what he wanted, trotting up and down the rooms to fetch him some perfectly useless thing or another, *blushing* when he spoke to her, willing to dwindle to a pin's head of insignificance for Naren's sake. There often were signs of sniffles on her face. But this evidence of a secret grief in no way diminished Mila's habitual scorn of her aunt. She wanted her to go back to Grandma; and with all her heart she wished Mother would return.

'And destructive,' her father was saying. 'We ruin lovely things. A book, for instance.'

Mila's eyes filled as she thought of what she had done to the book. It had sat on the hall table amidst the clutter of letters and bills she had checked through on her birthday to see if anything had arrived from her mother by post. There was nothing. She had given the table leg a vicious kick and was turning away when she noticed the brown-paper parcel and knew immediately what it was: a *Reader's Digest* omnibus, four books condensed in one volume. It had arrived almost a fortnight ago with a circular that said the reader was welcome to glance through the pages for a couple of days, after which would he please either remit the price if he decided to keep the book, or return it (postage prepaid) to the local dealer.

Her aunt had done exactly what Mila had expected of her: read the book from cover to cover, then wrapped it up in brown paper for its journey back to the bookshop. This was surely a violation of the terms of the bargain, and Mila had been filled with indignation. She had carried the rejected parcel to her bed, opened it and slowly, with implacable ill will, ripped out random pages from the book. Her fingers were strong. They gave her a heady sense of power; at the same time, she was a little frightened by the hidden violence they were expressing.

She had completed the mutilation to her satisfaction and was absorbed in replacing the torn pages in numerical order when the curtain lifted. Roma-masi had come in with a gift held behind her back and a placating birthday smile, which froze on her lips as she moved closer to the bed. She took in the scattered pages with a dawning horror in her eyes, and they looked at each other for what seemed a long time. Behind Mila's defiance all the winds of shame and fear were gathering. Aunty's eyes had been hurt, bewildered, her face pink with outrage. Then the storm had burst and the shocking tale was borne with hysterical dispatch to Father.

Mila was blubbering now. 'I don't know why I tore them.' She didn't know how to tell Father that although her adventures in learning were spasmodic, she *loved* books. Her ear always responded to words. Words had magic, Rayhaan had assured her when he quit his fat airline job to create literature. Oh, she knew words had magic! So why had she mangled the printed pages? Why was she in battle every hour of the day?

'I don't know why I do the things I do,' she mourned. She could not assemble her baffling anxieties to work any meaning into them. She wanted to shake them off, like a wet dog coming in from the sea, but did not know how to achieve this liberation except by persisting in an ugly striving to make herself disagreeable to everyone. By sailing into a fight with arms flailing, plaits swinging, feet kicking, mouth screaming. By baiting and tormenting her brother, two years older but by nature passive and docile, with a tense imploring look in his eyes because she knew about the state of his bedsheets in the mornings and had learnt to use Vikram's secret shame against him.

'Daddy, wh-what's wrong with me? Am I . . . like Soni said, cursed by malicious—'

'No!' His arms went round her, holding her tight. 'Nothing of the sort. Listen, Mila,' he whispered in her ear, 'listen carefully now. Quite early in life, and quite simply, we must come to this decision: *I am my own happiness*.' But this, too, was an act of the imagination, of faith, and Mila must have looked bewildered as he released her, for he added: 'Of course, at first it's a frightening decision. But it will help us grow tall and strong . . . And we will never feel cut off from our own power and value.'

I start as the grandfather clock in the living room begins to strike seven. The chimes cut across the high-falutin words pronounced by Father so long ago. Pushing aside the crumpled copy of the *Times* I heave myself up from the divan—almost knocking down the empty platter of jalebis—to switch on the lights. Immediately the handsome dimensions of the room are revealed, and I see how transformed it is from the one I remember: repainted, reappointed specially for my homecoming, Vikram told me—where the hell is he? Has my idiot brother forgotten about the dinner party? I dismiss Vikram and try to reconstruct the original living room in my head: the divan had been under the large picture window on the opposite wall and the hand-embroidered wall-hanging from Bhavnagar, which Mother had laughingly promised me as part of my dowry (I'd grown fond of its geometric stars, flowers and village girls), had been removed from next to the window to adorn the wall above the old rocker, which I was glad had survived the changes . . . But my mind skips back to Mila.

Isn't it kinder to a child to demarcate for her the good she must do from the bad she must not, in the simple Zoroastrian manner? To assure her that light is bound to triumph over darkness—as Baimai earnestly tried to convince me over dinner the other night? When we fight the good fight, Baimai had said, Ahura Mazda is on our side and angels rush to protect us. But that was not what Father tried to teach me that morning long ago when I had just turned thirteen. He told me, virtually, that I was on my own. Had it been his intention to put Mila on the sharp quick road to self-reliance because there was no other help for her?

All Mila knew that day was that her father was gentle and wise, proven and dependable. The fortress of the family, the place that could not be shaken. Will I one day recover this omniscient father? Make me feel *good*, I am tempted to plead with him as I reach down the years to touch this image of him. Let Sharmila stay secure within the charmed radius of your presence like Mila did when she was a child, when she could drive out hurt and fear because *you* practised denying them in yourself. Yet that image today has a brittleness that will cause it to crack before my eyes, disintegrate, if I get too close to it.

'So out of bed now,' Father said briskly to Mila that morning, 'to bathe, dress, breakfast . . . and enjoy the day. What are holidays meant for?' He bent over to kiss her forehead and Mila flung her arms round him. She loved him utterly! Over his shoulder she saw a movement behind the bedroom curtain, and even in that instant the thought crossed her mind—and immediately she was scornful—that Aunt Roma was tethered to the doorway, listening to them behind the protective drapery.

But the next moment the heavy curtain was swept aside, and it was Mother who entered the room.

3

Vikram was annoyed when I opened the door to him as late as 8 p.m. in my housecoat. 'I thought we weren't going to the party,' I said in defence of my *déshabillé*.

'What gave you that idea?'

'I was expecting you home by six.' Petulantly: 'At least you should have called.'

'Why? The invitation's for 8.30 and I take twenty minutes to shower and change. We would have been in good time if you'd been ready.'

I decided to sulk. 'Well I don't want to make you late. You can go without me.'

For a moment Vikram looked as if he just might gallop off like a willing horse, but he relented. By 9.15 I was dressed in one of my mother's saris, a blue silk with a riot of green paisley motifs, very fetching, but all my brother said was, 'Your jeans would have done just as well.'

And indeed they would have, for most things about parties in Bombay these days are incongruous. This one was a crowded affair in a penthouse on Cuffe Parade, where unabashed miniskirts mingled with sweeping sequined saris and jeans, trouser suits and ornate Punjabi outfits clashed with freaky sartorial innovations picked up from Fashion Street. I need not have worried about being late, either, because dramatic entrances by tardy couples continued almost up to midnight.

On the adjoining terrace, where the lights were dim and the amplified music deafening, the pelvic thrusts of arthritic elders (obviously the hostess's kinfolk) were in sad competition with more adolescent endeavours (by her children and their friends). One unbarbered nephew who asked me to dance was divine on the floor, but I've forgotten his name. And leggy teenagers who made a beeline for my brother would have soon discarded him as a stuffed shirt, I suspected, but for the scar across his right cheek which lent him a deceptively rakish air.

In the sizeable living room with the sizeable bar there was incessant chatter and laughter and smoke, but no conversation. Every time Vikram introduced me to strangers as Mila, I revised that to Sharmila, which rather irritated him. We were an ill-assorted group in an alcoholic haze with only one thing in common: our growling hungry stomachs, for our hep hostess was reluctant to serve food till the midnight hour had struck. Vikram wanted to leave immediately after dinner. We left before dessert was served.

'Why wasn't Urmi there?' I asked him in the car on our way home.

'She wasn't invited,' he said shortly.

'Oh.' I was wide awake despite the wee hour (my alcoholic intake had been minimal), and decided to pursue the subject from another angle. I was about to ask Vikram if unattached females were tolerated only at hen teas and girls' luncheons while only couplehood was honoured at superior repasts like the one we had just enjoyed, when my brother startled me by saying, 'You look good in a sari.' His eyes were on the road. 'Mother's, isn't it?'

'Of course,' I said, fingering the silk. 'I've not got round to buying my own.'

'She last wore it the day she came home from Panchgani. The day after your birthday, when we weren't expecting her at all.' And he fell silent. My brother never ceases to astonish me. Does his mind still dwell on vivid portraits of our mother while she, pale star, sank aeons ago below the horizon into the surcease of death?

My sleep was fitful in the pre-dawn hours. In my repainted bedroom, my bed was the same one Mila had slept in years ago and she began to claim me once more, though by turning on my side to face the wall I hoped to turn my back on her. Restless, I manoeuvred my head to steal glances at my mother's sari, now a shadow draped neatly on the back of my polished rosewood chair. How astounding that Vikram had recognized it and not I, though I had chosen to wear it to the party. I couldn't pick out its colours in the gloom, but yes, it was the silk in which Mother had swept into this room, intruding on a poignant scene between a father and his thirteen-year-old daughter. There Shivani had stood, to the right of the wardrobe, and wound the end of the sari regally round her shoulders.

It's she, Mummy's come back to me, sang Mila's heart after the first blank incredulous moment, and her hands fumbled for her glasses on the beside table. She had to be *sure*, for a confrontation so sudden, before she released the joy crowding within her.

Yes, she was real. Mila wanted to make a dive for her mother, cling to her feet in an ecstasy of love, but she could not move from the bed. Vikram and Aunt Roma now slid into view, non-linear phantoms. For about Mother there was a quality so egocentric that by some mysterious suction she drew everything to herself; and walls, tiles and sticks on furniture, light, shadow and human shapes seemed to deny their prescribed places to regroup round her, accentuate her, own fealty to *her*.

It required Soni to break the spell. She entered the room with loud cries, nosed round her mistress with sheepdog-like anxiety, gathered her into her wet fold, released her, then stood with arms akimbo, scolding her for having returned home without fair warning. In moments of crisis Soni had great eloquence. In the same breath with which she voiced her pleasure at the queen bee's newly acquired plumpness, she commanded the drones and workers in the room to rub their feet hard on the floor to ward off the Evil Eye. Then she turned to Mother and resumed her chiding. What did she mean, catching them unprepared in this manner, with their imperfections heavy on them? Why, her sari cupboard was in a mess, her silver hairbrush and hand mirror had to be polished, her pot of the auspicious red powder was dry, her mattress had to be aired! Muttering and threatening, Soni withdrew from the room to terrorize the other servants into performing miracles of order.

Shivani had endured this tirade with an unreadable little smile on her face. Perhaps she had not heard Soni at all and hardly knew that her daughter had encircled her knees, her face pressed into sari pleats, glasses cutting into flushed cheeks. Mila looked up from her haven, claiming affection as if by assault, only to find her mother's eyes fixed on Father across the room.

'Well?' Mother breached the silence. 'Aren't you glad to see me?' It was said with defiance. And as she devoured him whole with her eyes, her blouse seemed the thinnest covering for the nakedness of her breasts, her blue-green sari the sheerest drapery over insistent thighs. But on the bed her father held himself so still that Mila feared a delicate mechanism inside him had snapped.

At last something flickered in his eyes. 'Welcome home, Shivani,' he said. Was his voice composed, or hollow with resignation? Then he did an unexpected thing. As Shivani lifted one hand in a gesture at once assertive and suppliant, he abruptly left the room.

Above Mila her mother jerked herself free of her daughter's embrace, brushed past Roma and Vikram and followed Naren out. It all happened so suddenly that Mila found herself without a prop and trembling. The main actors had muffed their lines, deserted the stage. The scene was unrehearsed. No part in it was written for her; she had to find the cues herself and was filled with a nameless dread.

She turned uncertainly to Vikram. 'Isn't it wonderful,' she asked, her voice shrill, 'that Mummy is back?'

'Yes,' whispered Vikram, but he avoided her eyes and drew closer to Roma-masi. Aunt and nephew had a pact, it appeared; they shared an alliance from which she was excluded. When Aunty put an affectionate arm round his shoulders they seemed to close ranks against her and Mila was physically afflicted, in throat and belly and knees, by her sense of rejection.

The next moment her unwholesome excitement foamed over. She pushed her masi out of the way and began screaming at Vikram, shouting, sputtering malice, spilling venom, almost incoherent with hurt and a senseless, vindictive rage. She knew her face was ugly, her mouth contorted, her body shaking, her heart near bursting. Roma-masi tried to say something. Mila gave her a shove that sent her reeling against the wall and threw herself on Vikram. But before she could bite his hands, kick his shins, land a movie punch on his chin, rake his white face with her nails, she felt an arm tighten round her waist. She struggled madly against that iron arm, bending and twisting and clawing every way, but it held her secure. And her father—when had he returned to the scene?—lifted her completely off her feet, swung her up against his chest and sat down on the bed holding her writhing body on his knees.

At last her panic subsided and Mila grew quieter, though between sobs she still repeated Vikram's shame and poured scorn on his head.

'Be quiet!' Father looked down on her with anxious eyes. 'At once!' She turned her head against his chest and saw that they were alone in the room. And suddenly she was tired to her bones, bewildered and despondent.

He held her patiently for a long time. 'It is not something that Vikram can help,' he said at last. 'It is an involuntary habit. It is cruel of you to hold it like a stick over his head.'

Mila considered this. 'Very well.' She swallowed a hiccough. 'I won't hold it against him then. I'll pity him.'

'Pity,' said her father, putting her down on the bed beside him, 'is a secret gloating. To pity someone is to see him as far down the ladder as he can get. Here, take my handkerchief.'

She blew her nose loudly. 'What, then, should I do?' she asked almost humbly.

'Mila, you love your brother?' She nodded miserably, her eyes filling again. 'Then that's all you have to do. Love him. Which means you accept him as he is. Make no demands, impose no conditions. You don't judge— now, no crying again! That's the only way, Mila, you can help another human being.'

She stared blindly at his face, her heart swelling within her. Again she had not fully understood the import of his words. They had merely skimmed over her head with friendly, outspread wings and she passionately wished he would not stop speaking, but he got up wearily from the bed. 'I must go. Your mother will be out of her bath by now.' The prospect of encountering her again seemed to give him a leaden feeling, and Mila felt the familiar grip of tension in her stomach. She did not recognize this reluctant father any more than the mother who had walked out on her welcome. Were there two Narens, then, and two Shivanis?

In the nascent morning light I turn on my stomach and a fist tightens in my guts as I resurrect the two Narens and two Shivanis in this very room. I am thirteen again, and it is as though the first of each pair offers protection, my splendid father, my beautiful mother. But the second discordant couple is menacing my world and I see danger hanging tidal over it. The second Naren threatens his home because his eyes are fatigued: instead of seeing his wife, they are deciphering a secret code on a doomed wall. The second Shivani is on some extreme edge of herself. She is sick and frightened, so that before her Naren has to keep a perfect front, not only in moments of crisis, but every moment, every day, and all his tomorrows . . .

Naren has made his exit and I see Mila jump to her feet and hurry out of her room in pursuit of the daddy who guarded her childhood, the bulwark against the wilderness in her. And there, huddled on the telephone stool at the end of the passage, she found Vikram.

He stood up slowly. They stared at each other. Under his eyes the shadows were dark as bruises. Vikram had wiped away his tears but there was still a tremor round his mouth, which gave Mila a sense of her own power. At the same time she felt such tenderness for her brother that she flung her arms round him and held him tight. For a moment his trapped body stiffened and she felt he was going to push her away; but then they clung together and it was as if she, too, was being shielded. The clumsy embrace was strangely and stubbornly double-edged. They were seeking as well as affording protection. Against what? They were reaching out desperately for something—a virtue?—to share with each other. She loved him. She would have killed anyone who hurt her brother. It was sweet, this closeness. Unbelievably sweet.

But it did not last. Days went by, and Mila jealously watched Mother with Vikram. Of course Indian mothers doted on their sons; my *prince*, she called him, my *jewel*, my *peacock*. Beside him Mila felt as ordinary as a bunch of coriander leaves. But she was perceptive enough to see that certain things about him irritated Mummy: the way a sudden noise made him start visibly; the way he sidled into a room, as if he expected to deal with an enemy waiting in ambush for him; the way he hated to speak up or explain his difficulties—which was why at oral work at school he was the butt of his classmates' jokes. And clever Mila soon learned that Mother was mortified that a grown boy should wet his bed every night.

No, it did not escape Mila that Vikram was becoming more and more unknown to his mother. Sometimes her son's remoteness filled Shivani with despair, sometimes it bred in her a kind of baffled fury. At such times she warded off the rare, tentative caress and never realized the icy distances she set between them: that her withdrawal resulted in the freezing over of Vikram's whole world. She chafed against the fact that her only son was so solitary, shy and unsociable. A hibernating creature, burrowing into holes, hiding in corners. It made her angry, it nonplussed her that he was totally without the impertinences that could make a boy of his age so lively, such fun to be with.

Because Mila was excitable and impulsive, so much the enemy of constraint, Mother understood her better. Her shrillness did not offend her as much as Vikram's quiescence. 'Can you emit sparks?' the cat asked the ugly duckling in Mila's old English storybook. *She* could. Like a cat, she was all sparks and scratches when rubbed the wrong way. This Mother could understand because she, too, gave off sparks. But Vikram's long, self-effacing silences defeated her. She did not know that behind them a jungle screamed and winds howled, shadows lunged and lost birds cried. Father knew, and Vikram was the cause of a persistent battle of wills between his parents.

After lunch one hot Sunday afternoon Father tried to engage his son in conversation, to draw him out. At this time the only friend of his age that Vikram had was Kishore, Ritu's brother. What the two boys had in common was not at all obvious. Kishore was tough and pugnacious—every time he playfully jumped Vikram he almost cracked a rib or two. And he hated his father, while Vikram adored his.

For some reason Papa's inspired speculations in sugar and groundnuts, and other dazzling financial coups, had failed to impress Kishore. Perhaps because Mansukhlal Motichand dressed so humbly, spoke so meekly. And were it not for the exigencies of the female population of his tribe (clamorous wife, daughter, sisters, aunts, sisters-in-law), MM would have continued to live in conditions of anonymity, guided into such saintly conduct by his guru. Indeed, despite having amassed his fortune in just two decades, no one could be less *nouveau* in his *richesse* than MM. Was it his lack of richmanship (which almost succeeded in camouflaging his wealth), or his white garb of spirituality (which almost disguised his greed) that had alienated his son? Perhaps Kishore would have taken more kindly to his pater had the old man not differed so radically from his ulcerated counterparts in the West, who, equally agile in habitual fraud, as triumphant in compound deceit and clever brigandage, are distinguishable in any crowd by the quality of being rich. The indifferent gaze, the lips fixed in command or drooping with ennui speak boldly enough that cash has purchased for them the blissful state in which they can tell you to go to hell. But MM, mild as milk, with his benign smiles, palms joined in timid greetings, his simple white dhoti and Gandhi cap, was a different breed of dacoit altogether. An indigenous Indian breed that Kishore, tainted as he was by inexpert Westernization, could not stomach at all.

But that had not prevented him from helping himself to Papa's money for his latest escapade. Four days ago Kishore had run away from home, his pockets bulging with cash and wild ideas crowding his head: from Kathmandu he had intended to sneak into Red China. But, traced to his obscure hotel in Delhi by the police (with whom his papa had appropriate connections), he had been brought back to Bombay by the first flight that morning.

'You've spoken to Kishore yet?' Father asked Vikram.

'No.' Vikram averted his face. He sat with his knees and ankles crossed, making a kind of rope of his thin bare legs.

'But *I* spoke to Ritu this morning,' Mila volunteered. 'Kishore is not one bit sorry or anything.'

'You know what made him do it?' asked Mother.

Vikram shook his head, then numbled something about his friend being suspended from school for a week for smoking in class.

'And for refusing to cut his hair,' Mila chimed in again, officiously. 'Ritu told me so. I bet you've never tried a cigarette,' she said to Vikram with malicious intent. 'Not even one little puff.' Her brother squirmed and tensed in his chair.

'I don't see why he should,' Father came to his rescue. 'If he doesn't want to.' At this Roma-masi flashed him a grateful look, and Mila understood that for Vikram the fabric of security was woven by his father and his aunt. But this, for some reason, convicted them of failing *her*, and she was troubled.

She tossed her head. 'Well, I'm going to try everything just as soon as I can!' This bit of bravado came out shrill and spiteful.

'What I'm going to try now,' said Father lightly, rising to his feet, 'is an afternoon nap.'

They all got up except Vikram, who remained glued to his chair. In passing Mother brushed his hair with tender fingers, a gesture that made Mila feel so neglected that she cast about for some means to win adult attention. She remembered the watercolour drying on her desk and ran to fetch it.

Her masterpiece was a gooey sunset scene. It would have made a good poster for tomato ketchup, but Mila was very proud of it. Holding it reverently before her with both hands, she was about to walk into her parents' room when Vikram's name, spoken in a high, excitable voice by Mother, made her stop outside the curtain and listen. In such matters as eavesdropping and reading other people's mail, she had no compunctions. Given the opportunity, she thought, everybody did it.

'. . . but he's almost fifteen years old!' Mother's voice.

'Shivani, why can't I make you see that this is a symptom of some deep disturbance . . .' There were murmurs Mila could not hear.

'. . . for which I am to blame, I suppose!' Her mother was apparently pacing the room, and had paused before the thin divide of the curtain.

'That's not what I said.'

'That being so,' she went on, not heeding his protest, 'perhaps it *is* better to send him away from me. The Mayo College in Ajmer—'

'Is everything you say it is, but not for Vikram.'

'Rayhaan schooled there. He's practically spent his whole life away from his parents—here and abroad. It's made him grow into a young man of poise and confidence.'

'Vikram is not Rayhaan.'

'No,' she said bitterly. She moved away from the curtain.

'Rayhaan is . . .' Father spoke so quietly, Mila could not hear all he said, '. . . the product of a consciously sophisticated background . . . the supreme egotist. If he worships anything, it is his own talent.'

Impatiently: 'Why must you harp on Rayhaan? It is—'

'You mentioned Rayhaan.'

'What if I did? It's Vikram we have to decide about.'

'The boarding school is the right answer for boys of a certain temperament. For Vikram it would be a disaster.'

'And me?' Her voice rose alarmingly. 'Have you found the right answer for me?'

'Shivani—'

'Didn't I see how upset you were to have me back?'

'I was upset because you did not complete your treatment. The doctors—'

'But I'm absolutely well now, I keep telling you! You keep harping on treatment. Do you know what it's been like? Driving miles to the Wai hospital every morning, six days a week. Waking up at midday in a cold, clammy bed, soaked to the skin and made to drink heavily sugared tea that to even think of today makes me sick, *sick* . . .' She had paced to the far side of the room and Mila could not hear her. '. . . and put on this enormous quantity of weight.'

'That's because of the greatly increased carbohydrate intake. You'll soon shed it.' Low murmurs.

'. . . and with Mother sitting on my back, I just couldn't take it any more. I could not! In every letter I pleaded with you—'

So absorbed was Mila in her eavesdropping that she had forgotten where she was till footsteps in the passage, the jingle of bangles and the scent of soap brought her to herself. She wheeled round and almost collided with Soni, who, bedouined up to her nose with freshly picked clothes from the washline on the rear balcony, shouted: 'You can't see?

In your head you have eyes or marbles?' And she shook a fist crammed with clothes pegs at her.

Mila smiled weakly and, hugging her watercolour to her bosom, walked back to her room. The conversation she had overheard was far from reassuring. It echoed back to her as she stood before her mirror, examining the paint that had come off on her shirt front. Was Mummy seriously ill, then? Only very ill people went to hospital. Mila had a down-the-shaft sensation in the pit of her stomach. At the same time her mind struggled to carry high, like a tugging kite, the thought that Mummy was better, that she had quite recovered. Hadn't she said so herself . . .?

'You are getting up today or not?' Soni's voice again. I must have dozed off, for when I open my eyes she stands on the threshold of my room in bright daylight. 'Baba has to go to work'—even if you have nothing better to do than loll in bed, her voice implies—'and he's asked for breakfast.' She is waddling out of the room when her eyes fall on Mother's sari on the chair.

She snatches it up, muttering that it will lie there for days if she doesn't fold it and put it back in the cupboard where it belongs. After all these years, Soni is still possessive about Mother's things.

4

Since my return I rarely speak to Vikram (or anyone else) about Mother, but at the breakfast table this morning I said, with an enormous yawn, 'What a bore, the penthouse "do" last night. Remember the dinners Mother used to host? The party she threw for Roma-masi within days of her return from Panchgani?'

'Mother threw that party for herself,' said Vikram as he passed the toast. 'She loved parties—the visiting sister was only an excuse.'

'Mother loved people!' I rose to her defence.

'She was afraid of solitude,' said Vikram as he stirred his coffee. 'She had reason to be.'

I digested that slowly with my buttered toast. And it struck me that Vikram was more perceptive than I had ever given him credit for. Had he known even as a boy how passionately troubled our mother was, how vulnerable and easy to damage? I had been aware of her great beauty, her gaiety, her restless appetite for life—the more glittering facets of her illness—but had her son understood that she needed to be guided with active and affirmative insistence at all times? That the reins had to be drawn tight to keep her on the road to rationality, that care had to be taken to blockade the many devious routes to derangement?

Vikram had finished his coffee and was about to light up the first of his three cigarettes of the day when I said sharply, 'What are you doing? I thought we agreed the dining room is a no-smoking zone.'

'Sorry. Forgot.' As he replaced the cigarette in its pack his gestures had something of Father's imperturbability. 'I'll smoke it in the car. Tell me, Mila—'

'Sharmila.'

'*Shar*mila, was it the media hype in the States that made you forswear the habit? Because here you were all set to try everything. Remember?'

'I did try everything,' I said stiffly, disliking the sly gleam in his eyes.

'Even drugs?'

'Yes,' I admitted with reluctance.

'And?'

'And my first dream smoke made me so sick, I didn't have the guts to try it a second time.' Suddenly I didn't mind my brother knowing this. Suddenly it seemed pointless to offer him selected fictions from my exile, or to hide from him behind a complex of little accommodations and dishonesties. 'It was like breathing over a burning acrid rag,' I told him. 'I coughed and choked, my throat felt raw, my nose ran, my eyes ran, my heart raced, my stomach heaved. *This* a substitute for grace? Never again.'

'Why,' asked Vikram slowly, 'did your body put up such violent resistance, do you suppose? Because you dared not let go?'

'*Dared* not?' I nervously snapped up the last bit of my toast.

'You know, dared not lose track of yourself? Dared not slide down towards oblivion, cease to exist even for a short spell . . . because of what had happened to our mother?'

His observation stuck in me like a thorn. He was right, of course, but his words were pushing me against the uneasy conjunction of the known and the unknown and I shied away from the question with a shrug. He did not pursue the subject, and presently got up to leave for work.

But alone at the table, where I continue to sit after Soni has cleared it of the breakfast things, I am a prisoner of memory, feeling again the tug of a weighted plumbline. I see Mother laughing and talking with her guests, gossipy and witty by turns, shimmering and glowing in a tusser sari dyed a sunburst yellow. At the same party I see my aunt, ostensibly the guest of honour, wading through a sea of treacle, moving from trap to trap: Roma-masi is smiling painfully at everything said to her, her expressions uncertain, hands excusing her faltering speech with lame gestures of expiation. And of course I see Mila, sitting decorously alone on the divan under the picture window, looking up at Rayhaan lounging nearby, his dark head almost touching the border of the embroidered Bhavnagar fabric adorning the wall behind him.

Mila looked up at Rayhaan leaning negligently against the wall and thought how well he fit into her favourite daydream, which went something like this: she was out shopping in some kind of diaphanous drapery when she was spotted by an olive-hued, savagely handsome sheikh, also out for a day's shopping. Carried off in one swoop to his luxurious tent, she was made junior assistant to his fourth wife and lived her days in delirious happiness, except when she wondered if her classmates—Ritu in particular—ever thought of her, the jealous cats . . .

Mila's fantasy collapsed when her mother joined Rayhaan at the window. Dinner was over, and some of the guests had already left. 'Tired?' Rayhaan asked her.

'Not really,' said Mother. 'I'm so glad to be home again.'

From his great height Rayhaan stared down at her with impunity for a full moment. Then he said, 'I agree with everyone in this room, Shivani, though I always want to bite my tongue before saying it: you are beautiful.'

Shivani laughed. 'It's sweet of you to say so to an overweight matron like me.' She reached up to pat him lightly on the cheek.

Rayhaan flung back his head as if stung, then said quietly, 'You did that on purpose, to make me feel like a nephew. Do you mind not playing the beguiling aunt with me?'

'Well,' Shivani was smiling, 'I *am* a haggish forty, you know. And you a handsome stripling of—'

'Don't.' Then he added, 'What a neat gift you have for duplicity. You and all the other chaste wives in this room with king-size heroes for husbands. Never mind.' He was looking across the room. 'Who is that pretty new face?'

She turned. 'My sister Roma. Weren't you introduced to her as you came in?'

'No. I tried to catch her eye, but she looked away with becoming modesty. Married?'

'No. The youngest, and lives with Mother in Panchgani. Why?'

'I have this love-hate relationship with all fetching unmarried girls,' said Rayhaan, straightening up against the wall. 'My time is spent either pursuing them or eluding them. To meet one in your home is sheer violation of sanctuary.'

'Oh!' It was Shivani's turn to draw herself up. 'Are you accusing me of keeping pretty young girls away from you?'

'You would if you could.' He was grinning down at her. There was an air about him, always, of ease, of the privileged son of a privileged family. 'You know I almost followed you to Panchgani?'

'A mercy you didn't! Mother would have had you thrown downhill from Kate's Point. Or shot for a tiger on the prowl. But it's the best hill station for miles around and I had a splendid holiday. You can see the extra pounds on me.' She faked a laugh. When he did not respond, she looked away, and as her eyes rested on Mila on the divan they were troubled, they carried a hint of anxiety, of caution, and did not acknowledge her daughter's smile. Shivani turned back to the window. 'I like to look at the sky,' she said in a constrained voice. 'The stars make me conscious of the universe to which I belong. I *do* have a place in it and that is as reassuring as . . . love.'

'Did you say "love"?'

'But,' Shivani shivered, not heeding the interruption. 'I hate to look down, I'm scared of heights.' She was out in space somewhere by herself a moment longer, then turned to Rayhaan briskly. 'So, have you been working?'

'No.'

'Ah, the Great Novel's not shaping so well?' Despite herself, Shivani could not keep a punishing note of triumph, of scolding righteousness out of her voice. 'I told you it was a mistake to throw up that job!'

'We agreed not to discuss this.'

'If you hated airline work, your father could have set you up in some business. You only had to ask.'

'Don't nag me. You're not my wife.'

'Or come with Naren into the printing firm. The offer is still open.'

'For which I'm grateful to you both, but it's simply not what I want to do.'

'I know young men who'd jump at a chance like that. But of course *they* have to earn a living. Adjust to—'

'Money, quickly amassed money. To a merchant-class appreciation of things that makes for mediocrity.'

'Listen to you! You talk so high-and-mighty because—'

'I don't want to talk about it at all, I told you.' Abruptly: 'I called on Amrish a couple days ago. He's not so well.'

She sighed. 'Is it the same complaint?'

'Your brother doesn't talk about himself. But he called me a self-infatuated fool.'

She became animated at once. 'How right he is!'

'An indisciplined dilettante.'

'Ah!'

'He said my mind was still in a chrysalis. That I have only bouts of thinking, like he has bouts of asthma.'

'My brother can always size things up pretty well.' Her smile was entrancing.

'How right you are. About you he said you'd disown anything tinged with failure. Like your mother.'

She stiffened. 'You discuss me with Amrish?'

He laughed. 'Don't alarm yourself. It was just his way of shaking me out of my inertia, pushing me back to my word processor.'

'What else did you talk about?'

'Oh, with Amrish I usually hold my tongue. *He* treated me to the aphorisms of Patanjali—elaborated on the first one on concentration. Then, between bouts of coughing, he deprecated the fact that I write in English. My sad fate, he said, was never to be sung in the fields or acclaimed by multitudes.'

'Well, you should have talked things over with Amrish before chucking up your job.'

'I did, so shut up. The gravest danger for me, he said, is that I will produce books tailor-made for Western consumption.'

'Why not write in Punjabi, then?'

'Never learnt it.'

'Or Gujarati? You must have learnt some Gujarati from your mother.'

'That's the point,' he said with wry humour, 'I learnt *some*. You know the kind of mutilated Gujarati the Parsis speak... which never bothered my mother, she was so thoroughly anglicized.'

'But she fought to have your navjote ceremony done.'

'Dad allowed it to indulge her—rituals mean very little to him. But *her* community was up in arms. The old priest who initiated me almost got chucked out of his fire temple.'

'I've never asked you this, Rayhaan: do you think of yourself as a Zoroastrian?'

'Hell no. I try not to think of myself as *this*, for then I put myself up against *that*. The navjote is just a wonderful childhood memory: there was a band and lights and sumptuous Parsi food—and my mother. A year later she was dead.' After a pause, 'Why do you never go to see your brother?'

Shivani's face closed guardedly, as if his question were a breach of security. She looked round the room. 'There's my sister talking to poor Gita Seth. Shall we join them?' Then, sharply, 'What are you grinning at?'

'At the "poor" Gita Seth. You attach these neat tags to everything.'

'What do you mean? Gita's had a most tragic experience—'

'God, I've heard all that. But you know her real tragedy? Living in the wrong century. In the old days a childless Hindu widow could invite a brother-in-law or any available brahmin stud to father a child with her, without the least shame or prudery.'

'Rayhaan!'

'*And* in the interests of the Aryan community. A valid remedy based on a frank acceptance of the flesh, wouldn't you say? A woman has the right to fulfilment without having to scheme and cheat. Where are you going?'

'I have to circulate.'

'Don't run away, damn it. *Poor* Gita has only to say the word and the old Rajput sense of chivalry I lapped up as a schoolboy will command me at her service.' He gave a little mock bow in Gita's direction.

'A service,' snapped Shivani with flushed cheeks, 'with which you are generous to *all* petitioners, I've heard!'

'From whom? Ah, my gossipy landlady has been visiting you again. Did Mrs Choksy confide in you that I feed every night on a banquet of tarts?'

'Something like that!'

'To which you voiced no objections, I trust?' He was gazing hard at her.

'You're drunk,' she said scornfully. 'Choksy is going to write to your father about it—before she kicks you out.'

'Not she! She's not going to kick me out while I can afford her outrageous rent—which may not be for long, I admit. You aren't thinking of deserting me?'

'It obviously hasn't occurred to you that I have other guests.'

'To hell with them, I need you. So the officious old witch is going to complain to Father, is she? What if I tell you, Shivani, that Dad's always encouraged me to investigate for myself the truth that all women are basically alike—'

'I won't stand here and listen to you abuse your father!'

'I'm not abusing him, heaven forbid. Respect for our elders is the bedrock of our society.' He broke off as she made an impatient movement. 'Don't go.'

'I must go,' she insisted, but stood fast for a moment, fighting him in silence, angry and helpless, Then she flounced away so abruptly that the heavy coil of hair high on her head unrolled a little, escaping form the combs that sought to restrain it.

Rayhaan made no move to follow her but leaned back against the wall and surveyed the room. Like someone watching the stage from the wings. From her divan Mila called out to him.

'Why, hello,' he smiled down at her. 'You're up rather late tonight, aren't you?'

Mila explained that her vacation wasn't over yet. Mother had returned from Panchgani a day too late for her birthday party—about which she had been wholly penitent—and to make up for it had allowed her one late night.

'I see.' Rayhaan sat down beside her and went through the motions of lighting a cigarette. Mila stared at his mouth. It was a reckless kind of a mouth, she decided, one that could get him into all kinds of trouble. She liked the scent of his cigarette. She liked his nose, too.

'You don't have a proper Parsi nose,' she observed as she examined the prominent but shapely appendage.

'It's not quite like a trumpet,' he agreed, 'but almost there. A legacy from my maternal grandpa.'

'Baimai Buhariwalla from my class has a proper Parsi nose,' she volunteered. 'I attended her navjote. Vikram was invited too, but he was too shy to come.'

'And he's not here tonight? I don't see him.'

'Oh, he can't stay up late, he's such a baby.'

'Did he enjoy Nirad Chaudhuri's book?' Rayhaan encouraged them to read in several directions—some of them curious enough to have outraged the good nuns at Mila's school, had they come to learn of this bookworms' orgy.

'He hasn't finished it yet,' sighed Mila, 'and I can't start on it till he does.' But her mind was on other things. 'You don't think she's *very* pretty, do you?'

'Who?' Startled, he removed the cigarette from his mouth.

'Roma-masi. I heard you say she's pretty. Soni says she's so fair you can see the water trickling down her throat when she has a drink—but can't say *I've* noticed.' Mila tossed her head.

'Well . . .' He looked across the room in Masi's direction, then swiftly down at her. 'You don't like her?'

'She's all *right*,' Mila said disdainfully. 'She's your *age*, I suppose. But you won't let Mother talk you into marrying her?'

His dark eyes flashed for a moment and Mila thought he was going to be angry. But he threw back his head and gave a hoot of laughter.

'What's so funny?'

'I'm sorry.' He stopped laughing and looked at her intently. 'So you wouldn't approve of the match? Tell me, wouldn't you like me to be your uncle, Mila? Your Rayhaan-masa?'

'No.' She shook her head emphatically. 'I'd like to marry you myself when I'm old enough and you are famous.'

Mila could have bitten her tongue and for a terrible moment thought he was going to laugh again, but he didn't. Slowly he stubbed his cigarette in the brass ashtray on the window ledge behind him, then turned to her. 'I will remind you of this a few years from now, and Mila,' he took her hands in both of his, 'you won't believe me.' The eyes looking down on her were quizzical, but also very kind, and she found herself trusting the quality of his voice. But she also felt confused, and for the first time his beauty troubled her, made her shy and anxious and terribly aware that she was so plain and clumsy. She tried to pull her hands away, but he was looking at them. 'You have your mother's elongated hands,' he said. 'The lovely slenderness of her fingers.' Mila was rapturous. Thank God she no longer chewed her nails like Preeti Madnani in class.

He dropped her hands. 'So you think I'm going to be famous?'

'As a writer,' Mila nodded eagerly. 'I just know it.'

'You have no idea how good that sounds. I won't ask *why* you think so, your answer might spoil everything. But fame is the only condition on which you are prepared to marry me?'

Now he was teasing her and suddenly, inexplicably, Mila was close to tears. 'Go,' she said. 'Mummy is calling you.'

And indeed Mother was looking in their direction. She was laughing but her hand, raised to beckon Rayhaan, summoned him peremptorily. Rayhaan looked across at her with an almost burlesque scowl, stubborn, resistant for a moment, like one acting out his revolt in order to minimize it. Then he shrugged and left Mila to walk across to Shivani.

Mila saw him smile at Roma-masi, whose hands made little futile gestures. She saw him say something to Gita, who was doing her borrowed Hindi-movie-star routine involving teeth, dimples, eyelashes and a demure glass of Thums Up laced generously with rum. Gita's laughter trilled out as she gazed up at the young man. Mila felt a sharp stab of pain and wanted to scratch her eyes out.

5

For hours after Vikram left for work I chased up memories of Gita Seth at the same time that a more fastidious voice in me deplored this mental witch-hunt. But no matter what I did, painting my toenails or being called to the phone by Baimai, with a book in hand or at the lunch table polishing off the new cook's khandvi and khichdi and Soni's brinjal curry (the reverence accorded to homemade food in this household has resurrected my faith in the culinary art), one ear was cocked, so to speak, for Gita's footfalls.

She laboured for my father. Her desk was outside his cubicle on the first floor of a squat, two-storey building in a congested part of the city. SHIVA FINE ARTS AND LITHO WORKS had its offices on the first floor, processing and plate-making departments on the enclosed terrace and the press in the basement. As I look back I see Gita nibbling round the edges of the glass door that kept her out of my father's cell, nibbling round his teak desk, papers and files, round the elegantly framed picture of his wife and children, getting bolder and nibbling round their lives like a small, industrious insect till she had wormed her way into the very heart of our little family circle, a voracious *third* presence always with us.

I catch recurrent glimpses of Gita everywhere, like a dream image or a leitmotif: I see Father and Mila immersed in schoolbooks, and Gita too is bending over the child to help with the homework. The downpour of her perfume is heady, it makes Mila squirm, but Father sits stiff and unyielding in his chair. Now Gita is smiling at Vikram, now sharing our family meal, now presiding over guests while Mother lies in bed with a headache. Now she is with us in a skiff-light boat on a sunny lake during our last summer trip to Kashmir (before the trouble there put a stop to our annual visits), making herself endearingly small among the cushions in the shelter of Father's maleness. And wherever Gita manifested herself, at whatever point of time, she seemed to crowd out the people I loved. Without appearing to use her elbows at all, Gita shoved them out of her way. There was no solitude *à deux* that she did not invade and destroy.

The strange thing is that before I met Gita, my imagination had reached out to encompass her shattering experience: her husband had been killed in a car crash within the first month of their marriage. For some inexplicable reason the tender core of my heart—on which I was learning to plant thorns, briars, thistles and cacti for my protection—had been touched by the plight of this unknown woman. I had visualized her with naked, bangle-less wrists, forehead bare of the vermilion marriage daub, in a borderless sari that declared her widowhood in every austere fold and spoke of sanctity, joys renounced. I had pictured Gita as a woman folded over her past, re-reading letters, clasping a photograph to her quivering bosom, caressing old clothes... And when at last I met her—she had brought home some papers from the office for Father to sign—I searched her face for the ravages of sorrow I felt must be indelibly stamped there. But the young face was unlined.

'You don't look like a widow at all!' I blurted out.

I shall never forget that Gita was not wounded by my words, but furious. Her eyes narrowed and she glared at me. I think in that moment we recognized one another. I knew at once, with the intuitive secretiveness of a growing child, that Daddy's secretary was not to be trusted. And Gita knew in that instant that the daughter would fight her, always. I had continued to stare at her solely in the hope of finding nourishment for my hostility, for Gita's apparent fragility had not deceived me: she was not so much pretty as cute, with her rounded girl-body, her pouts and sulks, her shrugs and skillful little self-flatteries.

Father walked into the room then, and Gita's eyes promptly filled with tears. The clever bitch was now a wounded doe. He asked her a question and she was attentive to the point of trembling. She answered him haltingly, her eyes misty, and further demonstration was curtailed only because they were not alone. Father looked puzzled. He threw a quick, questioning lance at me. Clearly he felt awkward and defenceless before Niobe while she wept her silent, copious and becoming tears. And clearly Gita felt the power of her tears as she advanced against the daughter behind their silver shield, while demanding to be rescued by the father.

My face betrayed nothing. I watched my adversary coldly, unmoved by her being so small and vulnerable. Perhaps she had hoped I would leave the room, but I held my ground, and it was Gita who was routed.

After that first encounter, Gita tried to be nice to me whenever we met. If she had wanted a return match it was okay by me, but it was obviously part of her strategy that I should like her. Her moist eyes were shrewd enough to see that the daughter had to be handled with tact. And I was equally polite to her. But neither of us was fooled, and the war we had begun continued to rage underground.

Gita had chic and sophistication, and at the party for Aunt Roma she arrived late enough to make an entrance. There was that brief, calculated pause at the threshold to check that all eyes were on her, and then she made a beeline for her hostess. Mila heard the excuse she offered for her tardiness: a last-minute print order had kept her glued to her desk after office hours. Then she said with false warm cordiality as she extended both hands to Mother, long nails bloodied like some terrible Goddess Durga after slaying the demon Mahisha: 'So *good* to have you back, Shivani!'

With that Gita walked away, her rump luscious in her magenta sari, and for the rest of the evening rendered herself useful in a variety of ways. Saw to it that the guests' tumblers and goblets were not empty. Helped Mother with bowls of cashew nuts, peanuts and potato crisps. Fussed round in circles to empty out ashtrays. After dinner she even found the time to reduce Dr Bakshi, a good doctor but an appallingly pedantic man, into a state of feeble helplessness with her girlish smiles, spoilt-child pouts and modest tugs at her sari tail each time it wantonly descended her shoulder to flash a make-love-not-war signal. Knowing she had an appetizing bosom, Gita had no qualms in putting it to work.

Mila yawned loudly. She was bored with the party, depressed by sitting on the divan like a wallflower. Unable to ward off a feeling of abandonment after Rayhaan had walked away, she stood up and crossed the room to her mother and squeezed herself against her on the chair. Mother made room for her absently. An argument was in progress and Shivani's attention was claimed wholly by Naren the philosopher.

'One is tolerant,' Father was saying to Rayhaan, 'when one can see the fact behind the appearance. Which is not to be confused with the laissez-faire attitude you're complaining about.'

'So what you're saying,' Rayhaan's tone was belligerent, 'is that we are not given to sitting on our asses, but are a tolerant race.'

'Well, look at what we Hindus came up with,' said Father mildly. 'We allowed contradictory doctrines to flourish neck and neck at one go. The Buddha's philosophy does not demand the existence of a Supreme Being. Vedanta does not require a personal God. Yet the devotee's submission to the Supreme embodied in a personal form has always been accepted. What is this if not tolerance? And I don't need to mention that India is home to many religions and lifestyles—'

'But,' Rayhaan interrupted, 'all that's over, all that's gone, the "glory that was Ind", the philosopher kings, the verities of the Vedic Age—all the old perfections, going, going, gone!'

'You're right,' said Father after a pause. 'Hindu dharma is being replaced by a sterile Hindutva. But perhaps what killed the old perfections *was* their perfection? Since what drives us on are our imperfections.' He added reflectively, 'That is why our omniscient rishis never prophesied doom.'

'Great!' Rayhaan gave a short laugh. 'Then let us be happy that there's no danger our present culture will cease through perfection.'

'Yet our imperfect age,' Gita piped up unexpectedly in her high voice, 'gave us a man like Mahatma Gandhi!' The name came out too pat. And Gita looked smug, as if its invocation out of all context was enough to lend her the virtues she did not possess.

'For God's sake,' Rayhaan turned to her impatiently, 'can't we Indians forget Gandhi now?'

'That you can say such a thing amazes me!' Gita was a child choking on an intense emotion. It often suited her purpose to turn everything into theatre, and there was a break in her voice as she said (to a nodding accompaniment by Mrs Rinky Thadani, who had come to the party without her husband but with his fortune dangling from her earlobes): 'How can we forget the Mahatma? That great soldier of liberty! That great seer of human destiny, martyr of the world's sorrow . . .' She turned to Father for approval, embellished and expectant as a bride, the shameless hussy.

Father was silent, but Mila's accusation rang out loud and shrill: 'She's pinched those lines from Sarojini Naidu!'

'I was wondering,' Rayhaan murmured, 'where I'd heard that mellifluous flow of words before.' He gave Mila a quick wink as she transferred from Mother's chair to the pouffe at her feet. 'A grand woman, Sarojini, but she sometimes hurt her message by overstating it.'

'I was only quoting from her,' snapped the filching female, her face so red, her cuteness all but curdled.

'Of course,' said Rayhaan silkily.

'I think it disgraceful, you see,' Dr Bakshi stepped into the breach, 'that Britain has unveiled Gandhiji's statue in London, and that in the capitals of Mexico, Italy, Norway and Guyana, the Mahatma's work is commemorated—and still Delhi is not having a prominent enough statue of the Mahatma!' He swelled with indignation in his seat and skinny Mrs Thadani condoled with him, her diamond earrings oscillating like a seismograph.

'Put up more statues of him by all means,' said Rayhaan. 'Turn him into stone or consign him to our history books. But let's stop using Gandhi for the buying and selling of votes and other sordid manoeuvres, dragging him into our hypocritical speeches and grubby preoccupations.' And he added, 'Let him not be handed down to us by teachers who don't know their souls from their elbows.'

Dr Bakshi rose majestically to his feet. His stalwart wife of many years rose with him. 'Oh, must you leave so early?' Mother protested.

'Assuredly,' said the worthy doctor, 'for Mrs Bakshi and self are not used to excessively late nights, you see.'

While her parents walked the couple to the door, Mila watched Gita from her pouffe. There was something about the poise of that soft body among the cushions that she resented. She wanted to pry her out of the big armchair, but was too sleepy to plan a strategy. Gita's cheeks were still flushed and the sari end had strayed down her arm again, revealing twin eager cones of flesh. She was a desirable woman, she had *volupté*. On her exposed neck Mila noticed a semi-circular bruise, a stippled discolouration. She squinted at it through her glasses and was about to jab a finger and ask Gita what had caused it, when an overwhelming tide of sleep blurred the woman and the room.

'... go to bed.' Her father's voice came to Mila from a great distance.

'No!' She sat bolt upright on her pouffe.

'You are ready to drop ... Goodnight, Mrs Thadani, you must come to us again when Mr Thadani returns from his tour.'

Gita now rose from her chair and said in a voice in which sweetmeats could be preserved, 'It's rather late and I'm a poor working girl. If someone is going my way, may I please ask to be ...' And she stood there, looking like a little girl lost. What she needed was a husband, everyone in the room was secretly thinking. How simple things would have been if Gita could have won a spouse in a lottery, bought him through a mail-order catalogue or bagged him as a celestial wicket at Fate's second throw, in a heavenly game of cricket. As a widow she had made a virtue of the legitimate anxieties of her condition. There' was something about her that cried out for a warrior on a white horse; she beeped powerful pleas for succour that lured good men into bondage and made even women feel gallant. Mrs Thadani offered to see her home in her chauffeur-driven car, nodding and shimmering at her encouragingly.

As Gita murmured her thanks, Rayhaan bent over Mila. 'Her voice is so purry tonight,' he whispered, 'doesn't she give us paws for reflection?' Mila giggled, and twisted her right hand into a claw. He flashed her a smile that told her how delighted he was to be sharing this moment with her. Mila was transported. It was enough to exchange a look with this man, to partake of a total communion denied to lesser mortals. But the next moment she was shy and felt a panicky urge to escape him. What was there about Ray that made her so painfully happy? She knew, even in her confusion, that she would never again declare herself as she had earlier in the evening. The fear of rebuff was all too real. Her naiveté was gone, this was the abrupt end to her innocence. She got up and took a hesitant step towards her father.

'I thought I told you to go to bed,' he said.

'In a minute, Daddy. Please.' She tried to blink back the waves of torpor. 'Everybody's leaving, anyway.'

Gita had turned to Mother, all velvety attention. 'Thank you, Shivani, for a lovely evening,' she purred. 'But you must take things easy. Didn't you keep well in the holidays? It worries me to see you looking so pooped.' As Gita delivered this poisoned dart, Mila saw waves of fatigue wash over her mother's radiant face.

Brusquely clasping her arm in a grip that was too tight, Shivani had without a word marched her daughter to her room. Her manner, as she helped the child undress, was grim and distracted, as if in yanking the party dress over her head and pulling her hands out of the sleeves of her nighty, the mother was battling some destructive force that threatened her life. Mila was frightened. Mother's hands were not normally rough, they touched even inanimate things with delicacy and compassion. So what . . . ? Questions milled in her head, but Mother would not meet her eyes. And Mila was sleepy, so sleepy. She fell into a deep slumber the moment her head touched her pillow.

She was torn out of her sleep by a scream from Vikram's room. It was a cry of terror. Mila's heart began to thump in huge, fearful beats, then stood still as ice closed round it and she lay paralysed under the sheets for long moments. She heard another scream, dying into a gurgle, then running footsteps outside. Fear had made her rigid; now she was trembling uncontrollably. She forced herself out of bed and made her way on bare feet to the passage outside. The lights were on in her brother's bedroom.

Vikram lay on his bed. The sheet had been removed, exposing the zebra stripes of the mattress under him. Mila could not see his face because Father was bending over him. There was an unpleasant smell in the room. Aunt Roma, looking dishevelled, stood some distance away from the bed. Her head snapped round as Mila entered and she stared at her niece for a moment before saying harshly, 'Where is your mother?'

Father looked up at her words. 'I told you Shivani's taken a sleeping tablet and I don't want her disturbed. Come in, Mila. There's nothing to be alarmed about. Vikram's had a nightmare.'

'But I definitely heard—' began Aunty.

He cut across her words with 'You're all right now, son, aren't you?'

Vikram was silent, one hand at his throat. Mila drew nearer the bed and saw that he was driving the knuckles of his other hand into his wet forehead as if to free himself from some appalling memories that lingered there. Dad gently guided the hand away from the white face, and worked his fingers in and out of the thick mass of damp hair. Vikram closed his eyes. Mila felt no particular compassion for him. He had been known to wake up screaming before.

The minutes ticked away. Quite groggy now with lack of sleep, Mila was like a marionette, her strings manipulated by invisible hands. She found that she was swaying slightly and rubbing her palms up and down her arms, though she was not cold. She heard Daddy say, 'Go back to bed, Mila. I'll stay with Vikram till he falls asleep.'

'No need for that,' said Aunt Roma sharply. 'I'm sleeping here. On the floor.'

'Roma, you'll be uncomfortable—'

'I'll sleep here tonight.' There was an obstinate note in Roma's voice. 'Tomorrow I shall have my bed moved back into the room.' At her own request her bed had been put out on the adjacent balcony. Mila couldn't read the expression on Aunty's face without her glasses, but why did she stand so far away, holding herself fiercely, almost ominously, aloof?

It wasn't like her at all. Roma-masi should be fluttering hysterically round Vikram's bed, magnifying the incident into crisis proportions. It was very strange. But it was also very late. Mila turned, tripping over the muslin skirt of her long nightgown, and left the room.

She had almost gained hers when something made her hesitate on the threshold. The corridor on which she stood, and which flanked the three bedrooms of the flat, was not lit. Insensate with sleep as she was, Mila stiffened suddenly for she had felt, rather than heard, a stealthy movement—a soft, menacing rustle, a fractional displacement of air—as if someone had brushed past her.

'Roma-masi?' she called out. Had her aunt followed her into the corridor? There was no answer.

She listened. It couldn't have been Soni; she would have heard the jingle of bangles. Besides, if awake, Soni could never have remained silent. Suddenly Mila was unaccountably afraid. The dismal corridor was static, empty. But as she took a step forward, shadows loped towards her with open arms. They enfolded her.

Moving within their embrace like an automation, Mila entered her room and climbed into bed in darkness. The night was opaque, like her classroom blackboard. Her eyes were aching and heavy, but they would not close at once. A light went on in the tall building opposite, and now Mila could see the curtain at her open window swaying silently, back and forth, back and forth. Then a gust of wind blew it inwards till it was like a horizontal net, spread out to catch a falling body. Quickly she closed her eyes.

6

Father flew in from Delhi this evening and decorum prevented me from inquiring whether Gita had returned with him or stayed behind in the capital for a brief holiday with friends. Not that I had ascertained, earlier, whether he planned to take his concubine-cum-secretary to the printers' conference; his baggage was none of my business and I had behaved with commendable tact.

As it happened, the same evening brought me a letter from my cousin in Los Angeles, in which Carol had enclosed a forgotten packet of photos she had come upon when clearing out my old closet. The pics proved a welcome diversion in the hour after dinner when most families let down their hair—usually a trying time in this household, with leaden moments and awkward breaks in our rather tenuous accord. Things get particularly sticky when Aunt Roma is not here to manage a kind of détente. In her presence we are content with conversational staples like the weather, or her yummy mango pickle, but she has not returned from Pune. Mercifully, then, I remembered the pictures.

'That's Red,' I said to Dad, handing him a photo of an unkempt giant with flaming hair. 'He lives across the road from Carol with his hard-drinking mother. She was constantly in our kitchen bitching about what-all she had sacrificed for her son while the lousy bum, like his slob of a father before him, was bent on messing up her life.' It's strange that when I address Soni in Gujarati, I feel she wants to reach out a hand to burp me, so haltingly do I speak the words. Right now I had switched to fluent Americanese.

'Red's a dropout?' asked Vikram.

'Yep.'

'Does no work?'

'Sometimes—as a postman.'

'He looks grubby,' said Father.

'Red stands for instant mysticism,' I said. 'Don't we in India make a connection between dirt and saintliness? At the highest level of spirituality all things must be equal to the devotee, the most commonly cited opposites—*you* know—being sandalwood and excrement.' What tongue was I speaking now?

'Quite,' said Father dryly. He studied the photograph again. 'Is Red a saint? He looks dirty enough.'

I plucked the pic from his hand. 'A gentle soul is Red. He plays the guitar and believes in non-violence and the expansion of consciousness by joyous song and natural herbs. His dream is to come out to Goa one day.'

'Of course,' nodded my know-all brother. 'Plenty of "natural herbs" on the silver beaches of Goa. Bhang, ganja, charas—'

'I've promised to send him a bracelet of hippopotamus hide,' I interrupted Vikram, 'as a talisman against all diseases.'

'Including AIDS?'

'Any idea where I can get them?'

'You must be joking,' said Vikram.

'Okay, this is Subu,' I said, dealing out the next snapshot.

'Indian?' asked Vikram.

'Absolutely. A bigoted brahmin from a small village near Trichur. Balaram V.T. Subramaniam's only true passion is mathematics.'

'Why "bigoted"?' asked Dad.

'He didn't let on in so many words, but Subu made me feel I should have stayed at home after attaining puberty.' I didn't like to add that despite the release of his hitherto repressed libido, Subu had clung to the diseased belief that a woman who looked him in the eye as his equal was a slut and therefore a legitimate object of his lust. Incapable of injecting 'love' in the Western sense into his sexual exploits, he continued to regard her meanly, with compulsive prurient interest and greed. And I currently possessed a diary of his, as Carol had asked me to mail it, on reaching Bombay, to an address she had scribbled for me. I hadn't done that yet, intrigued by Carol's comment that Subu wouldn't mind me peeking into it myself before parting with it.

'And this is Mike.' I put another photograph in Vikram's hand.

'You mentioned him in your letters,' said Vikram, 'as verging on a genius and something of a grouch. But not that he was so good-looking.'

'Oh he's very clever and articulate,' I said, glossing over the latter part of Vikram's comment. 'Mike believes in the new sensibility and has tried Zen, quantum healing, scientology, electronic music, hydropathy . . . you name it. He's marched in march-ins, sat in sit-ins—'

'And loved in love-ins?'

I glared at my brother for his levity and hurried on, 'Mike works in a lab now and is always on the frontiers of the *next* idea.' Once, for a period of twenty-seven days and twenty-six nights, he had scarified sex to yogurt and carrot juice, but I didn't bring that up.

'He sounds very . . . progressive,' said Dad cautiously.

'Oh, that he is, but I had to accept his intellectual assessments or he reduced me to pulp—verbally. He was a rebel, but as his serf I was expected to bow to his edicts and obey.'

'And you did?' Father looked sceptical.

'No.' What I couldn't confess in this company was that I had been more vulnerable to Mike's physical presence than to his words, though he could wield metaphors like bludgeons. One evening in his parked car with his mouth clamped on mine and his hands navigating the terrain under my shirt, I had been reduced to moaning sweetly in my throat—but the next moment I had pushed him away.

That did it. Mike had often voiced his genuine concern that as a malingering spinster, I was on my way to becoming a neurotic and retarded old maid unless I forthwith got rid of a certain unwanted physical fact. And no doubt that evening he saw, sitting behind me in strange garb, a row of forbidding preceptors—and they were there, I suppose, a pure force of censure. So with lucid rhetoric the iconoclast had torn to shreds the doctrine, folklore, religious cant, moth-eaten pieties, hang-ups, delusions and fairy tales that had been fed into me in the underprivileged country of my birth.

When Mike paused for breath, I had accused him of trying to brainwash me with his masculine ethics. *He* was in strong possession of his *mind*, but all he was asking of *me* was that I should be in strong possession of my *body*: why? So as to be able to render it more fully to him? Right?

This application of cerebration to a field where cerebration was not required of a bedworthy female made Mike sit taut with anger for a moment. It then sparked one of our highbrow quarrels. He called me a 'barricaded spinster' and 'pontificating Indian'. I called him 'the ugly

American'. The drama had a farcical ending when he started his car with an abruptness that flung me against the dashboard. He drove in vengeful silence while I felt the bump on my forehead and wished for a gooey pie to smack into Groucho's face.

In the following two weeks as Mike and I ignored each other it came upon me, sadly, that we were not of the same age, though contemporaneous. I understood that despite his sophistication Mike shared with his peers in that richest country on earth a naive belief in happiness without end, amen. Their optimism shone like the sun, untouched by the dark powers of sickness or deprivation, while I was isolated in a paleness of spirit, infected by my knowledge of what can be denied us. My mother had proved to me how plausible it was to die. Hope was always within hollering distance for them, but not for me . . .

While I was thus crouched over my past like a bomb-squad detective intent on defusing something delicate and dangerous, Dad was saying: 'Aren't you going to show us the other pics?'

'Sure,' I said, promptly dropping my pincers and detectors. 'These are some of Carol, playing handball on the beach with our usual crowd. This is an older one taken in their dining room. And here—'

'Wait,' cried Dad. 'What's that monstrous thing Harish has on his plate?'

'Let me see.' I peered closely. 'A steak-and-tomato sandwich, looks like . . . his favourite food.' I didn't tell Dad that in my heart I had for years nursed the idea that his brother was an escaped convict—the way Harry (to use the name given him by his clan at home and colleagues at the real-estate agency) never reminisced about India, never referred to his antecedents, the way nothing in the house betrayed his origins. I had dreamt up a whole sequence of scandals that had made it imperative to deport this family black sheep in dreadful secrecy from native shores right around the time I was born. But what I said aloud was: 'And the lumpy mess on my plate is vegetables cooked by Aunt Martha—this was before I turned carnivorous. See, here's Carol again. In the pool with Kenneth.'

'Her boyfriend?' asked my brother.

'The current one. As far as I know.'

'She's very pretty,' he mused.

'She's gorgeous,' I said with an inaudible sigh. It had added to my early woes that at an age when my body was still rectilineal, my waist not yet truly nipped, Carol, older by only eleven months, had been a svelte beauty. It wasn't fair. Her quicksilver loveliness had made me ache under the weight of my plainness. In her lissom grace I had repeatedly read my doom.

'She's very American,' observed Father.

'Oh, it's preposterous,' I exclaimed, 'how Carol doesn't look like us at all. There is so much of Aunt Martha in her that she could have been hatched unassisted from her rib.'

'You got on well?' asked Dad.

'Well, Aunt Martha is a most resolute woman who felt I should put my time to noble use—like typing out her protest letters to newspaper editors on sundry subjects in which she saw room for improvement. Like her urgent pleas that something be done about the poverty in India.' I knew I was not answering Dad's question.

'I've invited them over on several occasions,' he said after a moment's pause. 'Martha has never been to India.'

'Yes, well, they're sure to take you up on it one day. They both keep very busy, you know. Aunt Martha votes Democratic—and gives little lunches for lady Democrats.'

There was a little speculative silence from the males, at the end of which Dad said gently, 'I was actually asking how you got on with Carol.'

'Oh, Carol. On the day we first met as schoolgirls, I locked myself in the toilet and sobbed in misery at the thought of having to share a room with her.' Now why was I telling him this?

'You must have been very homesick in those early days.' My father was hesitantly venturing into territory he should have known was out of bounds for him. Looking up, I caught him off guard and saw myself imaged in his helpless eyes: the source of worry and bafflement, the child he had desperately wanted to secure against life.

'Yes, homesick,' I answered shortly. It seemed to me that I was suddenly in danger of recovering my young Daddy from the treachery of his years, something I must never allow. Let him reserve his compassion for people his own age! So I looked away and was silent about the lonely girl nobody ever got to hear of. Who stood with elbows planted on her window sill, gazing up at a sky that, even without its familiar curtain of smog, seemed more remote than her Bombay sky, intoning with an absurd passion the names of Indian rivers: the Jhelum, the Ravi, the Sutlej. The Yamuna, the Ganga. The Gandak, the Gogra, the Sarda. The Tista, the Kosi, the Sabansiri. The Godaveri, the Krishna. The Kaveri, the

Narmada ... She was a priestess weaving a spell by melodic incantations to exorcize her homesickness ...

But Vikram was tugging at my sleeve. 'Does Carol never think of herself as a Hindu?' Bless him, he looked kayoed by his smashing cousin after poring over her profile in a bikini.

'Oh, no. Carol's too smart to be caught in dilemmas of race and identity. You know, to be troubled by anything as profound as blood. Or burdened with choice. She's not to be trapped!'

'She's not curious about our shared ancestors?' persisted the smitten swain. 'Our common set of grandparents, flocks of mutual aunts, uncles, cousins?'

'Carol avoids such dangerous knowledge,' I said solemnly, 'in good conscience.'

'Like the forbidden apple,' Dad suggested helpfully.

'Yes,' I nodded. 'Intangibles she ignores. The unseen powers are extraneous. She requires no fresh stratum of ideas to feed on, she's healthy as she is, thank you. Enjoys playing ball in an uncomplicated emotional climate.'

'But you two became friends?' Daddy was doing some agonized probing of his own. 'Over the years?'

His voice asked for reassurance, so I said, 'Sure.' Carol had remained as serenely unaware of my inner turmoil in the last months of my exile as she had been of my initial hostility towards her. She had included me in all the fun things right away, I told Dad. 'All the parties, movies, evenings at the drugstore with her gang.' The truth was that I had been obliged to tag along and contain myself in a role she had not very perceptively chalked out for me. I hadn't liked her friends. In my nervousness I had felt had they were all prowling round me, making judgements, and any suspected condescension on their part made me shrivel up inside. I almost panicked. I was more clever and serious, I thought, than they, but in their presence I felt diminished and wanted to be like them, quickly—to propitiate them and disarm them from attacking my singularity, at the same time masking my timid overtures with a touch-me-not demeanour. So in those early months I had clung to Carol, in terror of being abandoned.

But now, to dissipate my memory of those ancient misgivings, I gave a prodigious yawn.

7

Our after-dinner session ended when that yawn prompted my father to his feet, saying he wanted an early night. Vikram also stood up and handed me the last of Carol's photographs he had been meditating on. We said our airy goodnights and, gathering up my pics, I repaired to my bedroom. I undressed quickly, brushed my teeth and went to bed. There, waiting for sleep, I was again waylaid by Carol.

My early months in LA had been painful. I had felt my greenness in her presence as a shaming thing, but under her tutelage I could have learnt fast, for Carol was very knowledgeable in certain matters. I was not entirely innocent, but there was much she could have taught me, many opportunities she could have tossed my way, had I only extended myself a little. But her schoolgirl confidences, whispered to me in the privacy of our room after the lights were out, had a strange effect on me: they left me flushed and uneasy. I wanted her to stop the bedtime stories forthwith, yet anticipated them with an unbearable excitement. I rolled over on my stomach, dug my teeth into my pillow, hardly daring to breathe, and listened in magnetized silence to the details of her body's apprenticeship. The how-do-you-do with sex. The blatant explorations. The contracepted thrills—assignations proposed, and those casually consummated.

I participated vicariously in everything Carol described, what she had done, how, and with whom, but gave no sign that I did so. Because in a curious fashion I wished to resist such knowledge, to not know. To remain aloof, safe. I didn't want to join the herd. I wanted, quite fiercely, to go on being a little girl. There was a woman struggling to escape from within me, but I clanged the doors shut in the prisoner's face. And there was my unto-death allegiance to Rayhaan. I wanted him on hand when the girl let the woman out.

So I had tried to lie chaste and still, but my ears turned traitor as I pretended not to hear. Voices admonished me *No, Don't, Mustn't*, my own among them, but my body overthrew me. Stretched out there, hugging my pillow, the bed giving off animal heat. I felt a tingling in my breasts, a lonely, unlocated hunger, a terrible need to cry.

'You've never touched it?' Carol would ask, a hot whisper that seared me. I bit deeper into my pillow and waited in agony for her to go on. 'They like you to touch it.' I felt like a receiver of soiled goods.

'It beats like a bird caught in your hand.' I couldn't breathe. 'But that's afterwards. First it's limp, sort of wilting, like leftover lettuce . . .' From the depths of my spurious unconcern I wanted to shout, go on, go *on*!

'In your country they shape it out of stone and worship it. You've seen it? It's true?' So she knew about elephants *and* lingams. Carol had once pestered me about the pachyderms; now she had to know about phallic emblems as well. Crafty girl! What other shreds of knowledge had she secreted away in her pitiful squirrel's hoard? But I had no breath for questions. In the dark I silently kicked my bed, savaging the mattress with my lunging desire to know more, *more*!

Her whispers were like an avalanche. 'Garland the thing with flowers? I don't believe it. How can you? I mean, in public? Have you ever with your tongue . . .' I wanted to hit her on the mouth, stifle her words, stuff them back down her throat, but I lay there devastated, motionless as a wreck.

Those nocturnal whispers should have prepared me for an incident that took place when I had been with my new family a little over a year. It was not unusual for me to wake up some nights from a dream about my mother in which I had gazed wide-eyed at a trickle of blood running down from her nose into her mouth. In the shape of her dead face I clearly saw the shape of my own living face, and when my eyes opened my pillow would be wet with tears.

This was a recurrent dream, with some variations, from which Carol shook me awake when my whimpering disturbed her sleep.

'Want a cigarette?' she would say.
'No.'
'Glass of water?'
'No.'

She would pad back to her bed, jump in and fall asleep while I lay awake, confused and stung that no one in this family understood my misery. They might as well have been strangers, and how can one rehearse one's history before strangers?

But this night, as I switched on the lamp on my bedside table, I saw that Carol was not in the room. I turned off the light and lay still for a moment, trying to shake myself free of the dream in which Mother's closed eyelids had appeared pale and full, her nostrils dark with clotted blood, her mouth lifted at the corners in a kind of sardonic grimace. I groped for my watch and held it close to my wet eyes. The luminous hands showed 11.15: too early for my uncle and aunt to have returned from their bridge game. Carol would be in the kitchen downstairs, fixing herself some coffee. I got out of bed, put on my robe but not my glasses, and opened the door.

The blackout was startling. It was like standing on the edge of an open trap door. Who had switched off the light? I peered myopically in the dark, and with my right hand felt along the wall for the button that lit up the landing. But before my fingers could locate it, I heard an odd gasp close to my feet, followed by what sounded like a heavy groan.

Thin spikes of ice slithered down my spine as I stood there, transfixed.

Something scraped the floor, then hit the banister barely a yard away from me with a soft, dull thud. Then that low moan again, followed by a kind of suction noise, a snarl that made me think of a wild animal, little rustling murmurs that made me think of sundry jungle birds, and raucous breathing that had for me a visual accompaniment from the past.

'Who's there?' I called out, my voice shrill with panic, my mind still a lap or two behind my hearing. At the same time my blind, nervous fingers found the switch. The subdued light went on, identifying the narrow dimensions of the landing that communicated with the two bedrooms on this floor.

'Who did you think it was?' said Carol, hard-breathing, as she rose from the foot of the banister. My mouth fell open ludicrously as I stared in utter disbelief at the second figure who got to his feet behind her. In the dim light, without my glasses, and with all that hair on his face I couldn't quite distinguish his features, but I could have sworn it was no one I knew. There was a moment of silence in which he buttoned the waistband of his trousers. Then I heard the unmistakable sound of a stifled giggle.

The boy turned his back on us and, leaning his hands on the banister, began to laugh, his hunched shoulders shaking. 'Shut up,' said Carol sharply. He shook his head, stopped, then was off again, fizzing and spilling helplessly, bent double, clinging to the wooden railing for dear life.

Carol walked up to him. 'I said shut—' She broke off with a gasp, struggled briefly against the rising paroxysms of mirth, then supporting herself like him, gave vent to peals of almost hysterical laughter. I stood there, paralysed by decorum. Like Queen Victoria, I was not amused.

'You better go,' Carol gasped at last, pushing him towards the steps. He stumbled down obediently enough under her watchful eye, braying all the way. The front door opened and shut. A moment later we heard the purr of an engine, now the flabby crunch of tyres as whoever it was drove away. Who? The boy she had smiled at in the park the other day? The boy encountered outside the drugstore the day before, in trousers that fitted like a ballet dancer's at the bulge of his crotch? Her list of alternates, reserves, was long.

How could she, I thought dully, how *could* she? I clung to the door, feeling the need for some support myself, as memory identified parallel sounds borne to me from the summer of my great betrayal, when I had been fourteen. I translated the present into the past: Carol was no better than that other bitch, no better. Rigid with an excess of dislike for my cousin, I hung on there, the wood strange under my hand. Then I turned back into the room.

I was standing beside my bed in the dark with lowered head, stupidly concentrating on nothing, when Carol came in. I flinched as she snapped on the light. I did not want to see her, listen to her lies. I knew what she had been up to. On the landing, like a servant girl! I heard her go into the bathroom. And as the painful dislocation of time—the past helplessly entangled with the present—persisted, I struggled to get out of my robe and, before she came out of the toilet, to dive into bed and pull the pillow over my eyes.

But I must have taken too long over it, for now Carol was standing behind me and she did an unexpected thing. She suddenly put a strong arm round me, and with an irrepressible giggle turned me to face her.

'I'm sorry we laughed, but if you had *seen* your face . . .' Her smile was not quite focussed on me, but was a secret savouring of her own proud condition of animal bliss. She was vividly elated. 'Hey, you look good without your glasses, did you know?' I hated her for saying that.

It was as if my physical imperfections were so generous that she could afford to be kind about them. A damp curl was plastered to her forehead, a smudge of dirt extended over one shoulder strap to the skin of her back, giving its shameful data, and I saw them prone, supine, intertwined, climbing over each other... 'Of course,' she said, eyeing me judiciously, as if I were a prize heifer, 'you need to knock off a few pounds—'

'Don't!' I said so violently, and threw off her encircling arm and protective patronage with such contempt, that she stared at me in amazement. 'What's the matter, Sharmila?'

I tried to speak, but her beautiful flushed cheeks, her tousled hair and breasts like heaped-up cups of jello pushing out of the plunging V of her high-waisted gown, were a horrible affront to me. She looked like the inmate of a harem. A caliph's delight. 'Don't tell me you were doing nothing wrong,' I managed hoarsely at last, 'because I won't believe you!'

'Wrong!' Carol stared at me, expressions chasing across her face, one moment the commedienne's exaggerated surprise, the next, virtue's indignation over unmerited reproach. It was as if she had to mime her own powerful sensuality or it could not be sustained. 'Shit, I don't have to tell you anything,' she said at last, biting her lip. Her face changed for the last time. The chin remained insolent. And there was a look of such deadly experience in her eyes that I withered before it.

She walked regally back to her side of the room, her high buttocks not huffy but mocking me through the sheer white fabric. 'You want the light on, or shall I switch it off?' I did not answer, and she switched it off with a disdainful flick.

As I tossed and thrashed about in bed that night I could not understand why my heart was laid waste. My desolation had no clear meaning for me. Why was I so gutted by pain?

The answer was somewhere in my head, of course, demanding release. But I did not wish to set it free. It was too dreadful to confront. I was racing towards Rayhaan instead, as I did whenever I was hurt. He was my shield. I wanted Ray straight away, determined that he should make love to me on the successive landings of the Empire State Building. I need not be sad, I had Rayhaan!

But the fact was I had nobody. How does one grow up, I wondered bleakly? How does one get disentangled, so that life is not so hideously serious? Why was I so bereft, how could it feel like a betrayal of loyalty that Carol chose to do what she did? On me, a sultan would have solemnly conferred the Order of Chastity, while to Carol he would have been delighted to offer the most opulent divan in his seraglio. Yet *I* was on the rack, while the scarlet woman of my indictment enjoyed impregnable sleep in bed.

I felt a great stirring of resentment: *she* did not grant anyone or anything the power to make her unhappy! I was jealous of such self-possession. I grudged Carol her talent for finding pleasure, the directness with which she met living. In a country where youth was sovereign, I was, in my teens, anxious and middle-aged!

It seems grotesque to me as I am today (seasoned and mellow?—what a laugh!) that it was my need to demolish this sad self-image that led me to commit the extreme folly of accepting, towards the end of my stay in LA, Mr Johnson's invitation to dinner despite the rather unsavoury reputation the pedagogue enjoyed. The other reasons were: Mike had not called, after the last spat in his car, in thirteen days. Carol was down with the flu, and Red had disappeared on one of his protracted 'inner trips'. I had received word from home that Uncle Amrish was seriously ill, and my umpteenth letter to Rayhaan had been returned in the post with the remark 'Addressee unknown'. It also happened that between 10 and 11 a.m. that particular Monday morning the balding but still handsome Archibald Johnson, who took the summer class in comparative literature, had been in scintillating form. Strutting to and fro between the confines of two walls, hands linked over his sacrum, he had dwelt on the fallibility of great writers when it came to evaluating the works of their contemporaries. Archibald was eloquent, witty and unsparing of acknowledged masters, whose harsh or gauche judgements he exposed and annihilated with zest.

I had been entranced, as much by the brilliance of the discourse as by the clear, clipped accents in which it was delivered. It had brought to mind the bell-like articulation of Sister Matilda at the convent in Bombay. But this affectation of an English actor's diction did little to endear the Yankee-foaled-and-bred professor to his American audience. Sidney Davis, who was black and earnest about his work, interrupted the flow of Oxford vowels by calling loudly for 'Translation, please!' There was some sniggering, and the discipline of the class threatened to disintegrate but, undaunted, Mr Johnson had concluded his talk with a vivid little disquisition on how it was the task of the original artist to *create* the taste by which he was to be enjoyed.

I got up in a daze, his willing slave; and in the noisy, echoing corridor

Mr Johnson had caught up with me to ask if I would meet him for dinner that night. Before I could quite get over my astonishment, I said 'yes', then suffered a near heart attack.

We ate, I remember, in a remote, gloomy but rather charming little restaurant with red-checked tablecloths, cloudy candles and fake Victorian carriage lamps on the walls. The décor was discreet enough to be reassuring. So was the bland food that catered to Mr Johnson's ulcer, for who could plan strategies in seduction with boiled chunks of meat and potatoes on his plate? (I myself dined sketchily on salads those days, for Carol had at last made me conscious of my calories.) Most reassuring of all was the conversation, for Archibald was still harping on the subject of his morning's discourse.

Speaking between energetic mouthfuls with more and more self-conscious enunciation, he was making mincemeat of the great Voltaire for his obtuseness in condemning *Hamlet* as a barbarous piece. This, I told myself delightedly, was part of my liberal education. A true encounter with knowledge. The master continuing his brilliant dialogue with the star pupil outside the classroom. From Archibald to Sharmila, with love. You didn't forget your notes this way. I relaxed in contentment.

Then it happened.

'. . . fruit of the imagination of *a drunken savage*, Europe's most brilliant man called the most subtle and profound of the Bard's works,' Swami Johnson was saying, when I was startled by a hand exploring the pink folds of my Bangalore silk as it groped for my thigh under the table. Above it, the neat, dry chiselled face claimed total ignorance of any subterranean manoeuvres.

I tried to move subtly out of reach as I attempted a deferential smile at this example of the vulnerability of great minds. Above the table it was returned with a thin, pedagogic twitch of the mouth, while in the area of darkness below, Archibald's fastidiously manicured fingers persisted in their quest. 'What do you think of that?' he asked, referring, of course, to the Frenchman's blind spot and not to his own labours in the nether region. I was beginning to feel a bit angry at his fraudulence, but the pupil in me pleaded extenuating circumstances for her professor. Apart from suffering from anglomania, I reflected, he was also schizophrenic—though at the moment attempting a valiant synthesis between life and literature. 'Pearls before swine,' he was saying, 'don't you think?' His mouth gave a thin twitch again before he resumed shredding away at his food like a supercilious rabbit.

'Absolutely!'

'I adore your chaste British accent,' continued Mr Johnson, his hand becoming more predatory in the underworld, while above the table he behaved with perfect correctitude. It was a situation to be endured with a stiff upper lip. 'Where did you learn to speak like Julie Andrews, if a chap may ask?' I resisted the temptation to tell him that he spoke like James Mason, actualleh!

'At the convent, I suppose. In India there are still some opportunities to ape the accent . . .' At this point I had to slap away his pat-a-cake baker's hand. He must have found my attitude a trifle obstructive, but I couldn't help it. And it was rather unnerving how Archibaldus did not bat an eyelash at this bit of *sub rosa* unpleasantness. He even managed to intrude a large, booted foot between my gold sandals despite the encumbrance of the sari, and while in the Antipodes it was all I could do to refrain from fetching him a kick in the shins, in the northern hemisphere he was graciously offering to show me his early folio edition of *The Merchant of Venice*.

'A bloody good buy when I was last in London. I'm devilishly fond of London,' he said predictably. He added in the same breath that on his mother's side he could trace his ancestry to one of the early English colonists of Connecticut. I nodded. He belonged to a pioneering breed, I had reason to know.

When the meal was over, his pilgrim hand resting briefly on the table, Archibald said with Oxonian suavity, 'My place, then, for coffee, shall we?' It was not compulsion, not recklessness, but a kind of doped passivity that made me acquiesce in my teacher's little ruse. His wife, he had told me over his toothpick, was out of town, visiting her sick mother. I had clucked my tongue in sympathy, and avoided his eyes. We had all heard echoes of his marital discords. I tried to dismiss my qualms as we rose and made our way between tables. Dr Johnson was only helping me to experience the Age, I told myself. We were making the scene, the erudite professor and his gifted pupil.

At the door of his flat, while amorous Archibaldo fumbled with his key, I didn't know why it was so reassuring to be told that Goethe had found Dante's *Inferno* abominable, his *Purgatorio* dubious and his *Paradiso* tiresome. I tinkled merrily, as at some witty, face-saving jest, but when his rather portly back was turned on me my laughter trailed away. I was struck by the incongruity of such mirth. Dear God, what was I doing here?

The scene now took on the macabre quality of an unpleasant dream, in which reality is mercifully off-centre but you can't get rid of the feeling that a vile experience awaits you just round the corner. Why was he bent so long over the latch? Soon I would be called upon to switch over from spectator to participant—ugh! I had a moment of panic and was staring in dismay at the dyed semi-circle of hair on the back of his head when the door was violently thrown open from within.

A large blonde of warlike disposition stood framed there in a black negligée. In ominous silence, strong arms crossed over her ample bosom.

I did not wait to learn whether she was his wife or her counterfeit. I did not wait to exchange civilities—to ask if she called him Archie or Baldy, or if his mother-in-law had turned the corner. Heaven had sent me succour in the shape of this statuesque creature, and I smiled at her in sheer gratitude before I whirled round. On flashing heels I walked (resisting the impulse to break into a run) the entire length of the corridor to the elevator doors.

The next day I had called Mike. He was gracious on the telephone. We met for coffee in the morning, and made love in his parked car in the evening.

There were moments, in the glamorous darkness, when I thought—hoped—he had cast a spell over me. But they passed. And when his hand became too busy under my sweatshirt, I pushed it away. 'Still looking for a soulmate?' he asked hatefully.

I did not answer. A heavy, ungainly squareness descended on me. I felt stolid, unresponsive. I was tightly virginal, passive and, I suppose, insulting. He became aggressive, verbally, whereupon I grew hostile. And again we quarrelled. He made a gesture like Hamlet ordering Ophelia to enrol in a nunnery before starting the car, and once again maintained a formidable silence all the way back.

That week two letters arrived together from home. One was from Aunt Roma to inform me that her brother, my Uncle Amrish, had died in his sleep ten days ago. It was a terrible blow, for he had been my friend. The other letter was from my father. He did not mention Amrish-mama's death, but said it had been such a long time, hadn't I better come home?

I heard a plaintive note between the lines, and it was so unlike my father that it scared me. I sat down to reflect on him. He had not married his mistress, though for years I'd left the field clear for them. True, Vikram was there. But even if he was not the appeaser I had once unjustly suspected him of being, the collaborator with the enemy, on the verge of treason if not downright perfidious, he could have been feinted out of any defensive posture he assumed. Out-clawed, like Afzal Khan by Shivaji. It was asking too much of Vikram to have him outwit that obscene female. So why had my father not married Gita? He wasn't growing younger . . .

And suddenly I felt I owed it to no one to tarry in this land of great opportunities. With each passing year in this country I had become more irrelevant, displaced. There was, about my life here, a humiliating inconsequence, a lack of design. From which Hindu forebears had I inherited this troubling need for coherence, connections, patterns?

Surely it was my fault that living in the most *in* country in the world, I was yet *out* of it? Foreign in face, pace, accent, syntax, perceptions, I was not—what was the word?—contemporary enough to avail myself of the challenging freedom it offered body and soul. Something was very wrong with me, that I had not acquired the habit of liberty. I was lacking in drive, in the rebellious energy that blasts through barriers. Never in the swim of this Yankee business, never getting the hang of it, as nimble as a cow, unable to run, sprint, fly or swing into orbit without crashing.

I wanted to stay put—the folly of it!—like an old-fashioned, navel-gazing sage in a country where nothing held still from moment to moment. I longed for civility, good manners. For some *ceremony* in my approach to reality. And for some great, great kindness to be done to me . . . though I saw no reason at all why I should be singled out for such benevolence.

I wrote immediately to my father. I was on my way home!

8

Back home, one of the tough things I've come to terms with is Amrish-mama's absence. Keenly I regret him and silently mourn him. He was by no means a storybook uncle, being of an arbitrary and irascible disposition, but I had never thought of him as ephemeral. So to die like that, behind my back, was surely unworthy of him?

I said as much to Aunt Roma, who reminded me, gently, that her brother had been a sick man for years. 'My goose was cooked long ago,' Amrish had gasped in one of his lucid moments before the end. I think Aunty wanted to talk to me about the ravages of his last illness but I avoided the subject, it was too painful; and this morning when I was impatient for some answers, she was not here to give them. What was she still doing in Pune? Perhaps I should persuade Vikram to drive up the hills and bring her back, in chains if necessary.

There are days when I stupidly succumb to the fantasy that no vestige of Mila remains in Sharmila, but today was not one of them. I knew the moment I opened my eyes in bed that Mila was going to be around. But instead of exorcizing her I languidly lay back, and on the screen of my mind I watched her walking up an unlovely street with lean-to shops on either side, then turning left into a narrow lane where ragged boys played marbles under a brutal sun and called out rude things to her as she marched past with a set frown on her face. I cannot swear to the date of this excursion, but it must have taken place within a week of the dinner hosted by Mother for Roma-masi (an event to which I find myself attributing a historic context).

At thirteen, Mila's every visit to Uncle Amrish had required enterprise. There were risks to be encountered on the journey, at the end of which no avuncular amiability awaited her, for Amrish was a bully who enjoyed, frankly, his own truculence. He was poor. He suffered from cardiac asthma. But because he lived completely alone, with no concern for customs and habits, no irksome checkpoints of one-right-thing-in-one-proper-place, Mila adored him. His bachelor style delighted her. It was such an unpossessive way to live. And the subtle aura of family disapproval that clung round the solitary man further ennobled her trips into windmill-tilting expeditions. She embarked on them in secrecy and never talked about them at home—an exercise in discretion I now find remarkable.

On his part Amrish-mama treated his family with an undefined hostility. His references to his progenitors and their offshoots were either slighting or mischievous (he himself was, incredibly, unmarried though Nanima was already investigating a bride for Vikram). Roma was afraid of her brother's acidulous tongue, though she overcame this fear to nurse him when he fell desperately ill. At the mention of his name Vikram reacted like a turtle rapped on its nose. Shivani never went to see him, and Naren rarely so. It was Rayhaan who called on him with his precious manuscripts, only to find himself defending them like a porcupine against the old man's critical onslaughts.

Uncle Amrish was not his mother's favourite child, either. 'In a ditch he chose to bury himself,' Nanima said of him, referring to the years he had spent teaching school in an obscure little Maharashtrian village. 'A threadbare string his life is today, knotted with failures.' Her son was a middle-aged sell-out, she meant. Also she could not forgive him, that of all her brood he was the only one not conspicuously good-looking. His looks were, in fact, well on the way to being unprepossessing—rather like Socrates, Mila decided, a comparison that would have flattered her uncle. A Greek might have riled against the asymmetry of that face, but the more she looked on it, the more she approved of it. There was an irreducible something about this uncle that made up for his lack of physical beauty. As she grew older she began to recognize him by such fragile graces as taste and intelligence; and she knew instinctively that despite the scathing things he said about people, he had the power to dignify them. He was that rare and remote thing, a good man.

The ragged boys who played at marbles that morning called out rude things to Mila with much hilarity, but she ignored them. She marvelled that their bare feet could endure the burning asphalt, for its heat stung her through the rubber soles of the gym shoes in which she had evaded

Soni's sensitive antennae—the 'cockroach ears' Soni proudly claimed for herself—and sneaked out of the house. She crossed over to the blackened building on her right and mounted its dark, smelly stairs. On the third floor she knocked on a door—it didn't even have a bell, and Mila missed the feel of imperiousness that ringing a bell gave her—and entered a dingy room to find Amrish-mama lying without mattress or pillow on a short, coir-bound bed.

'May I come in?'

An unshaven, unkempt head was raised at her voice, and her uncle supported himself on his right elbow to glare at her with protruding, bloodshot eyes. 'It's you,' he said at last, ungraciously, and fell back on the bed. 'Will I ever get used to the impudence of people who drop in without an invitation?' he asked the ceiling. Then he closed his eyes tight, as if to shut out the unwelcome apparition at his door.

His greeting did not disconcert Mila. His confrontation was not with her but with the whole world, and to come under the breadth of his satire gave her a secure feeling. He opened his eyes and was now regarding her with an unfathomable joke in them—as if she were a curious animal whose tricks vastly amused him. But when she grinned back he rapped out, 'Well, what are you so pleased about, at your time of life? How old are you? Fourteen? Eh? Thirteen! God help you.' He shuddered. 'Miserable fate, being so young. Youth is a painful disease, a tug-of-war between what is and what seeks to be. Youth is agony, because it's the time when we desire blindly without knowing who we are. Anyone who denies this is a dull clod and does not deserve to reach my hoary age of forty-four.' He struggled into a sitting posture. 'But why aren't you at school? Playing truant, I hope?'

'Oh, no,' said Mila. 'I have a whole week of holidays left.'

'Tut, you disappoint me! I hoped you had deserted your classroom to come to the fount of all knowledge—but there, conceit is the only armour I can afford these days. Sit down, sit down, take that chair.'

There was only one chair in the room, a sagging, cane-bottomed affair that Mila was wary of because it had the nasty habit of toppling over on its face. One day Rayhaan had thrown himself into it heartily and the chair had just as heartily flung him out again, and her uncle had laughed uproariously. Mila thought it much safer to squat on the not-too-clean floor near his bed, and did so.

'Well, is your mother better after her long holiday?'

'Oh she's fine,' said Mila quickly. But a chafing note of worry had crept unbidden into her voice as she thought of Vikram's nightmare the morning after the dinner party. And how Mother had slept round the clock that day after having sedated herself heavily in the night—or had the dose been administered to her, and if so, why? Father had stayed home from work, and Vikram had wandered round the house like an estranged ghost in search of a more solid self.

'Hmmm.' Uncle Amrish was looking at her sharply. 'Parents are a trial and a tribulation, are they not?'

Mila nodded absently, thinking now of the other stray incidents that had disturbed her that week. Like the evening when, just before leaving for a new movie with the family and Gita, Mother apparently forgot Mila's name and had called her 'Sejal'. Mila had jumped, startled, but her mother's face was blank; she gave no sign that her tongue had slipped, and addressed Mila by her cousin's name again, with a smile this time. A sweet smile. But when it stayed too long on Mother's face something alien developed in it . . . The other time, waiting up late with Mother in her room for Father to come home from work, Mila noticed that she punctuated their conversation with abrupt glances over her shoulder. Suddenly Mother said, loudly, 'I tell you, there is a stranger in this house!' To Mila's surprised queries she made no answer, but stared rigidly in a corner of the room beyond the point where the bed surfaced out of darkness. Just as Mila was beginning to get really frightened, Shivani relaxed in her seat, as if the matter was of little importance, and continued to talk to her daughter as before. Only some shadows she had seen?

'I know all about parents,' Amrish-mama was saying. 'What chance did we have, Shivani and Roma, Ajit and myself, brought up by a woman who—never mind. One can always avenge oneself on one's parents when they grow old. Or one can forgive them . . . Did you know that it is said in the *Rig Veda* that the *child* gives being to his mother as he expresses himself in the various stages of his growth? Which poses an interesting question: is it the past that builds the future, or the future that projects its luminous shadow backwards into time—hey!' He glared at Mila. 'Have you the dimmest notion what I'm talking about?'

'No.'

'I thought not,' he said bitingly. 'Women have the fecundity of rabbits to supplement the brain of ants. But wise and humble men, Mila, have always asked *where* time begins . . . never mind.' And he interrupted one of his endless abstruse dialogues with someone unseen to say to her, 'You are not entirely stupid, thank God. Your intelligence—by some devious routing—has been derived from me, no mistake about it. Ha, you'll note that I'm a firm believer in heredity,' he said, slapping his thigh, 'when it suits me. What are you going to do with your life?'

'I don't know,' she mumbled.

'But I do. You'll get married. A woman's business in life—despite what the excellent nuns at school may have told you—is that of the hen, to rear the young.'

'No it's not!' Mila had countered with some heat. 'I'm going to write.'

'Write!' He made an impatient gesture. 'Who said you could write? Not the good nuns, I hope. A nun is, after all, a secluded female under a vow, and seclusion and devotion affect women in such curious ways that certainly the education of nubile creatures should not be entrusted to them.' He stared at Mila with cynical intentness. 'Who said you could write?'

'Rayhaan did.' Hadn't he praised her last essay on 'A Visit to the Zoo'?

'Rayhaan! That vagabond word-doodler! That delirious musk ox!' He hitched himself up, crossed his legs and scowled ferociously. Mila loved that her uncle was never willing to sacrifice his astringent wit for plump phrases of tact. 'Has that imbecile been stuffing your head with nonsense?' He thrust out his formidable chin. 'Did he tell you that writing is the worst indescretion one can commit?'

'N—no.'

'Did he tell you how dangerous the pen—okay, the word processor—is? That one may kill oneself with it more easily than with a gun?'

'Kill!' Mila was impressed.

'Did he tell you that you must die in order to live like a creator? That a writer must stand in a cool, fastidious attitude towards humanity, that she must have a corrupted nervous system, that a properly constituted, healthy, decent person never dreams of writing? No!' He paused for breath. 'Of course not. Rayhaan is a . . .' He went on to use a number of descriptive adjectives and expletives that were new to her, and thus interesting, but not complimentary to Rayhaan. She was not dismayed. It seemed to her that her uncle despised people with much tenderness and belittled many things he secretly admired. He liberally mixed what he believed with what he didn't, for the sake of effect. At his best he was a humourist: he overstated half-truths with a kind of comic, self-conscious wrath. At his worst he was a benevolent despot.

'No my dear,' he went on, 'you will not write. You will get married.

That'—he jabbed his index finger in the air above her—'our scriptures say, is the whole duty of woman. Religion was invented to provide pious Hindus with servile wives.' He chortled throatily. 'Do you know the very first chauvinist male? Shiva, who challenged Brahma to measure the limitless extent of his lingam. But I digress. We were talking of holy matrimony and woman's salvation through her spouse. "He for God only, she for God in him." You've heard of Milton?'

'Oh, yes, he wrote *Paradise Lost*,' Mila proffered smugly.

'Well!' He allowed himself a moment in which to be staggered by the extent of her erudition. 'You also remember reading how the housewife reprimanded the sage Kausika? She kept the holy brahmin waiting while she insisted on serving her husband first.' He laughed again. 'Your husband is a mystic symbol—no matter how vile, stupid, gross or monstrous he may be. Hasn't your mother taught you that?'

'No.'

'Or Grandmother? I received a letter from your Nanima this morning'—he waved an airy hand in the direction of his desk which was overloaded with toppling piles of dusty books and papers—'in which she complains bitterly of her daughter-in-law, your Saroj-aunty. After fifteen years of marriage to your uncle Ajit, Saroj at last mustered up enough courage to walk out on him. This perfectly justified act has raised a howl of execration from my mother. Being a woman, your Nanima can see only the virtues of her degenerate son and the defects of her brilliant one—me, if you believe in calling a spade a spade!' And again there was that hint of a private, inward joke in the sharp look he gave her.

She saw no reason to argue the point, but sat there silent in the knowledge that there was a benefit in being near her irate uncle. He was a man most obviously above most men. She learnt this anew every time he told her tales of 'the sane men of the world', and of men 'wondrous in compassion'; or as she sat quietly on the floor with her arms around her knees, her back hunched in a manner that would have distressed Soni, and followed the inflections of his voice as he read out Sanskrit shlokas in sonorous tones. He himself seemed to be as hypnotized by the wealth of sounds he uttered as by the profundity of the ideas the verses expressed. He was a great articulate puppet, moved by the magic of his own voice, and she felt guilty that her presence obliged him to stop and make laborious translations when the words alone gave him such joy. She wondered if she dared ask him to read to her today. No, he was too restless, she decided, his eyelids heavy with pain.

'Tell me the story of Upali the barber,' she said instead.

'No!' He flung himself down on the bed. 'Not now. Not again. You heard it the last time you were here.'

'But I want to hear it again.'

'Well, you shan't,' vowed her uncle, his face to the wall. 'And that is final. Irrevocable. Wild trumpeting elephants won't drag it out of me.'

'Please?'

'I won't be importuned in this manner!' he shouted. 'Don't act like a woman who must have something only because she is denied it.' He turned round and raised himself on one elbow to glower at her in greater comfort. 'Long before you were born, I learnt to be impervious to female wheedlings—besides, don't you see how bad my cough is today?' And he flung himself back to cough so violently that it was impossible not to suspect that he took a fiendish delight in it.

'Upali was a barber,' he gasped, coming out of his feint just as Mila thought she had lost the battle. 'One day he was sharpening his razor when a Splendour passed by his house. It was the Buddha. The fat oaf dropped his razor and—confound his impudence—ran after the Blessed One.

' "Is nirvana even for such as I?" he asked, panting for breath, for much eating had made the hungry sinner a corpulent man. And the Effulgent One answered him with a gentle, "Yes."

'At this the overgrown barber trembled in all his chins and belly folds, for what is stronger than gentleness? "May . . . may I follow after Thee?" he stammered.

'And the Buddha said, "Oh yes."

'And Upali could hardly believe his thick ears. He said, "May I stay, O Lord, always near Thee?"'

Uncle held up one hand theatrically as he declaimed, 'And He who shone like a thousand suns smiled upon the dismal barber as He said—'.

But what the Enlightened One said remained unspoken that day, for Mila saw her uncle frown darkly over her head as he interrupted his story with, 'This is intolerable. Not to be borne. To have my privacy invaded twice in the course of one morning!'

She swivelled round on the floor in some perplexity. 'Rayhaan!' she cried, for it was he who stood at the door.

Yet it was not he. True, he was unshaven and his shirt looked as if he had lived in it for days, but what made Ray appear so strange to her was his air of vulnerability as he hesitated on the threshold, with a desperate need spilling out of him. This was something new. Inconsistent with the man, and therefore alarming.

'Hi, Mila.' Rayhaan's greeting did not take away the brooding in his eyes. 'So you have a visitor.' He waited with a wry patience for his friend to speak. When Uncle maintained a punishing silence, he added, 'Perhaps I had better make myself scarce.'

'A splendid idea!' Amrish-mama concurred heartily, folding his arms across his chest.

'No,' Mila cried, 'don't go!'

'How this welcome,' said Rayhaan, 'gladdens my sad and bruised heart.' But he was not looking at her. His eyes were fixed on Amrish, and he was not yet released from his strange irresolution. A tension started in Mila's stomach as she stared up at his defensive handsome face. She did not know that it was his tension she was feeling.

Uncle was watching Ray's every move with sardonic, inflexible attention. With a bright, obstinate suspicion. Each was taking measure of the other, wary and alert. 'You look as if you've not slept all night,' Amrish-mama observed at last.

'Maybe I just forgot to shave,' said Rayhaan. He touched his cheek. 'I did forget!' He sounded incredulous.

'And if you have hunted me out in my lair,' Uncle went on, menace in his voice, 'to help you nurse another hangover, you've come to the wrong place. Not again in my house you don't!'

At the incipient growl in his words, the younger man relaxed visibly. He grinned. 'Perhaps you have a sure-fire remedy for my condition? You have infallible cures for everything.'

'Try the sauna bath,' Amrish spoke contemptuously. 'Get yourself whipped sober with silver birches.'

Rayhaan attempted a laugh, but there was a fatigue in him that resembled defeat. And smudges under his eyes. Did he, too, have nightmares? 'Aren't you well?' Mila asked.

'Oh, he's well enough,' Uncle answered for him. 'Here you see Rayhaan renewed in the flesh at the expense of his spirit. Behold life's darling!—with the rascal's fallacy that charm excuses everything. You have been drinking like a fish, among your other dissipations.' It was a statement, not a question.

Rayhaan shrugged it away gracefully. 'May I sit down?' He walked to the chair without further invitation, and Mila held her breath as he bent over and gave one of the legs a deft outward twist before sitting down quickly. The chair received him meekly enough. 'Well, don't look so grim,' he called out to Amrish as he stretched out his long frame in the chair. He was lordly again: himself. 'The best of life is intoxication, didn't a poet say that?'

'Byron said it,' Uncle replied dourly. 'And you have all the Byronic ennui, I note, with only one of the Byronic palliatives: fornication.'

Rayhaan suppressed a yawn. 'You mean *he* had another?'

'Yes! Work!' Amrish-mama pronounced the two words sharply, as though sharpness, toughness, and a pitiless clarity were demanded of him at the moment as spiritual values. 'I see you've brought no pages for me today.'

Rayhaan pretended not to hear. 'What I would like now,' he murmured languidly from his chair, 'is a cup of strong, black coffee. And today's newspaper.'

'There is no coffee in the house,' snapped Uncle, 'and when ignorance is bliss, perhaps you'll tell me why I should borrow my neighbour's newspaper?'

'I wonder why I come to see you, when you never give me what I ask for,' sighed Rayhaan.

'Precisely because I give you what you *need*, and that is more than you have the wit to ask for.'

Rayhaan sat very still, and for a moment Mila thought he was going to say something awful. He was decorous enough on the surface, but something was rasping against his taut nerves and it was as if he longed to explode in irrational rage. But he said, with an air of insouciance, 'Well, if you don't have coffee in this Spartan household, and no newspaper, you can talk to me. Of cabbages and kings. No Patanjali today, please, or songs of Zarathushtra. I'm here for relaxation.'

'And what makes you think,' retorted her uncle, 'that I'd spend my morning in idle chit-chat? If you were busier with your work, you couldn't afford the time, either.'

'You think it a joke to see me in print anyway,' said Rayhaan after a pause. 'So we will not talk about my work today, Amrish, if you don't mind.' His voice was carefully purged of all emotion, but Mila still heard the constraint in it. Uncle seemed to have heard it too, for he said abruptly, his tone less disciplinary, more concessional, 'Very well. Let's dissect a scandal or two, for your entertainment. How's this: last week in Pune my brother's wife walked out on him after fifteen years of marriage.

Fifteen years of unmitigated hell, I can tell you, for Ajit is a selfish, unprincipled brute.'

'You've never talked about your brother before.'

'I avoid disagreeable subjects.'

'Neither has Shivani.' There was a little silence, in which the name sounded very loud. 'Tell me about him.'

'Well. Picture to yourself a rooster-chested officer in a swell uniform, absorbed in drinking, gambling, horses, women and keeping up with the swank of his regiment and his pressing debts of honour—a bloody stupid tin soldier. That's Ajit.'

'Children?'

'Three daughters. My mother's never forgiven Saroj for not presenting her favourite son with a male heir. Though why she's anxious to propagate a family with a long history of neurosis behind it, I'll never understand. But my mother is an obstinate, fanatical woman.'

'I've never met her.' Rayhaan sank deeper into the chair, and it creaked protestingly.

'You will. She's made up her mind that Saroj is hiding out here, in Bombay that is Mumbai. She threatens to come after the girl and drag her back to the bosom of her family. To the chaste duties of a hip-spreading, vegetating Hindu wife. Tell me, why do we Hindus lock our wives in, vault them, stifle them? Even pickle them?'

Rayhaan laughed. 'I'll answer that when I get me a wife. Unless, like you, I succeed in evading my domestic destiny.'

Uncle gave him a sour look. 'You might do just that, despite horoscope-hawking mothers ogling you for their simpering daughters. By now you must have perfected a neat method of ending liaisons, avoiding the trap—'

'We were talking about Saroj,' said Rayhaan with a disarming smile.

'Poor Saroj. As a bride she was a slight, gentle girl with a brimming heart.'

'Bombay is a big city. Perhaps your mother will never find her.'

'Ha, you don't know Mother. She'll find Saroj. And haul her back. Like a shikari on a long, careful stalk, she will follow every sign, every spoor that will bring her prey into focus.' He paused. 'My mother is a singularly determined woman. The secret of her strength is a complete lack of imagination and a mutually defensive alliance with God. That makes her invincible. I remember . . .'

Uncle so seldom used those two words that Mila sat up.

'I remember once when I was a pimply youth—ugh!—we got caught in a food riot in Calcutta. This was during one of the really bad famines. We were walking on this street late one evening, Mother and I, past a restaurant, when suddenly a stone flew over our heads. A windowpane gave way, and glass splintered in all directions. A crowd gathered on the pavement in a trice, drawn out of their haunts by the magic scent of food.

'Now things happened quickly. Clods of earth flew into the air, and clubs and sticks appeared out of tattered pant legs and sleeves. Before we knew it, the crowd had cut off our escape. Stones flew, blows were aimed and delivered. At whom and for what? For all their viciousness, these were poor creatures, weaker than sick cats but driven by the demon of hunger and despair.

'I felt my first spasm of fear when I discovered that my mother was no longer by my side. I felt hot breath against my face and smelled the foul odour of lice-ridden clothes. The slaps and thumps gathered momentum, and blood began to spurt from torn nostrils. Teeth engaged the flesh of bare arms and a mad, savage frenzy pervaded the crowd. "Food, we want food!" they were raving. Spittle flew from contorted mouths. They were chinless starvelings for the most part, with sunken faces and clumps of matted hair, but they were desperate and they had shed their humanity. Their grimacing faces were of ghouls and fiends, and if I couldn't get out of there quickly with my mother, death awaited us. Pain, beating, lynching . . . and death. The dread of extinction under the stamp and mash of ill-nourished feet was upon me . . .

'Then, like a miracle, I heard Mother's voice behind me: "We must get out of here." She was swaying with the crowd about two feet away. "Reach out your right hand."

'I stretched out my hand. The crowd pushed first one way, then another. We were in danger of being swept back or carried away. "Now," cried Mother as her hand clasped mine, "push behind me. We're getting out."

'Inch by inch we battled our way out. She took the worst of the buffeting herself. She hewed a way out for us by hurling her body against the heaving wall of flesh. Strength was in her, the strength of mules and horses, of powerful waves pounding the rocks. The crowd was now shouting with the ferocity of beasts. Over the din a scream of anguish rose in pitch till it seemed to pierce my very heart—the scream of death. But Mother did not falter, and I pressed on blindly behind her.

'At last, unbelievably, we staggered out in the clear, and I sank down on my knees on broken glass, but Mother dragged me up again. We had come out of the crowd on the side of the restaurant. We were safe.'

So breathlessly had Mila followed Uncle's every word that when he stopped speaking she was surprised to find herself at the foot of his bed.

'For days,' he continued after a long pause, 'food stuck in my throat. I could not eat. I could not sleep. I dreamt of skeletons, hundreds of them, shambling about in a kind of grotesque wedding procession, their faces lit by wavering flames . . . But in those nights a strange awareness of humanity grew in me. It was something I could not deny. The emaciated forms on the streets were no longer an abstraction. They were real. They were *my* problem. They were *my* guilt.' He seemed to be meditating between his sentences, yet the pauses were urgent. 'We left Calcutta soon. Time has blurred the pain, the indictment. But I have not quite forgotten.'

Amrish-mama gave a short, ironic laugh. 'My mother thought this reaction on my part a species of foolishness, impracticality and extravagance. She had no patience with it. Her God is a disinterested God. The mystery of the universe is a non-human mystery. She is satisfied that man counts for nothing to the divinity that shapes his ends. If he expends himself, there will be others to take his place. The play never ends. The source is inexhaustible. So she looked back on that evening with a sensible resignation, with detachment. These things happen in our country. The important thing is to assure yourself a favoured birth in the next life.'

Uncle stopped speaking and for the first time Mila noticed that Rayhaan was no longer seated in his chair, but standing by the small uncurtained window near the desk, looking out of it. Now his silence was different in quality. He seemed to be listening to something within himself: waiting for his star, so long hidden, to ride out high and shine again, newly silvered, above the earthly disorder of his days.

He turned round. 'Sometimes I wonder,' he murmured, 'whether I should be writing or you.' Then he announced abruptly, 'I'm going. I have work to do.'

'Work!' Uncle's voice rasped with sarcasm. Again Mila was aware that the scathing edge in his words would not be used for self-aggrandizement, as by so many people, but for something more valid. There was a sly flicker in his eyes as Amrish continued, 'Ho ho! Are you sure your head is clear enough of whisky fumes?' He pursed his mouth. 'You, a writer and a Zoroastrian by courtesy, must go freighted with fire, not liquor, in the region of your heart.'

'What would you know?' Rayhaan sounded amused, but at the same time threw his head back like someone reacting haughtily to an insult, 'What would you know of the fire raging in my heart?'

'And what you most need,' Amrish-mama went on unperturbably, 'is perseverence and steady labour, with no regard for yourself as a pampered human being. Your writing,' he added with insufferable condescension, 'is close enough to the real thing to be disconcerting.'

Rayhaan faced him with sudden force and animosity, stung out of his equanimity for a moment. 'You give nothing so profusely as advice!'

'It is a point which need not be laboured, I think.' Uncle looked smug as he flicked off an imaginary speck of dust from his sleeve. 'People look to me for right opinions and guidance on virtually everything.' He mocked Rayhaan with his voice, and held the younger man's gaze remorselessly.

It was Rayhaan's turn to cross his arms before his chest. 'Yes? I am now awaiting the final words of wisdom.'

'And you shall have them.' Uncle Amrish spoke with chin-jutting deliberation: 'By persistently coveting what we should not possess, we weaken ourselves without achieving anything.'

His words were like sparks struck in a perilous inner void, and Rayhaan's face flamed an angry red. 'Anything more?'

'Yes. A feather in hand is better than a bird in the air!'

They glared at each other with unfriendly eyes, and Amrish-mama looked like a malicious demon. The whip, the sting, the cattle goad, the picador's lance, he had employed all these to prick Rayhaan, needle him, lash him, drive him into revolt and combat him. Yet Mila had the confused notion that Uncle really wanted to rescue the younger man, put stepping stones over a dangerous torrent, gird him with strength, teach him to live alone, and it was possible to attempt all these things because he loved him.

'And you expect me to act on your advice?' Rayhaan was saying.

'No. Only wise men profit by advice. And you—who can doubt it?—are an idiot.'

Mila got up. She felt hot, scarred and uneasy on Ray's behalf and suddenly wanted to escape into a world that was bathed in sunshine, uncomplicated. Certainly kinder. 'I'm going home too,' she said.

'Yes, why not see the child home?' Uncle suggested.

'Do come home,' Mila turned eagerly to Rayhaan. 'Mother is out shopping, but I have nothing to do. And Vikram is at home and . . . and so is Roma-masi.' Rayhaan stared at her, but she knew he did not see her. He was circling round some terrible decision. Then he gave a nasty laugh.

'The pretty aunty is at home, is she? Let's go, then.' At the door he turned back to call to Amrish in a disagreeable voice, 'A feather in hand, you say? Well, I may follow your advice after all.'

9

But at the door of her flat Rayhaan had balked. 'I don't think I'll come in, Mila.' He stood tethered to the sunless landing under a daytime bulb that burned feebly overhead.

'Oh, but you must!' Mila's voice was throaty, as if a cough waited in it. 'Vikram's dying to show you his stamp collection and I've learnt to make coffee—'

'No.' The word was sharp with decision. 'I'm going away, Mila, from this stinking city. To see if I can get some work done.'

'Oh.' The thought of his absence emptied her. 'But you're not going *right* away?'

'I am.'

'Now?' She stared up at him till a tendon in her neck began to hurt.

'Yes.'

'But . . .' Her reluctance to see him go pulled taut the air between them. 'When will you come back?'

'I don't know.' Again Mila was struck by a certain helplessness in his posture and wanted to comfort him, completely, to grind his heart into her own. 'But when I get back,' he was saying, 'I'll come to see you and Vikram. That's a promise.'

She clung to his sleeve, and again she had the deep blind wish to give comfort. Reaching up she timidly touched a bristly cheek, and felt she had somehow sheltered him. Swiftly he caught her descending hand and kissed the inside of her wrist. Then he was gone.

Her hand tingled. She stood there exulting, not wanting to ring the bell. But the door swung open as if activated by photoelectric cells responding to her charged presence: as if Soni, who stood scowling behind it, had had nothing to do with it. Deaf to her brassy, scolding voice demanding where she had been, Mila walked in proudly as if conquering space, clearing a passage for herself—though of course she had only squeezed past Soni, her head in the clouds.

'Where have you been all morning, I'd like to know?' Soni was struggling, with incongruous results, to hold down her voice. 'Worry chewed up my brain like a centipede! Then I had to hide your absence from your mother—'

'Oh, is Mother back?' She smiled on Soni beatifically. Nothing could scatter her enchantment. That tight kiss on her wrist had put her in a mysterious relationship to the world. She felt bold, independent, gracious.

'Two hours ago she returned! You steal out again without a word to anyone,' Soni's loud voice attempted a whisper, 'and see if I don't tell your father—'

'Did Mother ask for me?'

'No. Stuck in her room she is with a headache, and I don't go there for fear she'll ask where is Mila, and could I have told lies? Your aunt is out, too—what are you hiding in your hand?'

'Nothing. Nothing!' But Mila could not help beaming at her.

'Show!' she demanded. Mila danced her empty consecrated hand before Soni's nose, then hid it again before the old faithful could grab it. 'What devil of mischief has got into you,' Soni shouted, 'that you ran out on the street without—'

'Oh, shoo! I went to see Amrish-mama. And I wasn't alone, Rayhaan brought me home.' The sound of his name brought her up short. She paused, going stiff and unheeding like a yogi. Then the irrepressible, secret smile must have played round her mouth again, for Soni said furiously, 'You are smirking about what? Like a cat that's lapped up the cream?'

Mila found it impossible to iron out the smug expression on her face, to dismiss the superior smile that kept hinting at a choice secret dreamily relished. So she said, 'I'm going to see what Mummy's got for me,' and made good her escape.

But for some time she lingered in her own room, tremulous with the discovery that Rayhaan possessed an ascendency over her. Not only was she prepared for this dominance, she welcomed it with a violent assertion of joy. Strange. From him she asked nothing more than a chance to smother him in thick layers of her devotion: and so round this provocative mote, this new entrant in her life, create a pearl of priceless value. But a corresponding response from him was inconceivable; it would have scared her silly at this stage.

When at last Mila found herself outside her mother's room, she hesitated. It was very quiet in there, but a surge reached her from it, conveying alarm. She could not account for it, and was suddenly filled with misgivings. 'Mother?' It required effort to raise the curtain and take the first step in.

And there she froze.

Her mother sat facing her across the room, her lovely hair tumbling about her shoulders and partly hiding her face. In her right hand she brandished a tiny pair of nail scissors. Her mouth working soundlessly, she was hacking away at the brown strands with vicious little snips and jabs. She had cut the right side of her hair till it hung in a crazy jagged curtain just below her cheek. She did not see Mila, so absorbed was she in her task, but abruptly her mutterings grew audible. Round and round went her words, a low rumble tearing out of her, impossible to grasp.

Suddenly she rose and darted across the room to her dressing table, on which she dropped her scissors. The mutterings changed to laughter. Leaning on her flat palms, her thumbs placed to make a kind of butterfly pattern on the table, Mother began to laugh. Her head hung lower and lower over her hands as she laughed; then abruptly the spasms ceased. And in the mirror, from under that untidy pelt, she at last saw Mila and her lips parted in a sudden awful smile. Mila quailed. The room spun round her. The smile seemed to contain some terrible mindless knowledge of destruction, of dissolution—where had she seen that smile before?

'Come in, Mila!' Mother cried in a voice so abandoned that another wave of fear went through her. The walls of the room grew dense. There was a threat in Mila's stomach, and sea-water in her mouth. As she stood rooted to the spot her mother picked up the scissors and shot back to her chair. 'Come in!' she whooped as she fell backwards into it. Mila winced at the voice, but she was commanded. With impaired, almost crippled steps, she went towards her.

'See this?' Mother shouted quite gaily, clutching a fistful of hair in her left hand and snipping at it with the mean, darting, frantic scissors. 'See it? I'm going to wear my hair *young*, like she does! And it doesn't hurt at all. Painless, see?' The scissors cut wild arabesques in the air, then pull, snip, pull.

Mila found her voice at last. 'Don't.' It was hardly above a whisper, forced through unshed tears. 'Please, Mummy, don't.'

'Please, Mummy,' mocked her mother. 'Don't.'

'Stop it!'

'Stop it!'

'Please?'

'Please?'

Mila could not stand the way her mother mimicked her, eyes snapping with malice. She had on occasion imitated Vikram's high voice, the earnest nodding gestures of his head, the little nibbling gestures as he bit his nails, but now terror washed over her. And Mother sat watching her from behind all that hair, expectant and crafty. 'See my face?' she yelled suddenly. 'Come, examine it! It has lost its meaning.' She looked momentarily confused. In a blank, vacuous way she passed a hand over her face, then clawed at it with cruel fingers as if plucking at an intolerable mask. 'You find it ugly? Objectionable?' Her voice fell to a confiding whisper: 'Have you ever overturned a wet rock by the sea? Found an obscene creature waiting for you in the shallow dirty pool, looking at you with alert, dangerous eyes set in the middle of its shapeless body?' She looked rapaciously round the room, at the door, at each of the two windows and whispered, her face sly and hyena-pointed, 'You know it has to be *killed*, don't you? So hold this bit of hair for me. So I can cut it easier. Just under here.' Mila did not move to do her bidding. 'Hold it for me *here*. HERE!'

'No.'

'Do as you're told! At once! You think I don't know all the scheming and whoring that goes on behind my back? He tries to hide his filth from me, but you think I'm blind? You think I don't see the dreadful flower growing in all that slime, the lotus with murderous roots? You think I don't feel disgust in the back of my mind, on the back of my tongue? All that *muck*? Hold it!'

The room had gone shrill and dizzy with her fright, but Mila managed to shake her head. Her mother's body shifted from side to side in the chair, gathered sap from some secret roots, and then she sprang upright, strong and terrible in her wrath. Her face contorted with a powerful rage. Muscles leapt and swelled in her long neck. Now she stood over Mila, the scissors gleaming in her raised hand, and once again that smile flickered across her face, derisive and remote, as if she were savouring a superb but barbaric jest.

'Mother!' Mila closed her eyes. And from an instinct stronger than any fear she blindly flung her arms round her, as though she were still the only possible haven, the only security in her tottering world. As if only one part of the child felt threatened, while the other still trusted her mother.

The next moment Mila was sent crashing against the wall. And that fall saved her, because it brought Vikram running to the door.

'Mother!' It was his shrill voice that now said the same word.

Like an animal at bay she crouched there for a moment, rigid fingers curled round the scissors, a frozen angle of the triangle completed by Vikram. Only her eyes darted quickly from him to Mila, and back to him again. Then, with a sound that was hardly human, she lunged at him.

He was shaking like a leaf, but he stood his ground. She laughed aloud and Mila saw the upturned blades inscribe a gash on his cheek. The scream that had risen in her throat refused to leave it, as she simply could not summon enough breath. She tried to hide behind her hands as she cowered on the floor, but through her shaking fingers and the glasses askew on her face she saw a curlicue of blood tracing a path down his ashen cheek. Still he did not cry out or move, but stared at his mother with despairing eyes. In silence he seemed to wait for the long fall, the final blow, the end. And yet it seemed to Mila that with one frail hand he was pushing back an ocean, for suddenly Mother drew back with a little stifled cry, her hands flew to her mouth and the scissors dropped from her nerveless fingers. She stared, horrified, at the blood.

'Go away!' she barked at Vikram. 'Go away, I don't want to see it—I can't bear to see it—go away, take him away!'

They did not know then that it was her abnormal fear of the sight of blood that had stopped the attack. They could only stare, unbelieving, as the strange transformation took place and she who had been wild and violent a moment ago was now whimpering. Mila rose shakily to her feet and went to Vikram's side. She took his hand. It was trembling as hers was.

'She hurt you,' Mila whispered. 'She hurt you!'

'Pick it up,' he said, and Mila saw that the silver cross made by the scissors on the floor was a magnet for his eyes.

Fearfully she bent for them while Shivani stood with her poor ravaged head buried in her hands, her shoulders sagging. She lowered her hands as Mila straightened up and their eyes met. And Mila saw that her mother was fighting to avoid a confrontation with herself, which she would now be forced to endure with a vengeance. And there was such pain, such hopelessness in her eyes that Mila desperately wanted to rescue her, make her safe. Yet in this, her mother's most terrible hour she was removed from her. Space howled between them like a flood, and as they stared at each other Mother was borne further away from Mila, like a prisoner aboard an enemy ship. And the distance between them was unbridgeable.

'Come,' said Mila to Vikram. They turned their backs on her and walked out of the room, hand in hand.

That night Mila slept in the same room as Vikram and Roma-masi. She was awake when Father came in. They talked in whispers.

'But why, Roma, why? Why did it have to happen again? Why did she lose control?' Father spoke with an unfamiliar impatience as he paced the room. With a sinking heart Mila realized that he was annoyed with Mother, as if he expected her, after all these years, to recognize symptoms of strain in herself and guard against them. He had hardened himself against her; he was deliberately driving a wedge between Mother well and Mother sick. If you were not a saint, wasn't there something unforgivable about sickness, weakness, senility, debility in those you must care for? And wasn't there, beneath her father's stoicism, a thick crust of reproach for such defection? It was becoming increasingly difficult for Mila to distinguish between a self-protective detachment in him, and this new coldness in his heart.

'What time did you send for the nurse?' he asked.

'Immediately on my return,' said Roma. 'Within two hours of it happening the nurse was here.'

It did not bear thinking of. Mother had been sitting in her chair, drumming the right armrest with strong fingers, when the nurse entered the room. Head forward, chin lowered, she had stared up with venom at the massive, uniformed woman in white, then shot up without warning. But the nurse had been quicker. That pugilist had thrown herself forward and on her, arms and body spread round her like a net, springing and jumping on her before she could take another step. They had gone down together and it was at this point that Soni, finding Mila standing at the door, incredulous, white-faced, trembling, had hustled her out of the room. Mila was sick in her bathroom. And she hated that muscular nurse forever.

'Roma, do you realize what this means?' Father's urgent voice. 'This collapse prophesies a new cycle, a new bout of the malady. She never completed her treatment. Dear God . . . My poor children . . .' As he spoke Mila knew he was learning to make himself empty of her mother. Mila also knew that Mother knew about this, the knowledge a murk inside her that she had to tint a bright colour by demanding from him a total commitment, an impossible devotion, at the same time hating him for her dependence and helplessness. *His* strength was endless.

'You were not at home when it happened?' he asked.

'No.' Mila began to notice a sullen backflow in Aunty's voice, but her father did not seem to heed it.

'Did she appear at all strange to you when she left the house this morning?'

'No, she didn't,' was the curt answer.

'Then why . . . why?' Mila heard the impact of his fist being driven into his open palm and wished she was fast asleep like Vikram on the opposite bed. He looked like a little Sikh, his cheeks and head swathed in bandages. Father's restless pacing was resumed, till it was suddenly interrupted by Roma-masi saying in a whisper so fiercely sibilant that Mila flinched under her covers: '*You* know why! *You* should know, if anyone does!'

A moment of silence. 'Now what does that mean?' Father asked very quietly.

'You . . . You . . .' Roma seemed to strangle on her words, but rushed on, driven by the propulsive power of a private wrong she must have long endured. 'You are a hypocrite! Yes, that's what you are . . . All these years I didn't know it. All these years I thought you were a . . . a god come down on earth! Worthy of worship . . . I thought of you as her saviour!' She was almost weeping.

'Roma, do you know I haven't the slightest idea what you are talking about?'

'Then you're a liar as well!' she screamed at him. 'A liar!' So her aunt was a woman of imperfect docility after all. She was not without fight, and her outburst made her more substantial, more real than the pathetic shadow of her Mila had carried in her mind for years.

'You'll wake up the children,' Father cautioned Roma. 'I must ask you to control yourself.'

'Don't talk to me like that! I am not my sister. I'm not that poor woman you've driven out of her mind!' Her voice rose in pitch and upbraided him so harshly that Mila imagined the skin peeling off his face.

'Roma!'

'You think we don't know what's going on? You think we don't know about that—your woman? And all this time I defended you . . . even against my own mother! Don't trouble to deny it, don't! I saw you with her this afternoon.' Roma's voice trembled. 'No, I won't listen to a word you say! What I saw with my own eyes . . .' The frantic, tearful voice trailed away. Silence, except for the sound of stifled sobs, during which Father seemed to wait patiently for peace to be restored.

Then Mila heard him sigh. Such a weary, heartfelt sigh that she knew just what it meant: would people never stop trying to involve him in their troubled imaginings, when it was only his steadfast resolve to stay clear that allowed him to help them? Must everyone beat against him over and over again until the warped patterns conceived by their sick minds were shattered on the granite of his detachment? Must they demand anger from him, and weakness, because to be undone and helpless was to be human, to be strong was to be suspect?

When he spoke his voice was as calm as usual. 'In a way, I'm glad this has happened. It's out in the open now, where it won't bother you so much, and that's a good thing. I have, in fact, long wanted to talk to you—'

'I don't want to hear it!'

Gently: 'Perhaps it could help both of us.'

Between sobs: 'It won't help. Nothing can, now.' There was desolation in her voice.

'The explanation is very simple. From what you said, I presume you saw me lunching with Gi . . . Mrs Seth this afternoon.' Mila tensed in bed. It was he who had suddenly crystallized the situation by mentioning a name.

'It makes little difference what you say.'

But he went on: 'At one o'clock we had to break up our conference with Sodani and Sons, from whom we are seeking a large print order, for lunch. And I welcomed this opportunity, as I had to come to a quick decision about a point raised at the meeting.'

'Don't trouble to go on—'

'Sodani and Sons is housed in Karmali Chambers, which is next door to "Ali Baba." Mrs Seth and I had no time to return to the office, so we decided on a quick lunch there.'

'All this means nothing. I saw what I saw!'

'Roma,' he said, still very patient, 'if you mean you saw our heads together at the table, it was because we were going over her notes.'

'Yes? And your hand was resting on hers because . . . ?'

'This is getting more than absurd!' He sounded angry at last.

'And you were smiling into her eyes for . . . inspiration, I suppose?' There was a note of pure jealousy in Roma's voice.

Heavily, after a brief pause, he said, 'People see what they choose to see . . . and perhaps you are as responsible as I am for the clay feet you chose to mount on a pedestal.' He was now picking his words very carefully. 'You are disturbed and overwrought, Roma. I will not pursue this further till you are more composed.' But for some reason he felt compelled to add, 'You may not know the circumstances in which Mrs Seth came to me for the job—in which Shivani sent her to me for a job. *Years* after the sickness had taken root in her.'

Was there a plea in his last words? An apology? Was he excusing himself? There must have been a new note in his voice, the voice Mila wanted to remain unalterable forever, because if ever it *did* alter, it would hurl her into chaos. There must have been something in his words to threaten her trust in him, for that night a new apprehension entered her heart. Had she been betrayed? Was her Daddy committing fraud with every schooled cadence of his voice? Was there something in him to be despised?

Sharmila knows the answers to these questions today, but that night all Mila felt was cold and lost as her father, a natural force of immense prestige, almost a deity, fell in her eyes to a more human level. And a new pain was lodged inside her. She lay awake a long time after he left the room, scratching and digging away at the topsoil of her mind like an eager dog, and unearthed a few bones: early impressions, things heard, seen, sensed but not comprehended. Fragments, memories, little odds and ends. But when Mila tried to construct them into any semblance of unity, the picture they began to form was so distasteful that she started to quickly bury them again, one bone after another, in the many hidden vaults wherein she had already buried secret after secret, particle after particle of herself.

Mila overslept. When Soni shook her awake in the morning, the sun had invaded the room and Aunty's and Vikram's beds had already been made.

'How is Mother?' She sat up as the events of the day before came crowding back.

'Resting,' Soni said shortly. 'You are not to go to her room.'

'And . . . Vikram?'

'Nothing that a paste of turmeric wouldn't have taken care of, but they had to drag him to a doctor.' Soni did not hold with doctors and was not impressed with the injection and three stitches that Vikram's wound had earned. Mila grabbed her hand and was about to ask a question she dreaded putting into words, when in the passage outside the phone began to ring.

'If that's *her* again,' Soni muttered under her breath, 'I'll tell the devil's daughter not to be troubling this household any more. I'll tell her to eat mud and drown herself.' She tried to pull away from Mila, who now held on to her with both hands. 'She wants to be in every pot that's cooking in this house, in the dal and the pumpkin . . .'

'Who, Soni? Who are you talking about?'

'Let go, can't you see I must answer the phone?'

'*Tell* me who, or I'll never let you go!' But as Mila spoke they heard the receiver being picked up and her father's voice saying 'Hallo?'

Soni no longer struggled to free herself, but stood there scowling and complaining. 'Spoke to her for half an hour on the phone, your mother did, just after she came home from the shopping yesterday, all smiling and happy-like. What the whore told her, I'd like to know, to bring that stare in her face and that bad headache. She had called me in to see the sari she had bought, but after talking on the phone she said, "What sari?", her face all bunched up trying to remember. Then she sat glued to her chair with that stare in her eyes, talking of this man who had followed her home, though I told her to hush and lie down.'

'What man?' Mila tugged at Soni's sari. 'Didn't she take the car?'

'Of course Shankar drove her all the way, but she kept talking about this man who walked behind her on the pavements and peered over her shoulder in the shops. "He used the most foul language," she kept saying, frightened like a child come in from a thunderstorm. "He might have harmed me." I tried to get her to eat but she refused, though she had asked for curd and mango juice before the phone call . . . That woman has an evil tongue, I know it, for all her sugary ways. She commands spirits of darkness and brings destruction with her'—Soni slapped her own quivering cheeks—'was her lord not snatched away from their marriage bed when they had hardly used it? Her karma is heavy, her mouth big enough to swallow us all! She must be stopped from coming to this house before—'

There was no stopping Soni once she was in spate. But as she swooshed on, Mila ceased to listen. For by now she had little difficulty identifying the calamitous witch who figured so darkly in Soni's narrative. And so it was that Mila marked Gita Seth for extermination.

10

Mila was determined that 'Operation Gita' be in full swing before the new school term began, but apart from slamming the front door once in the witch's face, muttering inaudible impertinences behind her back and drawing eloquent sketches of 'Gita the Gangster' and 'Gobble-Gobble Gita' that the greedy guts never got to see, she did not accomplish much. In her imagination, however, she was The Great Avenger: she saw herself getting Vikram to piss accurately into the mouth of the elegant leather handbag she suspected was the boss's gift to his lady secretary. In another clandestine fantasy Mila ordered the slyboots to disrobe, then turned her out on the streets with not so much as her boots on. Next, she sealed up the slut, frantic and struggling, in a capsule set for outer space . . .

But despite such fanciful heapings of insult and injury, despite Soni's purple scowls and Aunt Roma's glacial civility, Gita continued to telephone regularly and to turn up on impromptu visits home, all honey and Florence Nightingale. She was apparently consumed with anxiety about Mother, who, wrestling grimly with demons for possession of her mind, was incarcerated for weeks in her room. Which gave Gita time enough to convey to Father how noble he was to put up with this unbearable domestic situation.

As I look back on her now, I know that Gita succeeded in distorting, by barely perceptible stages, Father's attitude towards the prisoner in her cell. Flooding him with her generous concern, she left him with nagging doubts about *who* the real victim was—the patient, or he and his unfortunate children; and with gratitude for the highwaywoman who made her daylight robbery seem like a salvaging operation. If there were any finicky rules about what one may or may not help oneself to, such Geneva Conventions had long ago been repudiated by that tenacious little tart.

Strong words? Yes, because even after all these years I am angry that Father allowed Gita to use weapons invisible to him, and that he was not quite as sapient as I had thought him to be. How else could he have failed to see that when she was skittish with Vikram, when she chucked him under the chin or rested a hand with simulated affection on his sleeve, she was using her female body on a mere boy to seduce him? That through the son she was reaching out to grab the father, her ultimate prey?

Vikram was frightened to death of her. The more plumply she advanced, all her youthful flesh in motion, the farther he retreated. If she went after him with a butterfly net, he drifted out of reach. If she flung a spear after him, he went crashing past the furniture to seek refuge in his den. But I can't forgive my brother for drifting instead of fighting, for not meeting Gita head-on, for allowing her to use him instead of turning on the predator and chasing her off the home territory. Vikram was a wimp who might as well have deserted to the enemy camp.

What I still marvel at about Gita's performance in those days was its blend of helplessness with competence: a smooth, potent compound. Her frailty was her main resource, to be invested profitably in various schemes and stratagems. She was the wilting widow robbed by fate, ill-treated by destiny, in constant need of a strong hand with a drawn sword, a shoulder to cry on and a manly chest to snuggle against. She was so meek that she inherited my father!

At the same time her campaign was unmatched for sheer efficiency. She was industrious, neat, painstaking—like certain insects. The lady secretary projected a professionally packaged look, but she was also an amateur angel who took on all those nibbling little tasks that eat into the day of a busy man of affairs. She not only made his business appointments, she also rang up his dentist—and would have cheerfully impaled herself on the chair in his place, had that been possible. The seraph took charge of his laundry receipts, the changing of oil in his car. She remembered to book cinema seats and holiday hotels in advance for the family—taking care to be invited along herself. I suspect she even bought the birthday gifts that Father gave us, and chose and sent flowers from him to Mother. She was shrewd enough to see that these fond, proprietary gestures spelled power for her, and entitlement. For the same reason she disciplined herself to listen tirelessly to Father, though when speaking with others her eyes continually strayed to distant objects of interest. She was as devoted to him as the silkworm to the mulberry leaf. It was his sad fate to be desired by two fiercely possessive women, and had he not been Omnipotence itself, he would have been devoured long ago.

Mila had quite accepted that when Mother was unwell (which was often enough), she would come home from school to find Gita busybodying all over the place as if it belonged to her. Now she would be poaching in the living room, now in the bedrooms. She would jingle her mother's keys, order the next day's meals and queen it in the kitchen and the storeroom, much to Soni's disgust. Gita's exceeding capacity for housekeeping concealed a constant reproach to fate, which had deprived her of her rightful place and work.

One night early in the year, before the domestic crisis that had brought Aunt Roma to stay with them, Mother was called to the bed of a sick relative. Late in the morning of the next day, Sunday, she had not returned from her vigil and Mila was in the living room when a scowling Soni ushered in Gita, looking, oh, a real calico cutie in her fresh white sari with a wide primrose border. Mila greeted her perfunctorily, picked up her book and marched out of the room just as Father walked in with a file under his arm. Obviously the master and his diligent slave had arranged to meet for some homework, and had busy hours ahead of them.

It was near lunchtime. Restless at her mother's continued absence, Mila had wandered into her parents' bedroom to be confronted by this extraordinary vision: two smug, pouting faces converging on each other in slow motion—for a kiss?—the one imprisoned in the mirror (the only one Mila could view frontally, herself unseen) luxuriously contemplating its twin visage through half-closed eyes. Midway the pout turned into a beatific smile as hands crept up to caress with gliding touches the rounded hips, the tight waist, the high curving breasts . . . the face all the while smiling provocatively at its infatuated image, till Mila became confused and thought that the real woman was the one swimming in the reflective pool of glass while the one who had her feet on the floor was her doting shadow, mimicking her. Fascinated, Mila moved farther into the room to watch one maiden perform like two brazen hussies.

'Gita!' Father's voice had rung out like a pistol report from the open doorway, and the snake almost sloughed off her skin as she recoiled in a flurry from the mirror.

'Just exactly what,' Father spoke with tense controlled anger, 'do you think you're doing here?'

Tears. Trembling. Gita, gosh, was understandably unnerved, and liquid with emotion. Her voice came out in a dying whisper. 'Don't shout at me, please. I can't bear it. Don't shout—'

The angle of the door had hidden Mila from his view, but now Father saw her. 'Mila,' he said quietly, wearily.

At that moment Gita saw her, too, and her agile mind was quick to use the daughter to gain an advantage. 'I came in for a moment to see'—the strain of inventing lies made her face look older—'if I . . . I couldn't set the room to rights, with Mila's help. Shivani will need to rest . . .'

'Yes, of course,' Father cut in heavily. The seams in his face were marked. He quickly left the room.

Gita's tears dried mid-stream, and in her eyes there glowed an unquenchable hope. She was like someone eternally in a queue, awaiting her turn with excruciating patience.

All such domestic trespassing and encroachments were suspended, however, when Nanima sent Roma to keep house for them later that year. And Mila was singularly drawn to her aunt by her discovery that she, too, detested Gita. Perhaps niece and aunt could have become friends in the next two months as Mother slowly recovered from the latest bout of her illness. Weren't they in tacit league against the interloper? Their truce could have yielded a fine formulation of plans to deal with Gita; but Aunty's preference for Vikram was too marked. They had evolved a code of private behaviour to which Mila could not find the key. They had ways of talking, ways of silence, ways of exchanging glances that excluded her and killed her fumbling attempts to establish that communion between them in a few weeks that had not been accomplished in years—and which, in truth, did not exist at all.

But this was also a period during which, as Mother seemed to retire further into the shadows, Aunty emerged into light, grew vivid. As though, while Mother struggled in her private fog, all her animation and vitality were being transferred to her sister. Roma lost her pale, maverick quality, her air of knowing she was there on sufferance. Once so indistinct, a sketch done in very light pencil, she became more and more clear in outline as Mother disappeared inside the pale shell of her room. It was as if Roma had at last shed her senseless amiability and developed a more shapely human will. There was something exceedingly real about her now.

But she had also stopped being pretty. She was preoccupied with thoughts that left a permanent crease between her eyes, etched bitter lines round her mouth. Roma grew thinner. When she raised her head, blue cords stood out in her fair throat. Fine little lines branched faint-blue across her brow. Her movements showed a kind of impatience, as if she were constantly brushing away something distasteful that accosted her in the dark. No longer attentive to Father, Roma did not scamper from room to room, a nimble ballet mouse performing timid pirouettes in the course of trivial errands. She did not run to him with complaints, and clearly he was no longer prepared to swallow, in one obedient gulp, whatever she dished out. On the other hand, with Vikram she openly allowed herself tenderness. With Mila she was correct, and earned from her niece a kind of grudging respect.

For the greater part of the two months that Shivani took to emerge from the clouds that obscured her, the house was unnaturally quiet—as if padded with secrets. It was in a state of siege, with frantic preparations apace in induced gloom. Yet soon, by a kind of inertia, the unusual took on the guise of the normal. Vikram and Mila inquired routinely after their mother in lowered voices. For them the door (sometimes just the curtain) that separated her room from the rest of the flat was an effective barrier; beyond it they were not allowed. Beyond it some violent activity was going on, with the startling hush of a film whose soundtrack had broken down. Mother must have been kept under heavy sedation, for they heard no extraordinary sounds from the room. They saw Dr Bakshi, another bearded doctor, two nurses including the wrestler Mila disliked, Father, Aunt Roma and Soni flitting in and out. Their steps were light, urgent or purposeful, but they all seemed to be part of a pantomime going on behind the scenes, and without an audience. Mila felt that one day the drama would explode brilliantly and without warning into sound, but it never did. At least not in the mornings before they rushed off to school, or in the evenings that saw them home. What happened in the intervening hours they never knew. On weekends they were farmed out, on one excuse or another, to relatives and friends. Father slept in Mila's room, in her bed, while she moved into the next bedroom with Vikram and Roma-masi. And if Mila did sometimes struggle awake in the nights it was only the rain she heard, weeping without let: for now they were in the throes of the monsoon, and it was particularly heavy that year.

One evening early in August, Soni had the door open for Mila almost as soon as her hand touched the doorbell. Mila erupted into the living room trailing a wet raincoat, her heavy school bag bumping her hip, ribbons missing from her plaits as usual, her sneakers the colour of dirty wash with the laces undone, to find Mother established on the big green divan under the window. She stood still. To find herself suddenly in her mother's presence was a feeling so overwhelming that it forbade speech and action.

'Well?' Mother finally said. Her hair was tied back, so Mila couldn't tell how much of it had grown again. Her face was sallow and the skin of her full eyelids sagged a little. She sat there stiff and straight, no bending, no concessions to weakness, but the smile she attempted was so wan and uncertain that Mila flung her school things on the carpet, fell on her knees before the divan and covered her hand with kisses.

Mother smiled again and wordlessly stroked her hair. Then she chided her gently for not protecting her feet with overshoes in bad weather. When Mila attempted some excuse, she folded her closely in her arms while large, unwilling tears gathered in the corners of her eyes. It was raining outside. Again Mila's sense of her miraculous presence smote her so acutely that it created a solitude in which her mother alone existed, while she herself was totally absent. Only Mother. And now the room seemed full of a soft, perfumed rain and the cool uncarpeted strip of floor at the foot of the divan became a gathering pool under a green overhang of foliage. Mila held her mother's hand tightly. They did not speak. There was no need for words.

After that evening Mother's recovery was rapid. Flesh and colour returned to her wasted cheeks. Her dull eyes gradually lost their tendency to stare vacantly into space, or at an imagined presence in unlit corners of the room. She gave up her incessant melancholy nodding and pressing tight her quivering lips. Headaches and nausea became things of the past. When she began to sleep without sedation, the night nurse received her marching orders and soon the day giantess was doomed as well. Father joined Mother in their bedroom and Mila moved back into hers.

There was only one incident that marred Mother's smooth journey back to self-possession. For almost a week of fine weather she ventured out alone on a short daily walk before sundown, an exercise that did her visible good. On Friday evening she was caught in a shower and returned home early and bright-eyed. She changed her sari and joined the family in the living room, and very lovely she looked with her warm hair, warm eyes, warm skin. She chose the big chair. As she settled into its depths with a book, she remarked that a wisp of a boy, a street urchin, was in the habit of following her every evening, from the steps of the garden that crested Malabar Hill past the post office and down the winding slope of their lane to the gate of their building. She gave this information quietly, with some amusement, without the corrosive anxiety that had accompanied such statements in the past. But what she said was enough to inspire a shapeless dread in all of them. A secret panel to a hidden room seemed to slide back at her words to reveal to their shocked gaze the stricken creature within.

Mother did not appear to perceive their disquiet. She went on, 'A little chap of about six, painfully thin. In torn canvas shoes and khaki shorts too big for him. I stopped a block before our gate today to see what he would do. He halted right behind me and stuck his thumb in his mouth.'

They sat there, dissembling calm, while amorphous fears solidified, grew bones. The nightmare past was no longer safely the past, but incarnating before their eyes into a neurotic present. Father's hand shook slightly as he added a Y to Mila's M-E-S-S on the Scrabble board between them on the divan. A spasm crossed Aunt Roma's face. Was she in sudden physical pain? She made one restless motion of escape, then bent more closely over the square of unbleached duster she was hemming. 'It started to rain again so I walked on,' Mother was saying, 'but he was still there when I looked back. Getting wet and sucking his thumb.' With that she returned to her book.

The room had closed in on them. In the oppressive silence that greeted her words, Mother must have felt them furtively picking holes in what she had said—testing her story with a certain practised cunning for fact and fabrication, and even resenting what it portended. For the doctors had been explicit on this one point: they had to watch out for such telltale symptoms. When Mother suffered delusions, such as that of strangers following her, or was obsessed by their presence, it could be the beginning of a new cycle of her malady, a relapse into disorder. Sitting there they felt ruthlessly threatened, their silence screaming red inside them.

Mother read on but their appraisal must have blown scorchingly about her head, for at last she shut her book and directly addressed Dad. 'You have no faith in me, do you?'

He flinched. 'Why do you say that?'

'You don't believe I really saw that boy.'

'Of course I do,' Father said too quickly. Don't people lie to be merciful?

'I not only saw him,' her voice was growing sharper, 'he was *there*.'

'Shivani—' he began helplessly.

'You don't trust me.' A flash of the old fire was in her long eyes. 'I've become a millstone round your neck.' This was said in anguish.

'Not so,' he said hoarsely. 'You've done so well. You *are* well,' he added desperately as she stared at him with a hard face. 'And I want to keep you so.' He was pleading with her now.

'But you cannot.' She was gathered into herself like a cat about to spring. 'Because you don't trust me.'

'You know I do.'

'Do I? Tell me then: did I see the boy or did I imagine him?'

'You saw him.'

'He was not a hallucination?'

'No.'

She said after a pause, softly, and almost with compassion, 'You're lying. You don't trust me, you only pretend to.'

Father stood up abruptly, scattering some of his Scrabble letters on the floor. 'Perhaps you're right.' The words stuck in his throat like a rusty needle pinned in jute cloth. 'Perhaps I only pretend to trust.' His face was exhausted, drained of denials, evasions. 'Perhaps your illness lies like a knife between us, making trust impossible,' he said, his voice trembling, 'for which I ask you to forgive me.'

Fearful of the effect of his words on Mother, Mila kept repeating in a shrill voice, 'Let's play. We haven't finished our game, Daddy. Let's play!'

In the moment of truth Mother had closed her eyes. But now she opened them and quietly picked up her book again. Instead of kindling a blaze, whipping up an operatic climax, by this small courageous act she chose to distance herself from the scene. As if now that the worst had been said, now that she felt a sense of finality, of having reached a dead end, her painful option was to cease to be vulnerable; and her will was not yet so eroded that she could not summon it to do her bidding.

In response to such valour, and with a superhuman effort, Father sat down again. Mila bent over, blood drumming in her ears, to pick up the scattered letters from the floor. Aunt Roma sat devotedly over her duster, as if their lives depended on her giving neat edges to the coarse fabric in hand.

After that Friday Mother gave up her walks, but she slowly resumed control of the household. As she steadily became herself again, so did Aunt Roma. She began to gently fade, as if the outline of her form was being rubbed out by an invisible eraser. Once more she appeared structureless, lacking in significance. She suffered from a dreadful lack of vigour, an absence of straightforward, operative desires. Instead of a conflict of wills, there was again a frustration of wishes and mute entreaties—life was a Chekhovian drama in which she would grow old and defeated while life passed her by.

Thrice a week she accompanied Mother to the hospital for a mysterious treatment called 'shocks', but to the onlooker it must have appeared that it was Mother who steered the younger woman there. No two sections of an hourglass could drain and fill more evenly than the two sisters once Mother was on the road to normality. It was as if, in her rehabilitated presence, the newly discovered qualities of self-reliance and affirmation were filtered out of Roma to find their way back to Shivani, in whom they had their source. Once more Masi lay under the stigma of invisibility. Only for a brief, bright spell had she produced her corporeal shape, and now all promise paled away again.

It was about this time that Ritu's father bought a new car, a yellow Mercedes. With an extreme casualness that did not deceive Mila, Ritu invited her for a drive one Saturday afternoon. With an added sense of triumph she also produced for the occasion, on the back seat of the car, her cousin Vidyut, who had passed out of their school that year and who, by a clever parental coup, was betrothed to the eldest son of a prosperous Gujarati businessman. So Ritu had two trophies on display, and seated stiffly between the two girls in the car Mila had the sensation of being encompassed and plotted against. The chauffeur, Rao, was for some reason in a foul temper. He changed gears inexpertly, honked and swore at the traffic, stopped with a jerk and accelerated with a start. Such brutality seemed to amuse Vidyut, but it really bruised Ritu's sense of possession. She suffered, but did not reprimand Rao. He was from Kerala, with a face like a pot on fire—dark, greasy, encrusted—and he intimidated her.

Vidyut wore a hideous floral sari which she had pulled tight against her pumped-up bosom encased in the briefest of blouses. It could have been a bikini top! She was very fair, and so considered a beauty in the community despite her chunky hips and somewhat blunt features. Her movements were languid, and she had an unabashed self-esteem that Mila rather envied. It pleased Mila to note that her cousin's curves made Ritu look scrawny.

Vidyut inspected Mila curiously with eyes heavily ringed in home-made mascara, the kind prepared from soot with a lamp burning pure ghee. Her long, sticky eyelashes were spaced like the spokes of an umbrella. 'I know all about you,' she said. She had the trick of making the simplest statement sound like an accusation. 'And about your mother. How long has she been like that?'

Mila disliked her on the spot. 'Nothing's the matter with my mother,' she said shortly. It was an effort not to pinch the bared midriff, the white ridge of flesh between the choli's edge and the sari girdling Vidyut's pudding belly.

'No?' the heifer batted her eyes. 'Then why did my aunt, Ritu's mother, tell us—'

'I don't want to know what your aunt told you,' snapped Mila. Just then Rao swerved sharply in an ill-timed attempt to overtake a taxi, and Ritu gave a little squeal as she was thrown against her cousin. Vidyut disengaged herself in slow motion. Her movements were so fatigued, Mila was tempted to take her pulse to make sure she would not die on their hands.

'I know about your mother, all the same,' Vidyut said. 'And I've met your friend Rayhaan, too. We meet everyone. My sister thinks he's very handsome. But I don't think he could get into Hindi movies, no matter how hard he tried.' She sniffed. 'Not even a TV serial. For that you need *in*fluence.'

Ritu patted her hair, done up in a series of complicated knots and loops. 'Vidyut's father has a lot of *in*fluence,' she said.

Vidyut shrugged. 'People come to meet him all the time.'

'I don't think Rayhaan wants to get into any stupid movie,' Mila said resentfully, her face aflame.

Vidyut turned to look at her, and Mila had no expression ready to counter that direct gaze. She felt revealed, exposed, and dropped her eyes in some confusion. Rayhaan was her secret and now it was imperilled. The degree of her engrossment in him after their last meeting was remarkable, considering that she was always caught up in a hectic round of schoolgirl activities. He was everywhere—within her like something tugging, a flutter of silken wings round the heart. He peered at her out of cauterized textbooks and plush magazine illustrations. He was the hero of all the silly novels she read, all the idiotic TV soaps she sat through. He was ever present, not only with a childish haunting but with a sovereign insistence that at times left her confused and shaken, at others in a haze of enslaved delight. And the pain of physical desire was a deliciously diffused aching of her whole body.

Fortunately for her, to Vidyut every subject that came up in conversation proved to be, upon examination, unbearably tedious. So now she turned to Ritu and said, with a long-suffering air, 'Where did you say we were going?'

'Juhu beach,' said Ritu. 'You said you wanted to go to Ju—' She broke off as Rao took a wild swing to the left and the car seemed to keel over. Ritu glared at his back in helpless indignation, but Vidyut merely raised her brows.

'Suppose it rains?' she said.

'Look, you *said* Juhu—'

'Oh, all right. Let's go to Juhu.' Vidyut suppressed a yawn. 'Unless Rao manages to smash up the car first.' She turned to Mila wearily. 'School is a bore, no? Don't you think school's a bore? Am I glad to be out of it!' Mila merely looked away, and maintained a superior silence the rest of the way.

The afternoon sky was deceptively cloudless, the sand glossy, and the water scintillated in the hard glare as Rao raced the Mercedes down the sloping beach in one mad spurt, then brought it to an abrupt halt on a patch of level ground.

Vidyut sighed as they got out of the car and fumbled in her handbag for her dark glasses. The elongated corners of the tortoise-shell frames were encrusted with large synthetic gems. The beach, which inclined farther down to the sea, was over-bright, garish, like her brilliant sunglasses. In her transparent nylon sari Vidyut was, if anything, even more inappropriately dressed for gambols on the beach than Ritu in her raw-silk pant suit. 'Suppose it rains?' sweet Coz asked again, perversely.

'Then we can go to my father's shack,' Mila said, to hush her up.

'Oh, you have a place here?' Vidyut stopped in the sand to regard Mila with something like respect.

'Of course we have,' she retorted, then stopped in mid-boast, regretting her words. 'It's not very new or anything.'

'Far from here?'

'No, no. But it's locked up. In any case we can't go without Dad's permission, and he's in Delhi.' Vidyut sighed again.

They strolled aimlessly on the beach, under the headachy glaze of the sun. In spite of the season and boards proclaiming at intervals that it was 'Dangerous to Swim Here,' people were enjoying a dip in the sea. They watched a Maharashtrian lady plunge bravely into the water fully clad in her sari (all nine yards of it), but Mila's suggestion that they wet their feet was deprecated with a sniff by Vidyut, who didn't seem to be enjoying herself at all. She was too old for sandcastles, and too afraid to expose her white skin to the sun. A tan was no acquisition here.

As the afternoon advanced, the shore grew more and more crowded. Poverty sported on the beach in the garb of beggars and fortune tellers. Ragged entertainers with sand-coloured monkeys. Snake charmers. Rope walkers. Little-girl weight lifters picking up rocks with their plaits. Hawkers and pedlars. Sellers of ice-cream and crushed-ice-gobs-on-sticks sprinkled with sherbet. Vendors of vegetable sandwiches, grams and peanuts, popcorn and potato crisps, of savouries prepared with curds, raw onions, and chutney made from green chillis and coriander leaves, from jaggery and date pulp . . . all eking out a precarious livelihood. There was something graceless about Juhu, even vulgar. Pinched faces, emaciated forms, rags and a whining clamour for alms blended oddly with cellular phones, blaring transistors and elaborate picnic hampers.

'At least we should have packed something from home to eat, no?' said Vidyut, disdaining the fare on offer. 'Never mind.' She fiddled with her handbag. 'It's from Hong Kong,' she volunteered as she caught Mila eyeing the glittering clasp. 'Let's have some coconut water.'

The water was cool and sweet. But as the coconut seller was scooping out the creamy kernels for them with his knife, single raindrops as big as one's thumb began to descend from a sky in which the sun was still in command. It is a shameless rain that falls from a sunny heaven, Soni always said, like a wanton displaying her naked charms to all in sight. Mila looked up. A bruised purpling had intensified over the land side of the beach, and now a moving wall of cold air hovered over them on its way to the sea. The sun, wrapped up in gauze a moment ago, now disappeared traitorously behind a thick velvet shroud.

The thunderclap was sudden, ear-splitting. And as luminous cracks pronged the northern sky, people began a disorderly retreat on the beach. 'Back to the car, quick!' shrieked Ritu.

'It's no use,' said Vidyut phlegmatically. 'Too far away. We'll be *drenched*.'

'Let's try and make it to your shack,' cried Ritu.

'But—' Mila turned to stare at the level ground at the head of the sloping beach where some cars were parked. Behind them, in line with the hotels, stood the cottages and bungalows, with narrow pathways and creaky little gates. She blinked, her vision distorted by wet glasses and the rain scratching silver lines on a landscape of pigeon grey. Surely that dissolving red blur in the distance was the gate painted by Vikram during their last summer weekend? 'Yes!' she shouted in excitement. 'We're almost directly opposite my place! Let's make a dash for it. That red gate!'

The coconut man had hoisted his basket of giant nuts on to a coiled cushion of cloth on his head, and was off scissoring the sand with brown blades of legs, his lungi tucked in at his waist. Figures scurried crabwise on the slopes, seeking shelter. There was thunder again, a resounding thump to heave earth and sea, and Vidyut flung down her drinking shell at her feet. Mila thrust hers with its creamy contents into the hands of an unkempt little girl in a bedraggled skirt who evidently had nowhere to run to, and took to her heels as exuberant whoops, hoots, toots and even laughter rent the storm's ominous music.

Ritu streaked ahead of them. She reached the gate first and began to manhandle it as if it were a savage animal, tugging and wrestling with it every wrong way. Mila came up behind her and pushed it open, wet and yielding under her hand. As the three of them ran in a single file up the ribbon path between palms, an intense rising fragrance of damp earth and tree and mould made Mila stop short in the rain, which on her upturned face tasted salty with the tang of her sweat. She could no longer distinguish between air and sky. As she ran again to catch up with her friends, her clammy skirt clung as if with restraining hands on her legs, and black rain fell directly on her beating heart.

The cottage appeared rustic as they gained on it past flower beds in rectangles of whitewashed stones. 'The doors will be locked,' Mila panted, 'but we can sit on the front veranda.'

They cannoned up six stone steps, then stood laughing nervously on the oddly dark veranda under its sloping roof. Mila noticed, through misted spectacles, that clutched with her handbag and sunglasses Vidyut still held her sari immodestly high, and that her legs were thick and straight like the Ashoka pillar. Her white feet, as she kicked off wet sandals, had a fish-like sheen. They were flat and wide, like something washed up by the sea. Mila whipped off her specs, and though she flinched from the unpleasant contact with her sodden skirt, she tried to wipe them clean with its hem, for she could never find her handkerchief when she needed it. She put them on again. And now that the blurred vagueness had somewhat cleared, she saw that the door leading from the veranda into the living room gaped wide open.

Mila blinked in self-orientation. She was staring at it, puzzled, when a man stepped out of the inner room and stood rigid for an instance, framed in the door as for a full-length portrait. He vanished—only to slide into position again the next moment. She gave a little cry. It was her father.

For what seemed like a whole minute he stood looking at them with a powerful and angry eye. At last he parted company with the door and came forward. Her friends stared at him with some astonishment.

'Mila?' he said quietly. She had been mistaken, her father wasn't angry at all, a smile was coming into his eyes—but there was a distinct question in his voice. He was asking her to explain her presence there, and for a confused moment she felt she did not know him at all, this strange man who was confronting her. She saw him as closed, mysterious, other than himself. Not quite Daddy.

'I—I didn't know you were here!' she stammered. 'I mean, your fax from Delhi said you were returning tomorrow—'

'Yes,' he said. He did not seem to know how to continue. Then, 'I cut short my visit by a day.' She read in his face a quick reassembling of some inner elements, like the moving of stage scenery behind a scrim. 'On my way from the airport I stopped here.' Pause. 'To pick up some papers.'

'Oh.' For some shapeless reason she felt a weight roll off her back as he said this, and she smiled at him. 'Mummy will be so glad. But you didn't let her know!'

'No.' He stared at her. 'She knows you're here?' His voice was flat and quick. Again her father was both recognizable and out-of-joint.

'No! I mean—she knows I'm out for a drive in Ritu's car. We were on the beach when it started raining, and the car is parked so far away . . . so we just ran up here . . .' She could not interpret the expression on his face and suffered a strange pang of unease, of guilt: surely she was inventing all this, her spoken words were not composing things as they truly were? Her anxious curiosity seemed to have displeased him, as if she had put out a foot to trip him up, and he was struggling against dislike of her. Mila's mouth felt dry; she tasted sand on her tongue. 'We thought you'd be—' she continued helplessly.

'I'm glad you thought of it,' Father cut her short with a smile, and everything was right-side-up immediately. 'I hope you're not too wet. You and your friends?'

'Not very. This is Vidyut, Ritu's cousin. And you know Ritu.'

'Yes indeed.' He regarded the deglamourized trio before him with a patience that was willed, not felt, and Vidyut stopped sucking one end of her harlequin glasses. Ritu, with her natural reverence for clothes, began to smooth out her soggy sleeves, then fiddled with her lopsided tiers of hair, frowning in concentration. 'I don't know if you keep any clothes here, Mila, that you could change into,' Dad was saying.

'No,' she said, 'I don't need a change.'

'But perhaps your friends would like to.'

'No,' said Ritu, still fussing with her damp hair, which she would not admit was a lost cause. She looked as if she wanted to say more, but restrained herself. She's a little appalled at the idea of wearing my things, thought Mila.

'Well, perhaps you'll allow me,' Dad said, 'to get you something warm to drink.'

'Oh, is Balraj here?' Mila asked. Balraj was the servant who managed for them during their weekends at the cottage.

'Why should Balraj be here?' Father said in a voice so taut with sudden anger that Mila swallowed grits of fright that hurt her throat. The next moment he was saying quietly, 'No, I thought I could fix you some coffee myself.'

'No, thank you,' said Vidyut. She sighed, batted her messy eyelashes and looked infinitely bored. 'I think we ought to get back to the car, no? Rao will be worried where we are.'

'Rao?' said Father.

'My driver,' said Ritu.

'Her chauffeur,' Mila said with her.

Pumpkin-bosomed Vidyut sighed again. 'Perhaps if you could drop us in your car to Ritu's car—'

'I'm sorry,' said Father drily. 'I have no car. A taxi brought me here.'

'Then you might as well come back with us,' Mila was quick to say. 'There's plenty of room in Ritu's car.'

'It's a new Mercedes,' said Ritu.

'Thank you, but no.' Suddenly Dad's voice carried loads of weariness. 'I might as well get through those papers. I'll make my own way later.'

'But Dad—'

But he had abruptly turned away to look down on the wet garden where everything was gurgling, murmuring, rustling. He was still for a moment, he had withdrawn to a remote island of his own, mouth shut tight, knuckles of his fists together on the veranda railing. Then he straightened his shoulders. 'It's stopped raining,' he observed. It was true. The light had faded, leaving a premature darkness over the scene, but the rain had ceased. Only single drops splashed from eaves into puddles with a grey whispering.

'We'd better *plod* back to that car,' said Vidyut in her most adult voice. 'It's parked miles away.' With a sniff she stepped into her wet sandals. She did everything without pleasure.

'I'll come with you,' said Father. 'See you to the car.'

'Oh, no,' Mila protested.

'We don't wish to take you away from your work,' said Vidyut with the primness of a schoolteacher. 'And you might get wet.'

'I'll come.' Mila saw that he was determined to do so.

'Then let me fetch an umbrella for you, just in case,' she said. He stepped towards her quickly, but she smiled, darted past him through the open door, skirted the cushioned wicker sofa and turned left into the bedroom with the aged four-poster.

A light at the end of a long cord lit the room, and Mila saw that the large bed was crowned with a mosquito net. Now who, she asked herself in passing, had been careless enough to overlook the net when they had locked up the place at the end of summer? She made straight for the corner between the rosewood wardrobe and the wall, which accomodated a pail containing a tall beach umbrella and a couple of diminutive ones. She chose the one with the blue handle, and was about to leave the room when she noticed a long single key protruding out of the doors framing the upper half of the wardrobe. They were special doors, carved with thick smooth ridges of wood radiating from a round centre to represent the rays of the sun. The lower half of the antique Parsi closet was fitted with outsize drawers; to buy it Dad had outbid an American at a local auction. Mila stared at the key. On a strange impulse she reached up and turned it.

The sun centre was neatly bifurcated as half of the closet opened with a series of creaks. Immediately a pile of clothes tumbled to the floor. Mila bent down to pick them up, hampered by the umbrella, and as she thrust them carelessly back on the cupboard shelf with one hand, a gleaming magenta bundle slithered down at her feet again, uncurling like a preposterously dyed tail of hair. It resolved itself into a satin sari petticoat. This time Mila dropped the umbrella to pick up the slippery stuff with both hands. The petticoat was narrow at the waist and too short to belong to Mother. Mila frowned. She knew Roma-masi did not possess a petticoat of this shocking colour; she was such a pastel person. Who did it belong to? She did not face the question honestly, but banished it to the periphery of her mind. Bundling the petticoat into an untidy heap on the shelf, Mila closed the wardrobe and turned the key, leaving it in the door. Her actions, as she saw them reflected and multiplied in the triple-winged mirror of the dressing table against the opposite wall, had an air of thieving. Snatching up the umbrella she drew back, making herself small, then left the room with quickly averted face.

The journey to the car was uneventful. There was an ebbing of light over the low-slanting roof as they looked back on the cottage, but in the garden textures were sharpened by an ashen translucence, as were the gleams on the tiny water spouts that had mushroomed on the gravel. The sand, when they reached it, was spongy. The distant sea was wild, grey and desolate, with muscular waves reaching out to a blurred horizon. The umbrella was not needed, but a sharp breeze made the girls shiver in their wet clothes. Everything was chilly, soggy and blank without the sun.

They walked down the deserted strand to the sea, then, after about half a mile, up again to the land side of the beach. In the distance they discerned Ritu's car and a humped, camel-coloured figure making his way towards them. Rao.

As he came nearer, Mila saw that his face was surly. He was positively glowering. 'Where do you think—' he began almost with a snarl, but broke off when he caught sight of Father. 'I searched all over the beach for you,' he burst out again angrily. 'I'm all wet!'

'You're not the only one who is wet,' said Father, eyeing the grey splotches made by the rain on the chauffeur's khaki uniform. 'And see that you do not raise your voice.' He spoke, as always, with quiet authority. Rao's face, which was very thin, with a fierce angularity of nose and cheekbones, darkened perceptibly. But under Father's steady gaze he lowered his eyes, their whites inflamed by tiny blood vessels. He whirled round, marched back to the car, got in behind the wheel and slammed the door. As they piled in, he sat looking before him, smouldering with some strange resentment that somehow conveyed to them, without words, his aggrieved sense of being every bit as good as they were.

Father tapped smartly on the window pane. Reluctantly Rao unwound the glass. 'See that you drive carefully,' said Father. 'The roads are wet.'

Mila quickly lowered the window at her side. 'Your umbrella,' she cried. It changed hands. 'Shall I tell Mummy you're back, or will you surprise her?'

'I'll surprise her.'

'But you'll be home before dinner?'

'Of course.' He smiled his farewell. But as they drove away Mila caught a glimpse of his face: there was no smile on it now. It was pale, like a martyr's. Or like a sinner's?

11

To conceal her adoration of Ray from prying eyes, Mila reduced her secret to the size of a postage stamp, and carried it with her everywhere. Sometimes, though, it defied her and grew too large for her pocket. It *showed*. These were the times Mr Topiwalla, sticking out his little goatee, asked her to pay attention in class. Or Dad said at the breakfast table, 'Perhaps Mila will come out of her daydream long enough to pass me the butter?'

But by the time she was fourteen Mila could successfully stare past Rayhaan's face at the equation on the blackboard. Or she could smile at Daddy's pleasantries at the table while she drank her cocoa and reached for Vikram's shin with her foot, *and* retreat at breakneck speed behind her secret, which suddenly towered over her. Sometimes she cradled it. Sometimes it sheltered her. Sometimes it almost betrayed her.

Mila thus became an adept at living in different worlds simultaneously—or of streaking from one to the other. Like a spy, she wove in and out of plots and counterplots, extricated herself from double- and triple-crosses. Of her many aliases, only one was Mila Mehta, schoolgirl, roll no. 33. That image she had to hold up intelligently to the fellow pilgrims toiling with her in a world of textbooks and command performances. But she was also Mila Mitty, the hallucinator, savouring other existences in which thoughts of Rayhaan had a stop-go quality. They came and went, came and went. They flashed, they dimmed. And she could see him without closing her eyes, without pausing in her giggles, without ceasing to conjugate *je vais, tu vas*, without ceasing to cram for her history test on Chandragupta Maurya.

The theme of most of her reveries, with endless variations, was the next meeting with Rayhaan. In her private storyland she saw him stepping out of doorways, alighting from cars, floating out of a mist—only to materialize into a tall stranger every time he came close enough and reality intruded on her enchantment. Yet her extreme youth served her in her struggles against resignation; and there was always the next time she would see Ray mounting stairs as she stood nonchalantly on the landing, juggling a pearl-handled revolver, having just fired a round to save his life . . .

Delicious moments were given over to a montage of meetings with him in moonlight, for which Mila utilized all the backdrops of celluloid tourism: on Chowpatty sands, on the pinnacle of Malabar Hill, on the roof garden of a ritzy hotel. Next followed a collage of meetings in sunlight: flitting round a rosebush, standing before the Gateway of India, sailing across the harbour to the Elephanta Caves. One unforgettable interior shot had Rayhaan posing with her before the trimurti of Brahma, Vishnu and Shiva in one of the caves—a throbbing muscle in his prognathous jaw the only indication of his excessive passion for her, which he was manfully curbing because of her ethereal youth . . .

Mila was intensely, tragically in earnest, as an artist is when she creates her work. She was creating herself, learning who she was despite the paucity of means, the triteness of material at her command. She was searching her experiences for self-definition, for meanings of universal validity—though Sharmila can make these wise observations only in hindsight. All Mila knew was that her world was awash in thoughts of Rayhaan, which, like sparkling waves, gave it an astonishing brilliance. His long absence caused her pain—he had truly renounced 'this stinking city'—yet the wait was a pleasurable dalliance, a seasoning of the approaching delight, for with bliss just round the corner, delay can be intoxicating. So she was happy. She acquired religion. She made ridiculous promises to a multitude of gods, struck so many extravagant bargains with them that she ended up fearing she had antagonized the Supreme Being with too much propitiation . . . Krishna, let him come back to me like a bursting star! Govinda, send him back to me dragging my heart behind him! Balagopala, help me now and I'll part with the accumulated merit of all my past lives!

And then one evening Rayhaan was suddenly in their living room, sprouting up tall and straight from the Mirzapur carpet. Really and truly

Rayhaan, not just a hope. How trumpets blared and cymbals crashed in her ears!

Then he turned round. Ray turned round and the din was hushed. He had been too much in the sun, and was all burning gold and mahogany in his thin kurta. He smiled in greeting, but something was wrong. He was regarding her with guarded, speculative eyes. Something was horribly missing in his glance—the look that had in the past so graciously assumed her involvement in the private flashings of his mind. Her heart beat in painful thuds. He did not remember. He had forgotten the kiss he had given her months ago at the door of her flat . . . She had to lower her eyes not to glare tragically at him.

'So, Mila,' he said quietly, 'I've turned up again, like the proverbial penny. How have you been?'

A quick glance told her he was not really interested in her answer. He was looking over her head at the door behind her and frowning. 'I'll call Mother,' she said. She barely heard her own voice above the splintering of her dreams.

'Don't bother.' An odd emphasis in his voice more than his words, stopped her. 'I've just talked to her.' He didn't seem to know what to say next. 'She's been under great stress, hasn't she? I came as soon as I heard. Would have come sooner, had I known.'

'She's quite well now,' Mila said curtly. Mother's illness was not something they cared to discuss with anyone. Not even with Rayhaan who knew more about it than they liked to think, but who could not be made to speak of it in hushed tones because he did not see it as a skeleton in the family cupboard. To him Mother was the bold product of her disease. She consumed and digested it at times, and was consumed and engulfed by it in turn. She was essentially a modest woman compelled by unbearable pressures to live dangerously. Conventional as she was by nature and upbringing, Shivani's illness lent her a hell-bent quality that must have appealed to Rayhaan. He sensed in her a heroism not required in the tediously healthy. Driven by doubts, tracked by demons, she had to recklessly outstrip her own disintegration. Shake off pursuit by bounding from crag to crag. Dare a flying leap across a chasm or be demolished against the rocks below. Of her more violent or enervating symptoms Rayhaan knew nothing. Naturally; he did not have to live with them.

'She's quite well now,' Mila repeated sharply, for Ray looked as if he had not heard her.

'Yes, oh yes, thank heavens she's recovered now, she . . .' He bit his lip. 'She quite convinced me I need not have bothered to come.' He paused, then continued thoughtfully, 'You think, Mila, because we are, none of us, completely free, we fall sick and develop bodily symptoms—the *crise* of the spirit? In other words, all can never be well with us till perfection is reached?' He interrupted himself with a laugh. 'Forgive me. I must sound half-witted. Or like your father?' Then, with an effort, for he still saw Mila only through the prism of some inner turmoil, he said, 'Everything is well with you, then?'

'Perfectly,' she lied with dignity while inside her a poor, imprisoned creature—the builder of myths—was wailing and sobbing.

A faint echo may well have reached him, for some concern crept into his voice at last. 'You've lost weight, haven't you?'

'I'm fine,' she said in a brave high voice. Then she spoilt it all by blurting out, 'Rayhaan, I'm so *glad* you're back!'

'Oh, so am I, so am I,' he said, reaching for his cigarettes. 'In fact it was all a mistake, trying to run away. "The abstinent run away from what they desire. But carry their desires with them . . ." You know those lines, Mila?'

'No.'

'You must ask your uncle to explain them to you. Amrish will be delighted.' He smiled, and she found herself smiling back. She didn't want to, but the moment he reached out to her, she was not equal to the drama of resistance. The moment she judged him guilty, she exonerated him. She loved him so. He was watching her.

'What are you thinking of?' he asked suddenly.

For a dreadful moment she felt her secret accessible. Mila blushed violently, incriminatingly. 'Nothing,' she mumbled.

He reached out and traced a teasing finger down her nose. 'Well, don't stop, you're doing it charmingly.' She jerked her head away, hot-cheeked and furious with herself. 'But tell me, how *is* that uncle of yours?' He was gazing at his cigarette tip.

She knew he had asked to help her out of her embarrassment. 'Okay,' she replied gruffly. She had made several surreptitious trips to Uncle's room in the hope of some news of the beloved absentee, but had been disappointed each time.

Rayhaan walked to the window, looked out, then turned back to her. 'And your pretty aunty is still with you?'

'Yes.' She begrudged him that answer. Why did he waste time talking of aunts?

'She's not returned to her mother's home in Panchgani?'

Mila pushed back a growing uneasiness. 'No.' She waited for him to light his cigarette before adding resentfully, 'Roma-masi has been with us for months.' And she almost hated him as she said politely, 'Shall I tell her you're here?'

'Not this time, no.' He inhaled deeply and his next words struck Mila like physical blows: 'But tell her I'll call on her one of these days, will you?'

He was as good as his word. And soon Rayhaan was a frequent visitor to the house again—but it was not Shivani he came to see. Or Vikram or Mila or Naren. It was in Roma that he seemed to have found his new enchantress!

Here was treachery that took Mila's breath away. But how could she have known, at her time of life, that passion and fidelity are expensive? Mila assumed that everyone was supplied with equal rations of them. She had no idea that she was being inexcusably valorous in clinging with such constancy to her feelings, that she was a defender of faith! Or that practical affairs were hostile to such an aristocratic attitude and would soon nudge her into sensible adjustments. All she knew was such a sense of insult and violation every time she saw Rayhaan with her aunt that she could barely contain herself. How she detested them both, particularly her feeble aunt, who was like a bird fluttering in the network of the young man's will . . .

Today it strikes me as more than a little ironic that I am impatient to have Roma-masi back with us. When Vikram called mid-afternoon to tell me he wouldn't be in for dinner, I made him promise that we'd drive up to Pune at dawn tomorrow to pick up Aunty. Pry her free of her friend's clutches, abduct her if necessary.

Vikram sounded doubtful. 'Of course Dolly Pastakia is better, but I guess Masi is still needed there—'

'Well, she's needed here,' I cut short his protest. We argued some more, but I had his promise before he rang off.

But when Mila was fourteen years old, Rayhaan's courtship of Aunt Roma had caused her a compound injury, a multiple bereavement. Mila's first loss, of course, was of her secret: no longer did Rayhaan unwittingly, by the mere fact of being alive, illumine her world. Her beautiful affair was wrecked, her private idyll shattered. With a rival on the scene, Rayhaan became her enemy.

The other casualty was her aunt. Mila's feelings for Roma-masi had altered during the prolonged domestic crisis. She had been impressed by her dignity, her display of proud heart. Roma had not used the occasion of Shivani's illness to self-advantage when both the man and his children were at her mercy. For months she had quietly cared for father and son. Had helped the obstreperous niece with her homework, remembered her vitamins and, when she made a devastation of her room, tidied up after her without complaints. It was a fragile accord aunt and niece had reached, a set of civil concessions and minor accommodations that Mila had come to rely on . . . But now the woman tumbled down the ladder again, so fast that friend was indistinguishable from foe. And Mila hated her only a whit less than she hated Rayhaan, the author of her new confusion and torment.

And indeed Rayhaan's behaviour was outrageous. One day he would come to the flat impeccably dressed, masterful, his ego supreme midst a kind of despair: as if he had taken a terrific wallop and was too proud to show it. He was suave, eloquent, but there was something oblique about everything he said. All his words, it turned out, were irony in disguise, his visits to Roma a game, a charade that required a lightness of response from her to maintain the pretence. But either she did not know the rules, or she did not choose to play. Certainly Roma lacked the wit, but *he* played on with biting jests, sometimes silly through self-parody—the willful, controlled silliness of the Shakespearean fool, bafflingly faithful to a secret core of self.

On other occasions he would turn up with a three-day stubble on his drawn cheeks, alcoholic fumes on his breath. He barely spoke, but seemed wholly concentrated within a secret perception of self, like a sage. And thus he sat for hours in the front room with Aunty, his absurd *amorosa*, basking in her helpless regard like a crocodile in the sun, till at times he actually fell asleep where he sat.

If Rayhaan's antics were bewildering, Mother's reactions were equally so. Shivani seemed not to mind that he was paying court to her sister. Instead of sending him about his business, she encouraged the improbable romance, saw to it that they were undisturbed. Held long tête-à-têtes with her sister—and though Mila was miserable because she never knew what was said, she sometimes heard Mother use the kind of laugh with which one helps a shy child beyond the first line of *Mary Had a Little Lamb*. Mila understood instantly, with a sinking heart, what Mother was up to. She can't do that, it isn't fair, she told herself in a panic: she's throwing them at each other, coaxing her sister into his arms!

All this adult behaviour was devious enough, but suddenly Mother began to affect a connubial gushing that was intolerable, wifely effusions that were out of character and abashed her audience. She had eyes for no one but Father—if Rayhaan happened to be in the room. How meekly the wife deferred to the husband! She was cloying or implausibly arch, roguish. When she tinkled at her husband's mildest witticism, urging him on to more, when in all arguments she militantly sided with him, Rayhaan must have felt outnumbered, outlawed. And it was embarrassing, this transformation of a poised and demure matron into a bride of many blandishments. It discomfited Mila. It caused Naren to rest his eyes on Shivani's face with a thoughtful expression. She all but ignored Rayhaan. Only the brief flickering glance she sometimes threw at him, like the stinging tip of a whip, betrayed her . . . and Sharmila knows now that these guiles were used as so many provocations.

Could they truly be so called, I now ask myself, if my mother was unaware of the sadistic purpose behind her posturing and flattery? She must have believed herself justified in playing the adoring wife, whatever the hurt to the young man, for she was, before God, the adoring wife. And if she was challenging Rayhaan, even subtly chastizing him for what amounted to an underground revolt, she was also nervously defending her own vulnerability. And seeking reparation. Wasn't she, too, the injured party?

One evening, looking as seductive as the devil, Rayhaan was waiting for Roma in the living room when Mother came out in pursuit of a book. 'I had no idea you were here,' she said in cold greeting. 'Roma should be out in a minute—ah, there it is.' She held out her hand. 'That book beside you on the divan. Let me have it, please.'

He picked up the book but ignored the imperious hand. 'Hello, reading a Gujarati novel,' he observed. He turned it over, fingered the spine, flicked through the pages. 'Tried this author myself but my Gujarati isn't in his class. However, his air of pious respectability is unmistakable. I bet he divides his women into madonnas and whores.' He snapped the book shut, rather disparagingly, in his palm.

'Well, I like his work. Give!' Mother's voice was so peremptory that with a start Mila glanced up from her seat near the window where, doubled over a low table, she was dampening paint on paper, her box of colours and tumbler of turbid water at hand. 'I like it,' Mother went on authoritatively, 'because it enshrines old values and traditions. Chandrakant has a very clear idea of what is right and what is wrong.'

'Chandrakant?'

'The hero.'

'Oh. Most commendable,' said Rayhaan with a smile, 'very comforting.'

'Yes, it is,' she snapped.

His smile grew. 'And in the last chapter virtue receives her reward, I'm sure. And vice is fittingly punished. A most edifying book.' He held it out to her between index finger and thumb, as if with a pair of tongs. Clearly it was poised for descent into an imaginary wastebasket.

She had her revenge as she snatched it from his hand. 'Have you finished yours yet?' she asked, sweet-tongued malice in her words.

'My novel? No.'

'Well!' said Mother. And having made that venomous point, she turned to go.

'You don't want to know why?' he called after her, rising to his feet.

'Not particularly.' But she was facing him again, waiting to be told.

'The old conflict.' He spoke without stress, but was watching her intently. 'I can't seem to separate the mind that creates from the mind engaged in battles with—sordid reality.'

'I can well believe the last,' said Mother with a curl of her lip.

'You can?' he said mock-soberly, while his eyes went over her face. 'Then why don't you help me?'

'I?'

He shrugged. 'It has happened before, in the lives of other struggling writers that an older woman has been friend, adviser, guide, mistress. Balzac—'

'Have you been drinking again?' A look of genuine alarm crossed Mother's face.

'I'm not drunk, damn it!' But he swayed on his feet, deliberately, to give himself cover for what he wished to say next: 'Or perhaps *I* can help *you*. Take you under my disreputable wing.' At that she gave a derisive laugh, but caught her breath as he took a sudden step forward. He now towered over her. 'When will you begin to see the truth, Shivani? And do something before you bark your shins against it the next time?'

She stiffened. 'I've no idea what you're talking about.'

'No? What role are you playing now? Whose halo are you busy shining up, like a bloody little angel?'

'I, playing a role?' She spoke with vehemence. 'What about the stupid farce *you* are acting out?'

'Farce?' he softly repeated.

'What else do you call it?' she demanded. 'Why do you come? You are such an egotist, you don't care at all who you walk over, do you?'

'Ah!'

'What do you mean "ah"?' She was braced for a fight. 'What should happen to you,' colour stained her cheeks, 'is that you should be tied to a stake with a fire blazing under your feet. And with the flames licking your flesh you should be made to take an oath!'

'What oath?' he whispered.

'What oath?' She stamped her foot. 'That you will never again, on pain of death, raise your eyes above the feet of any woman!'

'What if,' he held her eyes, 'the foot thrashes like a heifer's in heat?'

'Then you will look away!'

'But—if my arms are needed?'

'You will keep them locked behind you,' she said hoarsely, 'as when they were bound to that stake!' They stood there frozen, staring at each other in a curious negation of movement, like two people on the brow of a precipice, afraid that the least change of posture would topple them over the edge.

At her table near the window, Mila added a little more ochre to the lemon of the syrupy sunrise taking shape under her brush, and heard them as if in a dream. Fragments of what she had witnessed would not suffer joining, but assailed her in crazy daubs and yellow streaks. Vigorously she plunged her brush into water and applied it to the paper. A horrible muddying ensued, a fading away of magic, as in detail after detail the skyscape entitled 'Break of Dawn' lost tone and clarity.

Aunt Roma came in then, and Mother slipped out of the room. Mila saw Rayhaan stare at Aunty for a full moment without recognizing her; then he bestirred himself. Ceremoniously he ushered her into the straight-backed Sankhera chair. 'How charming, how *votive* you look in white, my dear!' he began.

Roma was sunk in a strange apathy these days, and as she took the chair she looked like a bird hypnotized by a snake. Inarticulate, she was held by the persuasive rhythm of his voice, which, despite his expressionless face, promised so much. Did she really believe that after all the unlit, thrifty years, she was now chosen? Was she blind? Couldn't she see that this courtship was knitted from one long skein of know-how? He was wonderfully silky and appealing, but one scratch with a fingernail and the mesh would show a long run, hang in tatters . . .

How Mila despised them both as she mixed pigments furiously. She had not the slightest aptitude for this art, but persevered in it with a strange ardour. She cheated hours of schoolwork merely to satisfy a futile fascination with colours. It also provided the excuse for her presence in the living room. Her spectator seat near the window gave her an unobtrusive vantage point, and she looked so industrious, so withdrawn and absorbed in creative emotions, that no one saw a need for restraint before the dogged little apprentice. They forgot that Mila was there at all. They never guessed that she was watching them all the time, that her appraisal lacked charity, that she was both judge and jury and had a blistering contempt for their weaknesses. They competed bitterly, they jockeyed for position, they played dirty . . . she saw it all.

Who had Aunty dressed for this evening? Was it a hangover from her youth that she still cared how she looked? To Mila's early teens, a woman's late twenties appeared to be her infirm zone, and surely Roma's will was pathetically divided between her desire to run—from that lacquered chair, from her sister's home—and an inexplicable reluctance to do so? She could not resist that enticing voice but there was no joy in her surrender; her threadbare soul did not thrill to the words that limned her to the rigid wood. She just hung on there, like someone waiting to be released from a trap.

Now, however, I'm not satisfied that Mila's reading of the situation was accurate. She was skipping too many pages of the book: the characters were the same, but their actions made no sense because she knew so little about them after all. Perhaps Roma was playing a game, too. Pliable on the surface, she was not without her strategies. Not a pawn in someone else's scheme, but working towards her own ends. What were these? Was this charade a kind of therapy to free her spirit from an old bondage? If she was not bewitched, then Roma really knew what she was about. That was why she glued her bottom to that chair instead of taking to her heels, as was expected of her. She sat it out. And this fortitude is what has eventually made her someone to be reckoned with, though her little face would always retain a certain buffed, chafed quality.

What happened next no one could have predicted—except perhaps Amrish-uncle, who had once remarked to Mila that life has an elemental consistency, a way of forcing one incident out of the jaws of the preceding one, and that we are startled by the new phenomenon only because it has caught us napping. Well, they were all caught napping. For as Mila sat watching adults play their mad, incomprehensible games, her grandmother swooped down on their home in pursuit of Saroj, her missing daughter-in-law, and the personae were dragged willy-nilly into another circle of events.

12

In answer to a sharp ring at the door, Soni opened it late one evening in October to admit Nanima. 'To take Saroj home I've come,' the old lady announced dramatically to the startled family gathered in the living room as she stood centre stage in her widow's white sari printed with little black checks. She had a long ascetic face, very handsome, in which her eyes were twin dark gems that the dust of years had failed to dim. In her youth Nanima must have been tall and erect and spare. Now she was gnarled and tenacious and windswept: a wilful woman for whom the interests of the mind did not exist. For with her perfect intrepidity came a total absence of perspective, which made her deadly to deal with.

After a stunned moment of silence Mother and Mila and Soni began to speak as a chorus. Father raised his brows as he slowly rose to his feet. He walked to the liftman hesitating on the threshold, clutching Nanima's suitcase. Dad took the bag, put it down just inside the room, tipped Yakub and dismissed him. Only then did he turn to the old lady to bid her welcome. Were his gestures tinged with irony? Aunt Roma, who had been writing a letter on her knees, struggled guiltily to her feet, writing pad and envelopes sliding unheeded to the carpet in a slow glissando. She looked as if she had received a blow on her mouth. On the pouf, Vikram appeared to be nursing a scalded tongue.

As usual, within an hour of her arrival Nanima had upset the whole household, which remained in a state of upheaval till the end of her stay. Roma and Vikram were her immediate victims. Banished from their room to give her sole possession of it, they were to be accommodated in Mila's smaller bedroom. 'If I find the harlot tomorrow, I shall return with her to Pune,' Nanima said as her strong fingers stripped the sheet from Vikram's bed and threw it on the floor, whence Soni retrieved it and bore it away for washing. None of them dared ask the Tartar what she would do if she did *not* find her daughter-in-law, or how long she intended to go about looking for Saroj in this city of fourteen million people; or, having found her, how she would induce the desperate woman to return to a home where she had been so miserable.

Roma and Vikram trotted between their room and Mila's, removing their personal effects from the one and dumping them in the other. Mila did not offer to help. A battling self-respect made her want to show her granny that she was not to be yoked into vassalage like the other wimps. She decided to sit aloof in a corner of the living room but as she sailed in, head in air, she stubbed her toe against Nanima's suitcase—hard. With a yelp of pain and anger, she grabbed the bag and swung it over her shoulder like a stevedore; but it was heavier than it looked, and the handle promptly gave way. Before Mila knew it the bag had sailed over her head, to land on the floor behind her with a crash that brought Soni rushing to the scene. Frantic but futile efforts were made to mend the hasp before her grandma saw it. The task was abandoned in despair, but not Soni's string of reproaches as she propelled Mila, limping, to the divan and pushed her down on it with admonitions not to move a step. She then left to supervise the frenzied activity in the kitchen.

For Nanima was a strict vegetarian. Brought up by an austere Jain mother, she wore her lifelong abstinence from meats and eggs and root vegetables as a badge of virtue. Flesh was never cooked in Shivani's home, but her store of potatoes, onions and garlic had to be sent swiftly underground; the basket containing beets, carrots and radishes had to be suitably camouflaged till they could be disposed of; and eggs had to be whisked out of the refrigerator. None of these would find their way to the table as long as Nanima stayed with them.

Once, during one of Nanima's earlier visits when Shivani was very ill, Soni had dared to serve the children their usual breakfast of eggs after cautioning them never to mention the fact before the guest. Vikram had just stuffed the last of his fried egg into his mouth when he was startled to find the old girl standing beside him on bare and soundless feet. 'You are eating what?' she had asked, fixing her gimlet gaze on him.

Vikram was too petrified to answer, or even swallow his mouthful, but Mila had looked up from her empty plate and said, 'Potato chips,' remembering too late that even tubers were taboo.

'Indeed?' said the martinet. 'Open your mouth, Vikram!' Her voice curled stingingly round his name and the marrow congealed within his bones. In his place Mila would have swallowed the egg, but Vikram began to cry and his mouth opened weakly. Nanima thrust two cruel fingers into it and forced out the remains of the egg.

She had looked at the mess with disgust, locked herself in for an hour's purifying bath, then packed her clothes and left for Ajit's home in Pune, despite the fact that Shivani was not well enough to leave her bed. That was the briefest visit she had granted them. Shivani had wooed her mother for three years before she consented to set foot once more in her defiled home, and that grand concession was only made when the daughter fell seriously ill once more.

I think Nanima's strength had its source in her unyielding unreason, her mind fossilized by centuries of tradition into a rigid mould. Her security had grown with the years till she was now redoubtable. She did not fear old age; her children were there to look after her. It was the duty of children to look after aged parents, just as it was the duty of a river to flow, of a soldier to fight, of a merchant to make money. What if in her youth she had been heartlessly repressed by her elders? She had always known her hour would come. The wheel turned for everyone. The trembling bride, the terrorized daughter-in-law with time became the hard-nosed matriarch, the adamantine mother-in-law. So, with the onset of grey hair and wrinkles Nanima had begun to lay down the law, and very conscious was she that through her the whole Hindu pattern of virtue, obedience, endurance and ritual purity—all the intricate formalities surrounding food (what a person may eat, where and when and with whom), birth, marriage, death—would survive into the next generation. She was the venerable conduit of a culture that would never die. She immensely enjoyed being old.

'I should have stayed with Amrish this time,' said Nanima that evening as she arranged her white saris in a neat pile on a hastily emptied shelf in Vikram's closet. 'To stay in my married daughter's home, except in times of crisis, is unseemly for me. But,' she went on, paying no heed to Shivani's murmured remonstrances, 'you know how Amrish lives. When did he last set foot in a temple?' Reverently she touched the red-daubed cloth bundle containing her worship paraphernalia to her forehead. 'Even so I would have stayed with him but,' her eyes flashed, 'he has a hand in the disappearance of that worthless girl!'

'Mother, you're wrong,' cried Shivani. 'Amrish knows nothing about Saroj's affairs.'

'Not know!' Nanima turned round. 'If he stood shoulder-high in the Ganga and denied his complicity, I would not believe him. I wrote and told him that!' She looked larger than life as she stared at Shivani with quenchless self-assurance.

'You never listen,' said Shivani. 'Amrish is a sick man who rarely leaves his bed.'

'Sick, sick! Yes, Amrish is sick but also a wastrel. What has he done with his life?' Nanima abandoned the open wardrobe doors to settle cross-legged on the bed, and Mila knew that a long recital of Uncle's sins and derelictions was in order. They had been enumerated before. 'It was his duty to take up the cloth business your father left him,' she began, 'while I struggled alone to bring up three young children. But no, a doctor he wanted to be. He gave that up in the third year to study homoeopathy, for which he went all the way to Calcutta. Next, all his patrimony was consumed in setting up a free dispensary in some village no one had heard of. After the first cholera epidemic he had no money left, so he became a schoolmaster. A village schoolmaster for children of leather workers and barbers, washermen, grass cutters, water carriers, scavengers! In a ditch he buried himself, in a ditch!' There were no mitigating circumstances for Amrish's failures, because he had not shouldered his responsibilities as the eldest son. For the vision, the intention, the labouring will she had no use at all. 'I know Amrish,' she went on, 'only too well. A thwarted man he is, because only the performance of one's duties brings blessings, not the pursuit of another's *dharma*. Sick he is, and choking on bile! Could Saroj have taken this step, you think, without his connivance? A girl who is afraid of her own shadow?'

'Why can't you see,' said Mother impatiently, 'that this happened in Pune, while Amrish is tied here to his bed—'

'So that is why Saroj is here!' cried Nanima, whose stubbornness was related to something warped in her character. 'She is *here*.' And her eyes glowed with her determination, her need to be always in the right. She rose to her feet to unpack her gleaming cooking vessels and water pot and thali, all of which she carried with her everywhere. They had been scoured by her own hand with tamarind pulp and cow-dung ash, and they made a pool of light on Vikram's writing desk, which had been swept clean of his books.

'I wrote to you,' she continued, 'that Saroj's father died last year. Just as well, for never could he have survived this disgrace. And she has no relative in Nadiad who will take her in after this shameful business. I *know* the slut is here.' Her long, thin nose flared, exhaling such menace that Mila began to whistle nervously. 'Enticing his own brother's wife away from home! This cheap success will bode him any good? Long ago Amrish jeopardized his soul and now—' She broke off to fix on her grandchild a leech-like stare.

'She has grown,' said Nanima in the silence, not withdrawing her disapproving gaze from Mila. It was a crushing accusation.

'Not much since you last saw her.' Mother defended Mila hastily, indicating with a quick frown that she should pull down her skirt, which had ridden up her thighs as she slouched on the bed.

'Not much, Nanima,' Mila echoed simperingly as she hastily drew her skirt over her knees.

'Like a dustbin she has filled out,' pronounced Nanima. The smile disappeared from Mila's face. 'You know what Ajit found in the children's room?' continued the matriarch as she took an unopened cake of *shikekaye* soap out of her suitcase. 'The night she stole out of her house like a thief? A bundle of letters from Amrish to her. Tied in a pink ribbon!'

'I could almost laugh, Mother.' And Shivani did. 'Are you suggesting that Saroj has left Ajit for Amrish?'

'That I'm not,' snapped Nanima. 'Not even a brainless female like Saroj would leave a prince for a pauper, marble for mud, a lion for a sick dog! But you know how Amrish can talk! Twist things inside-out—you should read those letters!'

'I would like to! You're not saying they are love letters?'

'Nothing that can be produced in a court of law, Maganlal tells me.'

'Mother!' Shivani's tone was sharp. 'You showed those letters to Maganlal?'

'Why not? All these years who has helped me with the books and the estate?'

'But he's only a—a clerk. You should not have let him see them. Surely they're private? What opinion could Maganlal have on family matters—'

'The letters are enough to urge a girl to flout her duty and blacken her soul forever!' Nanima could override all protests by simply ignoring them. 'In one letter he writes that in this country women are treated like oxen. They possess nose rings and necklaces, but so do many oxen,

Amrish writes. And he talks of the revolt that must begin in the kitchen before it can hit the streets—what is such talk but coaxing a straying bitch with poisoned meat? In another letter he writes that she must demand respect as a person, and not because she is a wife and mother. *Demand*! What was Saroj before Ajit made her his wife? What is Roma today?' She snatched up a cotton quilt from the bottom of her bag and began folding it. 'And can you tell a wife that her husband has turned her into a dwarf? Can you say the only reason she is chaste and docile is because her mind is switched off, like lights in a disused playhouse? Yes, yes, that is said in a poem Amrish cut out and sent her!'

'Mother, if Saroj were not unhappy, Amrish could say little to—'

'He will pay for it!' Nanima's voice boiled with sudden rage. 'He will go blind and no one will give him alms!'

'Don't!' Shivani's plea was shrill.

But self-righteousness lent Nanima a flow of power that seemed to scream in her bowels, burn in her limbs and give a terrible accuracy to her words. 'He will be seized for the criminal he is and deported beyond the black water to the Andamans! He will rot there! He will become a leper!' The words wrapped a cold hand round Mila's heart.

It seems monstrous to me now that Nanima was blind to Ajit-mama's faults because he was her favourite son. She had never really allowed the umbilical cord to be cut. She had fed him at the breast and slept beside him long after he had ceased to be a baby. At the age of six Ajit was allowed to smoke bidis swiped from servants, his lies went unchecked, and if he refused to return his sisters' toys, well, they had to do without them. As a boy he had been insolent, demanding limitless service from the women of the house. As a husband he was discontented and surly with his wife, his children, his servants. Ah, but in company he was charming and mettlesome, high-spirited and haw-haw!

Ajit-uncle was ideally suited to army life. He rode and swam to perfection, entertained lavishly and could drink his fellow officers under the table. He was lucky at cards and, with his provocative good looks and conquering-hero air, successful in his pursuit of women. And for years, Saroj-aunty (who had grown up in relative seclusion as the late and only child of a small-town judge) had looked on with anxious humility and a hesitant smile on her plain round face while her husband exercised his fatal charm on bold and beautiful women. While he thus amused himself, she suffered. But she had remained modest and respectful because, from the scriptures and folklore and what her mother had taught her long ago, she had learnt that womanhood was a caste, like Brahmin or Sudra, a carefully prescribed role that the virtuous Hindu wife took to heart because it earned her not only society's approval, but also her soul's salvation.

After enduring fifteen years of this, what had made Saroj-mami walk out on her husband and the three little girls she adored? Was it Amrish-mama's letters, as Nanima insisted? She now slammed shut the doors of Vikram's wardrobe and added its key to the bunch at her waist. Then she turned briskly to inspect the bathroom, made exclusively available to her because of the repetitive purifying rites she performed—an ablutionary addiction she had inherited from her Vaishnavite father. Her need for ritual laving and lathering was compulsive. John the Baptist had nothing on her!

Daily she washed all her clothes, including the wet sari with which she wiped her body after her bath. She scoured the bell-metal pots she used for prayers, her drinking glass, her cooking utensils, her round platter after every meal, each of which she took by herself (after offering the first morsels to her deity) seated on a low wooden platform on the floor, never with the others at the table; and she even washed the floor space the moment she rose from her frugal repast. Nanima's ablutions echoed the interminable, rhythmic washing that goes on all over India on river banks and ghats, beside tanks and village wells and pumps, and at leaky water hydrants near open gutters on city streets.

Mila was also nosy about the other strange disciplines Nanima practised, and her esoteric spiritual resolves. Why did she fast on certain days, and on others eat food prepared without salt? Why did she give alms to rows of beggars on certain days, on others walk barefoot to the temple? Why, when Uncle Amrish took ill with the smallpox at the age of seven (because she had refused to have him vaccinated against it), had she rushed not to the doctor but to the temple, laden with gifts for an angry red goddess? Why, when a daughter or a daughter-in-law was with child, did Nanima not allow her to make new layettes for the baby, but insist that the squalling infant be swaddled in old clothes dug out from her nineteenth-century steel trunk?

If anyone had suggested to Mila that the old lady was running scared, she would have laughed. Who could be more doughty than her grandma, who had faced snakes and burglars and rioting mobs without turning a hair? But I now suspect that much of Nanima's devotional fervour was an antidote to the poison of fear. Thus even when the babies were born sturdy, it was not to be taken for granted that they would live, and the old clothes were meant to deflect the envy of kind spirits who could easily turn malign. For the same reason black beads were tied round fat wrists, eyes were carefully blackened with kohl—a black dot spotting each temple for good measure—so the toddlers appeared less attractive than they were. For who could say which vitriolic god or termagant of a goddess might be incited by good looks or talent or happiness?

That year Nanima was our guest for almost two months, and it was no easy thing to live in her shadow. For her shadow carried weight; it crushed those on whom it fell. Even the servants had a difficult time. Not that their work was greatly augmented, but she seemed to subdue them with her ferocious religiosity. Soni, whose voice at full volume could compete with a brass band, was reduced to fidgeting mutely with her sari end pulled hastily round her head as Nanima reprimanded her for chewing tobacco with her betel leaf. Maharaj, our conceited brahmin cook who went to the market with the houseboy because he refused to carry the groceries himself, was insulted that Nanima would not eat his food. Habituated to sulking for hours over an imagined slight, he resented her daily incursions into his kitchen. When out of earshot he muttered darkly about resigning the very next morning, but in her presence he was reduced to servility. And when she rebuked him roundly one evening for playing dice in the kitchen with his cronies and showed them the door, he bore the chastisement shamefacedly.

Nobody was exempt from her iron rule. Our houseboy Khushal, a cheeky and rebellious lad from a village near Surat, was prohibited from using his transistor (his pride and joy). From chatting (giggling, preening) outside the front door with maidservants from adjoining flats. From wearing his favourite shirt, imprinted with squares repeating the buxom figure of Mamta Kulkarni. And when Nanima sent him out for purchases, she flung the money at his low-caste person to avoid pollution by touch. Khushal's lively face grew dark and sullen at the indignity, but he always stooped to pick up the coins and notes.

That was the first year Mila became aware (and indignant!) that Nanima found much that was blameworthy in Father. He had married, caste-wise, below him—even if it was to her own daughter. He did not wear the brahmin's sacred thread, and when dining out he ate flesh and other such depraved things in the company of depraved people.

He did not insist on his wife living apart when menstruating, and he equated his daughter with his son, sent her to an English-medium school and in no way prepared her for marriage. By such means, not content with his own godlessness, Father was actively extending his condition to his wife and family, unlike many Indian intellectuals whose wives were barely literate and businessmen whose women did not reflect, in conduct or appearance, the new prosperity. If Father was aware of Nanima's hostility, in no way did he permit her to alter his plans or retard his purposes. He treated her with courtesy and deference (ironic?), but never allowed her to act as a goad to him, which was exactly what she succeeded in being to the rest of us.

For instance, it was strange how Nanima held the whip hand over Roma, despite being extraordinarily indifferent to anything her younger daughter did. If Roma's hair turned white overnight, or even purple or green, her mother would probably not fail to notice. Was it because Aunty had remained a spinster that she was nullified? For it was assumed that only marriage could fulfil a woman's purpose, and motherhood crown it. And since this reflected a *moral* order, Roma's plight was pitiable indeed.

Yet the chances must have been overwhelming that she could have found a spouse and attained the near-sanctity of motherhood. What had gone wrong? Had she lacked an adequate dowry? Had she— unnatural girl—resisted marriage, an indefensible posture in a culture where woman still functions as an adjunct of man? Had she suffered the pangs of unrequited love? Whatever the reason for her single state Roma, not yet thirty, was consigned to oblivion. And by this negation Nanima had been able to break, piece by piece, the structure of her daughter's desires. She was like a puppet on a string, and within a week of Nanima's arrival Mila could almost see the invisible filaments jerking her aunt this way and that, could see her slipping as she tried to find a reliable surface against which to brace herself. And Vikram, who held his grandma in dark distrust and to whom, after the incident of the egg, her acquaintance with his hidden deeds smacked of witchcraft, clung desperately to his aunty. They seemed to be slipping and drowning together.

Mila felt listless these days, as one feels after a school exam. A flabbiness, an enervation she could not explain to herself—something lay darkly buried beneath the ashes of her fatigue. Was it the weight of Nanima's disapproval? Nothing about her pleased the matriarch.

Not her skimpy dresses, for she was a big girl now and sometimes caught Nanima eyeing her rounding breasts with a frown that detracted from their budding importance and made her flesh feel immodest, gross, as if she were being catapulted with indecent haste into womanhood—a category that, compared to man's lordly estate, was itself a fall from grace.

Nanima did not like to see Mila sweaty and dirty at the end of a schoolday. She did not like her easy familiarity with the men of the family. Mila ought to defer to Vikram, the dowager felt, for an only son was absolutely crucial to a father's safe passage to heaven, whereas a girl child was merely an error. Vikram was an economic asset in his very sex, Mila a liability for the same reason. He was going to be his parents' support in their old age, while she would get married—expensively— and make her exit. But how could the sister defer to her brother when she was allowed to tag along with him to play raucous games in male company on a strip of open ground in front of the garages? Nanima had seen her race after a ball like a boy, and in the excitement of the game even grab a few shirt tails!

Daily Mila's tally of sins mounted. One evening Kishore rang the bell to borrow a schoolbook from Vikram. Her brother was out, and Mila was in the act of handing Kishore the volume of *Elementary Hygiene* when they found Nanima standing soundlessly beside them. Startled, Kishore grabbed the book and was off like a shot, slamming the door behind him.

'What did you give him?' the griffin demanded grimly. She made Mila feel that being a girl in a world of boys was a furtive business.

'The book,' she stammered guiltily.

'Keep your distance next time!' the old lady hissed. Mila looked at her in amazement. Did she mean the book should have been hurled at Kishore? Perhaps in her time girls and boys had hurled things at each other to avoid physical contact?

Mila opened her mouth to protest, then shut it. What was the use? She had been told she was far too argumentative. She lacked proper respect for her elders. Many things about her upbringing were deplorable: that she was allowed to wander into the kitchen during her monthly 'uncleanliness'. That despite Roma's pathetic example under her nose, Shivani was making no plans for her daughter's early bethrothal. That she was sent to a school where she learnt shockingly little about household tasks. Why, when as a bride *she* had entered her new home, her mother-in-law had dismissed the cook and the second servant so the thirteen-year-old could do all their work. In addition to milking two cows at four in the morning and the kitchen chores and the cleaning chores, she had every afternoon to beat the cow dung into large discs and dry them in the sun for her father-in-law to light the fire with the next morning.

'Oh!' Mila had exclaimed innocently after hearing her out. 'Were the cows kept for their milk or their dung?' To punish her for such irreverence Nanima made a point of summoning her to the kitchen daily to say things like: 'Your *Jejus* Christ isn't going to be angry if you shell some peas!' Which would have struck Mila as excruciatingly funny if it had come from anyone but her granny.

It is difficult to describe the sense of coercion that oppressed us that October. A weighing-down of all the things we wanted to say or do—as if she sat on them! With the exception of Father, we all felt troubled, and no one more dangerously than Mother.

No one perceived in those weeks that Mother was threatened not only by the old enemy within, but also by the abrasions we effected on each other. My mother was not disturbed in isolation, but as a member of a disturbed family. Her pyschosis was created, in part at least, by those grouped round her. Had this tragic fact been noted, the one person who should have been banished from her life was her own mother. Yet every time the dread symptoms appeared, or conversely Mother was on the mend, she was either despatched to Nanima's mountain retreat or that despot descended on us disguised as a ministering angel—thus perpetuating the sickness, or even sowing the seeds for the next one.

Before my eyes this minute is the picture of the brick-red curtain outside Mother's room. Exterior immobility as I stand rooted before it; interior agitation as Shivani paces the floor behind it; and a crescendo of voices raised in argument. Yes, that gloomy evening Mila was engaged in her favourite occupation: eavesdropping.

Nanima's voice rose sharply and Mila grinned to hear Mother reply just as vehemently. Then, to Mila's dismay, she heard an isolated sob. 'I won't!' Mother's voice was heavy with tears. 'I can't beg, I don't know how to.'

'Then the sooner you learn, the better for you,' came Nanima's tart retort. 'Too proud no woman can afford to be.'

'But what can I say to him? When I'm not sure of anything?'

'Say that you will never allow that slut inside this house again. Slinking in with the marriage daub on her forehead, bangles tinkling at her wrists. She has no shame?'

'Stop that! Widows are treated cruelly enough.' Desperately: 'I don't *know* anything against her. And nor do you!'

'Yes? In my days she would have been dragged off to have her head shaved to the scalp. Had that happened, perhaps she would not have strayed. Better even to be carried screaming to your husband's pyre to be charred to the bone, than to hover like a vulture over another wife's home. But you will not open your eyes to what is going on under your nose! You will not open your mouth!'

'You don't understand how impossible it is to say ugly things to him. He is not—Ajit!'

'Ajit is what he is for the whole world to see. He does not wear two faces.'

'Mother!'

'God will punish the jade,' said Nanima devoutly. Mila wished they did not have to wait for God. 'But if you don't have the courage now—'

'No! What are you trying to do?' Mila heard the note of hysteria in Mother's voice and trembled for her. 'Leave me alone. I won't listen to you.'

Mila too had heard enough. She turned from the curtain, raced to her room and threw herself face down on her bed. Something menacing was gathering shape again, and she was not prepared to meet it. She rolled herself into a tight little ball and dug into her bed, a foetus seeking the comfort of a womb . . . Presently she heard the front door slam. That would be Nanima setting off on her daily hunt for the absconding daughter-in-law. A long silence . . .

A sudden rustle in the room made Mila look up to find Mother standing before her. How long had she been there? Mother's eyes were grave with assessments as they contemplated the sorry huddled figure on the bed.

She reached down and, with one knuckle, lightly tapped Mila on her crown. 'Hey! Up you get, lazybones!' This was said with a teasing lilt in her voice. 'We're going for a walk!' She laughed outright at Mila's open-mouthed astonishment, for she had given up her daily walks since that wet Friday evening when she had scared them silly by reporting on a phantom street urchin. But this effort was for her daughter, and Shivani's laugh seemed to lift them both into a sunnier clime. Mila laughed too, and as she scrambled to her feet the capricious evening outside her window was drunk on a lavender light.

On the road Mila was acutely conscious of her mother's mood. They had set off without changing into outdoor things, without a word to anyone, and it was quite obvious that Shivani was on an impromptu holiday from cares. She had sprouted wings, and was discovering that life was a lark after all! At one point she abruptly pulled Mila back in her stride and, cupping her cheeks with both hands, gazed raptly down on her face as if to affirm that for this child life must be all grace, lightness, clarity, freshness, adventure!

Yet as they walked on again Mila was afraid that Mother's wave of elation was part of her illness, that it could be attributed to a chemical imbalance in her brain, that such excitation presaged a corresponding descent into black despair. But looking back I could swear that what surged in my mother that evening was pure joy—*ananda*. For she was mellow with it, not strident; and the healing it brought was instantaneous. In this way, by a spontaneous movement of the spirit, for that one perfect evening Mother disdained the trappings of her illness and embraced the luminous selfhood she had been fighting for all that year.

They sped up the hill to the garden that graced its summit. At the foot of the steps Mila saw him first: a spindly little boy in torn sneakers and outsize shorts that covered his knees. The next moment his eyes widened as he looked on Mother. Promptly he stuck his thumb in his mouth.

'The boy you told us about,' breathed Mila, 'the boy who followed you round.' So he was not the figment of a disintegrating mind. Tears welled in her eyes as she happily clutched her mother's hand.

Mother laughed delightedly. 'What shall we do with him now that we've found him? Buy him an ice-cream? We have no money on us.'

But they knew Mila at Café Naaz, farther up the road. 'Wait here!' She left them standing near the steps and ran to fetch him an ice-cream cone. He would not take it from her, his unblinking eyes fixed on Mother's face over his nose-flattening fist.

'Let me try.' Mother held out the strawberry confection temptingly. Anxious moments passed; then his thumb came out of his mouth with a moist *plop*! And with unconscious dignity he took the ice-cream from her hand.

When Father returned late that night from his bridge session,

Mother was asleep. Mila waylaid him outside their bedroom door and told him about the boy, her low voice wobbling dangerously, till she flung herself weeping against him. As he held her tight, in leaden silence, she knew he shared her desolation at the thought that they had failed her.

Mila pulled away and tried to see his face in the dark. 'We should have trusted her when she told us about the boy,' she mourned. 'Why didn't we believe her?'

'Hush!' He put his arm round her again. 'What matters is that she's well now, Mila. She's *well*! She will always be well,' he added fiercely, as if to convince himself.

13

As it happened, Nanima accomplished two things during her visit that pleased Mila enormously. One was the cool efficiency with which she sent Rayhaan the Gentleman Caller packing. The other was her victorious confrontation with Gita.

Evening after evening, Mila had watched Rayhaan with Roma-masi and suffered. His wooing was proceeding at a more distraught, frantic pace than ever, but Roma still appeared enthralled, captivated. Mila knew that Masi was not meant for searing glances, unblunted passion, the wrestling of soul with soul; even so, her behaviour was feeble to the point of being suicidal. Just as goats in the temple of Kali at Meher did not have to be dragged to the altar of the goddess (Amrish-mama had told her), but of their own volition placed their necks in the sacrificial frame to have their stupid heads chopped off, so by her own will—or rather lack of it—Roma was inviting slaughter. She was nothing more than a self-immolating goat. But Mila was terrified that one day she would wake from her somnolence, shake herself free of her drugged inertia to enfold Rayhaan in a tight embrace from which she would never let him go. Mila felt she could not survive that moment. If the aunt claimed Rayhaan, the niece would commit hara-kiri.

The first thing that came to Roma's (and Mila's) rescue was the heavy catarrh that had by now settled as a buzz in her ears and a wheeze in her bronchia. Aunty spent her days in a kind of stupor, almost deafened by aspirin. The bedroom had a perpetual Tiger Balm odour but, as far as Mila knew, she obstinately rejected other types of medication. At last the evening arrived when she declined to come out to the living room where Rayhaan awaited her. Mila thought this very wise of her, because she looked a fright with her nose so red in a sticky, waxen face, and the cleft in her short upper lip so deeply shadowed as to look like an incipient moustache. Thus, for a spell, the dreadful game was suspended.

At the time Mila hardly knew if she was grateful for this respite, for she lived in a jealous torment day and night. She could not even remember happier times. As a child she had missed Rayhaan if he failed to turn up at their parties and had been resentful of his solicitous regard for her brother—all the more real for being unobtrusive (Vikram, of course, shyly idolized him). But at least she had not coveted him. She had not dreamt of possessing him. Her desires had not been so frighteningly defined. The terrible agony began when she discovered that their lives were not plotted on separate or incongruous maps, after all. That he and she inhabited the same world, they co-existed on the same planet, as equals, and that she could love him if she dared! But now that certain barriers were down, new ones had gone up overnight to divide them.

And Mila could not confide in anyone. Impossible to go with her affliction to her mother, whose own frailty was always under threat. Or to Uncle Amrish, who had only nasty things to say about her prince charming. Or to Father, forever her mentor and guide, but who now troubled her by refusing to be drawn into a single focus. Whenever Mila turned to him, she had the uneasy feeling that the correlation between surface visibility and something lurking under cover could not be established and that *he*, somehow, was responsible for this cleavage. So she remained painfully tongue-tied and her father did not help her. Could she possibly fault him for that? No, but . . . Was there a subtle stepping-back, a quiet withdrawal on his part because he realized that her very dependency would one day breed hostility against him? Or was he just being wary, because he had something to hide?

Rayhaan the lady killer continued to wait on the inaccessible aunt while neglecting the available niece. But Mila's kinswoman, bless her, steadfastly refused to see him, pleading ill health. Why, then, did the swain still persist? About a week after Roma had sent out her excuses to him, Rayhaan sat facing the empty Sankhera chair, smoking cigarette after cigarette in a sombre communion with himself. Then abruptly he rose and came to where Mila sat near the window, trying to maintain a desperate artistic detachment with the aid of her faithful paints and a tumbler of water.

As soon as he came close enough, Mila flung herself bodily on the little table, acting on a natural impulse to protect her work from chilling criticism. In doing so she managed to spill some water on her painting, and in rising to make a grab for the rocking tumbler she knocked over her chair as well.

'All right,' said Rayhaan, steadying the glass with one hand and picking up the chair with the other, 'I get the message. I promise not to look.'

Furiously Mila said, 'Who cares if you do!' and flopped down ungracefully on her seat. She hated him. She hated his arrogant selfhood. She hated the iron constancy in his eyes, the aloof smile on his lips. He awoke chaotic echoes in her, and conflicts. She felt slavish and rebellious at the same time, so that she wished despairingly to inflict a grievous hurt on him. Tread him underfoot like a worm. Stamp him into the ground. 'I don't even care if you don't like it!' She added with all the truculence she could muster. She knew her lower jaw was trembling as she glared up at him. She wanted to lock her eyes with his in an exchange of pure hate, but with a queer wild leap within her found herself wondering what the warmth of his mouth on hers would be like. And she was profoundly shocked at herself.

'You have paint on your nose,' Rayhaan said as he circled the table. 'And yellow streaks on your dress. I'm sorry. My fault.'

Mila looked down at her technicolour bosom. 'You needn't be sorry! It's an old thing I hate to wear.' And she hated him even more, because under his gaze she was aware that her frock pinched at the sleeves and strained at the waist, while in a suit of some lightweight, dark-blue material (a suit!) he looked elegant enough to conduct an orchestra. She tried to fix a scowl on her face, but it kept slipping as she continued to hear the thunder and lightning of a strange music. How the treasonable woman, now wide awake in her, confused her!

With his hands in the pockets of his jacket Rayhaan observed, 'And I've spoilt your painting, too.'

'Who cares!' She snatched up the wet sheet and crumpled it into a ball. 'My teacher says I have no talent for it, anyway. So there!' She went on clawing and tearing at the paper ball with destructive fingers.

He watched her in silence. For the first time in weeks she held his attention. She felt he was irritated and concerned at the same time. She wanted to burst into tears. He must have seen that, for he said gently, 'She may be wrong, Mila. Teachers often are.'

She shook her head violently. 'She is right, right!' She struck the table with her fist and the water in the tumbler jumped, but he did not step back. She did not add that making crazy daubs on paper was a kind of harmonious accompaniment to the crazy world she lived in.

He was silent again for a moment, then said gravely, 'But you have talent in another direction. Why haven't you let me read your recent compositions?'

The duplicity of the man! As if he were in the least interested in her school essays. 'Because they're no good, that's why. Because I have *no* talent, *no* gift in *any* direction, so *there*!'

His face was expressionless as he said, 'Then you are a lucky girl.' He leaned against the window. 'Because a gift of the kind we mean is not to be mistaken for a birthday present, tied up in a pink or blue ribbon.' He was very serious. 'Such a gift is an unbearable load. A gnawing conscience. A scourge. A dissatisfaction with anything less than perfection.' Mila listened intently. Had he started writing again? There was a quietness in his voice, a certitude of power, that could only come from a fresh investment in his work. Did he now have the bad things under the control of his word processor?

After a long pause he went on, 'I expect to be forgiven for a lot of things, Mila. But for trifling with my gift I don't. For blundering in my art I don't. For economy of effort, for lack of clarity, precision, I want no pardon.'

Like a thirsty disciple at the feet of her guru Mila soaked up his words. He had revealed a new dimension of himself, and her identification with him for the moment was, implausibly enough, complete. She believed everything he said. She couldn't help herself. She had suspected this other Rayhaan, and now she understood him. And she was flattered that he had offered her a glimpse of this side of him. She looked up to find herself in his eyes—her reflection was there. She had not realized how closely he had been watching her. She wanted to stop this. She wanted to hate this man. The look had to end sometime. It did, just as he was about to speak again, for Nanima entered the room.

She sat down on the green divan, tucked the sari draped on her head behind each ear, and beckoned to Rayhaan in that incisive way she had.

He straightened himself against the window. Mila saw his eyes narrow—not in apprehension, but in something like suspicion. He stubbed out his cigarette in the brass ash tray, then walked across.

'Sit!' ordered Nanima, who could make a chair rock by merely looking at it. He took the one in which Roma sat with him in the evenings, and it seemed to Mila that it was now his turn to be held a prisoner. He was roped in. Ah, he was captured. Corralled. And it served him right. The chair contained him like a straitjacket as for a full moment Nanima measured him from the crown of his head to the soles of his shoes, obviously with the intent of assigning him his proper category, caste-wise and hierarchically speaking, and then to dole out the suitable degree of condescension. Plainly she was not impressed by the heavenly hunk of manhood opposite her.

Rayhaan was tensed in the chair but bore her scrutiny well.

'For my daughter you seem rather young,' Nanima began, 'but that is your business, not mine.' After his first, barely contained start of astonishment, Rayhaan sat commendably still. 'For me there are only two points on which I wish to satisfy myself. Your caste is what?'

He blinked for orientation, then said quietly, holding on to the armrests with both hands, 'I have no caste. My mother was a Parsi. Our scriptures teach "good thoughts, good words, good deeds", apart from which I do not believe—'

'We are not here to talk of beliefs,' Nanima interrupted him crisply. 'The second thing I want to do is match horoscopes, and if they agree, we can begin all formalities of marriage while I'm here. To take the tedious journey to Mumbai a second time this year I have no wish.'

Mila saw the sudden gleam that leapt in his eye and was in despair that Rayhaan would now overplay his hand. She picked up the tumbler and put it down on her table again, not too loudly, but loud enough to sound a warning.

Rayhaan's voice was dangerously bland. 'You have put your cards on the table. Excellent. For my part I would like to—'

'In my day these things were decently done.' As if rebuked by her voice Rayhaan's hands, with which he had been gesturing, fell back on the armrests. 'Parents were approached by parents, horoscopes read, before the matter went out of hand.'

'The old order changeth, as I believe you may have—'

'The priest must be consulted at once on the wedding date. Within two months it must take place, after which there are not many auspicious days for weddings. Also I am planning a pilgrimage to Kashi, Vrindavan and Prayag. Your parents must be living?'

'My father. However, and with all respect, I must tell you—'

'Good. A meeting can be arranged.'

Rayhaan's grip on the chair tightened. Mila could see that he was pulled in two ways. His itch was to clown, to seek the clown's traditional immunity by bluffing his way out of the situation. But he was also tempted to conduct this meeting in a decorous manner, to mouth unctuous platitudes—a ritual he would have managed better had his temples been touched by sanctifying grey. Solemnly he cleared his throat. 'Apart from the fact that my revered mother is no more on this earth, my father does not reside in this country, so I'm denied the advantage of both their—'

'Relatives you must have who can act for him,' snapped Nanima. 'I have heard that you have chosen the profession of writing.' She looked at him with patrician distaste. 'How you hope to support wife and family on what you are earning by that, I do not see, but again that is your business and her business. From our side you must not expect anything much—wait!' commanded the czarina as Rayhaan made to rise from his seat with undisguised impatience. 'You must be knowing that Roma's father died when she was very young. There is nothing much to her name, only a girl's share. But Shivani has agreed to give her sister a proper wedding.' Rayhaan was on his feet and stood before her in a single movement, all but eclipsing her, but she went on unwaveringly, 'So, it is settled for now. When I'm leaving for Pune I cannot say. But the earlier the horoscopes are read, and the two families are meeting, the better. That is all I have to tell you.' She got up from the divan and made a decisive exit.

Like an actor who had lost his sense of timing Rayhaan stood there, floundering. He had missed his cue and was unable to improvise, while Nanima's words echoed strong and loud in the room. He looked across at Mila. She stared back at him, her lips parting to question him, but no sound came from them. Her face must have been working in an agony of interrogation, for Rayhaan shook his head at her violently, once. His sudden laugh was a reaction to his bewilderment and anger, a late cover-up.

'Come here,' he said, and sat down on the divan.

Feeling as though she had been all but swept away by a storm, Mila marched across the room and stood stiffly before him. She felt ill, worn to shreds with love and hate for him.

'You look almost as frightened as I am,' he said. 'Sit down beside me till the brain fog clears, Mila, and tell me what to do. I need orders, prescriptions.'

She would not sit. 'Run away!' she said hoarsely. 'Run away and don't ever come back till they're gone.'

He looked up at her quizzically. 'You don't believe, then, that a man can do nothing but bow to the will of God?'

'Oh, no!' She clasped her hands together. 'Go away, Rayhaan, please.'

'You won't enjoy watching me played like a hooked fish?'

'No!' So tense was she for him that, although she had recognized his question as a wan piece of jest, she answered him in earnest.

His hand grasped her forearm and pulled her down beside him. 'My little friend, I think you're right. If not hooked, I am caught in a web of my own making.' He sat still for a moment, then took a handkerchief from his pocket and applied it vigorously to her nose. 'Sit still, you little monkey. It's the paint. A moment and it'll . . . all be . . . gone.' Mila struggled indignantly to free her head, but now he was calmly stuffing the soiled handkerchief back into his pocket. 'She's an arbitrary lady, your grandmother, isn't she? One of those absolute monarchs. Would you say, Mila,' he was musing aloud, 'that a coward is a man in whom the instinct of self-preservation acts normally?'

'I don't know what you mean,' she said, then added grudgingly, 'but you are not a coward.'

He took her hand in his and gave it a squeeze. 'I'm grateful for that.' She tried to snatch her multicoloured paw away, but he held it fast. 'As for your advice, which I am about to take only . . . will you tell your mother—' He stopped abruptly, and Mila was startled to see the intense, almost wild expression in his eyes as he let go of her hand. The next moment she thought she had been mistaken, for he was smiling. 'No, hell, don't let's say a word to anyone. This will be our little secret.'

'Nanima will go as soon as she finds Saroj-mami—which could be tomorrow,' Mila caught herself whispering in his ear like a conspirator. 'And Roma-masi will leave with them. She's been with us for *months*. Now that Mother is here and well again, we don't even *need* her.'

Rayhaan stood up abruptly. 'Quite right. We don't need the aunt at all now that the mother is here, do we? Then . . . this is goodbye again, Mila?'

'Yes.' Her mind was so blanked to everything but the horror of the consequences if he remained here, that she was in a fever of impatience to see him gone. She sprang to her feet and almost propelled him to the door. 'I will let Amrish-mama know the *minute* they've left. So he can tell you when it's safe to come back.'

He laughed, and somehow the gravity of the situation has not remained as vividly with me as that laugh, so that even today, when I hear a semi-tone of this laugh reproduced anywhere, say in a darkened theatre, I turn my head sharply and my heart behaves crazily.

'I'm sure Amrish will keep cave for me,' said Rayhaan to Mila. 'Yes, that's exactly what the bastar—what your uncle will enjoy doing.' He added bitterly, 'He always *said* I was a fool.'

An anxious thought struck Mila as she opened the door. 'You *do* like Amrish-mama, don't you?'

He raised his brows. 'Inasmuch as we are asked to do good to them that persecute us—' He broke off, reading her face. 'You know, Mila,' he spoke thoughtfully, 'most people have a kind of pocket, or bulge, in which they amass things exclusively for themselves—their worldly goods, accumulations of wealth, power, whatnot. Rather like the room in which your mother or a complacent Gujarati housewife stores her year's ration of grains, spices, oil and so forth. But Amrish needs no such locked-up place, and that is rare. Very, very rare.'

'Oh. Like Mahatma Gandhi?'

Slowly, 'Yes, I never thought of that. Rather like Gandhi—' A door slammed somewhere in the house. Mila flinched. 'I think you better go,' she said.

He nodded, but did not move. He had heard the door, too. 'Do you think, Mila, I could see her just once before I left?'

She felt a painful stab of jealousy. 'No! She has a dreadful cold.'

'Who? No, I meant . . . your mother.'

'Oh.' She looked at him, saw the oldness and sadness beneath the authoritative poses he struck, and felt for him something softer than desire. She wanted to take his hand in both of hers, cradle it in her neck, press her cheek down on it, shelter it there like a bird that had fallen out of the sky. But other matters were more pressing. 'You can see her if you want to, but I don't advise it,' she said briskly, and threw a quick glance over her shoulder to see if Nanima was approaching them with a trap, bait or a bomb. 'Besides, you said your going away was to be a secret between us.' Her voice was resentful.

He drew a deep breath. 'So I did. So I did,' he repeated, two fingers testing the wood of the door before he dropped his hand. 'You will . . . look after her, Mila? See that she is not troubled again?'

'Yes, yes.' In her distraught state, this dilly-dallying made her gauche and gruff. 'Go please.' She was all for speeding him on his way.

He stepped out. 'Right then, I'm off.' He bent over her. 'Goodbye little friend, for now,' he whispered in her ear, so that the warmth of his breath on her cheek was the only part of her that was not cold. She remembered that she still didn't know what the warmth of his lips on hers would do to her.

She threw her arms round him and kissed him full on the mouth. He was startled, she could tell, unprepared for such an embrace. His answering kiss was no more than a comforting response to a child, but she could feel the trembling begin deep inside her as gradually his lips took complete possession of hers. She had taken him over the edge and clung to him hungrily, her heart betraying itself in thud, thud, thud . . . till he gently but firmly disengaged himself. He stared down at her, very sober, a man fully recovered from a heady moment of disorientation. Then he said softly, a question in his voice: 'Mila?'

She turned her head away, and the next moment she had slammed the door shut in his face. She stood against it, trembling. Would he knock? Would the bell sound in her ear? No, he had gone. What a genius he was at going away! Mila wanted to race after him, charge down the stairs, yelp out his name and run abreast of his car like a dog. But the click of the latch made her feel that something had fallen into place, distantly and irrevocably, and there was nothing for her but to stay there without him, alone. All left-behinders are weepers. Her tears came.

She brushed them away angrily with the back of her hand, and tried to hug to herself the comfort that Rayhaan was safe. That was all that mattered, wasn't it? And indeed, he had not escaped a moment too soon, for Nanima entered the room, this time dressed to go out. At the door she gave Mila a finely honed look that made the girl feel unkempt, maudlin, brainless, guilty. Then she opened the door and banged it shut behind her in Mila's face.

Nanima ventured out at least twice a day, and though she never let on where she went, it was understood that these expeditions were connected with her efforts to find her missing daughter-in-law. Father had not offered to help her. Uncle Amrish, while disclaiming all knowledge of Saroj's whereabouts, had stoutly declared himself on her side. Mother's remonstrances that she was engaged in a fruitless search—like looking for a needle in a haystack—were brushed aside by Nanima, who had not even bothered to enlist the local police in her investigations. But every time she set off, it was evident to all that she experienced something of the hunter's instinct. She felt no grief for her abandoned son and three grand-daughters, only a sense of satisfaction at finding the despised daughter-in-law so palpably in the wrong. Saroj had only proved what Nanima had always suspected of her. Not only was she stupid and feckless, she was also a slut.

But the second month was drawing to a close and there was still no trace of Saroj. Sometimes, when Roma-masi's unrhythmic snoring woke her in the middle of the night, Mila would lie in bed thinking of her other aunt. Where had she found refuge? Had Saroj-mami become one of Bombay's millions of pavement dwellers? Amrish-mama had told her of people who shared a poverty too great for even the slums, who belonged to no one and nothing, who ate, slept, loved and died on the streets. Was Mami now one of their number? If so, wouldn't it be better if Nanima did find her and take her home?

As the days went by, Grandmother was still hopeful, still in command of the situation. She was so confident of her power over the absent girl that she believed she could manoeuvre her even from a distance. She had a fanatical single-mindedness, a terrible, crushing certainty that she would find Saroj.

One evening Nanima returned home rather early to find Gita ensconced in the big padded chair in the living room. For once Gita had ill timed her visit. It was a gross miscalculation, a strategic mistake. The serpent had strayed into paradise at the wrong hour. Father was out. Mother was in bed, nursing one of her sick headaches. Aunt Roma and Vikram were playing cards in the bedroom, and not likely to emerge to entertain the visitor. Mila sat in her usual place near the window, pretending to be absorbed in her homework. She had been answering Gita's tiresome questions in single words.

'What are you studying?'
'History.'
'Such an interesting subject, don't you think?'
'Yes.'
'Indian history?'
'Yes.'
'We had to do English history as well. Quite boring, the Magna Carta and all those acts of Parliament.' Mila made no comment, and Gita went on, 'Which period?'
'Moghul.'
'One of the most exciting periods in Indian history!'
'Yes.'

'All those opulent emperors. All that grandeur.'
No comment.
'You remember we took you to see the Taj?'
'No.'
'But of course we did! The very first night we touched Agra, how many years ago was it? Oh, I now remember you were tired and fell asleep in the car . . . Your mother was not feeling well, but we took you to see it, Nar—your father and I. By moonlight.' A sensuous haze descended on her face as she said this, and her bosom rose and fell as she re-lived her moonlit memories in a Moghul garden. Mila was resentful at being used as an audience for the bitch's feelings for Father. He existed for her in dimensions of which the daughter wished to know nothing. The minutes ticked away; then the doorbell rang and Soni opened the door to Nanima. Gita rose hastily from her chair, and with a hand tinkling nervous bangles she draped her wanton sari end modestly over her head. It made Mila want to snigger.

Nanima stood rooted near the door. From that distance she looked at Gita with such a terrible silent confrontation as would have made another—less hardy—female faint. (Actually the wench would have dropped in a graceful faint anyway, if Father had been there to hold her.) Gita, who had hastily sawed off tender memories to assemble her most buttery smile, was literally put out of countenance. Her face toppled like a vase, and broke without a crash. Ingratiating words of greeting froze on her cracked lips and the condemnation of that silence seemed to render further speech impossible.

Gita edged towards the door. Her aim seemed to be to dart past that ominous figure, but so damaged was she that she stumbled, like a dancer tripping over herself to spring offstage after an embarrassing debut. She turned round, and with effort raised a lame hand to wave to the audience on her way out. It was a valiant gesture, but Mila would not acknowledge it. Her head was buried in her history book.

Gita had been outmatched, her flight was inglorious, but Mila could not savour her defeat for she, too, was shaken. It was a mortal combat she had witnessed. Would the vanquished die of it? Mila tried to concentrate on her work. She read a few more sentences about Noor Jahan's adroit intrigues behind the throne—hadn't Swami Vivekananda said that woman was a fox because she was oppressed, but when free she would become a lion? What avatar would Gita take when they met again, now that the vixen had been stripped of her mask?

14

The next time Mila ran into Gita was on a crowded street, and she looked no different.

On the bus on her way into town that Saturday morning, Mila had seen herself as an adventurer rocking bravely through a hazardous world. Even the obstructionist bus conductor—she had to squeeze past him to a vacant seat—had added to her sense of being undeterred by obstacles. Stationed in the aisle, his arms raised above shoulder height like Dracula, he was appealing to his passengers to vouch for his probity, his unblemished record in their service, while at the same time a seated buxom woman was verbally assaulting him for having touched her person with dishonourable intent. She continued her tirade, he his pleas, but nobody responded. Neutral faces gazed resolutely out of side windows but Mila could not see past her neighbour, a seat-hog who had spread his bulk on two-thirds of the available space, leaving her to balance precariously on the very edge. Graciously she forgave him, for this was *her* morning. Hadn't she wheedled Roma-masi and Vikram into seeing a replay of *Gone with the Wind* at the Regal Cinema that afternoon? And when Father refused her the use of the car during office hours, hadn't she with much guile persuaded Mother to allow her this lone ride on the bus to buy the tickets?

The queue before the booking-office window was long, but Mila was content to wait her turn. Now she was carefully picking up her change; at last the matinee tickets resided safely in the black plastic handbag she clutched to herself in a sticky grasp. Flushed with a sense of achievement, she stepped out of the theatre.

She loved this part of the city, a hotchpotch of shopping centre, residential quarter and business district. Clean, busy and lively, it had a temple, a church, a mosque and a neat housing complex for Parsis called Cusrow Baug, where one of Rayhaan's aunts on the distaff side lived. Then there were cloth shops, shoe shops, betel-leaf shops, department stores, jewellers, hotels, restaurants and a transport depot that sent buses on their different routes all over the city and housed them when they crawled back in at night.

She was walking the pavement, humming untunefully under her breath, when a maroon Fiat drew up alongside the curb and stopped. Mila stopped, too: it was familiar. She pushed up her glasses, which had recently acquired the habit of slipping down the sharp incline of her nose. That was Shankar behind the wheel. Had her father relented, after all, and sent the chauffeur to pick her up? Daddy's brusqueness that morning had been out of character. She took a few steps towards the car when the back door opened and out stepped her natural enemy, Gita.

Quickly Mila retreated and wheeled round to stare at a shop window, very excited, for to be thrown into sudden proximity with your enemy is like coming upon your beloved without ceremony. Certain that Gita had not seen her, she stared with theatrical concentration at the saris behind the glass. She scrutinized the price tags with an eye worthy of the Internal Revenue man, and with the other watched Gita approach. With wiggling hips Gita climbed the three steps of the shop. Her hand had just touched the square wooden handle of the glass door to push it open when she gave a little start.

'Mila!' she called. 'What are you doing here?' Her eyes narrowed. 'You are alone?'

Yes, Gita looked just the same, all fake innocence in her virgin-white sari, her dark skin glistening like a temple in the sun. Her little-girl eyes so moist. Her mouth pouting, lascivious. As Mila mumbled a reply, with the odd sense of telling lies though she was speaking the truth, she glanced instinctively to the right and left for an escape route.

'Come inside with me for a moment,' said Gita. 'I've taken time off for a little shopping. Then I'll get off at the office and the car can drive you home.' She gave the swing door a push.

Mila shook her head. No, you spider, you scorpion, you rattlesnake, I'm going nowhere with you. Besides, wasn't the bondmaid supposed to be chained to her desk, earning her daily bread? How dare she use Father's car, irrevocably dedicated to work at this hour, for her shopping sprees?

'Come on, Mila.' Gita allowed the door to swing close again. She waited, one hand holding her sari end tight and rather affectedly away to one side, like a matador contriving an artful pass. Did she expect Mila to charge past her like a bull?

'No.'

'All right, then.' Gita dropped her sari tail, her impudent bangles merry-making, and undulated down the steps. 'I can shop later,' she tried to make her voice agreeable. 'Let's go and have some ice-cream.'

Mila pushed her glasses up her nose. 'I don't want ice-cream.'

'Of course you do.' Gita forced herself to smile, while in her wide eyes was pinned this little sharpness, watching Mila's face to see what she was thinking. 'You love ice-cream. Come on now.' Mila was undecided and obscurely frightened, but allowed Gita to grasp her upper arm and steer her along the pavement into a restaurant. The grip was too tense to be friendly.

It was cool and dim inside. There was Western music on a tape, but inferior equipment or bad acoustics gave the tune a vacant, swallowed sound. They sat in a far corner of the partially deserted room. Gita called the waiter and ordered a chocolate ice-cream for Mila, tea for herself. 'A plate of chicken sandwiches?' she asked with the air of a conspirator.

'No, thanks.'

'Why not? Your father won't mind.'

'I don't want it.'

'I *know* he won't mind.' Again that malicious acuteness in Gita's eyes. 'No one need know, at home.' Mila saw what she was doing. She was feeding her, grooming her, building her up. Taking the green filly over the small jumps, nurturing young confidence. Then, once she got the animal going, she would raise the bars bit by bit until they were positioned where she had wanted them from the start, and it would then be too late for Mila to balk: she would have to spring at her command.

'Six chicken sandwiches,' Gita told the waiter with a smile.

'Eat them all yourself,' said Mila, 'because I'm not going to.' She then plagiarized Gita's smile, and that seemed to bother the bitch.

'No sandwiches,' said Gita to the waiter, her mouth a bit strained.

He left to execute the order, and Mila would not raise her head but stared at Gita's hands resting on the table. Small, soft, helpless hands. But that was a lie—Mila knew they were strong, dexterous, pirating hands. Hadn't they manoeuvred her into this dark cavern? Suddenly she felt ambushed, sitting opposite Gita the manless bandit. Ah, she was a bandit *because* she was manless. There were stories in Sanskrit literature of women undergoing severe penance to secure a desired husband. What self-flagellations did Gita practise?

Mila attacked her ice-cream reluctantly when it came. Soon she was ashamed to find herself enjoying it very much.

'Has your Nanima gone?' asked Gita.

'Gone where?' Mila looked up with an ingenuous air, though she knew what Gita meant.

'To Pune. Or back to Panchgani.' Gita was gazing at her with a watchmaker's face, intent on learning what ticked inside her head.

'No.' Of course the hussy knew Nanima was still with them, but the humiliation of her last meeting with the prioress must rankle. Mila suppressed a grin, fortified by that memory, but Gita was staring down into her empty cup like a gypsy reading tea leaves, and two tears coursed down her cheeks. Hello, what was this? Gita's annual downpour was comparable to the rains in Cherrapunji, and she found it rewarding to weep before Father, but why would she think it worth her while to perform for the daughter?

'Did you notice how she treated me?' Gita's voice trembled. 'She insulted me! Drove me out of the house as if I were a . . .'

Mila could have supplied the word she wanted, and all its synonyms, but she silently watched Gita fill her cup with a shaking hand. 'What has she against me? What did I ever do to offend her?' Mila's answer was to spoon her ice-cream methodically.

Gita looked up at last. 'What has she been saying behind my back?' Her wet eyes held a joyless glitter, her words a vague threat. 'What vile things are whispered about me in that house? What wicked lies? *Tell* me!' Her voice was sharp and shrill, and louder than people ought to speak in restaurants. Gita must have realized this, for the next moment she was whispering. '*Tell* me! What do they say?' The vixen's devious moves had been detected, she had been tracked down, and wanted to learn how this had happened. She wanted decoded intelligence. Stop-press news!

Briefly Mila raised her eyes to allow Gita to read the contempt in them, then picked up her bag. 'I'm going,' she announced.

'Oh, no you're not!' Gita's original animosity had long ago turned into active dislike of the boss's daughter, but she made a last valiant effort. 'Have another ice-cream. Would you like strawberry this time? Vanilla, pistachio?'

'Nothing.'

'Oh, come.' She tried to play the brisk, jocular aunt. 'All girls your age adore ice-cream.' Mila gave a resigned shrug. 'Waiter, a plate of strawberry ice-cream.' And Gita began to stir her untouched tea, on which a sad scum had formed. She was now a sorceress vigorously stirring dubious ingredients (like 'eye of newt' and 'toe of frog'?) for an evil potion, and Mila's head was filled with dread images of magic rites, witches' cauldrons and monosyllabic spells. With mutterings and mantras, *'om, haum, jum, sah'* invoked for the perdition of all rivals . . .

'Mila,' cunning flickered in the black eyes, 'you know your mother hasn't been well ever since your Nanima came to stay with you, don't you?' She can't forgive Nanima, thought Mila with an inward giggle. The waiter's arrival with her pink ice-cream saved her from making a reply. 'You know that, don't you?' Gita persisted after he left.

'Nothing's the matter with my mother,' Mila said scornfully as she reached for her new teaspoon.

'You haven't noticed how strange she gets?' Gita whispered.

'No.'

'How she imagines people follow her?'

'They sometimes do,' she retorted stoutly. 'She's so beautiful, my mother.' But now Mila had the sensation of several eyes trained on her concertedly, inimically. So the accused must feel, innocent or guilty, with cruel lights trained on her while the inquisitor is embalmed in velvety darkness.

'And you don't remember what she did to Vikram with the scissors?'

Mila sat still. The words were having a strange effect on her: she was standing on a tightrope across a chasm, her hands clutching the rails of a support that she knew she must soon relinquish.

'And how the night after the party,' Gita whispered, 'Vikram woke up screaming because he felt hands reaching for his throat?'

Vikram has nightmares, Mila wanted to scream at her. Nightmares!

'You have noticed,' Gita was saying softly, 'that funny expression in your mother's eyes, haven't you?' She sipped her tea with satisfaction, while hoisted far above her Mila had the sense of an infinite circus arena below and upturned, slit-mouthed faces hushed with expectation.

'She's been like that ever since Vikram was born.' With Gita's words an ice-cold shower was turned full on Mila, so that every inch of her froze while the ice-cream melted in her plate.

'There was a procession of doctors and drugs. Your father took her abroad to Switzerland, Paris . . . After a whole year in the Paris hospital she was better, and the doctors suggested a new treatment.' Gita whispered these things as if they were dirty, unclean. She was rushing on with frightful cruelty, not giving Mila a chance to interrupt. 'The doctors said care at home, uniting with her children, family life in a protected, undemanding environment would help. Simple responsibilities were recommended. The doctors didn't think she could hurt herself. They didn't think she could hurt *any*one. But they were wrong, *wrong*!' Gita's eyes gleamed with a terrible triumph.' You were not even three years old when she tried to *strangle* you in bed!'

A hammer crashed on Mila's heart, cracking the ice there. And she was falling from that rope, falling, falling, and there was no net below to break her fall, only the steepness of that plunge. With a choked cry she rose to her feet, knocking over her chair, but Gita's hand shot out and grabbed her wrist. She held on to it as with a clamp, and only when the waiter came running to their table to pick up the chair and Mila sank back into it did she release her hand. The waiter looked at them curiously, but Gita's smile was reassuring. 'The chair overbalanced,' she said. He grinned, ducked his head and hurried away to attend to another table.

Mila sat there, tears running down her face, blurring her glasses as she put up a last despairing resistance against a knowledge that had always infected her invisibly, but which now seemed to be emblazoned on all four walls of the room. The fiend opposite her was bent on spelling out the truth Father had tried to spare her, but Mila felt as if a secret voice had spoken to her straight out of her own bones, and never could she hole up again in the dark comfort of not knowing.

Perhaps Gita was now frightened by the enormity of what she had said, terrified by what would be reported back to Father, for she reached across and patted Mila on the hand. 'There is nothing to weep about, you silly girl. It all happened so long ago. Get on with your ice-cream. You know how fond I am of your mother, don't you?' Mila looked up suddenly through her tears and netted an expression of such intense cupidity on Gita's face that she winced. 'Shivani is the best friend I have. I would do anything for her.'

Here Mila's anger came to her rescue. She couldn't bear the air of nobility with which Gita said these words, the studied heroism, as if she were sacrificing herself so that they might survive. She wiped away her tears with impatient fingers and said quietly, 'You are a liar.'

'Mila,' Gita said in a quivering voice, 'you say you are sorry or I'll tell your father.'

'Tell him!'

For a moment she sat there silently, holding a snarling temper on the fraying leash of her own selfish interests. 'Your father,' Gita began at last—and whenever she spoke of him Mila saw her with a big padlock in hand, ready to snap it on him, the dirty cheat—'your father... knows how much I... value the friendship of your mother,' she finished stiltedly. Something in Mila's face made her hastily change this to, 'And I was the one to tell him how bad Nanima is for Shivani. You see, someone has to speak up! And he trusts me, tells me everything. He has to tell his troubles to someone, Mila, otherwise how could he bear to live?'

Mila stared at her. Was she really his anodyne against sorrow—like a Rajput warrior taking opium to prolong his callousness to this wounds? Mila was not conditioned to meet this new man who seemed to be ballooning behind Gita's talk, emerging from behind her allusions. Mila had spent her childhood checking and verifying the security to be found in her father, and he had not yet failed her, had he? This man who honoured ideals with beautiful words out of a lost world? Beside him she felt as safe as a furry animal curled up in a deep burrow. So who was this other man whose identity cancelled out the first? Were the two one, was her father's careful cover coming undone?

'Naren tells me everything,' Gita said again. She quickly bit her lip, ostensibly regretting the slip of the tongue, but Mila knew she loved to speak that name aloud, she *wanted* Mila to know how familiar she was with it. A secret is most relished at the point of divulging it, and Gita continued proudly, 'You see, I know everything that goes on in your house! And I'm worried about your mother. I owe so much to her! When my husband died so tragically'—her eyes filled readily with tears—'my in-laws cursed me for bringing sorrow into their lives. They blamed me! They could not bear the sight of my face. My stars were ill omened, they said, I brought disaster in my wake and when their son died I should have died, too...' Her voice trailed off.

With an effort she began again, 'My own parents did not want to take me back! I had to beg them on my knees. You know what my mother said to me on my brother's wedding day? "Gita," she said, "be careful your shadow does not fall on my son today." My own *mother* said that! A widow is an ugly thing, Mila, a cursed soul, not wanted on happy occasions. My new sister-in-law called me *kalmouhy*, with my black mouth she said I devoured people!' Her lips trembled. 'They made me do all the heavy work in the house. I had a college degree, but I became a drudge at home. I had to know my place, my mother said, or people would talk. This colour I was not to wear. That sweet I was not to eat. Not show my face when family friends visited. The day my nephew was born, I was not taken to see the baby in hospital . . . in case my presence worked some evil on him . . . I had no money. My husband had died before he could change the nominee in his insurance papers. The insurance money went to my father-in-law. I had no children, so he refused to part with it.' Her voice trembled. 'Exactly a year after my husband's death, my in-laws called at my parents' home with five elders from my husband's village—to solemnize my engagement to my fifteen-year-old brother-in-law! They would lose face in their village, they said, if I married again outside my husband's family.' Gita twisted her wet handkerchief in her hands. 'I refused to marry that boy, that semi-literate oaf who could not pass the fifth grade at school! I said I would die first. There was a big rumpus. My parents refused to take sides. I had nowhere to turn and it was only Shivani'—the floodgates opened—'your mother, who stood by me . . . and insisted on Na—your father giving me a job . . .' She turned her face away, looking helplessly at the wall. With her straight dark hair cut short, and all the trouble on her face, and her tears, she looked young, so young.

Mila sat very still. She did not know what to think. She did not know, then, that life often makes us do to others what we feel it has done to us. When Gita looked at her again, that horrid little predatory glitter was back in her eyes though she went on talking in her lost-waif voice. It warned Mila that this moist packet of helplessness and injury was out to get what she wanted. 'I am your friend,' Gita told her, lisping a little as she acted out a kindergarten drama. 'Poor baby, poor Mila! I want to help you.' She also wanted to help Shivani, her best friend. She wanted to protect the family . . . Mila heard the basic insincerity in all she said, but the light rhythm of her voice was as lulling as a song and she felt her caution melting, like the pink pond in her plate. And she was in terror because she was succumbing to that voice.

'I want to go home,' she interrupted the flow of words. 'Now. I want to go home now.'

'Yes, yes, of course,' said Gita, in tones so honey-sweet that she could have ordered Mila a waffle and poured her voice over it. 'I know you're hurting. I know what you must be feeling. We've spent so much time just talking together, haven't we? And you haven't finished your ice-cream. Never mind. We've got to know each other so much better, no? Just a minute, while I pay the waiter . . .'

Coming out of the restaurant was like coming out of a cave. Perhaps the sunlight was too strong for Mila's eyes, or the violent onslaught of traffic fazed her, or there was a dip in the pavement she didn't see, but she had taken only a few steps when her foot turned. She stumbled awkwardly, made a grab in the air. Nothing solid came to her rescue and she fell on her hands and knees.

Stunned, feeling the pain begin at her knees and palms, and the shock travelling dully up her spine into her brain, Mila stayed that way for a moment, her two plaits hanging parallel, her handbag and spectacles lying in the dust on the hot, tilting pavement.

Gita looked down incredulously at the kneeling girl. For a moment she remained an upright shadow in front of Mila, outlined in violet against the brilliant sky. Then with a little cry she bent forward to help.

'Don't touch me,' Mila said harshly, not looking at her. She picked up her glasses and slowly got to her feet. With a shaking hand she adjusted the tortoise-shell frames on her nose and the ground seemed to rise and waver and meet above the level of her feet. Her palms were bleeding. She rubbed them on her skirt, leaving dusty red smears on it. A little blood was seeping from the broken skin of her knees. Her left ankle throbbed.

'Oh dear,' said Gita. 'Oh dear, you're hurt! What happened? Here, let me help you wipe your poor knees.' Her wet lacy handkerchief fluttered in her hand as she bent over, but Mila turned away impatiently. 'I'll drop you home,' Gita went on. 'What happened? How did you fall? I'll come with you . . .'

'There's no need,' Mila cut her short. 'I'm not going anywhere with you.'

'What are you saying? The car is—'

'I'm going home on the bus.' With a blind, rough movement she snatched her handbag from Gita and began to walk away, the pavement jarring her heels with every stride.

Gita called after her but she walked on without looking back, her knees stiff, palms smarting, while her ankle tingled, grew hot, seemed to grow fat, then turned into a heavy lump of lead. She limped past a bus queue before she realized that these people were waiting for her bus. Stoically retracing her steps she took her place at the tail end of the queue, shivering in the sun. But when the bus came and people jostled her, she felt menaced by their proximity and panicked so badly that she had to hang on to the white railing at the stop. The bus drove away.

Another bus loomed into view. 'Move on, please,' said a man's voice behind her. Mila nodded and forced herself forward. The bus slithered to a stop and she was lifted into it by the press of people behind her.

Not till she sat staring out of a window in the rear of the bus did Mila's panic begin to subside, and she began to think coherently about what had happened. Her nameless burden now had a name. In a sense, she was liberated. She was like a soldier who had received marching orders after a long wait. At last he knew for sure where he was headed, what the odds against him were; but she was too young to take comfort in this. It grieved her immeasurably to think of her mother as a crazed avenger. Didn't she love them, then, that she had tried to strangle her and hurt Vikram? It was one thing to come to terms with Mother being sick; quite another to see her as a violent maniac. Mila's entire being rebelled. It was not true, not true! Yet she knew the slow inner parching in the wake of the worst, when that has been irrefutably established.

But it was not only her mother's derangement that was so fearful. Father rose before her eyes, and she desperately wanted to touch him, for luck, for immunity, like a child in a hide-and-seek game rushes unobserved from under cover to touch one demarcated corner of a wall and shout 'Tip!' But what if the solid wall that was to be her checkpoint and anchorage was not there as she made a dash for it? Her father, as she had known him all these years, dissolved at her approach. And this was more painful than her torn palms and lacerated knees, where the scratches and cuts were drying and puffing up.

15

Mila missed out on her third viewing of *Gone with the Wind* after all.

That afternoon her temperature shot up alarmingly, and for a week she did not attend school. She had fits of shivering that Dr Bakshi could not account for. It was not malaria. It was not a virus. It had nothing to do with her bruises, for which anti-tetanus shots were prescribed. It was nothing that the good doctor (who claimed direct descent from one of the seventy-two brahmin priests who had, with the aid of medicinal herbs, cured King Chamatkar of Anarta of his leukoderma) could lay his stodgy finger on. A nameless malaise had settled in Mila's bones.

In the first three days, when the fever was high, whenever she opened her eyes she found her mother at her side. On the fourth morning, when she woke up feeling much better, Mother smiled at her from near her pillow. Mila gazed up at her solemnly for a moment, almost woefully, then smiled back. A feeling of great comfort welled up in her as she basked in that tender, anxious regard. Mila felt herself relax, as in a warm salt bath. And in the long days that followed, she convinced herself that Gita had told her some real whoppers. Monstrous lies. It gave her a headache to recall exactly what she had said, so Mila drifted lazily on a tide of non-thinking. Shied away from the pain of those spilled secrets, corked them up tightly inside her and remained unresponsive to her father's searching glances and tense inquiries. (What had the bitch reported to him to ensure her survival?)

But to frame Gita as a liar, Mila had to knit back the fabric of her own being as if it had never been unravelled; and her arbitrary pigeon-holing of Gita helped to cancel out a cruel initiation. In the restaurant she had been Gita's victim, but now, somewhere inside her, a protective mechanism began to tick to prevent the truth about Mother from crystallizing. Or, more correctly, to banish it offstage so that it stood in the wings, waiting to return on cue. A small pocket of tension remained, but this related to Father, not Mother; and by the end of the week the only thing that really troubled her was her ankle.

To honour her minor bruises Mila had liberally tacked strips of Band-Aid on her limbs, but her ankle had escaped attention in the first days of her fever. Only when she tried to walk again did she discover how badly she had sprained it. At this point Soni took charge. Scornfully overriding all other suggestions, she prepared a paste of ground limestone and turmeric, and Mila's foot was encased in yards of dirty yellow bandage. In a couple of days she could put down her heel without pain, but a jealous solicitude over this particular injury made her hop and hobble from room to room.

The week came to a slow, leisurely end. The days had turned subtly golden. From her balcony the mango and tamarind trees appeared resplendent in a light that, even as she watched, grew brilliant one moment as at the touch of a wand, then softened the next. Butterflies made little unsteady circuits in the tawny air, birds streaked across the blue and Mila was almost persuaded that all was right with the world despite the dreary prospect of school the following Monday—when her mellow mood was shattered on the Sabbath, which turned out to be the date of a new insurrection and Nanima's most vivid triumph. It was also the last time that Mila saw her, except in her dreams.

That Sunday afternoon she had just appropriated the largest bolster on the living-room divan to rest her bandaged foot when the doorbell rang. Rather feebly, she thought. With her toes she gave her brother a dig in his ribs. 'Open the door, can't you?'

'Why can't you?'

'Because I've sprained my ankle, silly.' It didn't hurt at all now and she was due at school the next morning, but it was not time yet to ignore her wounds.

'Wasn't that the doorbell?' asked Mother, looking up from her book.

Reluctantly Vikram put down his stamp album and rose to his feet, but by then Soni had come wheezing in. In her laborious passage across the room she grumbled under her breath against the houseboy, who had not returned all afternoon from a single errand across the street: Khushal was a work-thief if ever there was one, pulling a face long as a pumpkin when asked to lend a hand with anything, worried only about the parting in his hair and the crease in his pants, the preening knave, while she had to run from one end of the house to the other to open doors.

The bell-shaped woman who stood on the threshold was familiar. Her printed cotton sari was gathered over her right shoulder and had a baggy, pillowcase look because it had not been starched. Her large eyes moved quickly round the room but she did not speak.

Mother was the first to recover from her astonishment. 'Saroj bhabhi!' she exclaimed incredulously. Mila fixed her tiresome glasses more firmly on her nose.

At the name, Nanima, who sat at an oblique angle to the door, looked up from her square of embroidery and removed her spectacles. Slowly she stood up, like a figure of doom, and it seemed to Mila that the chair she had just vacated had all this while been aimed at the doorway, from which her unwary victim would emerge.

When Saroj saw her mother-in-law standing in the middle of the room, the shock seemed to reach her diaphragm, for one hand leapt to a place under her breasts and stayed there. Then her whole body quivered, just once. It was as if she had been caught fast on the out-flung strand of an invisible web and Nanima, the grey old spider, had tugged the line, jerking her helpless prey momentarily dizzy.

'So,' said the spider from the centre of her web, 'you have decided to return.'

'I didn't know you were here,' Saroj's voice trembled between fear and defiance, 'or I would not have come.' Mila felt her aunt struggle on an unseen filament while Nanima stared at her, beady-eyed, from that terrible immobility she summoned to chastise stragglers.

The silence was mercifully breached by Soni, who, slapping her own cheeks, exclaimed to Saroj, 'My, oh my, have you looked at yourself in the mirror? Like a cow in the days of famine you look, with bones sticking out of your skin!' Indeed, what had once been a rounded countenance was stripped painfully by deprivation, and from under Saroj's high cheekbones the flesh had been pared away. 'You don't eat?' Soni continued vociferously. 'Everything is becoming so scarce and expensive, may our government be set ablaze! May the swindlers who rule this country drop worms! In my village—' She broke off, recalled to herself as Nanima turned her head towards her, and faltered, 'What, have you been sick?'

'You must come in, Saroj, you look very tired, you must sit down.'

Mother began to speak more quickly than she usually did. She was like a musician suffering an attack of nerves before an audience, who in battling for composure finds herself going faster and faster through intricate passages. 'Soni, fetch her a glass of water. No, make some tea. Or would you prefer coffee . . . why don't you sit?'

'So at last I have found you.' Nanima's mouth was shut tight, sutured into a straight line by thin vertical wrinkles. She opened it again to add, 'As I always said I would.'

Saroj's eyes, sunk deep in their sockets, touched Nanima's face in disbelief, then looked away wildly. 'You did not find me,' she said, and Mila could feel her efforts to hold herself together, as if there were a widening crack in her that would cause her final disintegration if not closed in time. 'I came to see Shivani.'

'It is all the same,' said Nanima contemptuously, 'now that you are here. Where is your luggage?'

'Mother, let her sit!' Shivani's voice was curiously off-key. Mila felt a wave of hysteria rise in her and kicked aside the bolster. Forgetting to limp, she walked to the pouf and settled on it at her mother's feet. Vikram, as if taking the cue from his sister, picked up his stamp album and left the room.

Shudders disturbed Saroj's body as if the fine, imperceptible threads that held her captive were pulled in vicious jerks. Her mouth was jelly. Gradually the trembling ceased. She had willed it. Mila felt a sudden respect for her. 'I took nothing from the house,' Saroj-mami defended herself, 'that was not mine.'

'Send for your luggage,' said Nanima. 'Our train leaves in two hours.'

Mila saw her aunt try to swallow, to restore the moisture in her mouth and throat. 'I am not going home with you. I am not going anywhere with you.'

'Home you are going,' said the hunter to the prey, 'with me.'

To give herself time, to gather her courage, Saroj-mami made herself examine the room, and her large liquid eyes eventually rested on Mila on the pouf. 'Mila . . . how you've grown. The last time I saw you was . . . when?'

'Last year, when we came to Pune during the Divali holidays.' Mila smiled politely. But Mami forgot to smile, and looked dazed. She took a deep breath to hold back her tears. 'Let me see,' she murmured, and her tardy smile was a painful grimace, 'are you as old as Sejal?' referring to her second daughter.

'I'm older,' said Mila with pardonable young pride, 'by three months.'

'But so much taller,' her aunt faltered, then clenched her hands at her sides and asked in a muffled voice, her eyes stunned with grief, 'How are the children?'

'*Now* she asks how the children are,' said Grandma harshly, a spiteful gleam in her eyes. She was convicting Saroj of failing her children, and was *pleased* that she had failed them. '*Now* the whore wants to know—'

'We'll talk about this later,' Mother said quickly, 'after Saroj has rested in my room.'

'We'll talk about it now!' Nanima slid down the silk of her gossamer web towards her victim. A skeletal hand seized Saroj's wrist and dragged her to the divan. 'Sit!'

Helpless, Saroj obeyed. Pain and terror passed across her face, and Mila realized that Mami had been afraid of her mother-in-law for fifteen years. Afraid every minute for fifteen years! 'I have nothing to say to you,' she said in a thin voice.

'But there are a great many things I wish to say to you,' retorted Nanima, still holding her wrist. They stared at each other, sat like a frieze taken down from the wall and placed on the divan. Saroj tensed herself and sat quiet, but Mila knew her mami could not match the other's will. She would be broken.

'So,' said Nanima, flinging away the wrist at last, 'I won't ask you where you've been for the past four months. No. What you've done I won't ask you, where you've lived, or with whom. These things can wait.'

Saroj looked up with a cry. 'I have done nothing to be ashamed of!'

'By penance only,' Nanima continued, 'can the soul be purified. But even if you lived for the next seven years in Varanasi, I doubt this blot of yours could be cleansed.'

This reference to her soul's perdition seemed to terrify Saroj. 'I beg of you, touching your feet, let me go!' One supplicating hand clutched at Nanima's sari.

Nanima shook out her sari with both hands, as if repulsing a scorpion that had dropped on it. Then she stood up abruptly, raging, her eyes slitted in accusation. 'When a mother of three children deserts them to—'

'I didn't desert them! I was driven out! By you! And by your son!'

'You lie, you wretched—'

'I was your servant for ten years! Ten years! For ten years your servant and then his, when he took us to stay in Pune. Yes! As a child I came into your house and my days were spent in cooking, cleaning, grinding, doing errands and being scolded by you! In your heart there was no room or tolerance for the smallest of my faults!' Saroj's words tumbled out in volleys of resentment. 'You even beat me with the cooking implements. One day you cut my hair because I burnt the rice, you remember? And because he liked to play with my hair, because he said it was my one beauty, you snipped it close to my head, though I screamed and begged you not to! And when I started crying, sitting in one corner of the kitchen, you jabbed me with a burning brand of wood and ordered me up again. It took a whole month for that burn to heal—look, you can still see the mark!' Saroj pulled up her blouse at the waist, and Mila pushed back her glasses to gaze, fascinated, at a brown almond-shaped scar on the pale skin. 'Many times you dragged me round the room—'

'Enough! Be quiet!'

'I'll not be quiet!'

'Silence!'

'I'll not be silent! I have been silent too long—'

'Infidel! Unclean! Viper!' shouted Nanima in supreme high-pitched wrath. On the last word her voice reptured into two, leaving a piece of sound hanging in the air.

Saroj stood up in a flash. 'Your servant! For fifteen years a servant, yours and his! What did he give me, though I worshipped the ground under his feet?'

'Give you?' shrieked Nanima. 'What did *he* give *you*, you ask? Ingrate! Rather ask yourself wherein you failed him. Wife and mother you are, and like a common slut you behaved—'

'Mother—' It was Mila's mother calling out to her own, in pleading accents, while Mila cringed on the pouf.

'About suffering you complain? If you have suffered, it is your fate to do so! Your actions follow you beyond the cremation ground as a calf follows his mother! From your fate you think you can escape?' Grandmother pronounced these words as if fatalism were not apathy, not atrophy, but a virtue to be cultivated, disassociation from the human predicament, a submission that was akin to pride. 'To all sense of duty you are totally blind that *suffering* drove you out of the house? Ah, a good thing your rotting, diseased womb was carved out before you could have a son! Because'—screaming—'the nose you have cut off your face you would have given him to hold! Set fire to his name and thrown the ashes in his face!' Yelling fit to burst her lungs, 'For you would have brought as much shame on his head as on the three worthless girls you've spawned!'

At the mention of her daughters Saroj sat down abruptly and stared before her. 'No matter what else is lost,' she said softly, 'my children I will not give up. I will not leave them with him or with you, who never had a kind word for them. You are as heartless as a butcher. In a brothel I will earn my keep, but I will come back for them and take them away.'

'Such words she speaks in my presence!' shrieked Nanima, her hair tumbling about her face. 'For my white hair the harlot has no respect! You think I don't know who is behind this outrage? You have been seduced by that idler, with your own husband's brother you have been unclean! Rolling and groaning on his filthy bed, spreading wide your legs for him! This body,' she clawed at Saroj's sleeve, 'this loathsome body will become ashes one day, but don't blacken your soul! If you drowned yourself in the confluence of holy waters at Prayag, you think the pollution of this sin will be washed away? Whore!' She raked at Saroj's hair, then slammed her head back against the wall and slapped her across the face as hard as she could. Tears sprang to Saroj's eyes, and her nose began to bleed.

'Stop it!' Mother was saying in a tense, unbearable voice. 'Mother, stop this at once, I won't allow it in my house. Stop it! I can't bear the sight of blood. Stop it!'

Mila suddenly noticed Vikram at the door, staring at them all, his mouth shapeless with fear. The next moment he disappeared.

Mother had covered her face with her hands. 'Take her away! Take sister-in-law to my room, Soni, help her, put her to bed.'

Soni pushed past Nanima to help Saroj, who was trying to throw back her head, choking and gasping, while thick blood fell on her lips and on her blouse and sari-front. 'Amrish is the only person I know,' she articulated with difficulty over her shoulder as Soni led her out, 'who has treated me as worthy, always. But unchaste with him I have not been, or with any other man unless,' she fought for breath, 'unless it was with my husband, because I allowed him to debase me.'

'May your tongue fall from its roots!' Grandmother screamed so loudly that the veins in her neck stood out and her face was distorted. She rushed to the door. 'May it shred into worm-eaten strips in your mouth! A piece of rope you couldn't find to hang yourself with? Harlot! Slut! Prostitute!'

All evening the battle raged, from room to room, echoing and resounding throughout the flat. There were pauses—gasps—for breath, then the shrill eruptions of hostility broke afresh, like splintering glass. Such wrath and sobs of fury. Such accusations and denials, challenge and vituperation, the flush of loathing on perspiring foreheads . . . They did not trouble to restrain their voices. They clashed at Wagnerian pitch, ransacking the vocabulary of hate, the words spattering the walls. Vikram cowered on his bed, armoured by his possessions, trying not to show how frightened he was as he buried his head in the trembling book in his hands. More than once Mila felt as if she were going to be sick; but at the same time a part of her was thrilled by the terrible ardour, the unsparing violence. Who could have dreamt that someone soft and pliable like Saroj could spit fire and defiance? Put up such a fight? It was tremendous.

But in the night the clamour subsided abruptly, in a way unforeseen by Mila. When Father let himself into the flat with his latch-key, he was just in time to see Saroj leave tamely for her husband's home with her mother-in-law.

This turn of the battle completely dispirited Mila. She felt Saroj had betrayed a great cause: herself. She had fought without belief. All that black murderous energy had meant nothing. The evening had not been a stern death grapple between two avowed enemies; rather, they had lived inside an improbable farce, which they had played out with a parody of heroism.

To this day I ask myself, why did Saroj throw in the towel that night? Why, when she had fought so hard, sacrificed so much, did she return to a man who had driven her to such desperation? I cannot conceive of a failure of courage more pitiful, a self-betrayal more wounding.

Do women like Saroj really cherish suffering—though to do that, according to our scriptures, is to succumb to *tamas*, unclean darkness? Deep down in her, in spite of the overwhelming protest of her soul, had my aunt believed that her first duty was to be a *wife*? That, as the merchant class ritualistically worshipped wealth, she must worship her husband as a mystic symbol that would eventually lead her 'straight to Krishna,' even if he was a monster of selfishness? Or was this acquiescence due to a lethargy imposed on us by the enervating heat, so that any effort beyond that of the vegetable asleep in the sod, demands an improbable resilience of will?

What I found even more inexplicable, that night, was that the other members of my family were content to be passive witnesses to such oppression. With the exception of Amrish-mama, not one voice was raised on Saroj's behalf. If my mother was too afflicted to do more than protest, why had not Father rescued her? (Where had he been that evening, why had he come home so late, *after* the battle? Where was that most virtuous of men on Sunday night?) Why had he not offered Saroj temporary shelter? Why had Roma, who was also suffering martyrdom, not joined forces with her sister-in-law? If this unconcern on their part was not callousness but fatalism, an acknowledgment that they were not answerable for others' sufferings because of a moral law in operation, so much the worse for them! In bed that night, Mila seethed with indignation and resolved, before she fell asleep, that she had no connection with these switched-off people who did not care enough. She would have nothing to do with them when she grew up!

But the saddest part of it now is that Saroj-mami never truly believed anyone *could* help her—unless a kind Fate intervened on her behalf. The fact that she was suffering could only mean that she did not deserve benevolence, that her sorrows were just retribution for some misdeeds in a past life. And who was she, a mere mortal, to protest against her stars? So the battle was lost even before it began.

Nanima's noisy, swirling departure that night was like a tide that had passed, leaving a shore littered with the débris of broken wills, shattered nerves, exhausted spirits. Roma, also a casualty, was to have followed her mother to Pune the next morning (was there no *limit* to our docility?), but she did not leave. For the next day Mother took ill again. Her first symptom was that she was unable to hold her breakfast. The bitter duel that had so thrilled Mila had scraped on Mother's taut and tangled nerves till they had snapped, and as the new day advanced she went charging again down the road to unreason: to end, before the month was done, in a brilliantly staged dissolution.

16

'Mummy! Mother!'

Sometimes in my dreams I still cry out her name as I stare up at a tall building in the sun. I am sickened by the weird angles at which the endless, swarming walls climb into the sky. The glittering lines waver, they run in the bleaching light. Diamond-edged, they swim in the blank radiance. They hurt my eyes. And again the cries 'Mummy! Mother!' ring out like an animal's howls of pain. Had mother heard me, would it have stayed her dark purpose? Or is the end plotted by stars at birth, as my elders believe?

As it happened, that morning when everything came to a screeching halt, Mila did not cry out. She had stepped out into the sun from the porch of the building, feeling curiously blank without her glasses and probably looking it, too. They were sitting out the weekend at an optician's, where a fat man with padded palms and conical fingertips had promised to mount them in the jazzy pink frames she had selected over Aunt Roma's protests. Without them she felt subdued, exposed, like a tribal belle with the tattoo marks erased from her face.

She was walking up the paved incline towards the vague green oval of the distant lawn when a man brushed past her, almost knocking her over, shouting, 'Look up there!' Mila wanted to say something rude to him; the maniac could have maimed her for life! But he had already shot past and was welded to the ground some distance away, staring up at the house and gesticulating frantically. So she looked up too, but could see nothing but the dense geometry of the eight-storey building. She shrugged, and turned to walk on, but something held her back. She retraced her steps towards the man and he took pen-and-ink definition as Gopalan, a retired solicitor and their antipodal neighbour on the third floor. His open-mouthed, upturned face registered alarm.

'What is it?' Mila asked him.

He threw a perfunctory glance at the girl. Either he did not recognize Mila or he dismissed her as a harmless hallucination in pigtails and faded denims, for he continued to stare up at the building, hand to his mouth, his brahmin's capacious middle draped carelessly with a checkered lungi. He had now ceased his insane exertions and was cast in the mould of a question mark, his stomach protruding, his round hirsute torso coffee-coloured in the sun.

Again she followed his gaze. After a long, eye-aching moment, she thought she saw a figure in blue poised on the parapet of the terrace. Was it dressed in blue? Or was she merely staring into the blue haze of the intolerable sky?

'What's the matter?' she asked again. Before he could answer a man came dashing out of the building. 'Sahib,' the liftman addressed Mr Gopalan, 'will you phone for the police?'

'How long has she been up there?'

'She called the lift to the fourth floor an hour ago—to take her up to the terrace.' Yakub sounded agitated. 'How was I to know? Will her family blame me? They did not even know she was gone from her room till I rang their door just now. Could I have refused to take her up—'

'Never mind that! Get back up there at once—'

'But I've just come down! She's locked the door to the terrace from the inside and will not open it!'

'What about the door from the north side?'

'Mehra sahib has the key and he is out of town. Six o'clock this morning he left for—'

'Well, break open the nearest bloody door!' Gopalan had raised his voice to a shout.

'As you say, sahib!'

'Take someone with you to help. Get Ram Singh up there with some tools. I'm going for the phone. Hurry!'

Both men ran into the building.

As Mila stood there in the full bloom of ignorance, a knot of apprehension slowly began to form within her. She eyed the building with false insouciance. It seemed too pale, consumptive, taking a sun cure in the intense light. Was its apparent solidity deceptive? Was it going to come down? No, not even the white glare could disguise its sturdiness.

It was strong and sound but . . . there was something aberrant about its familiar shape today and yes, it posed a *threat*! The sky was hurtingly bright. Spots of colour began to dance before her eyes, and she looked away.

She was surprised to find people gathering in little clusters round her. An excited hum of voices grew louder and louder. Windows were dotted with anonymous parchment faces looking out and up. The terrace parapet had acquired a stagey significance. People began to pour out of the building. They milled round, a shifting, vagabond audience. Nervous eyes jumped in hot, excited faces within the narrow orbit of her vision. Everybody stared up at the terrace but did not know what the overture was about, and were asking to be told in tones that rose, with panic and a quite delirious avidity, higher and higher.

'Have the police been informed?'

'Who is it?'

'From the fourth floor? That's the cancer patient.'

'You've got it wrong. The lady's been in and out of mental hospitals.'

'We'll need an ambulance.'

'The fire brigade, too. I'll run up and do it.'

'No, use my phone. We're on the ground floor.' Two figures detached themselves from the crowd.

'God, she'll kill herself,' said a voice behind Mila.

'Who is it?'

'Why not dash up to the terrace?'

'The door's bolted from the inside.'

'God, I think I know who it is—'

'Look, she's walking the parapet again. Can't someone reach her?'

'They're trying to break down the terrace door.'

Fourth floor, they kept saying the *fourth* floor. Could they mean . . . ? A clammy chill invaded Mila's body, as if she had just stepped into a wet swimsuit.

Again she tried to see. She could discern nothing. Without her glasses she was blind. Her short-sighted sense of the unbearable distance of the sky, of dim faces fading into a grey fog, made it hard for her to breathe. But this same physical inhibition seemed to lend her a new intelligence, a powerful inner vision, as if Shiva's mystic third eye had opened suddenly between her brows, and in this strange flowering of omniscience she was simultaneously two people, one gazing up, the other down. One, a fourteen-year-old schoolgirl anchored to the earth before a brick-

and-concrete monster with tingling copper arteries and plastic nerves, the other walking a parapet in mid-air, intent on placing her right foot before her left, her whole woman's body aware of the sky rushing away from her at a million miles a second. Aware of the speed and the void round her as a world of bright lines drawn swiftly in parallels, a vast rapid river of scintillating strokes that made her dizzy, hurried her forward to the point where she would have to *jump*.

Don't, Mila pleaded silently as she stood tethered to solid ground before the building, *don't*, a girlish plea that failed to ascend to the tilting parapet where, with frail hands, the woman was trying to grab the earth as it spun round her. But perhaps a pitching vision of a water tank, quick glimpses of a television aerial or a pastiche of tar and concrete helped momentarily to check the wild swoop of her vertigo, for death was again a word a mile long as she resumed her precarious pacing.

'Thank God the parapet's quite broad,' said a voice behind Mila.

'Not for someone who's determined to jump.'

'He's got to be crazy.'

'It's a *she*, not a *he*.'

'How can you tell, at this distance?'

Exactly, said Mila's foolish heart, *how can you tell*? And quickly she repudiated her earlier knowledge, cheating herself with hope. But the spasm passed. She knew. She knew with such crushing certainty that murk welled up inside her, despite the vibrant noonday sun, and in that moment she thought she saw her father pushing his way through the crowd. An urgent male voice said, 'Narendra, I'm afraid they think it's—'

'I know,' snapped the man, looking up. It did not sound like her father, but she knew it was he. The next moment she expected his calm hand to fall on her shoulder, telling her that everything was *all right, Mila*. That the woman poised up there would pull a secret ripcord to end her free fall, and float to earth with the sun making a translucence of her chute; and Mila would wake up from this nightmare to find herself kneeling again before the living-room divan, where they always brought her mother after each crisis had passed. Mila looked round for Father, but she had lost him. No, that was he, rushing violently into the building, his footsteps echoing. She wanted to follow him, but could not. There were sly, tentative movements in the crowd towards her now, side glances, nudges, but no one approached her. As in a dream, no face beckoned and she could reach out to no one, nothing.

She found she was biting her hand. Somewhere in the swimming green foliage an ambushed bird began to give out piercing, reiterated notes. As they ceased, the figure on the parapet must have moved spectacularly, endangering her vital balance, for Mila sensed the shudder that went through the crowd. A boy began to cry. Vikram? No, he was spending the weekend with cousins in Bandra. She closed her eyes and opened them on Grandma's ravaged face three paces away, but Nanima had left for Pune two weeks ago, dragging her daughter-in-law behind her.

Now there was a commotion near the rectangular space between the gate and the outskirts of the lawn. With a loud grinding, an ambulance backed to within a few feet of where Mila stood. She did not move, but the crowd parted before it like blundering cattle. Three men jumped down from the vehicle, then stood there staring, useless. A group of curious stragglers had wandered in from the road despite the main gate having been roped off by two policemen. A constable was bundling them out again. A man behind Mila was actually taking photographs, his camera making amiable clicking sounds as it recorded—what? The performance on the high wall? The audience? The building? Mila's fear, which smelled so hot in the sun?

What followed she registered with confusion. That was her house standing there, and though she was straining myopically at a relief map of balconies, grilles, pipes, air-conditioners, washing lines, they all hung before her in the flat dimensions of a poster, which bulged and dimpled as the woman walked the parapet. She was pursued by invisible demons, Mila knew, tracked by hounds, while faint sounds from below tried to claw their way up to her: the crowd-sounds, the traffic-sounds, the bird-sounds, the knocking on doors, the hammering on doors, the tearing of wood, the hum of the elevator. Ah, someone had mounted the last flight of stairs to the terrace. Someone was coming for her in evil haste, and again there was an ugly sliding to everything. Again all was sneeringly and debasingly caricatured as, with a queer rising disgust at the back of her mind, almost on the back of her tongue, she saw herself as the thing-to-be-destroyed. Ended. Her effacement was a must. They had entered her skull, explored each memory to its last lair—a monstrous invasion of privacy—and now was she expected to crawl back the long way to recovery? How many times can a path of agony be walked? All had been tried, and all had failed. Jump she must, eight storeys down. Where a crowd churned in various stages of dress and Sunday undress to watch the power of destruction. Down where in her denim jeans Mila stood pinned to the ground by a mountain of sensations, and where suddenly a woman began to pray: old Mrs Vaz, who looked like Nanima.

Old Mrs Vaz alone had the courage to acknowledge young Mila with a trembling touch on her head, before she began to mutter a Christian prayer aloud. So Mila, too, closed her useless eyes and from under her clenched lids sent voiceless crimson prayers in terror to a faceless Third Person, imploring Him to do something. But He was a complete stranger, and stone deaf.

With a sudden and heart-stopping cry the woman threw herself down from the parapet.

Mila opened her eyes and thought she saw her go over, head down. She felt the ugly physical sensation of a sharp drop, the treacherous hole opening beneath her, the betrayal of the wind as it disavowed its burden and the woman landed with an unearthly sound close to the ambulance.

Everyone began to run to and fro, cannoning into each other. Dismayed cries arose, and a new strange sound, as if a number of people were summoning enough breath for a yell which never came.

As the crowd closed in upon the place where Mother had fallen, with a furious clanging of bells a red fire engine drove in at a reckless speed and braked near the ambulance. The firemen jumped down and did nothing. The sleeping ladder and the water hoses, slack and coiled, hung stationary above the wheels.

Like a motionless stump Mila stood where she was, petrified by what she had witnessed. In her every bone she felt the fragility of that broken body, and between her bones and her clothes there was nothing. No flesh, no blood. And she was impaled to that spot by the limitless volume of her loss.

17

It was her father who helped Mila to walk to the still form under the blankets. People tried to shield her from the confrontation but he, knowing her better than they did, fought them. The figures grouped round the inert shape, like those at an anatomy lesson, heads thrust forward, shoulders hunched, rose and dispersed at her approach. A police officer, standing there with an open notebook in hand, also walked away. And Mila was permitted to gaze down on that silent face.

She saw it through a fog. It was turned slightly away from her, one ear and the plane of one cheek fully visible. She blinked hard at it, willing it to yield her some explanation for its uncharacteristic stillness. Why? Why? Mila had expected to find Mother splintered like a crystal; but except for a thin trickle of very dark blood that traced a lane from her nose to her mouth, her face was composed as in sleep.

It conveyed nothing. There was nothing here that Mila remembered. In no way was she indebted to that face. This was not her mother. She looked round her scornfully. Who were they trying to fool? This woman was intact. The body of a queen lay here, sheathed in purple blankets. Clumsily Mila knelt down, feeling strange and dreamlike. No, not a queen; a rag doll, with that arm folded at the shoulder at an odd angle to disappear under the wool. Perhaps they would allow Mila to paint a fresh face to replace this ruined one—not a face to rival its beauty, that was beyond her skill, but at least one that would smile again, a stitched smile. And she'd put something heavy behind the eyes, like the lump of lead in a doll's head, to make her open and shut them. And with the flat of her palm she could tidy out those peculiar bulges and swells under the purple membranes. Smoothe her out. Then fill her up with life.

Substitute bone fragments with clean, fresh straw. Use nylon thread because it holds better than veins, the stitches fine enough to be invisible. Use the needle with a magician's hand to trick the eye by keeping something moving—the illusion of an eyebrow lifting, false eyelashes fluttering, nostrils flaring with breath that wasn't there . . . Mila felt her father's hand on her shoulder and stood up numbly. Amazing how unsteady the ground was, with brown splotches crawling towards each other to meet at her feet. She stumbled.

Her father quickly put his arm round her and was leading her away when she glanced back over her shoulder. What was this? Naked feet stuck out from under the blankets. At the sight of them, so helpless and doomed, an absolute terror came over Mila. Her mother lay there entirely alone, entirely deserted. Without anyone or anything. Abandoned by all. Mila made to rush back to her, but this time Father would not let her.

She struggled. She screamed. Tried to tell him how vital it was for her to be with Mother, to press those feet against her cheek. She pounded his chest with both fists, then threw herself, kicking, on the ground. He picked her up, and after fighting him some more she suddenly lay still like a wooden idol carried in a procession. She lay inert in his arms all the way to her room, but once in bed she again began thrashing about. Dr Bakshi was sent for. She was held down while he gave her a shot that put her to sleep.

When Mila's eyes opened it was dark and there was a kind of suspension in the room, as if it had stood empty for years. She lay in bed, feeling oddly passive. Now she was floating, floating . . . her bed was a raft that rose fountain-like to the ceiling, swayed, tipped, then dropped so steeply that she began to whimper.

A hand steadied her raft till she was floating again. But before she could surrender to the gliding motion, the thought of prayer presented itself. Pray? So violently did Mila reject the notion that her craft lurched out of control and began to spin elliptically. She cried out loud. As it slowed again, she saw Nanima swimming alongside her with a laborious sidestroke, like a swimmer lost at sea, her face corpse-pale as she exhorted her to pray. Pray! Sobbing defiance at Nanima, swearing she would never pray again, Mila floated away . . .

The next morning my eyelids were resistant, like adhesive tapes, to light. Invisible bales of cotton seemed to weigh down my arms and legs. A thick fog pushed down on me, its presence almost palpable. Faces were pale moving clouds, voices were abstracted; so I missed out, mercifully, on many things. Like the endless drill of photographers, newsmen and policemen in and out of our flat and building. Death, the most downbeat of all endings, sets up a cacophonous flourish if it has been spectacular, and acquires a distinct commercial-pop potential for the survivors to cash in on.

For me that morning all sound was muffled, all sequences confused. Things happened in a flood, or not at all. I remember telling my wet pillow, at some point in time, that Mother was dead, and seemed to hear a distant chanting and wailing, as if they were carrying her beneath my window on a bamboo stretcher. In brand-new clothes, perhaps, with flowers in her hair, adorned like a bride, the sari and coconut and red *kumkum* powder provided by Uncle Amrish, according to custom. Yet I don't remember Amrish-mama's presence in the house at all. I do see Roma-masi sprinkling the floor space before my mother's bed with water, then placing a burning oil lamp there, because that was where the body had rested after its bath, before it set off on its final journey. And I do hear Soni insisting that she could discern footprints on the drying tiles, indicating that the soul had already taken rebirth: my mother was born again as a cow, the hoof marks were there for all to see, and hadn't she been as mild and gracious as that auspicious animal? I wanted to cry out to Soni not to be such a fool, but then I knew she didn't see anything because her tears blinded her.

And so, while many details are lost in a misty wash, as in Japanese paintings, others stand out like tall clumps of reed. It is fixed in my mind, for instance, that the body was left with the coroner for twenty-four hours. I am positive I was not shown Mother's prepared face, the still centre of the maunds of jasmines and champaks and Bangalore roses heaped round it, but then how do I know that the body had come back stitched and swollen? Neither did I see her borne away on a bier high on the shoulders of our kinsmen, tied to it by coarse ropes, but I distinctly remember someone proposing that Vikram be one of the pall-bearers, and my father emphatically vetoing this suggestion. But didn't Vikram carry two mud pitchers of burning coal to the crematorium? A jolt of electricity must have reduced the body to instant ashes, yet the picture before my eyes is of a cold wind playing with sandalwood fire fed by ghee from earthern pots. And a peepul tree bending over the pyre to drip slow tears on it, a drop at a time.

Everything diffused and muted and disjointed gathered into clear focus the day Mila received an early visitor. Gita walked unannounced into her room, and Mila awoke to alarm bells on danger. The first thing the intruder did, as Mila squinted up warily at her, was to open her handbag and hold out a glossy brown plastic case fitted with a zipper. Mila stared at it. Gita had remembered to pick up her glasses from the optician! Such forethought. So much provident care bestowed on an orphaned child. She had taken time off from a million distractions to do this for her. No one else had bothered about it. What a treasure they had in her! An indispensable genie.

Mila sat up slowly. Did the meddlesome witch expect her to beg like a grateful puppy for this tidbit? With a sudden movement she plucked the proffered case from Gita's hand. She wants me to put on my glasses now, Mila thought, because she wants to put on a mighty act for me. Surely Gita had rehearsed a big sincere show, she was going to play the Grieving Friend, feign syrupy despair, overwhelm the daughter with elegiac tears. Well, Mila would not give her that satisfaction. She dropped the case on the bedside table, sank back on her pillow and closed her eyes. She pretended to snore, zzzzz. But then she could not resist a swift glance up.

She trapped Gita in an extraordinary look. The mouth was trembling—that must have been in the script, too—but the appraisal in her eyes kept Mila posted on her real purpose here. Sitting up again she grabbed the case, tore open the zipper and inspected the false face more accurately through her glasses. Yes, Gita was inconsolable. Her hair was uncombed. Her bosom, decorously covered for once, heaved with noble distress.

'Mila.'

Mila turned away angrily, feeling justified in her evasiveness. Was Gita going to hang round here all morning?

'Mila?'

Why answer her? Why answer her at all? Mila felt a tremendous necessity for resistance.

For a moment longer Gita stood before her, irresolute. She was performing with the caution that comes of being miscast in a role. Poor awkward bitch, she could bring to her part nothing but a change of costume. But hello, she was snapping into it, she pulled up a chair to the bed and settled foursquare in it. Mila stared at one knee draped with the folds of a white sari. White for virgin. White for mourning.

Suddenly she felt like smiling: what audacious fiction, her coming to see her like this. What grotesque parody!

But Mila didn't smile and Gita suddenly seized her arm, like a policeman making an arrest. 'Let go,' muttered Mila.

Gita released her arm but brought her face so close that the room got claustrophobic. 'Mila, I tried to . . . in my own way, warn you, didn't I . . .? Even though I knew you would hate me for it?' Two tear trails appeared dramatically on her chaste, unpainted cheeks. 'You remember I warned you?' she repeated obstinately, bludgeoning Mila with her words while washing her hands of her guilt, like a female Pontius Pilate. 'I warned you, Mila, but you hated me for it.'

'Please go away.' She should have sprayed that moist face with pesticide years ago, or unleashed predatory bugs to eat up the whole insect and end the infestation. 'Go away!'

Gita didn't seem to hear her. More tears rolled down. Why was she making all this fuss, anyway? How archaic was a solitary jump from a parapet, compared to the sophisticated machines of self-destruction at man's command? Deliberately Mila instructed her thoughts to wander. Once during morning assembly Mother Superior had spoken to the girls about the nuclear weaponry that could obliterate *all* human life. And of the poisoning of man's environment, till there was nothing for him but to adjust to living with poison, like the carp in Lake Erie. Well, better that than the fate of the masses of dead fish off the Volcao beach in Goa, because they could not stomach the arsenic in the sea. Or the plight of the brown pelican, whose eggs collapsed with weakened shells because of DDT . . .

'Remember? Remember how your Gita tried to warn you?' For some reason the lachrymose lady was insisting on this admission from her. 'You never believed me!' Gita went on in a schoolteacher's voice, scolding, repetitious, as if she had at *last* arrived at the kernel of her lesson, while her pupil sat there in a brown study over the pelican.

When at last Gita left, Mila came out of her meditations with a sigh and a sense of escape. But not for long.

That afternoon—and on successive afternoons till Father insisted she return to school—Mila sat with sundry female relatives on a mat unrolled on the living-room floor. Towards evening they were joined briefly by the men of the family, who took their place in discreet rows apart from the women. A rotund brahmin pundit presided over them from a wooden platform at the head of the room, holy books and incense sticks at his side, chanting Sanskrit verses from the *Bhagavad-Gita* or reading from the *Garuda Purana*.

Not quite belonging to the female ranks, yet not as sharply divided from them by gender as the other kinsmen, sat Kailasbabu. A distant relative, he was welcome on the feminine fringe because, though gap-toothed and shabbily garbed, he could embellish the texts with toothsome little sermons. A mortal ripens like corn, he told them with a wonderful air of wisdom, withers, and like corn springs up again. And his whispered parables helped to shorten the long hours, while he, chronically unemployed, had all the time in the world. The congregation of captive matrons accorded him an arm's-length respect, and appeared to be in nodding agreement with everything he said. This did not happen often to Kailasbabu. Growing ambitious, he spoke at length of the Self which is inborn and inviolable, part of the universal Self to whom all perishable forms deliver themselves up as food, with death as the condiment . . .

But this was too much. His morbid discourse lost him his seraglio audience; it grew restive. Vast posteriors and narrow flanks heaved on the hard floor, seeking more comfortable positions, and voices, not necessarily hushed, rose from different parts of the room. 'Where did you have this sari embroidered?' And 'Turn your head, let me see. What, this earring was given by your in-laws at your marriage? The stones are not all that big. Its value must be what?'

On the twelfth day the spherical pundit was fed large yellow laddus (the holy man had a healthy appetite) and paid off. His gifts included a string bed and mattress, a water pot and dhoti, a sari and a garland of jasmines for his daughter-in-law to twine in her hair. On the thirteenth day more sweets, fetched by an aunt-by-marriage who lived conveniently above a sweetmeat shop of local repute on Grant Road, were distributed to the devout congregation, and when it trooped out the four corners of the floor mat were dog-eared—to indicate that the mourning was at an end.

Still they came, the visitors. I remember that cohorts of commiserating relatives and friends swooped down on us, dressed in white, intent on pitying us, opening their arms like benign ghosts but forcing us to our knees, doubting we could ever take hold of life again. Mr Jayantilal Prasad, kingpin of the Bharatiya Janata Party, turned up in a jeep painted fore and aft with the lotus symbols of his party. It was mounted with a giant garlanded photograph of himself, and fitted with loudspeakers bedecked with orange flags for auditory assaults on his voters. He had taken time off from his election campaign to call on my father.

'I do not believe in pseudo-secularism,' said the chauvinist Hindu by way of consolation, 'all our policies being based on ancient scriptural precepts honoured by Ram when he ruled from Ayodhya. Which is to say,' here he cleared his throat, 'that it is not for us to deny that the stars shape our ends. That which the gods have written on the forehead, who can reverse?' I watched him drive away in his caparisoned vehicle with his retinue of volunteers, who had sat out the visit in the jeep.

Others came. Hands touched my head, poor child, to learn of death so early . . . but I would have none of that, and turned away brusquely.

But it was not so easy to turn my back on a new, precocious knowledge: we are all transients, though we choose to forget. We are all dying, even those to whom death does not come with a ready clap of cymbals. A little at a time, I suspected with growing horror. Piecemeal. A fingernail today. A corpuscle tomorrow. Slowly. Perhaps your liver the next year. In secret. My smooth belief in eternity was rucked up, puckered, the creases permanent. We were all doomed. Fear lumped in my stomach at the thought. And my mother, so cleanly burned to ash, was now a dead weight on my heart.

At last Rayhaan came too, the laggard. Mila had expected him all along, and late one evening he stood before her in his thin muslin kurta. He did not speak when she rose from her chair to greet him, but rested his hands on her shoulders, and to her their weight alone implied a strength that did not require a grip. Ah, this magical power would help to assuage, to dispel the dread, the heaviness. He made her sit again, and she was alone in her room with Rayhaan.

But the first thing he told her was that he was going away. Again! He kept pulling the same old stunt over and over. Mila nodded politely, then bit her lip hard. What a disappearer he was, she told him in a shaky voice, always making off, always in flight. Where now? He gave her a penetrating look and sat down on the edge of her bed. Then he stared at his hands and answered her carefully, as if allowing for her youth, her vulnerability. He did not lack cosmopolitan experience abroad, he said, but needed to get closer to his roots.

'Then you'll be going to Iran?' He looked confused at her question. 'Your mother's ancestors came from Iran, Uncle Amrish told me.'

'Y-yes. But that was thirteen hundred years ago.' He needed to dig into his roots here, in this country. It was vital, for his work, to do this.

Mila nodded again, sagely, as if she knew how eminently sensible it was to give top priority to one's work in all circumstances. He was going to travel vastly in India, he went, on, from north to south, east to west.

'Oh.' It took time to compose her voice, to keep her faucet of tears tightly turned off. 'Like Tulsidas and Kabir?' she asked at last, brightly.

'Something like that.' Rayhaan smiled, but there was concern in his eyes, as if he knew he was hurting her. So she looked away and began to see him on his monastic tramp through India, routing and re-routing his march along paths that holy feet had walked in ancient times. She watched him approach the boundary of a village, call out the monk's salute, *Om Namo Narayana*, and stand still. A woman would place some rice, dal and curd in his bowl, but the jade was not as old as she should have been. Her eyes lingered on his face, her hand began to unbutton her blouse . . .

'Mila.'

She looked up in alarm. Rayhaan had risen to his feet, they had not talked about Mother and he was going away. He was like one of those figures in a dream, endlessly receding, and she groped for some means of holding him. 'No please, please,' the words were out before she could recall them, 'don't go!' She went into a panic.

He stood there looking at her with a dull gaze, and that was when she knew that behind the tautness, the fitness, the spine-straightness, there was misery. He was as wretched and lost as she was.

As Mila stood up it crossed her mind that if she sobbed and screamed loud enough, tore her hair and blackmailed him with emotion, Rayhaan would have to stay. She was debating whether it would be theatrical enough just to burst into tears, when he forestalled her. With a little inarticulate sound he covered his face with both hands. She gasped. She felt a strong internal resistance against accepting such a reversal of roles. She was shocked. With a beating heart she tugged at his wrist. 'Rayhaan?'

She did not know how it happened but she was sitting on her bed with Rayhaan at her feet. Was it possible for a grown-up man to weep? Alert to the peril of such a thing, about which there was something awesome, shattering, intolerable, Mila cradled his head against her breasts and held him, held him. Held him warm in a young city of strength. To shut out the pain. Smother the anguish, which was heavier than the enormous shoulders she tried to encompass with her arms. She held him so, and wished she were old enough and beautiful enough to have been the woman he had loved so well. As her capacity to share his pain reached a terminal point, new nerves jumped into life inside her, so that she ached with him all over again. Her entire body was filled with his aching. It settled implacably about her heart, forced its way down to her thighs, weighed down the bed under her. She held him so for a long, long time, till he was quiet. Then she opened her arms and in an ecstasy of renunciation she let him go.

18

Mila knew that a telegram had been despatched to Nanima bearing the awful tidings. Gita, so distraught with grief, yet with the admirable self-possession of one who keeps her head when others are losing theirs, was the one to nudge Father into performing that sad but inescapable duty. Perhaps she even signed the missive herself, her fingers tingling. And every day Mila expected the front door to crash back on its hinges, the matriarch to sweep in like a storm. She carried this dread into her dreams and saw Nanima, her head shaved, wandering alone on the banks of the Ganges. Drinking water from cupped, skeletal hands. Launching marigolds in coconut shells, casting offerings of milk, fruit, and her own hair into the sacred river. At one point she pulled Mila to the water's edge, intoned verses from the *Rig Veda* in her ears and exhorted her to embrace a watery grave if she wished to attain immortality. Forcibly she immersed the girl up to her nostrils, then walked away screeching, 'Jai Ganga Mata!'

But the dreaded visit never took place. To this day I'm grateful, for Nanima would have been too powerful to take.

The truth, which we learnt a few days later, was that she could not come. She had blacked out upon reading the telegram. When she came to, her mouth was pulled down at one corner, she had lost her speech except for a few dragging syllables, and the right side of her body was paralysed. A stroke. What malevolent mantra had Gita breathed over the arrow that had sped to find this mark? Aunt Roma was summoned by a frantic letter from Maganlal, the estate clerk, but she quietly and steadfastly refused to leave Vikram's side. So it was Aunt Saroj who perforce had to answer the call of duty. In obedience to her husband's wishes she tore herself away from her daughters, with whom she had been so briefly reunited, and journeyed on a rattling State Transport bus from Pune to Panchgani. There, with brainless benignity, this martyr nursed her mother-in-law back to health.

If change can be viewed not as a series of modifications but as a pair of photographs captioned 'before' and 'after', I'd like to think of Saroj-mami *before* my grandmother's stroke as enduring the purely tribal life of drudgery, childbearing and subjugation; and of Mami *after* the illness as someone who had succeeded in establishing a new autonomy. Surely her role of sole nurse and guardian (except for a rushed weekend or two, Ajit-mama kept away from his ailing mother) could have acted as a catalyst, allowing her to summon enough liberating energy for a new self-portrait?

But soon it was obvious that Aunt Saroj was attempting no such thing. She suffered, but did not feel she owed it to life to arrange things differently for herself. Let me take it for granted, then, that no stealthy thoughts of arsenic-in-coffee, or asp-in-the-bosom, or fatal falls-from-the-bed ever crossed Aunty's mind during her command mission of succour and mercy. For of course no one had thought of engaging a nurse. Why import an alien *paid* creature, a bossy low-caste minx in uniform into the house when there was a daughter-in-law to do all the work? Were women today lost to all sense of duty and shame, virtuous matrons reasoned with each other from a safe distance, that the old lady should endure the ministrations of a mercenary wench?

In Aunt Saroj's place, feeling murderous as I performed my grim, unaesthetic chores, I would have at least indulged in such tactics as delayed meals, scalding soup, unmade bed, blaring MTV—each an instalment of vengeance that traced a pattern of justice in my mind. I would have done anything, fed Nanima stuffed turkey, tied granny knots with her sheets, read aloud anti-religious tracts or erotic love scenes—even flirted with Maganlal, the estate factotum. He was a wizened shrimp of a man with a large cart-horse of a wife who presented him with a miniature Maganlal every year. (This was quite a scandal. Everyone knew that Kokila-ben, who brought forth men-children only, was so generously endowed that Maganlal feared his marriage bed as Christians had once feared the rack. The situation was only partially redeemed, it was whispered, after Kokila began to feed her husband a preparation of carrots fortified by the cerebellum of young male sparrows, a concoction of legendary potency. And when their third son met his death by drowning in the old-fashioned chain well on the outskirts of Nanima's garden—a favourite haunt of mine because it looked like a pretty little lattice house spanned by flowering bougainvillaea—she so overwhelmed the father with reproaches that in expiation he embarked on the next little Maganlal that very night.) Yes, there was much I would have dared in Aunt Saroj's place, but she accomplished nothing for herself.

At the end of the three months my grandmother recovered the partial use of her tongue, arm and leg. And at the end of three months Sarojaunty, spent and bedraggled, dutifully returned to her husband, children and repetitive household chores.

I think of her now as a Lost Cause. I grieve for her. And there is still this great, angry impatience in me that Aunt Saroj continues in vassalage to Uncle Ajit. Somehow she should resurrect her crusade against his dominion, and I would galvanize her into action if I could. Years ago, she wrote me in LA, at the time of Sejal's marriage, inviting me to the wedding. With my regrets I should have added slogans like 'Phalluses Are Fascist!' and 'End Penal Servitude!'

At home, Aunt Roma's overriding concern following Mother's death was Vikram. Even before the tragedy, she had sensed in him a severe emotional neglect, which was why he was flunking everything in grade IX at school.

Vikram was tall for his age yet gave the impression of smallness—as if perverse hormones caused him to ingrow, like an injured toenail. The shy, troubled eyes did not belong to that young face. He had a more refined, aristocratic nose than I did, marvellous teeth and a pale-olive pallor. He *should* have been handsome, even at that hobbledehoy age, but he wasn't. Something inside him was facing the wrong way and was arrested there. He did not step lively.

Aunt Roma seemed to understand that Vikram had none of the outlets available to a growing boy. He was a poor athlete, so the playing field held no magic for him. He had no talent for classwork. No close friends of his own age. He was not hooked on girls or drugs or fast cars or some exciting project like the preservation of the dying breed of lions in the Gir forest. Vikram showed no effort at independence, no search, however mindless, for competence or self-assertion. Instead of a battle for supremacy with the parent of the same sex, there was a pathetic dependence on Papa. At an age when he should have convinced himself that he was better than his progenitors, there was no hostility in him; on the contrary, he tended to reflect his father.

Surely life had been easier, now that I think of it, for Kishore. In the same class at school with Vikram, Ritu's brother had a vehement need to be different from his father. Where his pater was pious, Kishore strove to be profane. Where the père greeted everyone with palms joined in touching humility, Junior swore with gusto in three languages. Mansukhlal Motichand worshipped money. Kishore got rid of it as fast as he could and, with it, his father's honest-toil creed, his lip service to sweat-of-the-brow ethics when both knew very well that it was banditry that procured their wealth. MM bathed twice a day. Kishore despised water and could smell like a goat. The father was close-cropped under his Gandhi cap, and close-shaven. His dhotis were an immaculate white. The son grew his hair as long as he dared without getting into trouble at school, and looked scruffy as a matter of principle.

But Kishore's sartorial revolution had distinct phases. For one whole term he was seen in the evenings in psychedelic vests of varying lengths and frayed corduroy trousers, his non-conformist style a thorn in his fashionable sister's side. Then, overnight, he turned into a male model with carefully puffed glossy hair and neatly barbered sideburns, standing about negligently in beautiful floral shirts. This was how he had looked at the time I was deported to a foreign land. At his sister's wedding he had appeared, Vikram reported, in a fetching ensemble paid for by the widow he lodged with—striped yellow double-breasted jacket, pink shirt, wide tie and bell-bottom trousers in a bright brinjal shade. He had acted huffy when one of his father's guests mistook him for a film actor. This was unforgivable, for his soul was in turmoil at this time as becomes one aspiring to the divinity of art, not the commercialism of the movie industry . . . And so Kishore had devised enthusiasms of his own, illusions of his own. Slovenly, dirty and disgruntled, or spruced up and decorative in purple, he was as much in the swim of things as Vikram was out of them.

And this is where Aunt Roma stepped in, as Vikram's good fairy. If it had not been for her, Vikram's self-sealing might have taken a serious turn. His mother had made spasmodic attempts to understand him but, troubled in herself, had not listened to her son long enough. His aunt *listened* to him, and above all, she exuded warmth. He went to her not for pragmatic advice, but because with her he was a person. He came into his own. Strangely enough, the lonely woman was able to do this for her nephew. She was not able to teach him facts—which soon become obsolete anyway—but she gave him a kind of self-regard. She made him feel he was marvellous. She made him feel he was dear and delightful. As I consider this now it strikes me that my aunt is a woman of infinite compassion. Never at the receiving end of things, she has always been prodigal with her affections. And though I spurned her for trifling reasons, like the evening I found her knitting away while Rayhaan sat opposite her (when a young god beckoned, she could knit!), I now know that her life has been a saga of obligations fulfilled, loyalties honoured—why could I never see this before? And now that Vikram and I have subpoenaed her from Pune to Mumbai, I mean to hang on to her.

But after Mother's death, my aunt was the immediate focus of my resentment. I took it ill that she was alive while her sister was dead, just as it was an affront to me that my thick-set body ticked on, my little needs lived on, my heart persisted in beating, when fittingly everything should have come to an end. I hated the house, its fatal, menacing height. I feared the paved ground all round it, and to cross the spot where she had fallen sparked panic in me. I was outraged that Vikram willingly did odd jobs for his aunt, and thought it base when she smiled at him. What kind of second-rate grief permitted her to smile?

'Don't think you're going to take Mother's place in this house!' I screamed at her one evening when, finding me sitting huddled over a book in the semi-dark, she thoughtfully switched on the reading lamp. What I had been really doing was indulging in a weepy nostalgia for the days when things had been 'normal', and I resented this jolt into the present.

'You don't want the light?' Masi had asked gently. 'I'll switch it off.' But, suddenly vicious, I sprang out of my seat and clawed at her outstretched hand, shouting, 'Leave it alone! Don't touch it again! Go away, no one wants you here!' She quietly stood her ground, her eyes filling with sudden tears, and was about to say something when Father came in. At a nod from him she silently withdrew from the room.

There was a long silence. My father lowered himself slowly on the divan and motioned me to sit beside him. I shook my head violently and stood where I was. I did not want to go near him; I had stayed away for an entire month. I didn't want him to refer to Mother because I didn't want to see him exposed in any way. Were his nights for sleep, or did he lie awake and remember why she was not beside him? Did he re-learn her death, sweat over it in the indeterminate hours when night begins to bleach and your window is a growing luminous patch in the wall? His sorrows did not concern me. I could not bear that he should impose himself on me as the suffering widower. I wanted no confessions, regrets. He had mentioned her to me once or twice, naturally, in the context of one thing or another, and I had closed my face into a fist. I recoiled from any signs of unhappiness on his face.

I need not have worried. His calm had not deserted him. Was he a man overcome by his inarticulate grief? Was he making as little fuss as possible, or had he fundamentally not cared a damn? I had no answers. But if he was on trial by his own conscience, I did not wish to know it, but wanted him to retain the old manner, the old fortitude, the dispassion of a moral genius. Certainly his calm posture did not suggest the contorted emotions of men who play double games. Yet I was terrified of what I would find in him if I looked too closely.

He began to talk to me in a tired, oddly gentle voice. He had always talked to me seriously, man-to-man. Such speech was troubling but wonderful, and I now know that it was aimed at expanding my vision beyond the measure of my years. But for once I did not heed all he said. Stray words reached me. Something about moving over to a new flat. On Cuffe Parade. That's where Ritu lived. Where greedy building projects were devouring land newly reclaimed from the sea. I disliked that part of the city; totally flat, and barren of trees. Too self-conscious of having *arrived* to be informed by any kind of graciousness. And the girls who came from those tall new skyscrapers were a dull lot. Like all uninteresting people, they reflected nothing but their possessions. They—but I was now startled by what he was saying.

'Would you like to go away then, Mila? For a short while?'

'Go away?' I was stunned. 'Where?'

Patiently he repeated what I had missed out on. His brother Harish, settled in Los Angeles, married to an American woman, would be willing to . . .

'No!' I cried, trembling. 'No! I'm not going anywhere. And you can't make me!'

'I don't want to make you do anything you don't want to,' he said quietly. But in the light of the single reading lamp his face was bleak. He rose rather heavily from the divan and walked out of the room. I stared after him. Even after Mother's death he had not opened, by a fraction of an inch, the door behind which he lived his secret life.

19

When Mila went back to school ten days after her mother's auto-destruction, she discovered that an epidemic of rumours had hit the convent. The spreading virus had infected not only the girls in her class but the entire senior school, and she felt a spotlight was trained on her. She wanted to hide. If her mother's fall had fractured her life, she was also subject to the violent shame that breeds in a school culture where singularity of any kind is shunned.

Eager eyes watched her at assembly. Necks craned to catch a glimpse of the motherless freak wearing a dark navy tunic and a wan glowering face. So far there had been only flying reports and newspaper stories—grotesquely distorted—so, naturally, much more could be deduced by just staring at her. Isn't her face too pale, do you think, girls? And goodness, why that scowl? See that girdle, deliberately flying at half mast—or had it always circled her hips instead of the waist? Quick, another look. How about her eyes? Dry behind the fancy new glasses, not particularly grief-stricken. The chin rather challenging than otherwise. Can't say she has lost much weight, isn't that funny? Expected her to look like a skeleton. You *did*? Didn't *you*?

She heard the thunder of their whispers. Felt their covert stares trying to define signs on her person that fate had dealt her a dastardly blow, that her world had convulsed. So in turn she made the viewers invisible by not seeing them, not hearing them. Yet in her own eyes Mila remained exposed: large, opaque, a mountain looming above schoolgirl hedges. So concentratedly did she scowl, eyes front, with a stiff British upper lip, that she could have been mistaken for the school bully by a new arrival. She could not help it. The feeling of encirclement was stifling. Even the lesson from the desk seemed to be chosen for her: the Lord giveth, and the Lord taketh away, blessed be the name of the Lord.

In the classroom she found it easy enough to deflect the quiet sympathy of her starched and rustling tutors. She resisted all their efforts to draw her out, to involve her in the mysteries of French verbs or the parliamentary system of government. Nor did she unbend with her classmates, though an orgy of friendship awaited her. She was the object of such swooning curiosity that Mila could have, in those first few days, commanded a bevy of page girls to fetch and carry for her. They were more than willing to share a textbook or a slice of mango pickle with so uncommon a creature. Or give her, *sotto voce*, the dates of Emperor Aurangzeb while Sister Mary Francis, becalmed before the blackboard, awaited her answer with chalk poised between her fingers. But Mila rejected all such advances, cultivating a self-conscious brooding to get away with inattentiveness in class, slipshod preparation at home.

She stared stonily at Nellie D'Souza when, attempting a friendly smile, Nellie offered to enrol her in the school choir, which she conducted at rehearsals whenever Sister Patricia was absent. 'I'm not *exactly* in the mood for singing,' Mila said with a nasty scathing edge to her words. Nelly stammered that it wasn't *that* kind of singing. 'What kind is it, then?' she asked, knowing well that to the Christian girl who sang a lovely rich contralto that soared to the rafters and the ceiling and beyond them to the sky, the hymns and psalms and cantatas were not singing, but something more. Prayer, a paean to life. But her mother was dead! She was right to wipe that idiot smile off Nellie's dusky face.

With the same harsh perverseness, Mila pulled away from Baimai Buhariwalla when she tried to press a tomato sandwich into her hand one afternoon. It fell to the floor and Baimai had to pick up the mess. And just to look at Ritu's face made her feel vicious. Mila hated the greedy glitter in her eyes. A morbid inquisitiveness showed through her mask of solicitude. Ritu wanted an intimate account of the self-slaughter, did she? What business was it of hers how Mother had dismantled herself? Was she expected to describe that drop to extinction in poetic images, to pretend it had been a blissful cop-out, like flowers drifting into the sea? Mother had been sick, for goodness' sake. The world had gone awry in her skull. What more was there to talk about?

But alone Mila worried like a dog with a bone: *Why* had she done it? What triggered the leap into oblivion, when they all had thought she was getting better?

Today I try to be wiser, today I discourage this unfruitful chase after reasons. I try to accept an existential rationale for such an act of dislocation—like the activist young who have no reason for their acts of violence. The act is sufficient unto itself. Who needs to seek beyond it?

Then I have to admit, miserably, that I still do. And get dusty answers for my pains.

I remember that my weekly marksheets faithfully recorded my falling scholastic standards, and at last I was summoned for an interview with Mother Superior.

About the head of our school I recall a parent's cynical observation that she was making laudable efforts to turn out girls fully prepared to meet the challenges of an era that had died five decades ago. Even to the schoolgirls, Mother Superior manifested an unworldliness that made them laugh over the naivete of a grown woman. But on more intimate contact with her we were conscious of a softly applied power. A steel-like quality behind the apparent mildness, the ivory-tower isolation, the strange disengagement. And if we thought that anything could get past her inward gaze, we soon discovered that nothing really did. No problems could be pushed under the rug. No issues glossed over, no frailties disguised.

Her voice was soft. Whatsoever thy hand findeth to do, she said to my foolish averted head that morning, do it with thy *might*. I threw a covert glance at the rosary at her waist, where her hand rested. The rosary was of black beads, with the Lord our Saviour crucified in miniature agony on a dangling cross. Her hand was large and white, and stippled with liver spots. *She* was white and pink, unlike Sister Mary Francis, who came from Kerala, and whose skin was the colour of honey made by bees who feed on purple flowers. I know you carry a burden, said the gentle voice above my head, but release it to Him who is willing to carry all our burdens. Here I would have sniggered if I had dared. Wouldn't I *try*? I felt her caring hand on my head, telling me I had engaged her concern. I brought out my much-rehearsed scowl, but her touch undid me and the tears welled up.

I muttered something inaudible. She raised my chin with one finger and after a searching, enveloping gaze from piercing blue eyes, which I was forced to endure mistily, she allowed me to go. I remember that gaze today. And wonder if the challenges of one century are so different, after all, from the challenges of another when we still need to meet pain, fight panic?

My marks did not improve. Aunt Roma remonstrated mildly. My father signed the telltale weekly sheets impassively. There was no doubt that a major shift was taking place in his mood. Was he emotionally exhausted? Was he human after all, did he need time to examine the meaning of what had happened, to contemplate the future? Only once more did he broach the topic of Harish-uncle in Los Angeles, and I made him a scene. And Father, whose words were always anchored in sanity, whose direction was towards equipoise, who could by a look swing clangorous outcries back to reason, got up and left the room. Flat in the middle of my wailing, he walked out on me.

His silent retreat was not reassuring. It was a kind of defeat. I picked myself off the floor. As I splashed my swollen face with cold water, I wished wretchedly that I could pull the washbasin's plug and swirl down the drain. I consoled myself by making faces in the mirror. Mocked my own verdict that I wasn't beautiful. Then I sat on the chair in my room and took off sharply, without a seatbelt, into my reveries.

Rayhaan. Shaped like a Y. I imagined the muscle-play of his broad back. There was nothing watered-down about him, as there was about other Parsis of pale pigmentation. I willed his hands on me, fluid and sure, knowing every detail of what they wanted and prepared to plead or fight for it. But he was drifting away . . . I flung myself at his feet, begged him to take me with him, made him abject promises. Offered to wash his saffron robe, rinse his begging bowl, cook him spartan meals under the sky—for there was confusion in my mind between Rayhaan the omnipotent lover, Rayhaan the wandering monk, and even Rayhaan the defrocked Zoroastrian—why did I insist on his Parsiness when it meant so little to him? But since in any disguise Rayhaan was pursued by beautiful and amorous women, it was more comforting to think of him preaching salvation to congregations of the faithful than to imagine him collared by eager virgins to conduct private services in bed.

But where was Rayhaan?

He had taken off abruptly one morning, carrying only one small travel bag. So we were informed by Mrs Choksy, her face smug when she called on us to release this bulletin. He had left her with instructions to have his books crated; he would send for them, and for his word processor, as soon as he could. That was all. And his landlady buttoned her mouth virtuously, as if to say you can't expect much of young men these days. The rest of his effects? She could do with them what she pleased, he had told her.

'Even his clothes and things?' I had persisted.

She gave me a sharp look, the way a shopwoman looks at you for size, before she said shortly that he had asked her to give them away. I knew instantly that she would sell them. Choksy had an itching palm. But being also a woman of ramrod morals, she would give part of the receipts to her favourite charity—a home for fallen women.

'Did you know,' she suddenly shot at Aunt Roma, 'that Mrs Shastri cooks flesh in her home? Never mind the holy airs that woman puts on.'

Roma looked bewildered. 'I'm not even sure who Mrs Shastri is—'

'Shivani used to have them over, I believe,' and here Choksy gave a high, neighing laugh, 'for *vegetarian* meals. Mr Shastri weighing two hundred pounds, she a faded creature. But I can always tell.' And tell she did, at length, on poor Mrs Shastri. And then on a neighbour's daughter who had slept with her husband-to-be before the lawful wedding night— and the poor mother believing she was marrying off a virgin! 'Eating sugar in her mind,' as Choksy put it, 'that her daughter was Sita pure and simple!' As she spoke I imagined her training a powerful pair of binoculars on other people's kitchens and beds, or poking around with an umbrella, disturbing maggots and starting wriggles at ferrule point.

Rayhaan had been a generous lodger, meeting all her demands though he knew she was fleecing him, but when she spoke of him again it was to complain of the hussies who still turned up at immodest hours to inquire after him, or kept her running to answer the phone. She ran a respectable house, she would thank them to remember. Here Choksy rose stiffly, sour with duty done, and took leave of us.

Even today I have no idea where Rayhaan is. Which is why whole scenes seem to be missing from my life, like a bad movie made from a good book—not with spare elegance, but with careless editing and desperate abridgement. There are times when the fear that I may never see him again arrests me in mid-action. My life stands still at such moments, without even the illusory movement of a stationary train that appears to be coasting only because another train is speeding the opposite way.

20

That the drama of the triangle cannot be sustained indefinitely is common knowledge. It cannot be borne as a permanent reality; it has to be resolved. Thus when the apex of the triangle I had glimpsed was sliced off by my mother's death leap, I seemed to be waiting, grimly, for the denouement. The wife had been eliminated from the cast. What was to follow?

The movement of the next few scenes was arthritic. The stream of mourners slowed to a trickle. Even Gita's visits were infrequent, though when she did come I noted the new keenness with which she appraised our household items, from the antique wall mirror in its intricately carved wooden frame (Father had picked it up on his last trip to Cochin) to the raw-silk draperies in the living room and the embroidered hangings from Bhavnagar. And I could almost hear her mentally listing Mother's collection of silver: Three dozen engraved fruit-juice glasses. Ten round platters, sundry trays, mugs and sweet dishes. Two wall plates, and one plaque of beaten silver from Tehran. One pair of silver elephants with raised perforated trunks to hold a quiver of incense sticks. One jar of long-necked elegance to be filled with rose water. One tiny pot balancing a dancing peacock on its lid, in which Mother had moistened the vermilion powder for her forehead. One hexagonal silver box with segments for betel leaves, nuts, lime paste and a gleaming nutcracker . . . I did nothing to interrupt Gita's stealthy inventory, but was determined that she had no future in my father's house.

Then things began to happen. Gita fell ill with the flu—as a neurotic bid for attention? She had been fiendishly energetic, I imagine, and her solicitous employer bundled her off to Pune for a fortnight of well-deserved rest. I heaved a sigh of relief at her departure. Gita had brought with her Pinteresque touches of menace: of veiled intentions and smiling masks hiding the same sinister face. All her attempts at friendliness were thinly disguised adventures in self-promotion. I would have vilified her at point-blank range, had I dared, but I had to watch my step now. Nothing and no one could be trusted.

The days of my respite sped by too quickly. At the end of two weeks the angel returned minus her wings (I saw at once that Gita had decided to leave them behind, and take no more of my nonsense), plus a few extra pounds in the right places. Yes, she had put on weight and she threw it around as never before. Now that she had made up her mind to handle the brat differently, she no longer played games with me; she was just the brisk contender.

In a sense the games had been fun, and I had perversely enjoyed the lines of dialogue Gita had scripted to bamboozle me. For instance, when she had striven mightily to play Best Friend to the poor motherless child I, instead of acting the Grateful Waif, had played the Threatened Orphan and so manoeuvred Gita into playing the Child Persecutor. If, in her recurring dramatizations of the underlying struggle, Gita had cast herself as Guardian Angel, I needled her into enacting the bloody-minded Thirteenth Fairy. No matter how often Gita changed her script, I had managed to sabotage her efforts.

But now all this was at an end. The *bhai-bhai* phase was over and Gita had severed all diplomatic relations, all pretence at effusive accord with me. Her about-face was truly acrobatic. Overnight she turned militant. In the euphoria of sudden power (what had intervened to make her feel flush with success?) the female commando took charge. Pointedly—as if she had already ousted her rival in a successful coup—she ignored the continuing presence of Aunt Roma in our home, her legitimate role in family affairs. She was not in residence, and it must have frustrated her bitterly not to be installed in state, but she nevertheless functioned as the Establishment. Vikram, somehow, had a natural insulation against her, but my defiance never failed to invite a repressive response. We were at last in frank collision, Mila versus Gita, and we suffered quite openly the pangs of requited hate.

The result of all this was that I became, to myself, an instant heroine. But not painlessly; not without a sense of desperation and confusion. It is horrible to be embattled when you are so young. It is sad to learn hate at any age. For all my bravado, I was really no match for the woman's cunning self-serving. I was made miserably aware, at times, that all I could do was yelp and bark at her like a resilient and mistreated pet. I kept it up only to make a competing and attacking noise, and I know that Gita really bested me in every major confrontation.

Moreover, the loneliness was costing me dearly. My greatest need was to be able to lean, body and soul, on people I trusted. I wanted the ground to be firm under my feet, the branches I swung from to be safe, my universe to be warm and friendly. And I felt, with a childish groping, that behind the people I valued there should be another being, hugely concerned with me, and that these lovely people had been ordered for me simply to pass on the gift of His presence.

In the homes of most of my friends, with a profusion of aunts and uncles under the same roof, cousins and cousins-in-law, parents and grandparents, I had felt this warmth from one or another source. But my father's parents were dead, and between the three sons and their wives and broods there had been dissensions and factions. One brother had emigrated to the States, and the joint family had splintered into separate Western-style units before I was born. But always there had been my father. Throughout my childhood his voice had rung out sure and deep, like the notes of the conch I heard echoing at sundown in the hills of the Kashmir valley during our stay there. But now I could not tell whether Gita's warlike stance met with his approval and was a conspiracy hatched by them to bring me to heel, or if he was so anaesthetized by the perfumed female at his elbow that he could not see he was selling me short.

When I look back on this period, on my feelings of grief, anxiety and anger, I understand how difficult I must have been to live with. I was aggressive—and I still don't believe that the meek are blessed. After a week or two of average conduct, which was already contentious enough to alienate a saint, I indulged in bouts of rage. I was merciless with my victims—anyone I could bully—and used every opportunity to abuse Vikram, as one does a weaker neighbour to affirm what is left of one's dwindling power. But my brother was learning to stand up for himself. I remember that once, after being worsted in an argument, I flung his stamp album out of the window. Vikram rushed to the door to retrieve it, but on his way out did not hesitate to empty the tumbler of water on my painting, left to dry on the coffee table.

I was turning out these messy watercolours every day. It was a kind of rehabilitation rite, an instinctive therapy of some sort. Perhaps it was good that I could work out some of my rage and frustration by making these grotesque daubs. They were something of my own, not pretty, not engaging, but an offshoot of my interior life. What was not so good was that I pretended the distressing results were wonderful to behold. Any criticism of my work, so frightfully vivid to me, made me indignant. And I defended it passionately against the blind and the thick-skulled.

One Saturday Roma-masi had the unfortunate idea of inviting Ritu to spend the day with me. I was far from grateful to my aunt. Why did she persist in the fiction that Ritu and I were great friends? Ritu arrived sprouting on her chest a huge bow of some shiny material in lieu of other, more genuine blooms. All morning she bored me with her giggle-chat. Her talent for fraternization almost prostrated me. I couldn't, in decency, ask her to shut up. I couldn't run off by myself to the next room and read or paint. Valiantly I struggled not to allow my feelings to overcome my manners. How does one learn to listen with a vacant ear?

Once I yawned frankly and cavernously, but it had no effect on Ritu, who nourished, in her flat bosom, a great desire for romantic entanglements. She was recounting a first-person experience in an interminable monologue, giggling and grimacing in a manner intended to be arch, while it was plain to me that she had pinched the whole episode from a story she must have read in a cheap magazine. But what really incensed me was that she constantly tossed her head sideways in an effort to turn her profile to me when speaking, because a boy had recently complimented her on the shape of her nose. It showed traces of Moghul nobility, he had told her. Or so she told me. But I had met Raju, and couldn't believe he had said anything as poetic as that. He was too stupid and illiterate, I told Ritu. He didn't have that grasp of language or history. And his face simply blazed with pimples, I added spitefully.

'Suppose I tell you point-blank that he's in love with me?' Ritu had said with a desperate toss of her head.

I told her, coldly, that I didn't believe that either, and I stared at her nose resentfully. It looked like an ordinary nose to me, but she thought it was something to take pictures of. If anything it was a little too assertive, a high Pathan nose; and with that hint of a bump in the centre of the bridge it barely escaped being a Parsi nose, which was almost as bad as a Jewish nose. She now tilted her head back and gazed at the far ceiling, conscious of her audience as she narrated her rehash of spurious passion. From her point of view she was a Moghul beauty. She looked ghastly to me. Should I slap her face? Unravel that neon bow? She made me feel so gloomy. I had no impulse whatever to communicate with her. I was getting ready to do something outrageous when she herself gave me the opportunity.

Propped up on my desk between the Hindi-English dictionary and a pile of exercise books was a painting, two days old, which now caught her attention long enough to interrupt her monologue. 'What is *that* supposed to be?' She pointed a rude finger. 'A *house*?'

'It happens to be one,' I said with a touch of loftiness. It wasn't as if she were horribly artistic herself. In school Ritu's art book was covered, simply covered, with hideous blotches. So this was an obvious case of sour grapes.

'It doesn't look like a house,' she giggled.

'It does!'

'It doesn't.' She got up. Resting a meagre flank against my desk, she went up on the toe of one foot, as they do in ballet classes, for a better look at my haunting work: at yellow vertical lines suspended precariously in a smudged blue void, at the drunken, runaway roof, the single star dislodged from its orbit to lie on the crazy doorstep, the moon overhead disguised as an alarm clock. All of which seemed to excite her mirth.

'What's so funny?' I was standing close behind her in a state of suppressed fury.

'*You* painted this?'

'It happens to be my painting,' I said with icy dignity, making it clear enough, I thought, that I did not care to discuss its artistic merits with her.

'It's like no house *I* have ever seen.' And she got the titters again.

That did it. I got hold of her dress at the back and a good grip on her hair and shook her. As she screamed and tugged, I let go of her hair and seized her famous nose between my fingers and gave that cartilaginous Moghul appendage a good tweak. But she struggled free, so I grabbed the nearest thing at hand—an old Japanese parasol that hung from a nail on the side of my wardrobe—and, seemingly divorced from any personal decision about it, I hit her a crack over her right shin. She gave a little yelp of astonishment, then began to howl. Shouting that she was jealous of my artistic potential only because my paintings were good, *good*, did she hear?—I whacked her again. The brittle rod snapped just under the handle and, shrieking, Ritu shot out of my room as if on castors. I raced after, yelling, waving the severed head of the parasol.

In the living room Aunt Roma caught up with her. My friend's back was half turned to me, her cranium convenient to the trajectory, so I threw the handle at her from the door. I missed only because the hysterical fool was dancing up and down, as if on a hot griddle. And despite all of my aunt's efforts to quieten her, Ritu continued to scream and shout, as if thugs were after her blood; and between her cries she insisted on being sent home at once.

'Hush! She didn't mean it,' said my aunt. 'Come here, Mila, and say you didn't mean it.'

'I did!' I was panting and puffing, but I felt just fine. Never better in my life.

'Say you are sorry—and go back to whatever you two were doing.'

'But she was hitting me!' cried Ritu. I delivered a superior half smile in her direction. It afforded me a base kind of satisfaction that she still cowered behind the slight figure of my aunt.

'I am not sorry.' I was adamant. After all, I was the injured party.

'I want to go home!' cried the ninny.

'Do! And stay there next time.'

'Later, after your lunch,' said my good aunt anxiously, and even fetched a Band-Aid packet to honour my foe's invisible wounds. But the ass was unappeased.

'I want to go home *now*.'

'Let her!' I folded my arms across my chest. 'Makes not a jot of difference to me.'

I hovered on my balcony and watched, stiff-rumped, as Ritu stepped into a taxi four storeys below, accompanied by Soni. When it drove away, I burst into tears. All fight was suddenly drained out of me. She would tell on me, I knew. She would tell her mother. The girls at school would hear of it on Monday. Well, let her call the papers, too! As I turned back into the room I stumbled on something. A shoe. It was quite old, with tiny holes dotted in a scalloped pattern across the broad toe. I scooped it up and flung it at the opposite wall, found its twin under my chair and despatched it in the same direction. Then I picked up my painting from the desk and tore it in two. Slowly. As if I was performing a rite.

At school on Monday Mila swaggered and strutted in the lunch hour, to prove that she in no way feared the whispering campaign Ritu had unleashed to malign her. But in class she did not shine. She had not prepared her work. The second time she was reprimanded, very sharply, by Sister Mary Francis, she cheeked her back and was ordered to stay behind after school. Mila awaited her in the deserted classroom at the end of the day, hostile, rebellious. Sister Francis set her a portion of history to learn, then floated serenely out the door.

Mila leaned her elbows on her desk and blinked back sudden tears. Everyone and everything had been hateful. At home there had been a rumpus over Ritu's visit, though it was *her* palm that had been scratched by the thick spokes of the parasol as she brandished it. She had welts to prove this, she could die of a poisoned blister, but no one had thought to nurse her hand. No one loved her. If only she could provide herself with a rescuing prince: Rayhaan. But princes were perennially in short supply. With a sigh and a sniff she picked up her history book. The Taj Mahal, she read, was a rich blend of Islamic and Hindu styles of architecture. The red sandstone used by former Muslim rulers for their forts and palaces had been rejected by Shah Jehan in favour of white marble . . .

Mila's hind quarters were paralysed with too much sitting, her stomach rumbled with hunger by the time her jailor came to release her. With stately rustles Sister Francis advanced to her desk and handed her an envelope addressed to her father. She was told to pick up her book and be off.

The letter open in his hand, Father was speaking gravely to her after dinner that night when Gita breezed into the room. Mila scowled. She had not heard the doorbell. Had the intruder been awaiting her cue in the wings? She was emphatically not welcome in Mila's sanctum but Gita sat on the bed, swinging her legs. She learnt quickly of Mila's disgrace, held out a proprietory hand for the letter, shook her head over it and sighed as she looked up at Papa, allowing him to see the depth of her anxiety over his offspring. At the same time the sari end slithered down her shoulder, and the topography thus revealed was interesting: high round breasts with pointed nipples in a white katori-style choli apparently made of cellophane, under which she wore no bra. And on her neck: a purplish bruise where, no doubt, a gruesome vampire had feasted his fill.

Papa's and Floozie's glances collided and held. God, what was this? What were their eyes saying? Though Dad stood aloof from the bed there was a sense of dalliance, of distances overcome between him and Gita, of a coming together over obstacles that had once barred the way.

But now Gita was looking at her again, asking pointed questions, and it troubled Mila profoundly that Father seemed to find this reassuring. When the phone rang in the passage, he hastened to answer it.

Mila adjusted her face for polite, blank listening as Gita berated her for her shocking behaviour, then seemed to offer herself as a model for future conduct. Mila raised her eyes about four inches above Gita's head, to the halo that was not there. Gita caught her squinting into space and chose this moment to recall her dearest friend. How would Shivani feel, she asked, her voice suddenly tremolo, if she saw how badly her daughter behaved these days? No worse than if she caught her conniving 'friend' at her game, Mila muttered under her breath. Gita would not have heard her even had she been loud and clear. These days she never heard what wouldn't please her, and accepted all but the most deafening dissents as unanimous agreement. She now sprang from the bed, adjusted her sari before the mirror, used Mila's comb briefly on her hair and left the room in pursuit of Father.

The next morning, for the first time in her life, Mila dreaded going to school. She was haunted by a feeling of betrayal, convinced that the girls had formed a defensive alliance against her. Ritu had come out with barbarous accusations, the sneak. What gossip were they wickedly whispering? For the first time she was grateful that Baimai Buhariwalla's desk was next to hers. Baimai gave her a nervous, timid smile as she unpacked her bag and Mila smiled back. She was only bluffing, but Baimai was dazzled. So Mila 'forgot' her hymn book in her desk and smiled again at Baimai in assembly as the singing began:

> Where the dear Lord was crucified,
> Who died to save us all.

Mila sang lugubriously. She felt chastened and virtuous, and wondered if she was destined to join the Carmelites. Baimai was already in heaven, because they were sharing her hymnal. When by lunch Mila hadn't said anything unpleasant to her, Baimai mustered enough courage to dig out a photograph of her parents from her desk and drop it in Mila's lap.

What could have prompted Baimai to do this—except, of course, a filial love that she wanted to share with her orphaned friend? She was a late child, almost ten years younger than an only brother. Mila was sprightly and blasé as she inspected the photograph. The father was jowly, his face elongated by baldness. He had a large nose so hooked that its tip pointed at his chin. A true Parsi beak, she commented, and golly, only two sizes larger than Ritu's. Baimai giggled dutifully, with a kind of baffled affection. Then Mila turned her attention to the mother, a fat Shirley Temple, with a wealth of tumbled curls elaborately and rather incongruously framing the elderly, unattractive face—and suddenly she was catching her breath from a sharp pain, a kind of shredding in her breast. At that moment she hated Baimai, who was so pale and whose gums showed when she smiled, because she had this wonderful mummy with the stupid bovine face, while hers was dead. She crowed over those curls. Of course it was a wig, Mila said to the cluster of nosy girls who by now pushed against her. She made ferocious fun of that face. The girls laughed. Too late, Baimai snatched the photograph from her faithless hand and slammed it shut inside her desk. The bell rang.

For the next hour Mila tried to concentrate on hazy hieroglyphics on a misty blackboard. It didn't help that she caught a side glimpse of Baimai surreptitiously wiping a tear from her cheek with two pale fingers. Why the hell was she crying? Mila wanted to twist her arm to stop her from crying. Helplessly, she tried to cut off the vision of suffering from her guilty heart. She did not succeed. A piercing sense of shame filled her. At the end of the day she tried to waylay Baimai at the school gate to tell her how sorry she was, but the girl evaded her. The next morning Mila could not bring herself to say a word, and for the rest of the day Baimai averted her gaze every time she caught her eye, as if *she* were the trespasser. But on the following day, with characteristic generosity, she seemed to have forgiven Mila, for she offered her a Cadbury Krisp at break without a word. Mila could have burst into tears, but she took it nonchalantly, even attempted to whistle a tune, while Baimai smiled at her with pleased deference. Baimai never knew that she had freed her friend from a hook on which she had been wriggling for two days; but Mila was so grateful that she was nice to her for a whole week.

But at night she did not sleep well. She had bad dreams from which she awoke not screaming, like Vikram, but in silent terror, not knowing where she was, struggling to figure out the latitude and longitude of her bed. Sometimes she woke up with a start to think of Rayhaan in an accident, Rayhaan destitute, Rayhaan dead. At other times she lay there feeling she had done him, quietly and anonymously, a great good. Given him something of such incomparable value that he would be happy forever. And this very possibility made her almost faint with bliss. There was one morning when she opened her eyes and the day was full of promise, as if the last months had never been, as if her mother would walk in any moment to coax her out of bed. Then everything came sweeping back, and she knew this day was set aside for emptiness and defeat, like the others.

What saved me from serious mischief in those days was Amrish-uncle. He was a brick. A rock of avuncular grace-under-pressure whenever I stormed in on him with all my pain, battered him with my misgivings.

'Shame on *her*,' he would say, having for some reason fallen into the habit of not addressing me directly (self-defence?). 'Shame on her for giving herself up to mopery and drift and tantrums. Is that the way to behave?' He had the good sense not to pamper me, even in my darkest moments.

'You are the only one I can talk to, Amrish-mama.' Desperately, 'The only one I *like*.'

'Hmmm. How can it be helped? To know me is to love me.'

'And I *hate* school. I don't want to go to school any more. I won't!'

For the first time I realized his talents as a listener. Nothing I said surprised or dismayed him. He didn't hearken to my litany of woes only to top it with a dirge of his own, nor did he offer me a first-aid kit or an instant panacea. When at last I ran out of breath and blues, he said quietly, 'We cannot listen to such drivel, can we? We know that no price is too high to pay for education. Who is not better off in a convent than in a kitchen?'

'But if you heard our teachers! You think Sister Mary Francis had the right to say to me—'

'The less a woman says,' he pronounced firmly, 'the more sense she makes. Invariably.'

'But you don't know, if you were to meet the girls—'

'Spare me!' He gave a delicate shudder. 'At the prospect of meeting strange females I experience this frantic urge to rush off and view myself in the nearest mirror—with disastrous results. Why, the last time I was threatened with such a visitation, in terror I—'

And he would go off into a complex and prolonged tale, his voice as tart as lime cordial, permitting himself an outrageous freedom with facts, all recited in the most erudite language. I would listen to him dubiously at first. I knew it was all largely fabrication, perhaps based on minor incidents that had befallen him at different points of time, but all woven together into a single impossible adventure for my benefit. And though

I never quite believed everything he said, I would soon get engrossed in the story. Sometimes he made me laugh outright, while he sat there unsmiling, and the sardonic formality of his words comforted me when nothing else could. And if sometimes I was particularly incoherent and he did not know just what to do with me, if his improvisations failed him, if I was too restless to be read to, if his bachelorhood was a bar to an intimate understanding of my psychology, his imagination never quite ran out.

Poor man, my complaints were endless and never played pianissimo. Such clangour must have numbed him, but his counsel was always ready and pungent. Mostly he performed by ear as he sat cross-legged on his string bed, watching me with the pitiless eyes of a highwayman as he relieved me of my pain. He was so kind, though he could still be a terrible bully. And he alone, singly, helped me with my decision to jump continents and make my home with Uncle Harish.

But I anticipate. This happened after an incident about which I have wanted to be totally amnesic, but which I remember, even today, with an embarrassment of details.

21

This painful episode had a preface, a quiet morning in May after I had crossed my fourteenth birthday. We were at breakfast. My father had just announced that he was shortly to go to Nagpur for a conference of printers. It was hastily convened, he told us, to challenge an arbitrary decision by the paper mills to put up their prices.

'Can you insist on a return to the original prices?' asked Aunt Roma. She made heroic efforts to encourage such general conversation as part of the duties she had assigned herself. I don't think she would have addressed a single word to Father if she found herself alone with him—a confrontation she scrupulously avoided.

'No,' said Father. 'Not quite that. But we'll try to wrest some concessions from the mills. The print order we booked last year, for instance. It will be difficult to get our clients to compensate us fully for the rise in paper prices. And it would be unfair to make the printers bear the entire burden. The mills must meet us halfway.'

There was a little pause, in which Roma-masi was no doubt forming in her mind her next careful question, when I said abruptly, 'Is Gita going with you?' The words slipped out before I could stop them.

'Yes,' answered my father. 'May I have the butter, please?' His voice was neutral, but his eyes, as I looked at him quickly and fully, were concealing.

The conversation threatened to end. My aunt passed him the butter. The knife glinted in his hand. It smeared, it scraped. Vikram took a loud sip of his cocoa. I put my cup carefully in its saucer and dropped my hands in my lap. So. Gita was one up on me, was she? I suffered a sense of eclipse, then felt queasy, as if what I had eaten was curdling inside me. I said nothing and finished my buttered toast steadily, taking needlessly small and vicious bites, but crunching with a lion's jaw.

My father had answered me truthfully, yet I recognized that we were part of a masquerade. His terse 'yes' was a performance, as much as the deceptive calm in which I had received it. My question had disturbed him. His candour had upset me enough to bring on a gastric crisis. How I would have loved to scream out my sense of outrage that he should take that woman with him! But I had to sit there eating my toast while he ate his with a tranquil air. He was a crafty Machiavelli, and under his statemanship everybody behaved beautifully at the table. With great cunning we passed the butter, stirred the sugar, spooned the jam, peeled green bananas. Beside me Vikram sat with his usual inattentive air— but wasn't that, too, an impersonation? He distanced himself from emotions that would otherwise feed on him like cankerworms. Like mine did. Even Roma-masi was up to these stunts, saying one thing and thinking another as she feigned interest in the vagaries of the printing business or the weather.

The strange thing was that when the date of the conference came round, Father didn't go to Nagpur. No reasons were given for quietly opting out at the last moment, and no surprise expressed; we were still living a masquerade. And when, about a week later, at another simulated tableau of the Happy Family at Breakfast, my father announced that he was flying to Delhi the next morning on urgent business, something in the tone of his voice warned me against reiterating my earlier question: was he taking his geisha with him? Also, I dared not ask—though I was dying to know—because if he had said 'yes' it would have corroded my insides, and if he had said 'no' I would have suspected deceit. In both cases I would have had to pretend an equanimity I did not possess.

That evening Father returned late, and from my window I watched him manoeure his car into the parking lot. Why had he dismissed the chauffeur? Where had he been? Now it was done, and the parking lights went off. But why was he sitting so still behind the wheel in the gathering dusk, as if he could not move beyond some indecision, as if coming home was assuming for him the gravity of an astronaut's re-entry problem? At last the door opened and he got out of the car. He reached inside again to pick up what looked like office files. As he locked the car with one hand, a little awkwardly, he glanced up and I quickly withdrew from the window.

I stayed out of sight all evening. I was silent at dinner. At bedtime I shouted a perfunctory 'goodnight' outside his door and marched straight to bed, though I knew he expected me in his room. For on the eve of one of his business trips it had been my pleasure, when Mother was alive, to help her put out his clothes on the bed in a neat pile, ready to be packed into the open bag on the floor. I wanted very much to do this for him tonight, but I was sulking. Lying in bed, I ached to be with him. I jumped up once and went out on the passage with bare feet. There was a light in his room. Was he working? He ought not to stay up so late with an early plane to catch in the morning. Should I knock on the door and tell him so? I shivered where I stood. A feeling of catastrophe was upon me. Something threatened my father and I was powerless to help. I went back to bed, but not to sleep.

I reflected in the dark on my father. He was curiously disorganized these days—in disarray, in a physical sense, even while he appeared to be in command of himself. He was perpetually misplacing things or running out of them, or not finding them under his nose. He mislaid the paper samples he brought home, the proofs, files. Or he stashed a wad of bills in some mysterious safe place which then evaded him for days. His possessions baited him; they were bent on mischief. Every so often they staged a walk-out. His bookmark disappeared from between the pages of his detective novel, his cufflinks rolled under his bed. He could not find his socks in his closet and I had seen him seize with surprise a necktie he had himself laid out on the chair, as if it were his good luck to have chanced on it just when he needed it.

This was serious for a man whose one vanity was order—whose ideas and emotions were impeccably graded, pigeon-holed. Everything had to form a pattern: not only the shoes under his bed, the pencils on his table, but life itself, which was not a tale told by an idiot but a disciplined composition like one of Bach's fugues. Never would he cease from the strife of learning the inner design, discerning method in the apparent confusion. For such a man, this physical disorder must have been particularly painful. He needed to be acclimatized to the house all over again. He had been the stalwart at the helm, the captain of his ship, and a law unto himself. But now he needed help and would not admit it. He refused to be 'looked after'. He hated people eddying round him. The chaos of his life was personal, to be dealt with on his own. You could no more assist him with it than you could complete someone else's poem.

The next morning, he left before I awoke. It was Saturday. I was in the middle of my vacation and spent the early hours in desultory tasks, with one nagging thought underlying them all. By eleven o'clock my war of nerves was too much for me. I dialled my father's office number and asked to speak to Gita.

'Hello?'

It was her voice, all right—girlish little Gitakins. She was chained to her desk while Father was soaring the blue in a jet. My sigh of relief was loud enough to be audible.

'Yes, hello, hello?' said Gita. Smiling broadly, I crashed the receiver down on its cradle, determined to hold my peace now that I had assured myself all was well.

Almost immediately the phone rang again, and as I answered it Gita's voice came over the wire in an angry splutter. She was like a kettle marvellously heated by a wicked rage, simmering on spite, and she could not resist this opportunity to blast some steam in my ear. I needn't pretend, she whistled and hissed alternately for fear of being overheard by the other office harpies, that I hadn't rung her up a moment ago, because the telephonist had recognized my voice, and what did I mean by disturbing her at work? If I thought I could do just as I pleased because Daddy was in Delhi—

'Soni wants to know,' I interrupted at random, 'if you are coming for her this afternoon.'

There was a sudden silence. 'What?'

'Today is Saturday,' I elaborated smoothly on the imrovised theme, 'and you know that on Saturdays you devote your afternoon off to dragging poor Soni to the market.' I gave her a chance to say something but she didn't. '"To buy a fat pig",' I added boldly, '"jiggetty jig".'

Even this last piece of impertinence did not make her hopping mad. 'I—I . . .' the voice was tepid, she had stopped spouting hot air. 'No, I think I'll be,' she mewed faintly, 'I don't think I can—can come in this afternoon—' Poor Gita, muffing her lines. Poor kitten.

'We shall miss you,' I said grandly, and hung up gleefully. Then I stood a moment grinning at the telephone, overjoyed that in her side I was such a fat, prickly thorn.

The rest of that day, I remember, I felt very hungry and made several sorties to the kitchen. I demanded an early lunch, which I ate on my own, insisting on more and more helpings of vegetables and curd and mango juice, and heaps of rice with dal and loads of pickles. Before teatime I was hungry again. After stuffing myself on biscuits I raided the kitchen for leftovers and was delighted to come upon a platter of fritters made from gram flour and whole green chillies. The *bhajias* were ferocious, so pungent they convulsed my mouth. I felt a passion for them and ate in gluttonous haste. I was devoured by an unnamed anxiety and could not fill up fast enough. I was thirsty, too. I opened the refrigerator and took long swigs of cold water from a sweating bottle.

'Shut that door!' shouted Soni from her corner on the kitchen floor. She was scornful of people who drank out of bottles.

I obliged her with a resounding slam, and in turning away craftily swiped another fritter from the plate on the table. But Soni had been watching. 'You have a goat in your stomach today, that you swallow everything in sight?' she snapped.

But with his red and ruined teeth the cook grinned encouragingly from the high step-stool on which he sat idly before the kitchen table, a wad of betel leaves swelling his right cheek. Maharaj was pleased with my appetite—it was a tribute to his culinary skill. But Soni continued her admonitions. I wanted a bellyache, did I? What was delicious on the tongue did not take long to become poison in the stomach. Her voice rose, as it always did under stress, and I quickly interrupted her with the news that she would have to forgo her conducted tour of the bazaar that afternoon: Gita memsahib was busy. She had other plans. She wouldn't be coming. I had received the message on the telephone.

Soni gave a non-committal grunt. Then her eyes flashed. Some ill-bred persons would mistrust their own mothers, she began. She was quite capable of buying her own brinjals and pumpkins and potatoes without anyone breathing down her neck to see she didn't part with an extra paisa or even pocket one herself! Not that it was *her* job to buy these things, she added with a meaningful look at the cook. Was she employed to carry out the business of others? She rose creakingly to her feet.

The cook was prompt to take offence. No one could accuse him of not doing his job, said Maharaj. It was not his fault that Khushal, who had helped him carry home the vegetables from the market, had been sacked for getting the next-door maidservant into trouble. Anyone with eyes in his head could see her belly swelling every month.

'Shut your mouth!' hissed Soni.

All right, his one mouth was sealed, retorted Maharaj, but was he a god with eight hands that he was expected to carry home unaided all the stuff required in the house? It was not his fault that instead of the daily shopping, the marketing was now done once or twice a week by car. The changes in this household were not of his making. Nor was it in every family that the cook did the dishes as well, he added with a glowering look at the dirty pots and pans in the sink.

What was he saying? shrieked Soni. Didn't she help him with everything? Didn't she wash the glassware and the cups and spoons—the slothful dog that he was!

Maharaj stepped down from his stool, pulling at his dhoti to cover one hairy calf. Who was she calling a dog? His voice rose in volume and pitch.

'You think your lion-roars turn you into a lion?'
'No bitch calls me a dog!'

I escaped from the kitchen, leaving them to nurse the row. They did not know that their smouldering anger, always dangerously close to the surface, was due to their unhappiness with their unproductive roles of servitude. Their voices followed me all the way to my room, and I saw Roma-masi race up the corridor to the battlefront. Then suddenly the warfare seemed far away. It was still going on, I knew, but my ears were deaf to the uproar. For I was listening, with undivided attention, to an indefinable thing within me.

What was it? What was it? Something within me was clamouring to be given a name. An unidentified object was struggling out of its private den, but my thoughts could not close in on its meaning. My mind was like a door that had been feebly shut, so that while it did not sit properly in its frame, it was impossible to tug it open again.

Then, with coldness and violence, I apprehended the truth that had been bedevilling me all day. Something clicked into place, touching off a connection in my mind. I saw them clearly, my father and Gita—in our cottage by the sea, where he periodically renewed auld lang syne with his secretary. Where I had surprised him last year on a wet Saturday afternoon when we had thought he was in Delhi. He was awaiting Gita there today. I heard, again, her flustered voice on the telephone. Half-remembered words and old fears coalesced, and I hit my head with the flat of my palm. Of course! She was with him in Juhu now. The shack was to be their refuge, their haven for the weekend. They had organized glorious hours in which to disport themselves in secrecy. And it had happened before, it had happened before!

22

I was dressed.

'But why,' Aunt Roma asked for the fifth time, 'must you leave right away?'

I turned on her a cheerless face. 'I've explained,' I said woodenly, 'more than once. You want me not to go to the temple?'

'I do—of course,' Masi said, one ear turned to the ominous rumblings from the kitchen, where our serfs were dishing out dollops of mutual abuse. 'But I do think you could—er—get a better school report if you applied yourself more. I mean, worked harder.'

'Then you don't believe in prayer?' I fixed on her an accusing gaze.

She looked pained. 'Mila, certainly I believe in prayer, but I believe in work too—' She winced at the sound of a falling metallic object. Had a demented Soni hurled a saucepan at the hysterical cook? 'I don't know how long this row will go on,' she continued nervously. 'I'd like to go with you. Or send Soni. But with both of them behaving so unreasonably—' She drew a sharp breath. 'All right, go. But come back soon.'

'It may take a little time,' I mumbled, adjusting my sling-bag over my shoulder with fingers that shook a little. Then I brushed past her out of the room.

'Wait!'

I stood still near the front door I had unlatched, my nails digging into the palm of my hand. I hope she's going to stop me, I thought. I don't really want to go. I want to leave everything in doubt, in darkness, in blank parentheses. In the external hell of not knowing. Please stop me.

'You can't go to the temple empty-handed.' Masi was holding out a lumpy, hastily tied brown-paper package. 'This is coconut, banana and sweet lime. For the temple,' she added as I stared at it blankly, trying to push down the thick pressure in my chest that made my forehead so hot and damp. So there was to be no rescue from this overwhelming thing I had to accomplish. I took the package and crashed the door shut in her face.

With a purring, bullying lunge of speed the bus began to overtake the other traffic. As it heaved its bulk round a corner, Mila dropped the brown bundle out the window. She saw the paper tear, the sweet lime roll out and skip across the road towards the open gutter skirting the opposite pavement. And she saw again her aunt's face as she told her by-hearted lies, heard the sonorities and eruptions in the kitchen and, strangely enough, the voice of the sea, muted, like the captured hush in a conch shell, humming under all the other sounds, though she was still miles from the sea. She had the feeling of being sucked into a dark orbit, of travelling at a rattling pace to a dubious, unhealthy centre. But Mila was only escaping to the sea: to sand that was warm in the hand and friendly between the toes, to a salty spaciousness, a glaring exposure to the sun. What harm could possibly await her there?

The bus conductor was anything but amiable. There were altercations all the way. Between him and passengers who clambered up in jostling groups at overcrowded stops. Between him and those who did not have the right change. Between him and those who disembarked in protest as he alerted the driver to shoot ahead even as they stepped out of the moving vehicle. But Mila paid little attention. She was in a distraught state from which she woke just in time to catch a glimpse, on her left, of the Juhu Children's Park. Her eyes passed indifferently over sculptured aeroplanes, monolith baby elephants, slides and see-saws before the bus swung out on an open road, consuming ground at a steady throttle.

An unfinished housing colony came up on the right, a movie house on the left. Other suburban developments unfolded: bungalows, cottages, a school, a crop of little shops, hotels. And between them all, dusty bushes, scraggy scrub and clusters of palm trees reminded her that they had reached the fringe of an island. Large advertising hoardings sat astride slim barks. Suddenly a curved expanse of the beach, with the sea beyond. More hotels. Stretches of shingle, glimpses of glassy water. The red beast drove on, deliberately heading for disaster, courting a catastrophe.

'Last stop!' barked the sadist.

So it was. With a tremor Mila recognized the plump white tomb on the side of the road—recumbent, upholding a dusty cross. It was a landmark, like the church opposite. She had arrived without misadventure; now there was no deliverance. She got off and crossed the narrow tarmac road. A hen ran across her path, clucking, into the grass verge on the inner side of a broken fence. Beyond the fence she followed a tan strip between thin palm trees. Indecision and repugnance fluttered in her as she thought despairingly: how angry Daddy is going to be! How would she explain her presence?

The dread persisted, and Mila's mind threw up a confusion of infantile images. She saw herself enter the cottage trippingly, announce her presence by singing out their names between giggles. A jocular air, a merry breezing-in would do the trick. 'Hi! Just dropped by to see how you two lovebirds are getting on. Oh please, stay as you are, stay as you are!' No, she could never sustain this in cold blood. The very thought of coming upon them together made her sweat and shiver as she walked. The next image, with props this time: she had the coconut and the fruit with her and entered trustingly, a wide-eyed Red Riding Hood lisping for her grandmother, only to find her swallowed up in a male embrace. Or she was the mortified Baby Bear who had just discovered Gitalocks in her father's bed . . .

A tree came rushing up smack in her face, and Mila went into a skid to save her glasses. Why were the trees so unfriendly today? She stopped. This was the moment to turn tail. Catch the bus back home with no one any the wiser, not even herself. The exit was that way! Yet it was essential to press forward; all of her fourteen years seemed to compel her to that decision. So her feet plodded on. She was being silly, needlessly punishing herself with disturbing visions. Of course she would find the two of them (if they were shacked up in the shack at all) at work, the width of the dining table between them, their innocence proclaimed by reading glasses, certified by 'Dear Sirs' on official letter paper, engaged in commerce that was not carnal at all. She would be reduced to the role of a penitent. Oh, they would forgive her—her paragon of a father would see to that—while she sat between them feeding on hot servings of lies . . .

The trees fell away abruptly and Mila was now in the small clearing behind the cottage. She felt conspicuous, like a fugitive driven by desperation into the range of hidden rifles. From which direction would the posse fire? But nothing stirred, only the gravel spitting out from under her shoes. She wanted to cover the distance at a run, but was caught in the familiar nightmare sensation of slow motion. Ugly tentacles were grabbing at her feet as she tried vainly to skim through space.

She now stood in the evil zone at the back of the cottage, facing the yellow kitchen door, which was never locked when the family was in residence. She pulled and tugged at the handle. Thank God! Thank God that despite its peeling paint the door would not open to violence, it had not lost its integrity. It was securely bolted on the inside, which could only mean the place was uninhabited. Hope raced in Mila that the shack was locked up, there was no one in there. It was curled into itself, composed for sleep. The earlier menace had been just a bluff!

She rounded the familiar corner of the building, her feet light and brisk. No lawn furniture was out on the front strip of green. Mila cruised round the garden a little, not interested in the phlox borders and bougainvillaea shrubs. No evidence of a car; she hadn't expected to see one. The veranda was patently empty. After blowing an airy kiss in that direction, she ran off at a tangent down the ribbon path between palms to examine the red gate that opened on the beach. A rusty, loosened prong had dug into the sand at its foot, and she was able to shift it only with effort. She remembered the wild dash up wet sand and humped grass through this gate on her last visit—a hundred years ago?—with Ritu and Vidyut her boon companions. That far-off day had been drab. It had rained, the sun had been stoppered inside a grey bottle, their clothes had been soggy. This evening was rich and balmy. Mila was half tempted to go down to the beach; but it was getting late, and her quickest route home was to return to the bus stop near the church. She ran up the slope between the palms, and this time when she faced the weather-beaten cottage, she decided to walk round its one unexplored side.

I wasn't really watching the house, so I flinched when my eyes fell on the open bedroom window overlooking the flower bed. I stood still. The window was curtainless, foolishly inviting salt air, sunlight and curiosity. Denying a decent barrier between me and whatever it sheltered. Distressed, I felt I was in league with those who laid low within, as if all along I had really wished to guard the very secret I had now come to filch. Even today I recall how cheated I felt by that open window. I took a nervous step forward. It was dim inside the window, temple-like, but for the performance of what sacrilegious rites? The latent menace had crystallized.

Gingerly I stepped on the flower bed, which had no flowers in it. Raising myself on my toes, one hand on the window frame to help my balance, the other behind me clamping my handbag to my hip, I peered inside. Revealed in half tones and shadows, the bedroom appeared ceilingless. The day, so brilliant behind me, was dusky within. Only some rafters showed. A light hung on one long, rootless cord with a shallow circular shade, but it was not lit. A segment of wall was visible, with the truncated head of the rosewood wardrobe resting against it. One fat, curving leg of the four-poster did not seem to reach all the way down to the floor, but was lost in darkness. I listened. Not a sound. The room seemed deserted. I felt oddly defrauded, oddly reassured.

With both my hands on the sill, I managed to raise one foot from the soft, yielding earth under me and half-straddled the frame. My skirt felt too tight. The sling-bag slipped from my shoulder to the crook of my arm and hung free outside the window. For a moment I was pinned to my perch, with my left leg inside the room, the other dangling outside, my body inclined more to port than starboard. I squirmed, trying to raise my haunches to ease my skirt free from under me. It did not help. I desisted, panting, and looking over my shoulder found that my right shoe had parted company with my foot and was embedded in the mud below me. I could see it from my precarious seat, gazing up coyly from the brown and empty flower bed. Damn! I was about to scramble back to retrieve it when I heard the splash of running water, followed by a gurgling sound. Someone was in the bathroom! In sudden panic I sat up and swung my unshod foot around. My skirt gave way with a wrenching tear and I fell in a heap on the floor, as if butted into the room by an angry goat.

I crouched on the floor. The thud of my descent seemed to have choked off the water, and the abrupt silence petrified me. I felt something of the circumscribed terror of the mouse as I darted quick eyes from shadow to shadow, silhouette to silhouette. The silence became unbearable. It pawed and prodded me till I was brought to my feet in an effort to fight it back. I stood up, trembling, and stamped the floor with my shod foot. The noise was startling, I immediately regretted it and collapsed on all fours. This time I saw the thread of light under the bathroom door, barely three yards from my nose. Someone was wallowing in water in there.

I lay on the floor, my body weighted with dread, fighting a desperate urge to announce my presence. The need for secrecy was no longer as compelling as the pressure to escape this fear of enclosure, of anonymity. I stood up again, walked past dumps of furniture and felt for the electric switch to the left of the wardrobe.

The sudden revelation of details impaled me where I stood, with one hand lightly touching the switch-board. Mirrors glared at me intimidatingly; the shadows cast by rafters were spectacular. The black four-poster wore a mosquito net folded over its head like a turban, and there was a fluff of hair combings in the one pink comb resting on the dressing table, reflected as three in the mirrors above it. The sudden sound of escaping, cascading water was like a stampede. It jolted me into action. Quickly I moved right, to the recess between the wardrobe and the angle formed by two walls. It was entirely taken up by the giant plastic bucket that held our beach umbrella, several smaller parasols and a clutter of walking sticks. I remember climbing in a panic into the pail, shoving aside masses of rods, displacing wads of cloth and folded nylon wings, setting off a little riot that sounded to my ears like thunder.

Nothing happened for a moment except that my heart began to beat in painful blows, with the odd effect of giving me a feeling of suffocation in the left side of my throat. The water continued to splash crazily. Then, through the front door, which opened into the living room, a man walked in with a lighted cigarette in his hand. He wore blue-striped pyjamas without the top. He was my father.

Mila watched him without surprise. She was only verifying what she had always known. He paused on the threshold of the room, then, passing within inches of where she crouched, walked to the bathroom door. She caught a clear glimpse of his profile, and recoiled from it. Should she have smuggled a pistol in her handbag, planned patricide? He hesitated at the door, half turned away, then faced it again to say, rattling the handle, 'Did you call for anything?'

'What is it?' came the voice of the strumpet, muffled by the roar of the water.

'I asked if you—'

'I can't hear!' The tap was turned off. 'What is it?' Gita's high voice was unmistakable. 'I'll be out in a moment. I've finished.' Mila was learning so fast. She knew, for instance, that Gita did not sing in her bath. Did she snore in bed?

'Right.' Father glanced up at the light and frowned in thought, his face creased and gleaming, as if alerted by a sudden premonition—or was he merely contemplating the light, wondering if it had been on all this time? Mercifully, he did not think of switching it off, but walked out as quietly as he had come in.

Now was the time to spring out of hiding. Mila longed to run away, but was too unnerved to do more than squat lower into the bucket. She was in a mess. She had corkscrewed her body to fit in with staffs and spikes and knobby protuberances, and was painfully aware of the strain in her half-flexed right knee with her handbag wedged tight against it. She felt the pressure of restless sticks against her neck, the prick of spokes on one arm. But the slightest movement threatened the delicate balance within the pail, and she had to endure a scuffle with wooden goads every time she stirred. What if Gita emerged from the door just as she extricated herself from the thicket? She listened in mounting anxiety and horror. Not a sound. She could not bear it. She was becoming demoralized by the moment, and had wild ideas of darting to the centre of the room and pole-vaulting (using the beach umbrella) out the window into the garden, thence landing with another brilliant jump into the sea beyond . . . when the bathroom door opened and Gita stepped out, a vaporous emanation, bringing a whiff of lovely perfume into the room.

Her short hair was pulled up in a little girl's top-knot. Wet tendrils framed her round and flushed face. Very small she looked, a rapacious little waif out to embezzle a fortune, damp and warm and glistening in Father's white bathrobe, which was too long and too big for her. The harlot had not tied it at the waist. At any moment Mila expected her to drop the robe (clearly an encumbrance) from her glowing body and shout: behold the woman! But she stood in the middle of the room, pirouetting this way and that before the dressing table, holding the garment bunched up modestly against her with both hands. Then she walked trippingly to the door and gave her mating call: 'I'm out!'

God, I remember after all these years that the agile wanton did not wait for an answer but returned quickly to the centre of the room. Raising her arms above her head, like a Spanish dancer, she stretched in a single voluptuous movement and the voluminous robe opened here and there to reveal her taut and treacherous body. The battery of mirrors obediently, in triplicate, recorded her every line and curve and groove. Her wrists still touching overhead, she now glided towards the bed, and out of my direct vision. But reflected in the last wing of the triple mirrors I caught a quick glimpse of a virginal bosom, faultlessly curved and tilted. And a static replica of the lower end of the vast four-poster, its red cover pulled back from its fat, gleaming legs to expose a narrow strip of a lilac sheet. A couch with a conjugal air: sturdy, patient.

The pseudo-ballerina had twirled back to the centre of the room, the flaps of her robe flying. This was a different Gita: not the secret schemer, but visibly flesh. And she was enjoying herself. She betrayed sheer exuberance in her posturings before the mirrors, in her seductive back bends in the direction of the doorway whence she knew male eyes would soon be glinting at her. She was a courtesan enamoured of the animal grace of her own body. Going to bed, it told her, was a supreme delight. Heigh-ho, said her ebullient body. No more slavish chastity! She suddenly stood up on her toes and the robe was severed as with a knife to reveal the resilience of her heavy thighs, the thick wet pelt between them, and her firm short legs on invisible feet.

At this instant her lover silently walked into the room. He watched her a long moment, and I knew she made him feel like a god. He threw away his cigarette and came and stood directly behind her.

His hands slowly drew her bathrobe over her shoulders till it pinned her arms at her elbows, and she co-operated by slowly arching her back. Bravely the bitch offered herself to his exploitation. His hands began to caress her out-thrust breasts, slowly enveloping them, moulding them with an artist's intentness, gazing all the while in the mirror, releasing them to run down her waist-curve to stroke her small protruding stomach, past her navel to the furry down, lingering there, then stealing up to cup her willing breasts again, while Gita leaned against him, head thrown back extravagantly, her teeth on her glistening under-lip, her erect nipples little nuts growing against his palms, watching her reflection from half-closed eyes as he repeated his caresses in a dreadful, absolute, silent, single-mindedness.

The next moment she had whirled round into his arms and was climbing all over him as a snake would climb a tree, entwining herself in every hollow and branch. With a little cry in her throat and a movement of reptilian grace she offered him her mouth. Now she was stripped completely of her robe and restraint, there was no more lyricism in her movements but a kind of frenzy. The muscles in his bare arms tightened into ridges. His mouth riveted on hers, he picked her up, writhing and convulsed, and carried her out of sight. Immediately the four-poster was the hotbed of tremendous horizontal activity, though all I could see in the faithful end-mirror were glimmers of bare skin and thrashing heels as they kicked and dented the scarlet covers at the foot of the bed.

As Mila watched and listened, half crouching in the bucket, a very powerful and curious excitement mingled with her terror, making the terror greater. Her heart seemed to be beating all over her body as the kneading and sighing and rearing compounded. Gigantic waves heaved, tidal, moon-maddened, to break on the bed, and Mila felt she had to move too, push against something, or she would die. Her right elbow came up blindly to hug whatever it could find against her chest, but in its restricted orbit thumped the side of the wardrobe, and was badly grazed. Not pain but fear arrested it there, while under her, sticks and rods inched on leather tips and metal ferrules to spear her unguarded toes.

The woman in the sack gave a loud, pleased moan. Mila shrank back, dumbfounded, but at the same time strange thrills rippled over her flesh. Her feelings of shame and terror, and the rhythmic pounding and bedquake only increased the intense, tingling sensations till she felt she would jump out of her skin. Gita's moans came faster and began to rise in pitch like a wailing guitar, and Mila's hands doubled into fists as she felt the need of a weapon to defend herself with, though she did not know what she had to defend herself against. Then the bed was suddenly quiet, like a safe boat, and she too went rigid. But the sounds were resumed, the creak of ropes, the flap of a sail in a whipping wind, the slap, slap of water against a wharf . . . and the murderous ferocity began again, more purposefully this time. Mila bit her knuckles as the song soared to a high-pitched crooning and feet drummed and dug into the mattress, and all undefined rustles and whispers and groans and lashings gathered into a tremendous tide till the doomed four-poster seemed about to be wrecked into two at its unseen centre.

Half-sitting in the bucket, Mila was everywhere at once. Rushing along the rim of the world, teetering precariously—there was no foothold for her, nothing to hold on to. So don't listen! Don't spy! You don't need your father any more! She was now determined to escape. The trembling sense of shame persisted and her one overwhelming anxiety was to leave the room unobserved. She could not decamp in the manner she had entered, for she would have to cross the bed to gain the window. Her only possible exit was the door that led into the living room; and from there through the front door to the veranda outside.

She stepped out of the bucket as neatly as she could, tugging gently at her handbag. Even so, her stealthy withdrawal activated a slow and audible glissade of spastic sticks and epileptic parasols within the pail, and she had taken the first few nervous steps across the floor when it lurched and overturned behind her with a reverberating crash. There was a little scream from the bed as Mila whirled out of the bedroom. Though hampered in her flight by having only one shoe on, she had reached the living room at a run when she stubbed her bare toes against a bamboo chair leg, hard. The pain was excruciating, and brought her down to her knees. At that moment her father came out, and they were trapped in an arena bounded by the suite of wicker furniture.

His face was white, his eyes blazing, his mouth hard and tight as he stood over her, holding a sheet draped round his waist. Mila whimpered as she stared up at him, and his face was distorted by the queer, ugly look he gave her. This was her moment of annihilation. She waited, with a kind of grotesque patience, to be savaged—for his anger to chew her up into so much mash, for the rain of fists to grind her into the floor. She marvelled at the interminable delay, at the extremity in which her father was visibly toiling, for all his features were moving as if to tear away from his face. At last he said something she did not hear because his voice was so terrible, like a volcano erupting, boiling and rumbling far, far away, while mephitic gases escaped from his lacerated mouth, from the agonized slits of his eyes and through his smoking pores.

Mila tried to speak, but her words were stillborn. A faint, green feeling stole over her. Tears did not threaten, they were irrelevant, but nausea plucked at the corners of her mouth. She had to strive not to burst open like a crater, but burst she did. Her hand went to her mouth as her cheeks ballooned, and she puked all over the chair legs and the cushion braids and the tiles. The odour was hot and sour. It was a most violent expulsion, and now she was engulfed in her own lava. The floor of her stomach fell again, burning lumps tore out of her, and she doubled over to spew them out.

23

Had my father been a conventional Hindu he would have, after such a traumatic experience, shaved his head and repaired on a pilgrimage to Rameshwar or Dwarka or Jagannath Puri to expiate his guilt, to purify his soul. To take vows in a surge of brahmacharic resolves, undergo penance in a passion of renunciation. For all Hindus are alchemists who long to end their lives as good as gold, to be in great shape on their deathbeds, and the process of transmuting common clay into that precious metal does not normally begin till the age of impotence sets in, or dotage is achieved. But some are nudged into acts of contrition early enough if their transgressions are brought to light. The sin loses its savour only when deprived of cover, and the sinner is now ready for redemption.

But my father was made of sterner stuff. He never could take the easy way out of an impasse, save his soul at a bargain price. He judged himself harshly. Not only because he cared very much that what I had witnessed had damaged me, but also because he saw his predicament from the point of view of a moralist, and that put him at a frightful disadvantage. This high-mindedness was part of his egotism (just as his extreme sensitivity to order was a vanity), and it was responsible for much of the torment he suffered. It forced him to do weak things, cowardly things, even when he was too honest to enjoy the benefits of such deception. It led him to an external conformity with norms that were no longer tenable in his life, involved him in a struggle for some impossible equation between the relative and the absolute when he should have been a law unto himself. For he, more than anyone else I know, was equipped to live his life at the point of coincidence of the inner and outer man, but somewhere en route got hung up on rules and regulations that told him that his love for his pushy little mistress was 'unconstitutional'. Hence the subterfuge, which put him in leg irons in his own torture chamber as we all are in our own.

But all this is hindsight, and I have no way of knowing what his thoughts were on the silent drive back home that night. Had his concubine stayed on alone in the cottage? She must have, unless my father had her salted away hastily somewhere else, out of very shame. Perhaps he had attempted to drown her in the sea? Anyway, she was not with us during the ride back in a sleek blue car I had never seen before. Where had it been parked? Not in our garden. Hijacked from a neighbour's compound?

Mila slumped back against the leather upholstery. It smelled new. If Gita was not a floating corpse by now, was she still cowering in the giant bed, moaning a different tune? Surely her crying, which had filled the bed, the room and Mila's skull with unlovely, unintelligible sounds, would have by now settled into pianissimo: a soft persistent un-un-un, that could go on all night?

She had not come out to watch the fun when the daughter spewed all over the cane legs and the cushions. But filthy as Mila was, her father had tried to pull her up to him, put a protective arm round her. He was not angry, then! She shrank from him all the same. With one desperate hand extended to keep him at bay, she tried with the other to clean up the mess with her square of a handkerchief, feeling like a swamp animal. He watched for a moment, then reached for her again. His big hands trembled on her shoulders and she cringed back against the chair, but he picked her up effortlessly and put her down on the cane sofa. She lay there, totally spent. She didn't hate him, she thought with something like surprise as she watched him go back and forth between the kitchen and the living room, bringing sawdust, newspapers, paper napkins and finally a bucket of water. He made himself very busy; he sprinkled sawdust on the dirty puddles, then with two sheets of newspaper, using one as a brush and the other as a pan, cleaned up the muck—very methodical and matter-of-fact, his face set and alien. With wet paper napkins he wiped soiled cushions and frills and spindly legs. He took his time over it. To give himself something to do. To exorcise what had gone before? Mila watched impassively as he sloshed water on the floor and a smell of disinfectant rose sharply in the air.

He left the room again. There were muffled voices from the bedroom, then loud sobs. This was when Gita started on her crying jag. Then he returned, buttoned up soberly in his pyjama suit. Mila could not meet his eyes as he helped her up, then walked her, on unsteady feet, to the bathroom, where she rinsed her mouth and washed her hands and face and the front of her wrinkled dress. She avoided his gaze in the mirror over the basin, which was warped a little anyway, but the light fixed immediately above it made it so silvery and undulating that her head reeled and she wanted to heave again. She clung to the bowl with both hands. His arm supporting her, he opened a creaking little cabinet in the wall and made her drink something from a plastic glass. She performed these motions of reality in an oddly unreal world. This man was a phantom, she wanted him to be one, stripped of all recognizable qualities. The liquid burnt her throat, but helped her nausea. She did not see Gita on her way out but knew she was huddled under the sheets, eavesdropping from her tomb between sobs. Mila was led to the sofa again. She lay down, and because she was still shivering he covered her with a blanket. Then she was left alone for what seemed a long time. She closed her eyes and pretended she was in bed at home and the last hour had been nothing but a nightmare.

But when Mila opened her eyes it wasn't morning, it was night, and Father was standing beside her dressed to go out. Someone had driven a strange car right up to the veranda steps, and as he helped her into it he asked her, gravely, what she had done with her other shoe. In the flower bed outside the bedroom window, she told him. He shut the car door without comment and went to fetch it. There was no moon, and under the cool stars Mila sensed rather than saw black shrubs, ghostly flowers. She imagined Father on his hands and knees, scrabbling in the mud for her shoe. She ought to go and help him, she thought, when he reappeared at the opposite door and slipped behind the wheel. Before starting the car he handed her the shoe. Then he was hollowing a golden tunnel in the darkness, headlights sweeping each turn of the winding path between palms. The trees fell away as they emerged on the straight road, and soon street lights were keeping abreast of her window. They were in the heart of the city still but had not found a word to say to each other.

From that night all meaningful dialogue between father and daughter ceased. I resigned myself to a sullen acceptance of the situation, he to the acceptance of his failure as a parent. I ceased to ask any questions, he to emphasize any authoritarian approach to anything. Oh, we did have several 'talks', but I could not find my voice. I muttered a 'yes' or 'no' by rote. Most times I sat there inarticulate, mulish, my face averted, not meeting his gaze. I just could not bring myself to encounter it. It was not that I did not feel sorry for him; I did. I felt all of his pain—but under an obstinate crust of ice. I could not take a common-sense view of what had happened. The thing seemed irreversible to me. It was done, no contrary order or position was ever going to change it, there was no way back through it. And it was as unsettling to me as if the earth's rotation had begun to slow down—when *he* had been the one to nurture my faith in its regular and harmonious motion. My agony was that I still wanted to steer by what he had steered by. As this was no longer possible, I was lost. And angry. Not once did Father upbraid me for spying on him, but in my mind I chastized him for many things. I wanted justice for my dead mother. How hideously he had deceived her! Or she had known, and the knowledge had mortally wounded her. He had *killed* her! was my hysterical verdict. God, my charismatic Daddy was like everybody else, doing something noble with his right hand while pulling a clever one with his left and covering it up. How *could* he be so flawed and imperfect? In despair I wanted to write him off and couldn't, so I began to punish him.

I sentenced him to a new kind of relationship. Because he had deprived me of my illusions, I convicted him of terrible crimes. Sitting beside him I turned myself into a solid square, rejecting every word of what he had to say to me, and the deadly efficiency of his own conscience did the rest—completed the estrangement. Perhaps he tried too hard with me, but I had him where I wanted him: under my thumb. I was merciless, full of mistrust and rancour and mute accusations. That made him a pleader for his cause, and because he was not the one for confessions with his head in your lap, that made him feel ashamed. Finally it was his own inconvenient sense of right and wrong that silenced him.

But I was passionately articulate about my woes whenever I visited Uncle Amrish, which I did frequently enough. He listened with a wry patience. He didn't ask me nasty little questions, as a lesser mortal would have. He did not kind-uncle me. I had sought the truth, hadn't I? And now that I'd learnt it, he told me, I should be worthy of it. I should be able to accept it, live with it without narcotics, and without making a nuisance of myself. It was time I stopped baying for the moon: that was what growing up was all about. But if I was too miserable and made others so, perhaps I should go away for a time? This suggestion always brought me up sharp against myself. It made me feel quite ill, so that I refused to entertain it even as a remote possibility.

Then one day I saw that my father couldn't stand for me to be hurt any more—that he feared for me the perilous years that stretched ahead, the things I had yet to face and which he could never hope to secure me against, because he had crippled me. It all came upon me one wet evening in the middle of June. School had re-opened, the summer vacation was over. I stood blankly before him after having submitted my weekly report for his signature. It was a miserable beginning. As he silently handed it back to me our eyes met only because I had not averted my face quickly enough and I was shocked to see how terrible he looked. His face had the gauntness of a man who spent his nights trying to tidy up his soul. Something dissolved within me. Inside the hour I was thinking of my cousin Carol in Los Angeles, whom I'd never met. What would she be like to live with?

Mila's exile to a foreign country was to be a hush-hush affair—or so she thought—but hordes of relatives came to see her off at the airport. Aunt Kamala came in from Bhavnagar the day before, and Saroj-aunty from Pune, with cousin Sejal in tow. Sejal was frankly envious about her going to the United States of America, and that helped, in a way, to cloak her apprehensions about the whole project. Mila preened before her. Aunt Muni, who lived above the sweetmeat shop, brought her a box of sweets and she hogged all the péras on her own before setting off in the car, despite Soni's dire warnings about getting sick on the plane. Soni had cried all morning and Mila had consoled her jauntily. The world was such a small place these days, she'd be back before anyone had he time to miss her.

Other aunts and cousins and cousins-in-law descended on Mila. She kept nodding to everyone like a stupid doll, and passing the gift envelopes to Roma-masi for safe-keeping. Kailasbabu, who lived always on the edge of debt, had managed a fresh dhoti for the occasion. Amrish-mama, who lived in perpetual hibernation, did not come to see her off, and she was glad of it because she would not have known how to compose her face in his presence. Ritu called with a garland of sandalwood shavings. Jayantilal Prasad drove all the way behind their car in his jeep bedecked with saffron flags and loudspeakers.

At the airport Mila was garlanded by Uncle Satish, a distant cousin on the distaff side, by Mr Chopra, who worked for Father at the printing press, by Jayantilal Prasad, who made a little speech about serving her motherland humbly (like him) no matter how far she wandered from her sacred shores, and by Ramanbhai, vaguely related to them, who had been deputed to perform this task by his wife, who was ill at home with jaundice. Before she went into the Customs shed Mila offloaded all her garlands on Mrs Bakshi, while Dr Bakshi gave her a parting sermon on the virtues of vegetarianism. Father said nothing, but held her close to him for a long, long moment. Aunt Roma's eyes were full of tears she did not shed. Vikram gave her a quick hug and looked away, embarrassed.

I do not remember if Gita's absence in the farewell delegation was remarked by anyone that morning. She had stopped coming to the house, though she continued to work for Father. Poor Gita. Could she ever have dreamt that one day her life story would do the rounds in an unauthorized version?

part II

24

Nine years later Sharmila zipped up her large beige bag and the small brown one and walked out of the Customs shed at Bombay airport. Home again, home again, jiggetty jig, recited a small irrepressible voice in her head. A crowd had congealed at the doors, but coming towards her unerringly through masses of people was, yes, her father. Her heart beat faster. How like him to have recognized Sharmila at once when she had been nervously hoping that her new avatar—compounded of feigned hauteur, semi-starvation, shredded hair and contact lenses—would enable her to pass muster as a beauty and cause him to swerve in the opposite direction for his missing daughter.

But as he reached my side, Father threw his arms round me and I wanted us to be photographed that very instant, I wanted some permanent record of our coming together. For in that splendid moment I was a filly transported back with risked, outstretched haunches into an old familiar dimension: I was Mila again, in school bloomers, and stupidly happy to have recovered this Daddy, who was ten feet tall and whose every statement was a revelation of the absolute order of things. So I smiled and went very still by his side, waiting for that calm to secrete out of him which had cushioned me so lovingly as a child. I waited, holding my smile. Till my mouth began to hurt.

Alas, there was no click. After that first rainbow moment Father moved away and offered me a diplomat's face. It welcomed me as a visiting dignitary, but I read no indulgence there. Pleasant, but aloof. The same aloofness that had been his only defence against Mila in their last weeks together. I was dismayed. Was he refusing custody of his own daughter? I wanted quickly to plead my case with him: it wasn't just my idea, leaving. Remember? *You* had wanted it too. I gazed appealingly into that impassive face, which showed few traces of elderly frailty. He had not even greyed as much as I had expected, and I felt an impulse of gratitude towards him for having braved the years so well. But wait—there are three new creases on his forehead in place of the horizontal stripes of ash worn by the orthodox Hindu. And in his eyes was a withdrawal, so that he could escape, in part at least, the presentness of whatever he was doing—like facing a daughter's anxious, knowing eyes which had long ago detected fissures in his elegant moral system.

All right, if that's how you want it. Sharmila quickly reassembled her features to put on the air of a celebrity who insists that no one fusses over her, that she would *much* rather dispense with the bows and the orchids, thank you. Without all of him there with her, and real communication between them outlawed, she was outside the pale of the old magic. Disqualified, within minutes, as his daughter. Ineligible. I wanted to weep. He had developed an allergy to me. My biological presence was threatened. My mother had disappeared from the face of the earth, and the continuity with my father was all but broken. Suddenly I felt a foreigner here, and in grief turned from him and walked on without a sense of direction. Was this the way out of the airport? I stared hard at the man and woman standing rather forlornly before a poster rhapsodizing the delights of a visit to Matheran, the 'gem of Maharashtra'. Then I was running towards them with a little shriek of recognition: 'Roma-masi! Vikram!'

My aunt's eyes held unshed tears as I embraced her wildly, and Vikram parted my back with stiff fingers, his face wreathed in embarrassed smiles as I caught him in a great bear hug. Then I stood back and my eyes feasted on them. Masi had allowed her hair to grow, and wore it in a low coil on the nape of her neck. How sweet the gravity of her face, but how tiny she was, diminutive, in the presence of the giraffe beside her. She had always been small and slight, with a girlish figure and light step, but now some terrible demands on the spirit had, along with the years, taken a double toll on her flesh. And my adorable prig of a brother, didn't he appear almost cross-eyed in his efforts to overlook my flagrantly foreign behaviour in a public place, by fixing his gaze on some consoling inner vision of feminine decorum? What he expected of his only sister was a maidenly modesty. But how handsome he had grown. He is too much. If Carol were to meet *this* cousin!

The garland of jasmines that had been in my aunt's hand now hung round my neck. The coconut with red and yellow daubs on its husk and the betel leaves Soni had insisted on packing with the flowers were pressed into my hand, and I was talking very fast, almost incoherently, as if it had fallen to my lot to cover up for the missing ones—my mother, Rayhaan, Gita—though actually Gita's absence was an unhoped-for respite. I knew well enough that over the years the vixen had doubled across her tracks—some neat footwork *that* must have required—and recovered all the ground she had lost. If she had been dropped from the farewell delegation of yore, she would have made up for it by heading the welcoming committee today: Gita was a born gate-crasher. But she was absent, and my spirits rose. I could not have stomached, just then, her air of part-ownership of my father. The harlot who had teased him out of his single-minded monogamy was the picture of Gita I had treasured for my torment all the years I had been away. And I knew that when we met, my memories would collide violently with her ambitions, and it would be a painful business for both of us. But as it turned out, this was one worry that need not have plagued me.

Today I fear no such head-on collisions, for I have discovered that my father keeps his houri in purdah. Oh, she still slaves for him in that office; but I have seen her only once since my return and that, too, by accident.

It happened on the street. She looked so much older that I almost walked past without recognition. At Colaba Causeway Gita was staring into the display window of a shoe shop. At that high-heeled gold sandal? Or that brown suede pair studded with brass cones . . . which one did she covet? I stood behind her for long moments but she remained unaware of me. So I took a step forward and stood alongside her. We stared into the window in unison, but she never knew of my presence. Such childlike absorption in one so patently middle-aged was disconcerting. I was troubled. Was she voracious still? I was tempted to introduce myself, but abandoned the idea and used the window as a mirror to examine her, my eyes swinging from the original to its reflection and back again.

God, she had thickened and eroded at the same time. Gone was the pleasing pointed firmness of her body. Heavy in the waist and haunches, this was no seductive nymph! The expensive voile sari was bunched too voluminously over her belly, giving it a protuberance that it perhaps did not possess. But the hips flared perceptibly. Her short hair, stylishly dressed, was darker than I remembered it, a dye job. The mouth was still full, but with furrows etched on either side. The cheeks were rather slack under the cheekbones, the jawline blunted, pebbled. I was shocked. Was it possible to change so much so soon?

Gita moved away abruptly from the window and I watched sadly as she stepped into the street, plunged hesitatingly into the midst of the blaring horns, obviously a little intimidated by the traffic. I had thought of her as bold, confident, crazed by desire, active overtime in her own little interests, brazenly planning piracy—not like this, growing old to no purpose, dulled by disappointments, gnawed by bitterness. Did youth always gallop off impetuously like a riderless horse, leaving you slow, your face fallen, your hands that had failed to rein him wired with thick blue veins?

How long I have hated her! For years Mila watched her pitilessly from a grandstand, not really seeing what was happening, what the contest was about . . . Ah, Gita is not as mettlesome as I had thought. Age is defeating her. She has outpaced my mother, she is still in the running, but she has also lost. I shiver. She is old, old, and I, further from the end, have won the race, I have bested her.

But have I?

Last Sunday morning, thumbing through our phone book to check Baimai Buhariwalla's new telephone number, I came across Gita's name and asked myself the same question. The digits printed next to it in indelible violet ink are in my father's neat hand. It had to be the old number, for she has since moved (Vikram tells me) into one of the tall concrete-and-glass buildings that have sprung up on the reclaimed land on the southernmost tip of the island. My papa must have propped her up there with a new phone and perhaps a poodle—how else could the widow afford a sumptuous fourteenth-floor apartment? I have a suspicion that this is the very flat my father contemplated moving into after Mother's death. And that when, after buying it, he changed his mind for some reason, he had installed his mistress there rather than sell it. It has three bedrooms, I understand, and Gita, who has a swindling soul, has rented out two of them for hugely inflated sums, thus qualifying as landlady and joining the ranks of Mrs Choksy and Mrs Dev. (I have in my mind this unfair association of landladies with the great madams of old: doughty women with money-counting eyes and parcels of real estate scattered over the suffering earth.) Did my father visit her there? Why hadn't he crossed out the old number in the phone book and put in the new one? Was it to be a secret from the rest of the family?

For a long time I sat with the book in hand. Had I, the evening I interrupted them in bed, really short-circuited a relationship? Perhaps Mila's eyes had put the curse of squeamishness on them—for much of what we call morals is the embarrassment of other people watching. Thus they had seen, with Mila's eyes, the lewdness of their stolen embraces. In the bad smell of discovery, their deceit had troubled them. Or just him. *He* had felt guilty and repudiated her. And so I had given their liaison a random ending.

But perhaps I was quite mistaken. They had been unrepentant. His blood brooded on the bitch. Even when his wife had been alive, without the second woman he had suffered an ennui not to be borne. (Was I getting warmer, nearer the truth?) And he had relished, despite his qualms, the mendacious excitement of a double life, the frugality of a ménage in which only one woman demanded the elaborate trappings of a home while the other was content with crumbs from his table. (Of course he never saw his doxy for the self-seeking schemer that she was.) Now, with his wife dead, fidelity was no more on test, continence a discipline without meaning, and this woman his insurance against a thinning of his sap. So perhaps he still met the jade in our cottage by the sea, and rode with her the sturdy four-poster under its white mesh.

And indeed, why not? I tried to be emancipated about this thing. Why should Father, living in the nineties and reasonably personable, reasonably affluent, sleep like a dry anchorite on a bed of nails? What, after all, was so reprehensible in what he had done? That instead of being as monogamous as the tapeworm, he had sought a partner in copulation? Or that he had turned out to be so shockingly Mohammedan, with wife and concubine, 'milking two cows at one time', as I had once overheard Nanima say with acerbic relish?

But the thing had to be judged by the standards (implicit or defined) owned by himself, by which he had reigned over my imagination all these years. I had loved being his student. Had it been a bag of wind, all that talk about self-sovereignty? I had loved his truth. That he needed a form for everything had reassured me. He had tiled the universe with order, which was an act of faith, for which alone he was worth cherishing. But it was equally true that because of him I had never been free of the threat and weight of moral judgement. I had been a victim of his virtue— when he had been as frail as the next man. And it was in trying to convert *his* ethical specifications into modern reality that I suffered hideously from my inability to bare myself to my own age. For if chaos, irreverence, experimentation, non-meaning, are the norms of life today, I have to be anaemic to pull a blanket over my head and moan, 'not for me, not for me!' However, there I was, prepared to concede that no blame was to be attached to him, that truly I was the culprit because I had invented an image to feed on, manufactured a fiction called Father—but now *he* would have none of it! He did not want this response from me, this permissiveness, nor a resumption of his old comfort. He was not a flabby man. He had his granite, too, in the matter of forgiveness. He had his pride—no weaselly shuffles for him. Mila had passed on him a judgement that Sharmila now regards as unrealistic and savage. He had been unjustly pilloried, but he wouldn't flunk his punishment. And wasn't it because he had the stuffing of a hero that he still grappled with his soul, and remained morbidly sensitive to me?

By the time I replaced the old phone book, I was in no mood to call up Baimai. I sighed. I was constantly betraying her friendliness, trespassing against her great goodwill—thinking of her slightingly. I couldn't understand why I behaved so meanly towards her, or how she could still be so enchanted by me. She had been so amicable since my return that I had avoided her like poison, hoping she'd return the favour. But she left telephone messages that I received grudgingly and did not bother to acknowledge. She pursued me with letters in which she planned enthusiastic reunions with 'old girls', a prospect that made me want to dig an underground tunnel. But I did reproach myself for not responding more generously to the strange trust in her eyes, which expected to find in me things uncommon and admirable. Her blind affection for me had scattered the little wits she possessed. Besides, she was a worried woman these days—on account of her father's retirement throes, her mother's nervous prostration, her brother's love life. Ten years her senior, Burjor had lost his head over Nellie D'Souza, the Goan Catholic at school with us.

'Black as a crow's wing, don't you remember her?' Baimai had asked the last time she dropped by to see me. Imagine—the family blamed Baimai for her brother's aberration, because it was she who had introduced Nellie to Burjor. 'How was I to know,' she demanded reasonably enough, 'that he would fall for her? He hadn't shown the slightest interest in girls before.' And now Burjor was smitten by cupid's jolly little darts. How tiresome of him.

'Why does your family object to Nellie?'

'You know how it is,' said the inadvertent cupid.

'No, I don't. How is it?'

She sighed. 'It's my mother. She's horrified that Burjor wants to marry out of his community. She is very pious. You know what I mean.' I had nodded. So that was it. A Parsi by birth, a Zoroastrian by fervent faith and descent, Baimai's curly-locks mother was devout after the manner of unimaginative people who have known little of human complications and the ensuing embarrassment. (Rayhaan's maternal grandmother had also stirred up a tempest over this issue, I've been told.) 'When she first heard of it,' Baimai went on lugubriously, 'she took to bed. Wept for days.' Of course; her most sacred instincts had been alarmed, shaken to the core. She had been annihilated by shame. Oh God, oh Lord Ahura Mazda, what had she done to deserve this? Burjor drooling over a sooty pagan! Love was a wonderful thing, but what would people say?

'I told her we're all Indians. I'm a Parsi, but also an Indian!' Baimai had exclaimed earnestly. 'But Mother doesn't understand. She feels all her years of devotion have been in vain, the fire in our home polluted, all her prayers nullified. Now nothing will ensure the safe passage of her soul out of the material body to spiritual realms.' Baimai sounded like a medieval theologian. She sighed again. It was a melancholy business, I suppose.

'But does Nellie want to marry your brother?'

'You bet she does!' I remember Baimai was nettled by my question. 'You know how things have been in that family. Four sisters. One became a nun. Two had to get married in a hurry. Nellie . . . by the way, Nellie asked me for your phone number.'

'And you couldn't remember it,' I said, but without much hope.

'I know it by heart!' she said indignantly. 'I think Nellie's anxious to see you.'

'I don't think so. We were not very good friends.'

'But she knows how friendly *we* are, and might want to talk to you about this thing. Ask your advice, you know, you having lived abroad and all that.'

'Which doesn't certify me as an oracle.' I didn't for a moment think Nellie would care to weep on my shoulder, or turn to me for sage counsel. I didn't voice my doubts, however, but asked Baimai to stay on for lunch, which made her get up with alacrity. Oh, she couldn't, she had to dash, she had no idea how late it was. She was full of protestations all the way to the door, where she buzzed round me in a rage of goodwill, like a maddening fruitfly. After expressing the fervent hope that we'd meet again, *soon*, she finally left. I shut the door, relieved but also dejected. Why was I so lacking in charity? Perhaps if I could get to love myself more, I could love her a little?

To exorcize Baimai from my mind, I rose from the telephone stool and wandered into the living room. Nobody was about. From the coffee table I picked up the half-read Sunday paper with its gloomy portents and imported comic strips, then tossed it down again. I should be scrutinizing the employment ads, but had no stomach for them today. I hated Sundays, when week-long impersonations were suspended, when each member of the family refused to play his appointed role but curled in on himself like a prawn, hugging the shell of his own room, while outside the windows the bright day shimmered like water in the sun. My father was in his room, my aunt in hers, and I had no wish to intrude on them. Vikram was away on an office picnic to Versova beach.

He had offered to take me with him, but I had declined with thanks. Despite the virginal aura around him, I was certain that my brother was having an affair with Urmi, and whenever they were together I felt like an eavesdropper. I liked Urmi and wondered if Roma-masi suspected the liaison. Maybe Vikram's shirts had already told her the whole story. A smear of lipstick under the collar, a long brown hair on the sleeve, a bobby pin in the pocket had painted a Japanese picture for our aunt. Did she disapprove?

I could not tell. I was just waking up to a stunned awareness of Aunty's niceties—to acknowledge, belatedly, her value to the clan. Since her return from Pune, I often caught myself watching her closely. How could anyone ask so little of life? Spinsterhood, which in the early years had negated her, seemed to have taught Roma self-reliance. I had learnt that my father had repeatedly offered her marriage (to expiate his guilt? for the sake of his children?) and she had steadfastly refused him. But what had she done with, how did she manage, the physical urgencies of her body? She was not yet forty. She seemed content. The same placidity that in the past had driven me to helpless fury now seemed to me a state of grace. Her eyes were as gentle as candle flames. She had made the best of things for herself—and worked quietly to make them so for others. Was it her selfless love for Vikram that had so redeemed her? She seemed to inhabit an indefinable sphere of goodness from which

I was exiled. And it was the touch of deference in this one relationship that showed up, glaringly, my apathy and impatience when dealing with other people.

From the living room I wandered into the kitchen. Soni and the new cook were exchanging shrill words, which subsided flatly at my approach. Maharaj swivelled his head, and when he thought I wasn't looking bobbed it down for a pinch of snuff. Soni's sullen face challenged my presence in their sanctum. She was being very difficult these days. My offers to relieve her of some of the laundry and dusting only made her as bristly as the business end of her scrubbing brush. Clearly these were not the occupations of the daughter of the house, and Soni expected me to be considerate and keep my hands off her work. The unambiguous stare she now gave me told me to be off, so I looked her in the eye and grandly announced that I intended to treat the family to a lemon chiffon pie for dinner that night. Yes, fashioned with my own brown hands. I glared at the cook. Put that in your snuff!

Before my courage could fail me, I had fetched at a trot from my room my American cookbook, a parting gift from Aunt Martha. I was already in a sweat, never in my life having conducted a culinary operation on my own (in Aunt Martha's kitchen I had always been the second assistant and dishwasher), but put a bold face on it. Undaunted by little setbacks like no baking powder, no measuring device (how much is eight ounces of butter?), no Grape Nut Flakes, no graham crackers, no nine-inch pie tin, I began with aplomb. Maharaj smirked every time I referred to the printed page and looked blank every time I set him a simple task, like softening the gelatine in water, or beating the egg whites into stiff peaks. But Soni snorted with open disdain that I should cook with an open manual propped up against the pots and pans.

Before long I was hot and dishevelled and knew that the pie was a terrible mistake. Rather than face up to the ultimate fiasco, I imperiously swept the whole sorry mess into the slop pail and offered to make puris for lunch. I wasn't routed yet! Ignoring the 'O' gape of Maharaj's mouth and his popping eyes, I helped myself to a vast quantity of wheat flour and enthusiastically manhandled the dough for nearly twenty minutes. Maharaj's smirks were transformed into almost audible giggles till I fixed him with a bold eye from my flushed face and ordered him to put some oil to heat on the stove. He belched loudly in protest but obeyed me.

But Soni, clearly outraged by the extent of my ineptitude, made herself a mug of tea and sat stoically in the far corner of the kitchen, to show me that if I was so keen to make a fat-ass of myself she wanted no part in it. I picked up the rolling pin and attacked the glutinous dough. It promptly adhered to the wood in untidy smears. I was ready to cry when Roma-masi walked in to supervise the lunch, which would now be late because of me. She said nothing, out of kindness, though no doubt she was surprised to discover me in the kitchen smog caused by the now overheated oil. I dropped the rolling pin. Smacked down the wasted dough on the platter for the last time. Washed my gooey fingers at the sink. And marched out of the kitchen, head held high.

In the living room I had found Father standing beside the huge brass urn-lamp, playing absently with the beaded fringe of its raw-silk shade. He acknowledged my presence with a start.

'Lunch is going to be late,' I announced shortly.

He nodded pleasantly, picked up a book from the shelf behind the lamp, and handed me the Sunday papers. When alone in the same room with me he invariably gave me some reading matter and opened a book himself. His assumption that I didn't want to talk to him exasperated me. I accepted the papers gingerly and, sitting on the chair across from him, pretended to read.

But I was angry. Why didn't he allow me to share something of myself with him? Our affections had been arrested at the level of childhood. My father had become a myth to me, just as I must appear to him a changeling disguised as his daughter—an imposter parading as his child, a pretender claiming his paternity. I felt desperate, and looking up abruptly from my pages caught him staring at me with such a tender helpless regard in his eyes that I had wanted to blurt something out, I didn't know what—'It's all right, Daddy,' or 'I *know* you haven't sold your soul like Faust,' or simply 'I love you.'

Even as this mushrooming urge to speak agitated me, he took my breath away by saying, 'And how's everything?'

But immediately he seemed to regret the question, though I'm sure it was sincere. And by the time I'd mumbled my awkward 'Okay, I guess,' we had both frowned and looked away, as if our thoughts had already strayed into separate channels. He returned to his book, and I ogled the photograph of a plump movie hero with cow eyes. I understood that my father had a dread of seeming too nosy, of coming upon a detail of my secret life that would offend not him but me—as an assault on my privacy. He was telling me that he had not the minutest desire to interfere in my pursuits, that it wasn't my fault things had turned out as infructuously as they had. And as we sat on numbly, I wanted to yell, 'Talk!' Couldn't he see that there *was* a bond? 'Speak to me as you used to!' I wanted to whirl him round, to push him back into his own convictions, to forbid him from surrendering to his egotistical offspring, for if he pandered to *her*, I had no way of dealing with him except as my own invention. I wanted him to know that I yearned for the quiet authority that was now never exercised, even for reprimand! I was the supreme judge of nothing, I wanted to assure him. He was not obliged to render exact statements . . .

At this point Roma-masi announced lunch, and I jumped up as if released by a spring.

The meal began in silence. Green chutney made of mint, two kinds of pickles, and puris piping-hot and deliciously light were already laid out on our plates. Thereafter Soni walked in holding one gleaming stainless-steel vessel after another at the end of a pair of tongs, and with a shaking hand spooned out an assortment of vegetables, rice, lentils and shrikhand. The shrikhand that afternoon was superb and, like Bertrand Russell's first sponge cake, will remain a high point of pleasure in my life. The curds had been mixed to a pulpy smoothness, with a garnish of nutmeg, cardamom and almonds, and on the tongue lingered the yellow delight of saffron. My father was generous in his praise, and coaxed it out of Masi that the miracle had been wrought by her and not the imbecile cook. 'Home cooking!' I mumbled with full-mouthed enthusiasm. 'Nothing like it!'

My aunt smiled. Soni took this opportunity to heap more portions of food on my plate over my protests (she thought I was all skin these days, and looked on me with the eye of a taxidermist), till Father intervened gently on my behalf, at which point she left the room in a huff. I sighed. No one could convince Soni that thin was in.

'Perhaps,' Dad was looking at me, 'you would occasionally like to be served non-veg food—'

'Oh no,' I said quickly, knowing that this was one point on which my aunt was vulnerable, and Soni would kick up and Maharaj would walk out. 'Not at all, when I'm enjoying this so much. Eggs are good enough for me.' And to change the subject I had asked Father if I could visit the printing press with him the next day.

He looked very pleased. The atmosphere in the press room had always excited me, the Heidelberg machines toiling noisily to spew out calendar sheets, diary pages, greeting cards, labouring mightily to deliver posters, playing cards, pamphlets and other miscellaneous items. Why not a newspaper? I had plagued my father with this question since my return. Patiently he had outlined all the difficulties in the way of converting a job-printing plant into a newspaper plant. Well, then why not a monthly magazine, I asked. I could edit it, instead of seeking employment as someone's salaried serf. And Vikram could produce it, and that would entice him into picking up his father's trade instead of fooling round like a glorified office boy at Lever's. Dad laughed. It could be a good thing, he said wistfully, except that Vikram had always hated anything to do with ink and paper and type fonts and proofs . . . everything that so fascinated me about the work.

The meal had ended pleasantly enough. I rose from the table and for a moment stood arrested there, full to repletion, like some prodigious Bhima after a gargantuan repast, then retired to my room for some light reading before my Sunday snooze.

This was when I remembered Subu's diary.

Carol had entrusted it to my care, hinting that it would be worth my while to browse through it before posting it to Balaram V.T. Subramanian at his Esso office in Madras. And to my protests about the sacrosanct nature of another's private musings on paper, she had assured me that Subu (who spoke misshapen English with an unfortunate accent) had been more than insistent on reading aloud to her, and to sundry other female acquaintances, selected entries from the diary. And added, with a wink, that I would find it educative, and that it was destined for bestsellerdom if Subu ever decided to publish it.

I dug out the hard-cover notebook from all the litter on my desk, and carried it with me to bed.

I soon understood what Carol meant. I held in my hands a detailed journal of Mr Subramaniam's sex life. It was evident that much research had gone into the compilation of this document. It bore the impress of a mathematical genius. The language was spare and emotionless. Intimate particulars were precisely tabulated. There were equations to demonstrate the speed of orgasm in relation to sitar melodies as compared to Western orchestral music. Statistics to support the listing of variations in erogenous zones for different income groups and age brackets. Graphs to illustrate peak performances and their timings, and other athletic details. One set of performances was annotated according to the skin pigments of the coital parties, another according to their cultural affiliations. There were bizarre references to breathing exercises recommended by Hindu seers during copulation. There was an engaging discourse (by Subu, whose in-the-flesh conversation blanked out all thoughts but the nagging wish that he'd get up and leave!) on the sexual act viewed as a ritual sacrifice and the sexual partner as a cosmic symbol. And there were thirty separate dispassionate entries on the agonies of a month of continence.

I closed the notebook carefully. Why had Carol been so keen that I sample it? Maybe she thought she would give a nice girl a treat. To help me cut my mooring ropes, was more like it. To throw out the sandbags. Plan a mutiny. Embark on a wanton splurge of sex for sex's sake—destination unknown, ports of call uncharted—and about time, too! But I was already adrift on another current.

My mind journeyed back to my earlier humiliation in the kitchen. I craved to be of use, but where was I needed? Was I contiguous with my past, or merely a disruption, a threat to the future?

I had no ready answers, and late in the evening after Dad had left—on one of his cosy trysts?—I drifted into his room and from my mother's wardrobe pulled out all her saris. Silks from Kanjeevaram and Kashmir, Benares and Bangalore. Rich temple saris of the south. Oriya and Dacca cottons. Voile, calico, organdy. Handloom and khadi saris, patolas, hand-embroidered georgettes, shamous of unparalleled sheen, bandhnis from Rajasthan. The cache seemed bottomless. I stacked them on chairs, piled them on the carpet, all the colours of the rainbow. Standing ankle-deep in them, thrilled by all that profusion and richness, I arrived at a decision: no more Western clothes for me. I would banish all those smart pant suits, jeans and minis inside a trunk with a shower of mothballs. Only traditional garb for me, henceforth. I selected a few saris that would serve my immediate needs.

I was posing with them before the mirror when my mother seemed to take shape behind me, then enter me, occupying specifically the curved area from under my ear to my chin. Was this, then, my continuity? A physical extension. But what else, dear God, what else? The identifying relationships with members of my family were simply not forthcoming. Or with my neighbours. Or friends. I turned away from the mirror, troubled in my thoughts. Was it true, then, what Vikram accused me of the other day, that I deliberately hosed down my friendships? Stamped on the embers? Witness Ritu, Baimai. But they were hangovers from a dead past—keeping up with them was all repair work, maintenance, mending broken springs, pumping deflated tyres. What I needed was to scrap the old models for new ones. I needed someone to talk to in a tough, inflammable manner, I sorely missed Uncle Amrish. Who else was available?

Jyoti Wellingkar, so widely read and seriously informed, who taught history at the university? Just talking to her, you felt compelled to jot down a few notes. Alas, she had disliked me at first sight. Perhaps my accent bothered her, or maybe it was the mini-skirt. Then there was Chandra Dalal, plain, bespectacled, earnest, working with rare devotion for rural uplift, a socialist by personal conviction, a future Padma Shri. But I found her literalness too literal (she changed colour every time I used the word 'bloody'), her humourlessness too humourless. Who else? Urmi? She had offered to find me a job, invited me to talk things over, but my brother was the impediment here, in a strange way. And friendly relations with idle women involved too many politenesses, too many shopping trips, coffee sessions, bridge lessons, Ikebana, committee teas . . .

Boyfriends? I sighed. They caused raised brows, they caused gossip, they caused sex. I could thumb my nose at all of that, but there was my chronic ailment, Rayhaan, flaring up weeks and even months apart but still debilitating enough, so that while I was hungry for new experiences, I was too listless to pursue them. No, occupational therapy was the only answer. I really should work with Dad. Impossible, with Gita enshrined in his office. Travel? I had several aunts all over India, I could see more of my own country. Whatever the method, I told myself firmly as I began to re-stock my mother's wardrobe, I had to break out of this isolation, this arrogance. I *had* to exist in relation to others.

I was folding the last of the saris, the blue and green paisley affair I had partied in the week before, when Vikram came in. 'Had a good time?' I asked. His patrician nose was peeling.

'Yes.' My brother was not given to exuberant overstatements. He regarded me in silence. 'What did you do all day?'

'Nothing.' I banged shut the wardrobe doors.

'You should have come with us.' Pause. 'Urmi asked after you.'

'Perhaps next time I shall join you,' I said, then turned the key and turned to him with a false smile. But he was looking at me curiously so I surprised myself by blurting out, 'The trouble is, I'm not like one who belongs here, but one who is going to. Belong, I mean.' I sounded confused and rather desperate, I thought.

Vikram was leaning against the door watching me as if I were presenting a scene from *Much Ado About Sharmila*. 'You feel you don't belong here, Mila?' he said at last.

'Sharmila,' I corrected him. 'But I didn't belong *there* either.'

'Where?'

'The USA. Anywhere, for that matter.'

'And not belonging anywhere makes you classless? A world citizen?'

'I didn't say that!' I looked at him with some astonishment. What was he driving at? More and more these days Vikram revealed to me a further self, differing from the visible man of routine and decorum—perceptive, sharply critical and doggedly alert behind the prim, self-conscious exterior. It frightened me a little. A captious man lurked somewhere behind my good-natured brother.

'Come, *Sharmila*.' He was now challenging me. 'A misfit likes to think of herself as a rebel in a prejudiced society. And most rebels claim a superior mind.' He gave a sudden grin, his eyes concentrated on me in mockery.

I felt myself flushing. 'I make no such claims!'

'No? Then why can't you make friends? Or by sitting in one place do you hope to be discovered? Like a gold mine?'

I felt a return of the old impulse to box his ears. He must have sensed something of this, for he laughed, tweaked my hair playfully and left, saying he needed a bath.

It suddenly got claustrophobic in that room. As if all the forces that had shaped me were like a network of streams that, having met at a confluence, were now encountering a terminal dam. Somehow I had to breach it, if I were to surge ahead! And I wanted to run from there, run barefoot through the night with a rose bobbing over my left ear (do you see me, Carol?) into the arms of some ruffian who would proceed at once to instruct me in what a man was all about. And thus my unlived life would be avenged at last!

25

Is one always attacked where one is most vulnerable? The mating season is upon us. The bells are ringing, and what can be more damaging to a single girl's ego than her girlfriend's wedding day? Oh, I do trot out skilful arguments against female subjection to the domestic yoke. But what I always hear above the organ peals and the passionate wailing of the shehnai is my own silent, unliberated lament: what is the male of the species that I need him so? And on every nuptial occasion I feel a distinct and quite revolting desire to embrace the destiny for which I was genetically programmed: to be, until my dying day, man's obedient servant—ha!

Similar alarming thoughts raced through my mind the afternoon Baimai called on me with a youth in tow. 'This is Minocher,' she introduced her large, ox-like captive, and her next words took my breath away: 'We are going to be married next month.'

I made the usual noises. *How* wonderful, *when* did it happen, what a *sly* puss to keep it from her friends all this time. She glowed. I dimmed before her. She squeezed his hand with proprietory pleasure, with an air of licensed possession. I felt left out, eliminated. This was her moment of triumph, and I saw her leading her mate into her cave, then roll a boulder to its mouth before I could peek inside the fecund retreat. I tried not to scowl at Baimai. What had she got that I hadn't? Minocher, of course.

She was ebullient. She made fond, patronizing sounds. She was truly delighted with her prisoner, and his answering smiles seemed complacent till I noted that even with her hand in his, his eyes were appraising me. A detailed, analytical appraisal it was, which rather annoyed me as I walked self-consciously to the door to order the tea. It was like disrobing for my annual check-up. Baimai, of course, hadn't noticed a thing. Sitting back in her chair she told me of her devotion to serious shopping—of the saris she had bought, the carpet, the linen, the beds, the cutlery, the sewing machine and other such appendages with which she would transform her home into paradise.

'I'm in one giddy whirl,' she said dreamily, looking like an advertisement for an exotic sari in which the happy woman has effortlessly achieved that peace of mind for which the Lord Buddha renounced everything. 'Haven't a moment to spare!'

'Of course not.' I was back in my seat. 'I'm glad you so quickly found a flat to live in.'

'Oh, we'll be living with his parents.'

'To begin with,' he added quickly, on the defensive.

'I shan't mind,' said Baimai. 'I get on famously with Sheroo-aunty. She's a darling.'

'*Aunty?*'

'Yes. Minocher is my first cousin. His mother and mine are sisters. We've known each other all our lives.'

'Oh.' This wasn't, then, a runaway romance, as Baimai had somehow managed to imply. The ox had frowned at her words, then collected himself. She had seen the frown and was looking at him with an earnest smile and submissive droop: what had she said wrong when she was there to gratify his every wish? The next moment she was bubbling again. 'He's with life insurance in the claims department.' She went on to contribute more facts about his work, but this, too, seemed to displease him and I gathered that his job did not measure up to his own ambitions.

It was not for me to fabricate difficulties for her, but the situation was heartbreakingly clear to me by the time I poured out the tea. For years Baimai had been in love with this oaf, who belonged to a not-very-affluent branch of the family. She had the money, and this was an important enough factor for him to ask her at last to be his wife. But he was already chafing at the bonds, he was restless before the noose had tightened. I was angry with Baimai. Why did she always cast herself in the role of a victim? Such a simpleton Eve must have been before she ate the apple. There she sat, in limitless subservience, smiling demurely at him from the corner of her eyes as she described her chairs and dishes like a love affair, her kitchen (Sheroo-aunty's kitchen, but completely renovated for the dowered bride) like the Sistine Chapel. But his eyes were travelling over me again, and he interrupted her effusions with, 'I hear you've lived abroad many years?'

'Yes.'

His heavy face became animated. 'That's what I'd like to do.' He held my teacup in a hand that should be in a boxing glove.

'Live abroad? Why?'

For a moment he was taken aback by my question. Then he shrugged his burly shoulders and put down the fragile cup. '*Sala*, what is there left in this country?'

Now I disliked him thoroughly, and I was irritable with dislike of the whole situation. Baimai made it worse by chiming in loyally, 'I agree with him. There is nothing honest people can look forward to in this country.' And they continued in this vein for some time, deploring the corruption in high places, the lack of opportunities, etc. Much of it was true, but it was all generalization, they were ill-informed and parochial and too comfortable to carry conviction. Minocher was a critic by rote, and his future helpmeet echoed his empty phrases. It was all rather sad and provincial, for to them the word *foreign* guaranteed an unqualified excellence that was non-existent, it referred to a supreme authority whose opinion was to be cherished. I said very little, waiting for the moment they would finish their tea and leave.

But when they had left I felt like a snail with its shell ripped off by a cruel beak. Instantly I protected myself by thinking of Rayhaan, and as quickly banished him from my mind. The time had come to resort to desperate measures, or my stalled life would never budge. I would enlist the help of aunts and horoscopes to get married. Ask Vikram if he knew a nice expense-account boy for me—that colleague of his, low of brow and buck-toothed, would do for bread-and-butter reasons. No, I would jump into bed with my first attractive opportunity—for experimental reasons—and devote my declining years to literature. How about flying back to the States, sending urgent letters to Carol tonight? No, running away never solved anything. I was wasting my college education, I'd better stop flirting with the idea of a job and settle into one to test my powers in the world outside . . .

So there I was, my head ringing with conflicting resolves, at Baimai's wedding yesterday. Vikram, also invited, had let me down at the last moment.

'But why? You get sumptuous food at Parsi weddings.'

'Something's turned up,' he said.

'But this morning you said you'd go with me.'

'I'm sorry.'

'Can't this other thing wait a day?'

'No.'

He's had a tiff with Urmi, I thought, and wants to make up with her right away. 'All right,' I said sulkily. 'I'll kiss the bonny bride for you.'

It was a fine evening as the car dropped me at the gates of Albless Baug. The garden (really a paved ground between squat structures) wore a festive look, dressed in a myriad electric bulbs interspersed with bunting and streamers. An elderly lady with a white halo of hair above a narrow face greeted me at the entrance. 'So glad you could come,' she gave me a limp shake with her be-ringed hand. I made an effort to smile but she was already repeating the same words to the man in the queue behind me. He grabbed her proffered hand and gave her rings a hearty squeeze, which obviously caused her acute pain, for she did not extend her hand to his wife and two plain daughters. Cinderella they had left behind in their kitchen.

I walked up a narrow strip of red carpet past rows of chairs on my right jammed solid with guests, towards the dais crocheted with flowers at the farthest end of the garden. Fresh from their ablutions and prayers, the bridal couple sat side by side on brocaded chairs ordered for the occasion. On a tall tripod beside the bride glowed a table lamp that looked from this distance like a glass football with a light in it. Behind the couple the in-laws had taken their stance in two solemn rows, like figures in a family album. The ceremony was already in progress, but there was no ritualistic hush. Most of the chattering guests paid not the slightest heed to the two priests who, standing perpendicular to the bridal pair, intoned prayers in loud voices and pelted them steadily with rice. The bride's face was hidden from me by the white skirt of the priest's muslin gown, starched with holiness, and all I could see of Minocher was the shiny top of his *pagri*, the traditional headgear shaped like a cow's hoof.

Looking across the heads of the congregation on my right, I spotted Ritu. I edged my way between chairs towards her. 'Hi Ritu,' I said, then my heart sank as I saw that with her were faces out of the past.

'Ritu said you'd be here,' called out the very dark girl in an audacious red mini. It was Nellie D'Souza.

'Hello, Nellie.'

'I wouldn't have recognized you,' Nellie's voice was low and attractive. 'My, you've lost weight and look nice without your specs. I was just remarking to Ritu here how people change. Seen her brother Kishore recently? Decked up in saffron like a ruddy angel in flames, but with a shaven pate. And you remember him roaring up the streets on his mobike?'

I nodded. 'Marlon Brando himself.' I also remembered that I'd never really cared for Nellie, who was saying, 'How come we never see you these—'

'Must we sit here?' Vidyut interrupted her with a pout, thereby saving me the trouble of inventing an alibi. In a sari of many colours Vidyut was overflowing her chair; she had achieved such a ripe fullness at puberty that from then on she could only grow outsize. She inspected me briefly with eyes ringed with mascara before turning away her head with a petulance that set her bejewelled ears on fire. 'We're much too close to the band,' she complained. 'I hate sitting close to the band.' I now noticed the cement platform that began where our row ended, and on which a small group had assembled with their instruments.

'Never mind,' said Ritu, hugely pregnant and peevish, apparently having caught the pouts from her cousin. 'We can move back later, after they start playing.' Poor dear, she was so cow-heavy in her brown silk, not of the right shape to walk between rows at all.

'Twice I phoned you last week, but you were out,' Nellie was saying. 'I left my office number. Didn't you get the messages?'

'No,' I lied, still eyeing Ritu. Was it because I was a potential childbearer that I had not learnt to be alone in a fruitful way? It was possible that my virginity had alienated me from myself. It had no religious value for me. Only the Catholics—like Nellie here, whose second sister was a nun—honoured the mother of Jesus more for her chastity than her maternity. We never extolled an intact maidenhead over motherhood.

'It's sure to be a girl,' Nellie too was now gazing frankly at the amplitude below Ritu's waist. No expression registered on her face, but I thought Ritu blanched at the prognosis, her lips changed colour. 'She won't go for her sonograph,' Nellie went on, 'but I can tell.'

'How can you?' I asked combatively, knowing Ritu had resisted all tests that could have shown up the sex of her child. Determined not to know, she was yet terribly susceptible to careless prophecies. She had once asked me to pray that the child born to her would be a son. I had tried to argue with her. What was wrong with a daughter? Even Mahatma Gandhi had claimed a partiality for daughters . . . Ritu had made no reply, but raised her eyes to me with such mute scorn for my incomprehension, my stupidity, that I had been abashed into muttering that okay, if that's what she wanted, I hoped for her sake the child would be a boy.

'It's the shape of her stomach,' Nellie elaborated, 'pointing forward, with the flanks so narrow. I've never been proved wrong. One of my sisters has five daughters, so I should know—' Mercifully, she broke off with a start as the band blared out the first few bars of *Congratulations*. We all craned our heads towards the dais, now swarming with women. The ceremony was over.

Ritu rose suddenly to her feet. As she did so, she gave a minute involuntary gasp, as if something inside her had been displaced by a sly kick. Had the child's movements grown tumultuous?

'Now where are you off to?' Vidyut asked her in a scolding voice.

Ritu did not answer at once but sat down again, her face wearing a startled look. I was conscious of a little nagging thrill. Had she felt in her back a sudden atypical phase of pain? In other words, was the baby on its way? 'I thought we should go and wish the bride,' she muttered listlessly.

'Not yet,' said Nellie. 'All her relatives will be fussing round her and I don't enjoy being stepped on. Besides, I want to finish my orangeade.' She waved her glass pertly.

'You don't want to be jostled in a crowd,' I said to Ritu to placate her. She made no reply.

'There are over three hundred guests here tonight,' said Nellie, who seemed as well informed as my hairdresser. 'Thank God the band's stopped playing. I know the pianist, he's good, but in another moment I would have strangled the vocalist.' As she said this I remembered that Nellie had a beautiful voice, a rich, deep contralto, and I was about to ask if she had kept up with her singing when Vidyut said, 'Think of the expense, to feed so many guests.' She sounded impressed in spite of herself.

'That's why they keep wedding ledgers,' said know-all Nellie. 'Every gift is written down. Then when the couple is invited to a wedding years later, all they do is consult the damn ledger and give back the amount they'd received, plus a little something to take care of inflation.'

'Go on!' I said.

'Not a bad custom,' grinned Nellie. 'It helps the not-so-well-off parents to defray expenses. This is classified information, but then I have a Parsi boyfriend. We would have been married by now, but his mother is a bitch.'

'I know who you're talking about,' I returned coldly.

But Nellie was not abashed. 'I guess Baimai told you. They don't like me because I'm not a Parsi. And because I'm so dark,' she added with refreshing candour. Fair Vidyut darted a supercilious glance her way.

The band swung into another tune as flashbulbs went off blindingly on the dais. The bride and groom were on their feet, the centre of a group being photographed on the steps. Nellie waved brazenly to a short man at the end of the second row. 'That's Burjor,' she said, and actually blew him a kiss. Unfortunately he was not looking her way, but Vidyut began to stare at her in the most marked manner, turned to Ritu and began to converse with her in rapid Gujarati. The wedding party stepped down and the stage was bare except for the vacant chairs and the lamp on its tripod. Two small boys dashed up and romped round them like goats, and a little girl in a yellow dress whirled about so wildly that she tripped. Burjor had to leap back on stage to rescue the lighted sphere before it crashed to the floor. He was rather spherical himself.

'Ah, there go the bride and the groom,' cried Nellie, 'on their way to the fire temple.'

'I thought they were coming round to greet the guests.'

'Later,' said knowledgeable Nellie. 'When we're eating they'll go round the tables shaking hands and collecting their gift envelopes. Girls, did you see the gleaming boulders round her neck? That diamond necklace is an heirloom.' There was frank envy in her voice. From Nellie's ears dangled large glittering hoops that were patently not of gold.

'I'm tired of diamonds,' said Vidyut. 'Aren't you sometimes weary of wearing diamonds?' She turned her head to me, her gems ablaze.

'I haven't had the opportunity,' I replied gravely.

'And what a gorgeous sari,' Nellie was still contemplating the bride, dressed in diaphanous, shimmering white. 'She looks lovely.'

'Every girl is lovely,' I found myself saying tartly, 'in the hour of her victory.' Then I regretted the words. They sounded waspish.

But Nellie laughed. 'Did you see how she smiled at us just now? Look what I've got, she was saying, pointing to the trophy by her side.' She laughed again. I began to like her.

A very loud voice on the microphone announced in Parsi Gujarati (blaspheming the niceties of Gujarati diction and grammar) that the first round of the dinner was about to be served, that four tables on the enclosed veranda were set for the boy's guests, all the tables in the garden were reserved for the girl's invitees and vegetarian food was also available on request. All the information was repeated thrice, at marathon pace, and with every announcement fresh waves of people rose from their seats and made for the tables. The last clarion call was: 'You will come to eat, please!'

Vidyut rose to her feet with a sigh, pulling her sari of warring colours—perhaps she had a repressed desire for aesthetic expression?—close about her excess girth. 'Might as well eat,' she said as if the prospect fatigued her beyond endurance, but she was determined to do her best.

I received the idea without enthusiasm. 'So early?' It was barely 7.30 p.m.

'Ritu and I must leave early,' sighed Vidyut. 'The car is wanted by your mother-in-law, isn't it?' Ritu said nothing.

I came to a decision. 'I'll eat later with Nellie.'

'Nellie will eat non-vegetarian food,' said Ritu, after a significant pause.

'I love non-veg food,' I smiled, 'particularly Parsi wedding food served on plantain leaves.' When I marry Rayhaan, I thought, I'll persuade him to host a Parsi feast.

'You'd better hurry,' Nellie said, 'or all the places will be taken.' Ritu hesitated, then followed behind Vidyut who was already in full sail. Ritu made me feel that by not going with them I had, in some egotistical way, rejected her, when all I had done was to make a rational choice. I sat there feeling grossly culpable.

'Keep your chairs for us,' Nellie shouted after them. 'Don't get up till we come!' She turned to me. 'You have to stand behind the guests as they begin on their ice-cream, or you'll never get a place till the third and last session. And that is only meant for the bride's and the groom's families.'

'Won't Burjor want you to sit with him in the last session, then?'

For the first time Nellie looked troubled. 'No,' she said in a hard voice, then laughed. 'He wouldn't want to rub his parents the wrong way on their daughter's wedding day. My presence here is enough for them to throw a fit. He wants to sort of, you know, get round them gradually. Let's sit just a little farther away from the band, but in view of the tables.'

We moved further down the row and sat down again. With uncontrolled pathos, the crooner was moaning another pulpy love song into the mike. At one point I saw Nellie wince. 'I applied for a transfer,' she said suddenly, 'to our office in London, just in order to hear a real jazz vocalist. I work for Glaxo.'

'And they gave it to you?'

'Yes. But I turned it down.'

'Goodness, why?'

'Because Burjor promised me marriage,' she said drily. 'Oh no, oh God, why doesn't someone stop that woman from making a fool of herself?'

I followed her gaze and saw a grinning accordionist stretch out his hand to hoist Mrs Buhariwalla up on the platform, her perilous ascent buttressed by husband and son from behind.

'What is she doing up there?' I gasped.

'Going to sing. Jesus!'

Which was what the bride's mother, triple-chinned, fat-armed and over-hipped, did. With hands locked together stiffly away from her aggressive bosom, as if she were about to lead us into prayer, Baimai's mum stood at the mike. A young man with wild hair combed into his eyes strummed the opening bars on the piano, the other instruments caught up with him in a half-hearted manner, and the curly-locks lady burst into song.

Eyes avoided looking into eyes. A crystallization had taken place in the garden: each guest sat frozen in a spell imposed by the piercing voice, pulled taut by good manners and embarrassment.

'God,' breathed Nellie. 'Poor Brazzi.'

'Brazzi?'

'The pianist. My friend. Braganza is a fine musician, he plays brilliant jazz and hates these overstuffed melodies.' Finally the song came to an end. Growing bolder, the intrepid prima donna, after whispered consultations with the hapless pianist, now trilled out an operatic aria and Nellie squirmed in her chair. 'Thinks she's a bloody nightingale.'

Scattered rounds of applause greeted the diva at the end of the bravura displays in *One Fine Day*, *Because* and *Vienna, City of My Dreams*, and at last a smiling Mrs Buhariwalla was helped from the podium by a beaming Mr Buhariwalla. I saw the pianist take out a kerchief from his pocket and mop his brow. He looked gloomy and sullen.

My attention was now diverted to the long parallel tables in the garden where the first batch of guests sat at dinner. Servers dressed in white coats, like doctors, worked down the lanes between tables in pairs, one supporting a vast platter of yellow rice into which he dove with what looked like a spade, precipitating its contents on each plantain leaf, the other swiftly adding dollops of dal scooped from his deeper vessel with a ladle as long as a golf club. They worked with a kind of clockwork rhythm, all movements rehearsed and synchronized, fast and puppet-like, somehow reminiscent of the speeded-up action of a Chaplin film, of old silent movies and ancient pie-throwing extravaganzas. Nellie informed me that rice was the last dish to be served on the plantain leaves, and that the feast would conclude with a dessert of ice-cream, nuts, toffees and paan.

Soon the soiled leaves were being removed, at top speed, by nimble pairs of attendants treading on the heels of a solitary man who only just managed to whisk away the forks and spoons (their use was optional) ahead of his pursuers. It was like watching a three-legged and lemon-and-spoon race all at one go. In record time the tables were stripped to the bare cloth. Without leaving their seats, and in turn, the diners began washing their hands in warm water poured by a waiter from a pitcher that he handled like a watering can over the aluminium basin set on the table before them. Even liquid soap was provided. The dirty water was emptied into buckets, and the rinsed basin presented to the next diner with a fresh supply of warm water.

Now all was set for the ice-cream relay. A man was positioned at the head of each table holding a tray arrayed with plates of ice-cream aloft on his shoulder, his eyes glued on the fat Parsi in a velveteen skullcap who stood in full view on the veranda steps, holding himself with hauteur though his stomach protruded and his shirt was drenched in nervous sweat, so seriously did he take has duties. His 'Go!' was like a pistol shot. Away went the ice-cream bearers like a team of athletes. And though the officiating supervisor shouted like a sergeant-major, and in moments of crisis even came down the steps to hustle and push his men, his dignity was unimpaired.

'Ice-cream is being served,' I observed to Nellie, but all her attention was on the band, so I had to repeat myself.

'Right. Let's walk across, then.' She rose abruptly and we were on our way to the tables when we heard a shout.

'Nellie! Nellie D'Souza!' It was the pianist.

'Hello, Brazzi!' She stood where she was and they beamed at each other. Then she walked closer to the stand.

'Save my life, will you, man?' Brazzi called down to her. 'Come up here and give us a song.'

'Oh, no. Not here.'

'Why not?'

She stared at him. 'Brazzi, I mustn't.'

But he had already seated himself at the piano and was thumping out a frenetic beat. 'My crooner's having a drink. Come on, Nellie, I've been having a bad time. Help a fellow out.'

'Why don't you?' I said to her. 'I'll wait for you.'

Nelly hesitated, looked at me with suddenly shining eyes, then sprang up on the stand. The band swung into the solid tempo initiated by the piano, and someone handed her a tambourine. I sat down on a nearby chair, prepared to enjoy myself mildly.

The next moment I held my breath—and the seat of my chair. For with her first notes something strong and alive and electric swept over the garden, generating a tide. Nellie's voice was powerful in a way that I had not remembered, with a glad, golden, ringing sound. In life Nellie had the need to placate, to submit, to abandon autonomy—she couldn't move out of a chafing situation once it had trapped her any more than I could. But up there, her will was supreme.

Nellie sang as if nothing was more important in the world than to sing. She was triumphant in this secret knowledge, and hurled her glee at the audience. Her brilliant dark eyes flashed and she became the 'black magic woman' of her song, out to 'raise the devil' in us. She did not move her body much, except for the hand that beat the rhythm against her bare thigh with the tambourine, but now she wore her flesh with a new, alluring sensuality. She even closed her eyes at times, which added to her intensity and held me more completely captive. Why hadn't I noticed before that she was beautiful? She and the pianist took turns at improvising and embellishing, as if they had worked together for years. The experimentation was dazzling. They were having the most glorious fun, these two, and the guests were puzzled, but also admiring.

Voices behind me said:

'Where did he get his new crooner from?'

'She's a wow!'

'Come on or there'll be no place for us at the tables.'

'Wait!'

I sat through that song, and the next, and the next, before it dawned on me that Nellie was going to be a fixture up there for the evening.

I stood up and glanced at the tables. All the chairs appeared to be taken by new candidates for caloric suicide, and the ritual had opened again with servings of potato crisps.

'Mila—' A hand touched me on the shoulder, and the bride was standing beside me in all her glory. 'I'm sorry I haven't been able to sit with you. Why are you alone?'

'I'm not. I was with Ritu and Vidyut. There was such a crush on the stage when we wanted to come up and wish you—' I plonked a kiss on her perfumed cheek and fumbled with the clasp of my evening bag.

'But they've left! I just saw Ritu and Vidyut off. Didn't you eat with—' She broke off to smile her thanks as I crushed my gift envelope into her hand. Then she frowned. Enthusiastic cries of 'Bravo' and 'More, more!' had drawn her attention to Nellie, smilingly acknowledging the acclamation as she stood at the mike.

'She's great, isn't she?' I ventured.

Baimai compressed her lips. 'She got up there on purpose, knowing how much it would upset my mother. Such unpleasantness so mars an occasion like this.' And she looked dour, which is all right for a Scotsman but not a bride.

'You've got it all wrong,' I began. 'Nellie didn't—'

'She decided to announce her presence because the family ignored her.' Before I could protest further Minocher had walked up to us. 'Where were you?' asked the bride testily. 'I've been waiting to do the rounds of the tables.'

'Again?' said the disgruntled groom. His breath smelt of alcohol, and his headgear must have been tight for him for it had left a horizontal furrow just below his hairline.

'Naturally! This is the second lot—we are expected to greet all our guests!' She turned to me. 'Will you wait here? We have to get this over with, then we'll come and sit with you.'

I nodded. Minocher favoured me with a bold stare before he turned to look up admiringly at Nellie's legs onstage, and Baimai tugged at his arm impatiently. They moved away and I was left standing there alone.

Suddenly I felt the whole set-up was banal in the extreme, that society weddings were utterly without charm. The festooned garden, the lights and the colonial music, the gargantuan feast with beggars at the gate, the women wearing their ransoms on their bosoms and churning round on showcase duty in a vortex of noise and smiles and sentimentality, all the riot of expense, of waste, all of it dismayed me. Nellie alone blazed like a beacon, because up there, however briefly, she had come into her own.

I decided not to wait for Baimai. I waved to Nellie, but she did not see me. Still trying to catch her eye on my way out, I only just avoided a collision with a squat young man stationed in my path, staring up at the radiant creature on the bandstand. Burjor. Endowed with a nose Lord Ganesh might have envied, he undeniably looked better from a distance. He drew a silk handkerchief from his trouser pocket and blew into it with loud accents of emotion. He desisted, looking woebegone. Now his hand was engaged in pulling at the cute little bow that tied together his Parsi coat under his chin, almost shredding its tassels in ecstasies of fret.

I returned home hungry and in bad humour.

I had just discarded my finery when Vikram walked into the room, very bright-eyed, and gave me a nasty turn. He asked about the wedding, but I saw he had something else on his mind. Several times he interrupted as I obligingly sketched the evening for him. Then, with a sudden foolish grin that irritated me, he said he had reached the most important decision of his life: he was to be married.

'Married?' I echoed blankly.

'Married,' he repeated, and volunteered further information with the same maddening grin. Next month. To a girl called Hansa Desai whom I had never set eyes on, and whom *he* had met only twice in his life: once at an elaborate tea hosted by the girl's family, to which he was chaperoned by Aunt Roma, and this evening when he had been allowed to escort the girl *alone* to a movie—a magnanimous concession to the twenty-first century by his future in-laws.

I stared at him, outraged. 'But why are you marrying her?' My tone of bitter reproach had no effect on his asinine grin, so I added, 'I thought you had a terrific thing going with Urmi.'

Vikram flushed a deep pink and stammered something inaudible.

'What did you say?'

He repeated himself and for a moment I froze in my seat. I could hardly believe my ears. What my brother had actually said was that *Urmi's morals left much to be desired!*

'What does that mean?' I asked sharply. He remained stubbornly tight-lipped, so I went on. 'That she's been sleeping with you?' His face instantly closed against me and that made me even more angry. 'And that is why you can ditch her in good conscience?'

At first he tried to equate silence with dignity. Then he adopted an older-than-thou attitude, but I would have none of it. I called him, roundly, a hypocrite, an upholder of the double standards he pretended to repudiate. I could tell that this enterprise, marrying a *good* girl from a *good* family, had always been in his mind, even when he had been screwing Urmi. It was his project or plan for a happy life: a deliberate choice as well as a compulsive conformity.

My contempt only made him obstinate. 'There is much sense in the old ways,' he said doggedly. 'I would not disown them entirely.'

'Why the hell should you,' I retorted, 'when they allow you to eat your cake and have it too? Why are you marrying this girl you scarcely know?' Now I had pushed him further away. He didn't answer, and as I studied his buttoned-up face I realized again that despite his surface amiability, Vikram had never possessed that 'open' look. And now I understood that he had never really dissociated himself from his upbringing. Nothing that had happened in his past had made him look back in anger. Nothing could dislodge him from his old attitudes, not even the defrocking of his father. He had no muscle for protest, no sense of his iconoclastic generation, and therefore he had never moved to legitimize it against the elders who would still lead it by the nose.

'And how much dowry have they agreed to?' I said because he was now out of reach, behind a glass wall. 'How much cash, jewellery, shares, bonds and the best of kitchen utensils for a manager of Hindustan Lever? Did they also throw in a flat? A Mercedes?'

'It wasn't like that!' At last I had splintered the glass, and he was defending himself.

'No? Oh, I see, it was the horoscopes! Your stars are beautifully counterpoised to meet Hansa's!'

'You'll understand when you meet her,' he muttered, recoiling from me, hating me for having reduced him to such drivel.

'Ah, so now you are trying to say it was love at first sight?' My tone was offensive. I was quite prepared to regard Hansa with a jaundiced eye. Who was this little ninny who had used her wealth and horoscope to snatch away my brother from under my nose? 'Did she sing for you, Vikram? Or play the vina? Or was it the pakora she fried for your tea that went straight to your heart?'

He was on his feet, on his way out.

'Wait!' I bawled after him, wanting to rip his brain open, to reach the old ideas and suppressions there. 'So now will you write to our grand-aunt and ask her which days you're allowed to sleep with your wife?

Never on the days of the full moon and the new moon—never on a Sunday, for all I know! And don't forget it's unclean to touch a woman during a lunar eclipse—'

So suddenly did he turn on me where I sat, his face dangerously tense and hostile, that I flinched. 'All right!' he shouted in a voice of challenging fury, a queer, powerful light in his eyes. 'What makes you think *you* are so different? It may be fun for you to put on this act, but when Father wanted to marry his mistress, who was it who stopped him?'

I rose to my feet, feeling short of breath. 'Why don't you ask *him*? I wasn't there!'

For one exposed, inimical moment we glowered at each other, and I had a strange, drowning sensation of having done this exact thing before. I began to tremble, there was a red glare before my eyes, and I knew that what I felt could only be articulated by violence, that I wanted to rake that taut face with my nails because I hated what it represented at the same time that I recognized myself in it. But the next moment he had walked out on me, leaving me alone in my schizoid world, with the chastening reflection that in his steady adherence to the 'old ways' Vikram was more of a piece than I was.

I sat back on my chair, feeling strange in my knees, jarred to my bones as after a dreadful fight, wanting desperately to be made whole again but not knowing how.

26

This morning, dressed in one of Mother's saris, I was about to let myself out of the flat when the doorbell rang.

'Who—?' The man at the door was garbed in a saffron-coloured dhoti with more of the same material on his shoulders. The dim light on the landing fell on a shaven skull with a long central tuft of hair.

'I have a message for one Miss Mila.'

'There is no Mila here,' I said. 'I am Sharmila.' He did not heed my words but simply looked surprised that finding me had not proved a more tortuous exercise—mounting additional stairs, ringing a few more doorbells, more acute sleuthmanship. 'What message?' I asked impatiently.

'Ritadevi Aggarwal was delivered of her firstborn two days ago, and is requesting your presence in hospital.'

'What! Ritu's had her—why, of course, you are Kishore! Come in, please.'

Kishore walked into the living room, outrageously thin, and sat on the edge of the divan, not out of diffidence but with a kind of magisterial condescension for his temporal surroundings. I sat on the other end as if entertaining a distinguished foreign visitor: a delegate from the Dalai Lama or the Kingdom of God or some such friendly neighbour.

'Tell me about the baby,' I gushed like a newborn aunty. It was a shock to find that his feet, which should have been bare after the manner of saints and martyrs, were sporting dirty sneakers. Without socks. 'Is it a boy or a girl?'

'Girl.'

'Great!' I tried to gauge the avuncular pleasure in his eyes, but they were misplaced somewhere behind his glasses. 'I trust they're both well?'

He gave a slight smile. 'As well as may be expected of the eternal spirit imprisoned in an ephemeral material body.' I must have looked stunned, for he added, 'She had a difficult time. The child is female but,' he pursed his mouth in a pleased way, 'she will possess *shakti*.'

'Yes,' I said a little uncertainly. The Sanskrit word connoted cosmic force, creative energy, feminine essence, but I wasn't sure what he meant.

'Because,' he turned on me his opaque glasses, 'she was not born upside-down, like most people, but entered this world feet first.' Again that fishy motion of his lips.

'Oh, you mean a breech presentation,' I said glibly, relieved that nothing more miraculous had happened, and pleased to toss this tidbit of earthly knowledge at Omniscience, perched on the extreme end of my divan.

But Kishore did not countenance lay opinion on spiritual matters. 'Women are not men's equals,' he began. I looked up quickly to see if he was pulling my leg, but he wasn't. 'This child, however, will overcome such a handicap by having shakti and people will follow her. But only,' he tucked his mouth in and out primly, 'if she humbles herself at the lotus feet of Him who is the Supreme Absolute Truth, well-wisher of cows, brahmins and all living entities on this planet.'

'Of course,' I said blankly. The portrait of an ass was assembling at breakneck speed. The poor man was up to his long ears in holy hocus-pocus, but I was certain that about absolute truth he knew absolutely nothing. 'Let's talk about you, Kishore. What made—'

'I am now Sudama Dasa.' His shaven pate had a shiny, boastful pretension to holiness. 'Thanks to divine grace.'

'Quite. How nice we're having this chat, because the last time I ran into you in Los Angeles,' I looked him squarely in his glasses, 'you were stoned out of your mind.'

To my astonishment he laughed abruptly. It was a boy's laugh, high and abandoned. And for a passing moment other faces emerged from behind the mask he had surely filched from Bottom on a midsummer night: he was again the rebel we had once known, the aspiring artist, the sartorial iconoclast, Ritu's swaggering brother, his pious father's cross and retribution. Alas, something stilted again took charge of his features as he waved a thin hand at me and said, 'That was before Billy Potter alias Guru Bhaktiprem elevated me from such bondage to the highest spiritual platform.' His glasses focussed steadily on me. 'He taught me that Krishna Consciousness is the one and only Science that will simply take us back to the godhead of which we are constitutionally part and parcel.'

'That's nice.' I smiled weakly and asked him how much his niece had weighed at birth.

But his pedagogic spirit was not spent. Hating to let me out of school, he ignored my question and proceeded as if he were quite used to having his wisdom uncomprehended. 'This easy, sublime Science is today the principal benefactor of humanity at large.' His weather-proof smugness almost brought my patience to an end. 'It gives the most apathetic humans a taste of the nectar for which they are forever thirsty, and without which they can never be rid of lustful contaminations.' Here he smiled at me and his smile said: hope you are satisfied with the mess you're in, my worldly sister. 'The material world is simply temporary and inherently sorrowful,' he added with relish, then sat examining me acutely. On another man's face the look would have meant he was seriously considering whether or not a pass was in order; on him it meant he was estimating my ripeness to embrace the good life.

'That is why,' he went on after a weighty pause, 'I eschewed drugs to become drugged on God; and I await His white rays of benediction on the day I take my final vows as a full-fledged sanyasi.' He was some prose stylist, was Sudama Das.

'I see,' I cleared my throat. 'Ritu told me women are not allowed in your order.'

'There have been no bona fide women sanyasis in the whole of Vedic literature,' announced Sudama Dasa. 'Women sanyasis are humbugs.'

'Why is that?'

'Mentally and physically females are on a lower platform. It says so in the *Bhagavad-Gita*, which is acknowledged by each and every transcendental authority as authentic scripture, once and for all. But she can join up as the wife of a householder devotee.' His smile was a lordly nursing of his own superiority. 'This is because woman is meant to be enjoyed.' There were daggers in the look I gave him, but he was unscathed. 'Woman's real pleasure is to please the enjoyer. And Krishna is the Supreme Enjoyer of all blissful pastimes.'

I fidgeted on the divan and threw him another rancorous look, whereupon he resumed with cloistral calm, 'Like all Westernized Indians, you are doubtless prey to the Hollywood concept of love, which is humbug. Love is devotion to Krishna. That is why for His devotees, marriages are arranged today as in the Vedic Age.'

'But all marriages were *not* arranged in the Vedic Age!'

'Much of the history that has come down to us today,' said Sudama Dasa, rising to his feet, 'is humbug. Shall we go?'

'Where?'

'To hospital.'

'You are going with me?'

'Surely—I am expected there.'

He set quite a brisk pace on the road, hurrying bald-head-down, thin calves peeping from behind his orange dhoti, lotus feet encased in sneakers. Quickly I learnt that he had no intention of hailing a taxi or even boarding a bus but expected me to walk the miles to Bhatia Hospital. His assumption was monstrous, but for the moment I was enjoying my morning gallop. I decided to go along with him till I was tired, then I could always stop a cab.

We were passing a florist's shop when I said abruptly, 'Let's buy Ritu some flowers.' He was already a few paces ahead of me when he stopped. He seemed unwilling to break his stride. My suggestion had not pleased him. Perhaps he had no money on him.

I left him there, a standing colour plate from *National Geographic*, and entered the air-conditioned shop. Tables like great wooden trays held buckets of blooms. I walked past lush and full-blown dahlias, hesitated before preening gladioli in a yellow plastic pail, then decided on red roses leaning dewy-headed in cool water.

When I walked out with my bouquet wrapped in cellophane I found him on the pavement, a florid mother grimly awaiting a recalcitrant child. His forehead was perspiring.

'Taxi!' I hailed the passing vehicle. His face told me I had further offended him, but I wasn't going to expose my lovely roses to the scorching sun. He chose to sit beside the driver, presenting me his tuft as he gazed out the window, till abruptly he turned in his seat and began to talk about his sister. It seemed that Ritu had behaved less than stoically when in labour. He spoke austerely, as if displeased by her performance. She had fought them all at the hospital. She had entered its portals quietly enough, but then it had been like an explosion. She had kicked her cousin Vidyut in the belly. Tried to strike a nurse. Panicked at the moment of anaesthesia. She had hollered the place down. Most disgraceful of all, she had screamed that her husband was a brute. She hated him. Hated him! She had never wanted this baby, and if he ever touched her again, she would use the kitchen knife on him. Yes, she had shamed herself, shamed the family. 'Was this the way a devoted *pativrata* Hindu wife behaved?' he asked with grave disapproval.

I had a vision of Ritu's husband, his face one of those crude unfinished things that in sleep must look unforgivably gross—his fingers thick and hairy, the nape of his neck fleshy—and I shuddered. Poor Ritu, plundered so mercilessly of her romantic dreams!

In the front seat Sudama Dasa had not done with listing her crimes. 'And now, because the baby is a girl, she will not give it her breast. She will not pick it up. She will not look at it. Is that how a mother should behave?' His voice implied that *he* was the injured party.

'And you blame her,' I rejoined angrily, 'when the birth of a daughter is regarded as something of a catastrophe in most families?'

But it was like sparring with someone not there. 'She weeps in silence all the time, which is bad for the milk. And the baby keeps crying nonstop, which is bad for everybody's nerves. She will speak to no one— except this morning when she asked her mother to send for you.' I was startled. So this was a summons! In her distress Ritu had asked for me. I was conscious of the honour, but my instinct was to hide: was I equipped to share such intimacy, to partake of her open grief? My own life seemed too precariously balanced to move into close proximity to a life that was truly unhappy—as I now knew Ritu to be. Then I felt ashamed of such thoughts, and wanted to get quickly to her side.

'Failure to bear a son,' my front-seat mentor was saying, 'is simply the result of misdeeds in a past life. But devotion to Krishna will wash away all suffering. If husband and wife cooperate in full-fledged activities for spiritual bliss, who knows what reward awaits them next year? They are both young.'

How does one duel with such a man?

'There are persons,' continued Sudama Dasa, 'described in the *Bhagavad-Gita* as *mudhas*. The word means ass, donkey.' I sat up and stared at him, speechless. Could he read my thoughts? 'They are the gross materialists, who ignore God. They . . .' But I had ceased to listen. Two more quotes from some equally transcendental source and the taxi stopped at the hospital entrance.

I stepped out and opened my handbag, but Kishore had already removed a saffron cloth pouch from his waist, exposing for a moment his navel, a thick-lidded eye, and paid the driver.

27

It is remarkable how one can sense, without being told, that the Bhatia General Hospital is patronized largely by vegetarians. It smells and looks different from the Catholic Holy Family Hospital, with its air of resignation imposed on a fanatical cleanliness, which in turn differs from the conviviality that stalks the spacious corridors flanking the private rooms of the Parsi General Hospital (rather like the veranda of a ladies' bridge club), and which is entirely missing from the Muslim Maternity Home, essentially a place of sufferance.

I entered the green-tiled hall behind Sudama Dasa. The maternity wing was on the first floor. As we mounted the wooden staircase I began to breathe in the peculiar hospital effluvia of drugs, disinfectants and soup. I followed my tangerine guide for about a mile of corridor—evidently no one was taking family planning seriously—to Room 19. Just before the door we had to make way for a nurse trundling an oxygen tent on wheels, its coarse transparent sides buckling and snapping as she pushed it along.

Kishore did not come in with me. This was just as well, as Ritu's room was so packed with women talking loudly, blaring away as if all the stops of an organ were pulled out at once, that I just stood there, bewildered, trying to locate the bed and its patient. The clamour was incredible. How did the hospital allow it? Luckily, Ritu's mother spotted me in my state of paralysis. Braving the many hurdles in her path she reached me with a bundle in her arms that gave forth an aggrieved, barely audible sound, less crying than the nagging expression of a desperate need. I looked down in fascination at the pink skull and bulging muscles in the little forehead as the baby screwed up her face in a kind of listless but unceasing protest.

'Ritu has been asking for you,' said her mother loudly, breathing hard. 'No one from the in-laws has shown their face since they heard the child is a girl.' Her own lined face looked sad and resigned. 'And she weeps, and will not take the child to her breast.' Her eyes filled with tears. 'Her two elder sisters-in-law started their line with boys and she dreads going home with her baby. They have sharp tongues. They will treat my daughter like a dirty cloth in their wash basket, to be beaten against stones!' More tears. And although she had a maternal bosom and rocked the bundle and made all the correct noises, the baby's feeble crying was getting on her nerves. 'Come. But you must not take flowers to her bed, because of the unclean blood that flows from her.'

'Here!' someone yelled at my elbow, splintering my middle ear. 'Give me the flowers!' Ritu's aunt had pushed her way up to us. 'The nurse will put them in a vase where Ritu can see them.' I let go of my roses reluctantly. 'And mind you don't touch her, but talk from a distance.'

She held my flowers in a tight fist and steered me with two hard knuckles against my shoulder. Ladies parted like curtains before our onslaught, and I passed through quickly to the bed. A new Ritu lay there in exhausted maternity, flat-stomached, invisibly bleeding, head turned sideways on the pillow, one long plait of hair falling down the side of the bed like a rope, palms facing up over tightly drawn sheets, utterly empty. She turned her head slowly. She looked drugged. Tension had enhanced the wilful discontent in the set of her mouth. Her eyes paused on me, then looked away with an air of brave fatigue. But immediately they came back to my face, and this time they widened with such terrible pain and helplessness that I sat down on the bed and, putting my arms clumsily round her body, laid my cheek against hers. Her arms remained at her sides, but she pressed her face to mine, nuzzling against me with a desperate movement; and as I held on I felt her disappointment washing back and forth in her chest like waves.

'She has been asking for you since yesterday,' said a voice from floor level. I raised my head and looked down at the hospital ayah squatting at the foot of the baby's cot a couple of feet away. I nodded at her, then turned to Ritu. 'Look at the roses I've brought you,' I said with false cheer. 'In the vase near the window. Aren't they lovely?'

But she stared at them and looked away as if they hurt her eyes; and suddenly I felt they were all wrong for the room and the occasion—

they were too vivid, too cherishing of their own beauty, too immersed in their own colour, believing, in their vanity, that their brilliant hue would never fade.

'You should not be sitting on my bed,' Ritu whispered.

'Get up!' came her mother's sharp command. 'Get up from there!' She hovered over me with the bundle in her arms. 'And see if you can persuade her to take the baby to her breast! It is not natural, the way she is behaving!' At the sound of her voice, now plainly hectoring, the female audience congealed round the bed. I remained where I was, staring up at their faces.

'We must take things as they come,' cried a tall, imposing matron. 'My Shanti gave birth to five daughters before Yogesh was born. Five girls!' She shrieked like a Valkyrie out of Wagner. Five times her daughter had produced one error after another in her diligence to trap the elusive chromosome, and Granny had obviously commiserated with each mistake till the tardy heir took his place at the tail end of a queue of superfluous granddaughters.

'It happens!' A shrill voice took up the refrain. 'If it's a daughter, it's a daughter. Is that any reason to throw her into the Ganges?'

'Where would *we* be,' said another voice, 'if our mothers had refused to suckle us?'

'I don't hold with feeding newborns milk powder out of tins!' bleated a thin, flat-chested female. 'You never know what they mix in them!' I eyed her balefully: how would you know, you are only a woman.

'Mother's milk is best, everyone knows,' trumpeted the many-times-over grandmother, thrusting out her severe chin at us. A chorus of assents. Then a high-pitched voice was inspired to say, 'A daughter is another pair of hands in the home, let's not be forgetting that!'

'No, no!' the faithful clique of relatives responded like a blast furnace.

'And next year you will be washing her feet in milk,' shouted the stalwart grandmother, 'when following in her auspicious footsteps you will get a son!'

'Yes, yes!' sang the brainwashed band of hopefuls.

I had heard enough. As I rose to my feet I caught a glimpse of Kishore's lank ochre frame in the doorway. 'All right,' I screeched electronically over the din, 'why don't you all just leave her alone?'

Ritu's mother, two distaff aunts and one cousin-in-law looked at me in astonishment. In the sudden hush in the room the baby's unaccented wailing competed with a single subdued line of melody from a transistor that sat unheeded on the white bedside table, between the glass of water and the kidney tray.

'Yes, leave her alone!' My words were pitched entirely in high C. 'Give her a little peace and she'll manage all right, for heaven's sake! Kishore!' Several heads turned in that direction as I screamed across the room to the man of God, 'can't you get them out of here?'

The Lord's Elect looked startled, then stood enshrined in the doorway like an idol. 'They have every right to be here,' he at last called out prissily. But then he frowned and seemed to arrive at a decision. 'All right,' he raised his voice authoritatively, 'Let's all go for a few minutes. Leave the mother alone with her child.' At this the ladies bristled, murmured, orbited round the room, fussed in circles, walked a few paces and turned to each other in confusion. 'Come on!' Kishore lifted both his hands and waved the horde towards him like an attendant directing cars, trucks and station wagons in a parking lot. Intimidated, resentful, they inched over in a wavering phalanx.

'Give me the baby,' I said to Ritu's mother, and the very suddenness of my demand made her part with her burden immediately, without ceremony. Surprised by the meagreness of the buttocks in my inexperienced palm, strangely perturbed to feel her stir in my arms, and mortally afraid that I would drop the fragile little packet, I almost called out again in fright to her retreating grandmother, when the ayah stepped forward and took the baby from me.

I waited till the rout of the ruffled matrons, who were making a last-ditch stand in the doorway—clogging it so that Kishore had to withdraw before them into the corridor, from whence he must have directed operations—was complete. Then I switched off the transistor.

'Right,' I turned to the ayah. 'What is your name?'

'Ambi.'

'Give the baby to her mother, Ambi.'

Ritu's sulky face sharpened as she heard this and she turned, with a slithering turmoil of sheets, to face the wall. I waited. A pungent female smell rose from her bed. At last she moved her head on the pillow and I saw that she was sweating heavily. A creeping moisture coated her forehead and upper lip. She appeared to be in a panic.

'Ritu,' I said gently, 'take your baby.'

She closed her eyes and shook her head. Her cheeks were wet with tears.

I looked helplessly at Ambi, who said, 'We must help her to sit up.

Wait.' She deposited the baby in her cot, and walking to the foot of the bed she cranked it up to raise its head, then its middle, till Ritu looked as if she were reclining on a deck chair. She opened her eyes. She did not resist as Ambi undid the buttons of her pyjama top, then the front hooks of her feeding brassiere. Her small breasts were revealed and I was shocked to see how luminous and full they were, grape-bunched and milk-proud, with dark-brown circles round the flattened nipples.

'Press the nipple between your fingers,' directed Ambi, but as Ritu only squinted down stupidly at her exposed breasts, Ambi pulled at the right nipple with thumb and index finger, pressing it at the same time. Four round beads of milk appeared on the now elongated lip. 'Here, you wipe it clean with this piece of gauze,' said Ambi holding out the kidney tray. This time Ritu obeyed. The beads were wiped off with a sterile square of gauze, but other cloudy drops immediately took their place.

Ambi now picked up the snivelling baby from her cot and placed her in Ritu's arms. 'Hold her like this. This extra pillow will help.' She slipped one under Ritu's right elbow. 'Bring her up a little. Put your fingers here, yes, and give her your breast.' But it seemed that the baby was too dumb to do what was expected of her. She squirmed and struggled in her mother's arms, moved angry fists, distorted her face and wailed hungrily, greedy but distrustful, and refused to take the timidly proffered breast.

'She won't!' Ritu looked up helplessly.

For answer Ambi reached out and, pulling at the jutting nipple with one hand, she at the same time guided the baby's face towards it by a hand firmly cupped behind the little skull till the blind, avid mouth closed round it. Ritu winced a little as the baby at last began to suck. But slowly a strange look dawned on her face, consternation at what was taking place, then a kind of pleasurable drowning, a sensuous delight at her fecundity as she felt the accumulated richness flowing out of her into the voracious, insistent mouth.

A minute passed. Anxious faces appeared at the door, then retired. Kishore kept thrusting his head in like a house detective. I pretended to ignore them all. Ritu was evidently a good nurser, a tree of food. Our eyes met over the baby's head, and even as I smiled at her I saw I was no longer needed in this room. She was fully absorbed, locked in with her baby. This was the time to leave, or I would overstay my welcome.

I was greeted by beaming faces in the corridor. I could have preened like a heroine but I felt small and deflated. Ritu had stolen a march over me. Achieved a feminine victory—or at least an ascendency—by doing three of the things I abstractly desired and dreaded: copulation, conception, childbirth; and now, breast-feeding. I wanted to skulk home.

'You did well!' Ritu's aunt shouted in my ear, while the hatchet-faced granny nodded approvingly. 'Nowadays you give advice to young girls by the bucketful, but they listen only to friends and don't obey their elders! You will come again?' I smirked, and gestured non-committally.

'How many children do you have?' boomed Grandma. She looked strong enough to have belonged to the Praetorian guard.

'What you are saying!' The aunt burst into a shrill peal of laughter. 'When the girl is not yet married!'

Her crony cackled like a hen. 'How you can tell, these days? This one looks old enough for a husband!' I smiled stiffly again. I wanted to step on their toes and make a dash for it. You don't waste time bargaining for the esteem of unliberated minds . . . but the words rankled all the same. I felt their eyes inspecting me. She doesn't stammer or limp, she has no harelip or hump. So why isn't she married? They were puzzled. They sniffed closer: watch out for secret defects! Wasn't there something one heard about the mother, years ago . . . Like the poet's pride in being mistaken for a bank clerk, I wanted to pass off as a docile Gujarati girl and felt a cringing urge to ingratiate myself with these ladies. At the same time I wanted to turn the place into a shambles. What fun it would be to whip their sari ends over their curious faces and scatter them before me as I charged down the corridor!

At last I had circumvented the endmost clump of women standing between me and freedom when Ritu's mother waylaid me. Taking me by the arm, she pinned me against the wall and began in a whisper: 'She's a good girl, always has been, but,' throwing a quick glance over her shoulder, '*he* makes her do unspeakable things. I cannot tell everything to an unmarried girl'—her hand went to her mouth—'but her husband gives her no rest. No rest! Not even when she got pregnant. Sometimes three times the same night . . . Also on some excuse he'd sneak home from work in the middle of the day and lock himself in the room with her. They live in a joint family but he has no shame! Of course we women must submit, it is our duty, but in the first months she feared he would force her to abort if the sonography showed a girl foetus—which is why Ritu refused all tests, you understand? She's a good girl!'

'Yes, she is.' The corridor seemed endless. Where had Kishore disappeared? 'I must be going now.' I edged away from the green wall, but she clawed at my arm again.

'Like a whore he wants her to behave!' Her eyes were red and staring. The poor woman had lashed herself into a rage. 'He makes her life as bitter as the neem leaf! To think we gave the flower of our home to that widow-born butcher! They don't marry girls, they buy meat for the house to—' She broke off abruptly. 'But I mustn't tell all this to an unmarried girl.' Here her wits began to wander. 'How is it you are not married yet?' she demanded. And I could see that she was holding it against me, unstitching all her own arguments and complaints. 'The temple needs a bell to make it shine, and the girl a husband,' she went on illogically. 'May you acquire a husband soon!' And she actually pressed the knuckles of both hands against her temples in a gesture of benediction, and in the next breath continued, 'To an unmarried girl I mustn't speak like this . . . but you will come to see her again, no?'

'I will,' I assured her and made my escape.

Outside the gates I found Kishore brilliantly welded to a patch of sunlight on the asphalt (had he stood there, sucking in the heat all this while?), and without a word he fell in step with me. But this time it was he who had to keep up with my athletic stride, synchronize our walking styles. For I was raging at all the world. In my indignation I was ready to outpace everyone, everything.

'Mother has been talking to you.' It was a statement, not a question. 'About Ritu. I have been wanting to talk to her myself,' he said.

'To your mother?'

'My sister. I have to show her the right path in this impious age.' Of course, a brother's duty, but did he have to sound so smug about it? A gust of welcome breeze made my sari skirt fly in one direction, somewhat restricting my steps, but I pushed on. Nothing in the world was going to stop me. Demons were chasing me. Rage was my fuel. Not a sweet moment was I going to lose.

'The female principle has to be subject to the male, *prakriti* has to be subject to *purusha*, or the world simply cannot go on,' Sudama Dasa was saying with a pseudo-therapeutic air that was truly intolerable. 'This knowledge has to be imparted to Ritu for her own permanent happiness,' he panted. 'But you are in an exceeding hurry?'

'Yes!' Race you, sanyasi!

'I was hoping you would have something to eat with me.'

'Some leftover temple food?' I gave a derisive smile. But sarcasm wasn't going to get me anywhere, only my two agile feet.

'There is a Supreme Vegetarian Restaurant we shall be passing, where I sometimes eat. The owner is a true worshipper, and often spiritual foodstuff is available for mature devotees. Also his milk sweets are excellent.'

'No, thank you.' Enduring his prolixity in a noisy room with the clatter of plates and bark of orders for background music was not what I had in mind. I was damned if I was going to sit across the table from Suds and allow him to get supreme with *me*! 'I'm crossing the street here to the taxi stand,' I said. 'Bye!'

So impetuously did I cross the road that a plunging car succeeded in terrorizing me. Wildly screeching brakes sent me catapulting on to the pavement, my sari held immodestly high.

The driver of the car swore with great felicity in Gujarati, Hindi and English. I pretended to be deaf to his polyglot invectives till he thrust his head out of the window and exclaimed, 'What on earth are you doing here?'

28

It was Vikram. I recognized the car, if not the vocabulary. It was the first direct question he had addressed to me after our last spat and I answered with dignity, 'I was trying to get out of the way of your car.'

He glared at me. 'Where are you going? I'm on my way home for lunch. Get in! It's safer than unleashing you on the streets—for everyone concerned.'

I obeyed meekly. As we drove past I waved out to Kishore on the march, as gracious a salute as royalty would be pleased to bestow on a toiling serf. Only this one never looked up.

'Who was that?'

'Sudama Dasa.' I didn't add, né Kishore, your old school pal. I didn't want Vikram to stop for him. Though when the traffic condensed at the lights, I spoke up. 'That was your friend Kishore, in godly garb. Didn't you recognize him?'

'Kishore! Good heavens, I'd heard, I should have—why didn't you tell me? I could have stopped for him.'

'I didn't want you to.'

He threw me a curious glance, but the lights changed and we shot forward. 'This seems to be the morning for bumping into old friends,' he observed. The remark should have served as a warning, as it prefaced what was about to follow, but my mind was on other things. 'I've been to Bhatia Hospital to see Ritu's baby,' I said, ' a girl.' I waited for his reaction.

'Lakshmi,' he said musingly.

Would Hansa, I wanted to ask him, also regard the birth of a girl-child as a visitation from Lakshmi, the goddess of wealth? 'Would you mind if your first child was a daughter?' I said instead. It was my first reference to his approaching marriage, a tacit acceptance of the impending catastrophe.

'No, why should I?'

I tried to picture him as a father, reflected on the nearness and remoteness of kin, what they know of each other, what they can never know. Vikram would model himself on his own charismatic daddy. He had needed a father even more than I had—he had been such a helpless infant. Sensitive to all uncertainties, he needed authority even today, because it assured him that someone *could* rule the world. He needed to father children with a chaste woman he could dub an angel but treat as his slave, so that his sons would learn their male role from him, his daughters from her. And he would impose his will on them all, as he had been imposed upon: be king at last!

My brother drove his car with speed and control, and as I sat beside him in silence, my mood perceptibly changed. I relaxed. It was such a gorgeous day, I didn't have to muddle through it in a panic. But beside me Vikram began grousing about the taxes Father would have to pay next year. It was, in a way, his own confrontation with problems that would soon devolve on him, intimations of domesticity: a new appreciation of the breadwinner's burdens. My brother was clearly a bourgeois who would one day treat his wife as the proletariat. I was smiling at the thought, not paying particular heed to his complaints . . . when he suddenly pronounced the vital, he weighty words he had been cunningly working towards (no, no, how could *he* know he was releasing a dark precious secret), which shocked me more than if a small meteorite had fallen into my lap as the car sped on:

'I met Rayhaan this morning.'

With sudden unbearable excitement, with racing heartbeat, I sat upright in my seat, a bird tightening its claws convulsively on a twig.

'What did you say?' This came out in that unnatural croak in which we make our greatest declaration or ask our most poignant questions. The words he had uttered reverberated singly, in phonetic detail, through immensities of time.

'Rayhaan,' he said. 'You know, Ray Sharma?' My brother was a blockhead, he had noticed nothing. He smiled. 'This is obviously the day for auld lang syne. I met him coming out of—' I heard the snap of the twig, not the place name. I was dropping, plunging into chaos, my wings would not open. 'Is he . . .' I struggled to bring out the words, 'all right?'

'All right?' He seemed to consider this, while the news that Rayhaan was in town was spreading narcotically through my veins. I felt lulled, grateful as a dog, abject, weepy, ecstatic. 'Why shouldn't he be all right?' said Vikram, never the most articulate of men.

I took a deep breath. I had to think this out linearly, not get so fuzzy with emotion. Rayhaan's absence had for years given me an outline to conform to; what would his presence bring? 'He must have grown a paunch by now,' I said, inspired by a violent spasm of optimism. 'A bald patch, surely? He's turned into a fat slob?'

Vikram laughed. Little did he know that I was fighting for my life. 'He's pared down a whit, if anything. And he's still the handsomest man I've met. Which goes to prove that cross-pollination gives the best progeny—despite what the orthodox have to say about he purity of a strain.'

'Then perhaps you should marry a Hottentot—instead of Hansa.'

'Shut up,' said Vikram. Without batting an eye he added, 'I told Rayhaan you were back.'

I straightened my spine. Oh did you, Vikram dear, did you, I'll love you forever for this. 'You did?' I asked coldly.

'Yes. That surprised him. He'd heard you were in California and was planning a trip there himself.'

'And—?' I couldn't breathe. I was lying in water, immersed up to my nostrils.

'We barely had time to talk, I had this important appointment with the bank I was telling you about. He's travelled a great deal. Right now he's hibernating in his hotel room, waiting for reviews of his novel which he's already sold in England for . . .' My ears got clogged here, then I heard, '. . . an impressive figure by any reckoning.'

'Does that mean,' I cleared my throat, 'that he's famous now?'

Vikram glanced briefly at me: 'Strange that you should say that. His exact words were: "I guess I'm famous now. Be sure to tell Mila that." He wanted to drop by, so I invited him to dinner. He's coming home tonight.'

'Tonight?' I whispered. The man who had walked out on my adoration years ago was going to 'drop by' tonight!

'We can go to my club if you think the cook can't manage at short notice . . .'

I sank back in my seat, infinitely small. It was about to happen: my long dream was about to pop open. And for him? Did Rayhaan, too, feel there was some piece of unfinished business between us? 'Be sure to tell Mila . . .' Unbearable hope resolved into terror. He was not the vulnerable one, not for him the happy fear nor the embarrassment of an anti-climax. No, no, I was risking too much. The dinner would end in disaster. Stardust would turn into cinders and I saw myself walking away from the charred heap of a dream with measured, stoic steps . . .

I was growing smaller and smaller in my seat by the kilometre. Abruptly I reached out a hand and tweaked the mirror stuck to the roof of the car towards me. The rectangular slab of jelly revealed lips pressed tightly together—the lipstick eroded—to control an excess of feeling. The eyes had widened, darkened, they showed a queer mingling of defiance with fear. Would he be consumed with regret for the lost years when he saw the changes in that face?

'You'll break the damn thing off,' said Vikram peevishly. 'Besides, I need it for my driving, do you mind?' His hand shot up from the steering wheel and jerked the mirror back to its original angle. I was now invisible again and sat hunched forward, totally passive.

What, then, would it be like to meet Rayhaan again? A celebration of true minds, with violins in the distance, the zap-zing of heart strings in my ears? There was no time to build a welcome arch in my doorway (one of those loud orange-and-purple affairs) but I could keep a garland ready in the freezer. Suppose I *did* survive the first moment, what next? We would re-enact scraps of history, yes, but would the awful constriction of my life let up at last, new scenes open for me?

With an extreme exercise of the will, I fell back in the car seat and laughed. 'What are you laughing at?' said Vikram, irritated by the strange antics of his sister.

'Nothing.' And I laughed again because events rarely parallel the neat geometry of reason, yet the heart can bring anything to pass, so absurd and miraculous can life be. So here I was, hair flying in the wind, riding boldly forth to keep my tryst with a destiny of which I was (to put it modestly) a junior architect!

Brave words. But when I heard Vikram open the front door to Rayhaan that evening, I knew a moment of panic. I wasn't going out there! I would stage a sick headache, a nasty bilious attack to excuse myself from the dinner . . . Oh no, you don't chicken out now. Something in me promptly mutinied against such cowardice and, holding high my head, shoulders braced for a fray, I marched out of my room.

'Here she comes, isn't she something?' Vikram sang out, swilling his chilled beer. I did not need a flush-faced herald to announce my entrance and could have boxed his ears.

'Mila,' said Rayhaan quietly as he rose from the Sankhera chair to greet me. Now the room contained only him and there was a flash of light, as if a magic lamp had been rubbed, and in its prismatic glow I saw what my prince was all about: the courage of lions resided in him, the majesty of eagles, the constancy of stars . . . But immediately I admonished myself. What is there about this man that you are so mindful of him? Bah, such foolishness must end. My disobedient heart was a dog I must bring to heel. Across the room Vikram was shouting in a facetious vein that was not his style at all: 'You watch out, Ray Sharma. She'll get you to call her Sharmila!' How much beer had he been guzzling? With a weak smile I turned from Rayhaan to park myself on the rocker.

In a strained counterfeit of complete ease I rocked back and forth, back and forth, and talked without let all evening. I talked to camouflage my confusions. I talked to beat down the elation that would rise like a tide within me despite all my misgivings. I uttered inanities with Gallic shrugs, and at one point laughed aloud at the ludicrous expression on Vikram's face as he gaped at this weird new sister. I put asinine questions to Rayhaan which I then answered myself. Did he not agree with Naipaul that the trick to living in India was to allow the body to experience the stifling crowds, indigence and squalor, while the mind escaped to the mythic-historic land of saints and unspoilt forests, maharajas and elephants? He must surely agree with the literary giant, I babbled on, after straying from home long enough to become an outsider himself—but come, dinner was served . . .

At the dining table where Father joined us, I could barely eat. I was too drunk on my awareness of the god on my right to taste my wine, so I talked through the inspired meal the cook had rustled up, even without Roma-masi who was in Pune again, this time to help Sejal with her infant son. More than once I caught Dad directing puzzled glances my way, but my brother was too immersed in brinjal bharta and aloo-gobhi to look up from his plate. Dessert was just over (I had merely sniffed at the gulab jamuns) when Dad rose abruptly from the table and said to Vikram, 'Do you mind sending for your coffee to my room? We have some papers to go through.'

'Now?' protested my dumb cluck of a brother. 'Can't they wait till morning?'

'It's a matter of some urgency,' said Father, the most discerning of men, and he turned to Rayhaan. 'You must excuse us. But we hope to see more of you and look forward to your book. You must come again.'

'Thank you, Naren,' said Rayhaan. 'With your permission I intend to do just that.'

His words threw me into a tizzy. I surged up from my chair to seek refuge on the living-room divan behind the coffee table, where Soni had just landed a loaded tray. My nervousness increased as Ray settled beside me after neatly tipping over two fat bolsters to the floor. Inhaling the rich aroma of coffee for courage, I filled his cup with the brown brew, clouded it with milk and, ignoring the question in his eyes, was off again: how did he reconcile traditional Eastern values with the Western outlook—

'Mila,' said Rayhaan helping himself to the sugar, 'shut up.'

But surely the sense of alienation in the work of writers who located themselves in multiple spaces had to do with their unease over cultural boundaries—

'I know of only one way to shut you up.' Rayhaan put down his cup and I gasped as he pulled me to him and his mouth came down on mine. The earth roared past me, precipitate, plummeting down and away . . . I clung to him to save myself from drowning and heard distant flutes, bells, violins and a drum beating thud, thud, thud in my chest . . .

We came apart to stare at each other at close, mysterious range. He reached out a hand to brush back a strand of hair from my brow but I jerked my head away. 'What the hell took you so long?' I demanded, my voice petulant. Then tears threatened and I burst out furiously, 'I hate you! Hate you!'

'Hush.' He cupped my face in his hands. 'Look at me, Sharmila.' He kissed my wet eyes, my wet cheeks. 'I was prepared to fly continents in search of my lost love now that'—the old teasing look was in his eyes—'I've become so famous.'

I glared at him as he struggled to keep a straight face. His success sits lightly on him, I marvelled, and I began to laugh.